The Adventures of Alan Shaw

Volume Two

Craig Hallam

Inspired
Quill

Published by Inspired Quill: March 2018

First Edition

Contact the author through his website:
craighallam.wordpress.com

Chief Editor: Sara-Jayne Slack
Cover Design: Deranged Doctor Designs
Typeset in Garamond

Paperback ISBN: 978-1-908600-71-4
eBook ISBN: 978-1-908600-72-1
Print Edition

Printed in the United Kingdom
1 2 3 4 5 6 7 8 9 10

Inspired Quill Publishing, UK
Business Reg. No. 7592847
www.inspired-quill.com

Praise for Craig Hallam

"[*Old Haunts is full of*] Adventure, comedy, fiendish machines, dire plots and desperate heroism, with a charming side-order of subverting the action tropes. An excellent read."

– Nimue Brown,
author of *Hopeless Maine*

"*[In Greaveburn],* Hallam has crafted an engaging narrative with likable characters and a climax which makes a statement about human nature. However, one could argue the city itself is the real star of the story. Hallam's expert use of imagery helps us to imagine Greaveburn as a Gothic metropolis full of splendour."

– S. Kinkade,
author of *God School*

"Greaveburn is such a rich literary tapestry it would be a shame not to dip our toes into it at least once more. Fans of George R. R. Martin's Game of Thrones and Mervyn Peake's Gormenghast are certain to enjoy getting to know Greaveburn and its residents."

– Angharad Welsh,
Cotswold Style Magazine

"[*In Not Before Bed*], rest assured, there's something for everyone and each short story is unique as the last. Sheer brilliance this, one of the funniest horror collections I've ever read."

– Nathan Robinson
author of *Ketchup on Everything*

"Hallam puts so much into his writing and certainly produces entertaining and believable characters as well as thrilling plot lines. If you like adventure, fantasy or the Steampunk genre then Alan Shaw is a truly brilliant read."

– Occasionally Adulting,
Book Review Blog

Dedication

To my inner child who skips around my chair and sings
stories that I might write them down.

To the ailing old man that I'll become who urges me to
write with his failing breath.

The Adventures of Alan Shaw

Volume II

Contents

Alan Shaw and the Lovelace Code   1

Alan Shaw and the Wretched Revenge   83

Alan Shaw and the Vault of Hsekiu   135

Alan Shaw and the Blood Curse   207

Alan Shaw and the Lovelace Code

1

September 1861
Shanghai, China

PAPER LANTERNS BOBBED on the breeze, their rouge light making tricky shadows in the narrow street below. Steam rose from vents and grates as if Shanghai were a factory for creating the world's clouds. Plunging through the haze, a young man was visible only as a blurred impression by those he shoved; a whip of blonde hair, a muttered curse, and a glimpse of light on the steel of his revolver, boots pounding the slick mudslide that was the alley's floor. Covered with a mixture of dirt and blood, some of which was his own, Alan Shaw slithered across another alleyway's opening, throwing himself into the shadow, and bounced from the wall like a ragdoll. Managing to keep his feet, he careened into the opposite wall, which he clung to for a second's valuable rest. Sliding a hand into his coat's inner pocket, he found the small wooden box still nestled there, and gave a long sigh. Glancing back the way he had come, Alan wiped the stinging saltwater from his eyes.

On reflex, he jerked back.

Thunkthunkthunk

A trio of arrows thudded into the wall beside Alan's head, each one closer than the last until they were less than an inch from his eye. Their shafts were ancient, splintered, the feathers at one end mostly rotted by time. But damned if they weren't still effective. His Adam's apple bobbed with a near-miss gulp, and he was running again.

Shooting out of the alleyway's opposite end like a cannon shell, Alan exploded into a Shanghai market that choked the street with noise and the food stalls' mouth-watering fog. Paying the scents no mind, not even when his stomach made beastly protests, Alan slid under a stall's counter, ignoring the angry screams from the owner, and scuttled up and over a mountain of crates to the excited clucks and squawks of their inhabitants.

"Balls!"

The rotten wooden laths of a crate collapsed under his weight, swallowing his boot. The previous crate's previous inhabitant laboured into the air with a startled honk. Maintaining his balance by luck rather than judgement, Alan yanked hard, but nothing happened.

"Double balls!"

Behind him, above the sound of hammering cleavers transforming flesh to food and other human ruckus, someone screamed.

The Jiang Shi were coming.

Fighting the urge to look back, and still dragging the crate on his foot, Alan reached a ladder which led up to the distant rooftops. Taking a firm grip of the ladder, he smashed the crate against the wall as hard as he could, once, twice, and was finally free in a shower of splinters, feathers and goosey pellets.

"Ha!"

There was no way he was risking the crates again. His only option was up. Alan's limbs moved with simian dexterity, propelling him skyward at an alarming rate. Shanghai fell away as the mud alley turned to a vista of brick and dirty glass, foul gutters and shanty wood roofs. A stiff wind tugged at Alan's tan duster, setting the long coat whip-cracking behind him as his muscles began to burn.

This used to be easier.

Short winded, he vaulted the building's parapet and landed with a splash on the wet roof beyond. There was something about the chimneys, the sloping roofs, the strings of laundry hung like piebald Christmas decorations, and the grey sky above. If only there was a dome here, or a tower there, if only the hot stench of the Thames were in his nostrils, Alan could have been home.

The sound of powerful claws on the brickwork below roused him.

He was very far from London. And very far from safe.

From a sprinter's crouch, he set off across the rain-slick rooftop, building speed, and flung himself across the gap between two slums with as little thought as some might step from the pavement. As he landed, scraping his boots in a well-placed slide, he finally allowed himself a look over his shoulder.

There they were. One Jiang Shi landed on the rooftop behind him with preternatural confidence, another running along the wall of a tall building which ran parallel, both creatures moving like men one minute and like beasts the next, with bows and quivers slung across their backs. The stench of their moss-encrusted and tattered robes, along with their rotting flesh, preceded them. Eyes glimmered from under their hexagonal caps and tongues lolled like slivers of raw meat. Alan saw their claws digging into brickwork as if it were dough and he decided that he really didn't want one of them to get a hold of him.

Where do people find these things? he wondered. *Is there a crypt guardian guild I'm not aware of? And weren't there three of the buggers?*

A rush of air by his ear sent a sizzling line of pain across his cheek. If he hadn't dodged purely on instinct, the undead Jiang Shi's talons would have made bloody ribbons of his face. Alan made some wordless grunt of pain as his foot slipped on the wet rooftop and he fell, hitting the wood with his shoulder. For a second the roof creaked as if it might give up altogether and pitch him into the god-knows-what below. But it settled. With silent relief, he returned his attention to the sizzling mass of pain that was his face. The creature's rotting maw snarled. Holding out one hand to the creature, Alan made a placating gesture, and reached inside his coat. He knew exactly what it wanted.

The Jiang Shi, its tongue lolling like a barber's bloody rag, shivered with anticipation and began some tirade which was surely a villainous boast in its native Chinese.

"Sorry. I'm English," Alan muttered, and whipped his revolver from his coat in one fluid motion, bringing it to bear on the creature. All six rounds hammered into its face. The Jiang Shi screeched, reeling back as chunks of dusty flesh flew into the air. It spun, its ancient robes fluttering, one remaining eye roving in its pulverised socket until it found Alan already accelerating into the distance. It screeched, not seeming to notice when part of its shattered jaw dropped off, and made chase.

Across the rooftop, Alan fumbled in his empty trouser pocket. Unless he felt like firing lint, his offensive options had run out. He stowed his revolver in its shoulder holster, and concentrated on making it to the next street.

There would be a gap, he knew. A big gap. And in order to escape he would need to be at street level fast enough that falling was the only real option. Even the Jiang Shi wouldn't want to throw themselves off a building if they didn't have to. Strong as they were, the rot of the grave made them squishy. And that's where Alan had the advantage. Falling off of things was practically in his job description.

Vaulting a low wall and rounding a stack of chimneys, he caught his bearings by the Union Jack which poked its way high over a nearby roof.

Sanctuary.

Alan's rooftop was rapidly running out. He could almost feel the hot breath of the undead guardians on his neck. Every now and then he would catch one in his peripheral vision, moving closer, flanking him, expecting him to stop when the rooftop ended. The men, or creatures, or whatever they were, were panting hungrily. They could taste victory.

He allowed himself a smirk.

"You underestimate my stupidity," he panted.

The rooftop ended. Alan's lithe musculature bunched and shot him forward. He soared across the square below, arms cast forward, fingers grasping for every spare inch they could as the world turned topsy turvy and the ground began to accelerate toward him. His duster whipped out behind him, doing nothing to slow his descent.

He grinned, albeit maniacally, as the air tugged at his watering eyes and the familiar rush of impending death swarmed his body. Letting out a roar of exultation, he hit the flagpole and, locking himself into its orbit by his sweaty palms and muddy boots. Spinning downward helter-skelter he hit the ground with a choked scream, spread across the flagstones and groaning.

Lifting his head just enough that he could see beyond the high iron fences of the British Embassy yard, Alan made out three pairs of glowing blue eyes retreating beyond the rooftop, narrowed to slits and shimmering. He let out a laugh and laid back, letting the dull throb of his bones take over.

A rifle hammer clicked, followed by another. When Alan opened his eyes, he was staring down two barrels with Her Majesty's guards at the other end.

And so his day got worse.

2

THE LARGE OAK door bounced from Alan's shoulder as he was shoved into the office.

"Bloody hell. Mind yourself!" he yelled at the soldier, who he mentally named Corporal Shovey, as he dragged his duster under control and stepped onto the small rectangle of carpet which housed the office's desk and the only other inhabitant. The soldiers followed him in, rifles still raised. Corporal Shovey started to speak:

"Sir, we found this reprobate—"

"Yes, quite. Leave us, Corporal," said the rotund man behind the desk.

The soldier's mouth snapped shut.

"Quick as you like, Corporal," Alan sneered.

Shooting a look of amazement at Alan, both soldiers backed out of the room and the door clicked closed, leaving Alan alone with the man behind the desk. Gaslight slid over the man's well-oiled hair and winked from his silver tiepin, matching cufflinks and spectacles as he regarded Alan. His shirt collar was so perfectly starched that Alan felt choked by it all the way across the room.

The man's face glazed with mild annoyance as he cast a look down at Alan's boots.

"You're leaking blood onto my carpet, Mister Shaw."

"Don't worry, Rook. It's not mine. Mostly."

"Thank you. That has set my mind truly at rest. Take a seat."

Alan eased himself down into a high-backed chair opposite the desk. It wasn't until he tried to lean back that he realised he couldn't. With difficulty, he twisted an arm up his own back and found the problem. Shrugging off his duster, spilling more flecks of blood and mud onto the carpet, he poked his finger through the hole he found and made a little *humph* of annoyance at the back of his throat. Hand behind his back once more, he found the culprit and tugged it free. The arrowhead had embedded in the spinal support of his armoured waistcoat. At some point the shaft must have broken off. Lord knew when. The waistcoat had done its job, of course, but he'd need a needle and thread for the coat.

"Would you look at that?" he muttered to himself, turning the arrowhead this way and that. "The buggers bloody got me!"

Rook sighed. "So it seems. Aren't we lucky that you aren't so easily killed? Do you have the item?"

Alan gave a snort and dug into his coat pocket before tossing the box toward the man.

"Here. May it bring you great happiness."

The box hit the desk with a hollow thud and slid across the wood, stopped only by Rook's manicured hand.

"The money has been deposited into your account," the

spy-master said.

"Already?" Alan asked, twirling the arrowhead thoughtfully between his fingers as he sat down and reclined himself into a position that ached the least. Depositing the arrowhead in his duster pocket, he whipped out a fusty handkerchief, and began to dab at his bloody cheek. It didn't seem too bad. The gush had already turned to an ooze.

"Contrary to my personal feelings, my superiors have what can only be described as *faith* in you, Mister Shaw." Rook slid open a desk drawer and placed the box inside.

"Aren't you going to check it?"

"Do I need to?"

"I suppose not."

"Then I suppose I won't," Rook snorted, slamming the drawer shut as if it were a bank vault. "Curiosity would have me ask a question, if I might? Why didn't you show the guards your Letter of Marque? You would have been treated with much less hostility."

Alan humphed. "They wouldn't even let me put my hand in my pocket to draw it out."

A smile greased Rook's face.

Collecting his coat, Alan stood: "You done with me, then?"

"Two minor things before you go." Rook reached into his desk and produced a sealed letter. "Firstly, another task, if you so desire it."

Alan leaned over the desk to pluck the envelope from Rook's fingers. There was only a little resistance, but enough that Alan had to put some effort in if he really wanted it. He forced back a snarl as Rook smiled at him and released the envelope.

Alan held the Letter of Marque to the light as if deducing its contents, weighing the cost.

"What am I stealing this time?"

"Acquiring, Mister Shaw. You acquire objects for Her Majesty."

"Feels a lot like stealing to me. And I'd know."

Rook *humph*ed. "A young genius by the name of Lovelace has had personal items stolen by some Russian devil or other. A box containing a set of pristine white cards."

"What's he a genius of?" Alan asked.

"*She* is a genius in the field of analytic algorithms. The cards are the result of her life's work—"

"And I'm stealing them back. Got it," Alan interrupted.

Rook held up a finger. "Not quite, Mister Shaw."

"Oh bugger. You mean I'm stealing them *again*."

"Let's say that such technological advances shouldn't be left in the hands of the French." Rook's smile positively writhed.

Alan nodded. "Fair enough. There was another thing?"

Opening another drawer, Rook produced a pile of letters bound with string. He tossed them toward the edge of the desk where Alan let them sit.

Rook stared at him. "I am not your personal mailman. Answer your brother."

Snatching up the envelopes, Alan made for the door, muttering only one thing before slamming it behind: "Mind your own business."

Alan stepped from Rook's doorway with the Letter of Marque in one hand and a pile of mail in the other. After a moment's consideration, he stuffed the string-bound pile into his coat pocket and tore open the other letter with a little more violence than was necessary. Turning down the corridor as he read, he realised that he only had until tomorrow morning before his next adventure began.

3

GIVING CORPORAL SHOVEY a wink, Alan stepped back out of the Embassy gate and onto foreign soil once more. He stood for a moment, seeming casual with hands in pockets, but every fibre in his body was tense to duck or feint or dodge if the Jiang Shi reappeared.

They didn't. Not a single glowing eye or whiff of old meat.

As Alan had suspected, they were nothing but mindless bloodhounds, albeit rotting, stinking undead bloodhounds from an ancient Chinese era. Once he no longer had the box in his possession, they lost interest in him. They were Her Majesty's problem now; Queen Victoria the First, ruler of the Greatest of the Britains and all the territories of the British Empire.

A bloody long mouth full, Alan thought. *But I wouldn't want to tangle with her. Good luck, Jiang Shi.*

To any unsuspecting passer-by, Alan looked like a casual travelling gentleman with his tussled blonde hair and open shirt collar; unless they looked closer and saw the hastily sewn bullet holes and knife slashes in his clothing, the stains and scuffs that would never quite come out, and the crosshatching of pale scars on his knuckles.

Shouldering the duffle bag that the Embassy had stored for him, he stretched himself a little. He was between jobs now, and that meant he was somewhat without purpose. If he wasn't chasing, being chased, stealing, retrieving, or exchanging heated banter in the middle of some scuffle, life seemed just a little too dull for his liking. Still, it would only be until tomorrow, and then the game would begin all over again. Time now for some much needed rest. Even Alan knew he needed that from time to time.

Alan stepped down into the street from the Embassy's raised gates and crossed the road between a flurry of steam-driven bicycles that wove around each other in ever more dangerous proximities and speeds. His boots hit the opposite pavement and carried him toward the Shanghai docks. He had a few hours to sleep before his rendezvous at an airfield specified by the Letter of Marque, but he knew what he needed first. Taking a few more turns and twists through the city, Alan finally came to a squat wooden pagoda in its own square. Light spilled out into the gathering twilight from windows, wrapping the building in glowing bands, and water spilled from each floor of the bath house, tumbling down the sides in great cascades to a steaming lake at its feet just as a thousand pipes crawled back up like metallic ivy. Alan took the steps up to a humped bridge which carried him over the lake toward the bath house, surrounded by the rising steam and hush of falling water. To his right, only half seen through the fog, a great wheel churned the waters below and Alan could just make out a team of workers scrubbing with long-handled brushes at the workings. As the steam cleared he saw a tall, middle-aged woman stood in the open entrance.

"Ni hao," she whispered, and gave an elegant bow. Her blue cheongsam dress and tightly woven hair were immaculate. It was possible that her skin shone, but Alan couldn't be sure. He suddenly felt like the dirtiest pig on the face of the earth.

"I'm sorry, I don't—"

"Please, sir. Do not apologise. We welcome people from all over the world and are happy to accommodate your needs."

Damn. Her English was better than Alan's.

"If you wouldn't mind? Your boots, sir."

Alan looked down. Of course they were still crusted with every manner of filth imaginable. Popping them off using the toe of the opposite foot as a lever, he kicked them aside. His feet seemed somehow ridiculous in their stocking form and so he shed the socks and rolled up his encrusted trouser cuffs too. That was somehow better and utterly worse. His feet were pale, the skin peeling from places where his boots had rubbed, and there was a sprout of hair on each toe which hadn't been there a few years before. They weren't the feet of a boy any more.

The attendant said nothing, but beckoned him to follow. Wooden floors gave way to stone, blessedly cool on Alan's feet, as they passed through the bath house. They rounded two huge pools, half-hidden by the steam with groups of Chinese men in various states of immersion; all of whom seemed to think a towel was better used for shielding the shoulders than the genitals.

From those larger rooms, Alan was led through another where bellows taller than him were pumped by five or six mostly-naked children, forcing heat and more steam from tall, narrow tanks. Everywhere was the crackle and pop of coal fires or the rush of heated water; sounds which rumbled loud enough to drown out thought. The heat was such that Alan felt as though he were drowning without water, and he'd the sense that he had to hurry onward or die from the humidity.

Up a wooden staircase, which gave an unparalleled view of the city to one side and the cloudbanks of the bath house on the other, Alan's attendant led him through a sliding wooden partition which cut most of the heat and noise away as it slid closed. In the centre of the room was a single bathtub, looking something like an elongated barrel with a bar of iron binding the laths in place.

"English men prefer to bathe alone, this is true?"

Alan didn't answer. He could already feel the hot water on his body and he was eager for it. More eager than he had been for food on occasion. He nodded and the attendant bowed in return. The door hushed open and closed as she left him alone.

The duffle bag hit the ground without ceremony, his coat landed over a nearby chair. Then he began to unbuckle his armoured waistcoat. The thick leather creaked as the buckles released, and Alan could finally breathe again. It wasn't until he shrugged it from his shoulders that his body began to throb. The waistcoat's tightness had apparently held all manner of injuries in place. Bruises blossomed before his eyes. His ribs began to pulse. The aching seemed to spread into his arms and down his legs. His weary fingers fumbled at his buttoned cuffs and shirt front. Once victorious, he let the shirt lay where it fell, still wrapped in his shoulder holster. The revolver thudded as it hit the floor but Alan just left it. It had taken more beatings than that. He unstrapped the thick leather band around his wrist which held his triple dial watch, and set it aside on the chair. His trousers and underwear came off in one swoop.

He stretched then, feeling the complaint in every overworked tendon and joint, the heat in his spent muscles. Running from the temple and the Jiang Shi had taken its toll, it seemed. Since entering the third decade of his life, he was certain that these exertions were getting a bit more difficult. It took every ounce of his remaining strength to climb the few steps up to the bath and dip his toes in. Part of his brain swore his skin was peeling at the volcanic temperature, and another part screamed for him to continue. He lowered himself, catching his breath as the water touched a sensitive place. Soon the water was up to his neck, drawing every throb and swell in his body out into itself and flushing it all away. His face seemed to explode with the heat. A torrent of sweat began to ooze from him. He could feel the dirt of Her Majesty's most recent crime just sliding off.

ALAN LASHED OUT, catching the unknown hand as if it were a striking cobra. The water around him splashed as he fought to sit up, to stand, to brace himself against whatever it was that held him, which turned out to be just the bath water. He hurriedly wiped aside the hair that hung in his eyes, and saw the attendant standing there, her dainty hand still grasped in his.

He'd fallen asleep. When the hell had that happened?

He shook himself, and looked down at the attendant, who had expertly averted her eyes. He looked further down and realised that not only was he still naked, but sleep had resulted in the same effect it did every morning.

"Urm." He let go of her hand and sat down fast enough that water sloshed over the bath's edge, onto the floor and probably the attendant's sandaled feet as well. When nothing else seemed to be forthcoming from his sleep-addled brain, the attendant thankfully filled the uncomfortable silence.

"I brought shaving things, sir. And towels. When you are ready, of course." She gestured to the far wall, still not making any eye contact with him. "Through the door is a place to rest." She bowed once more and very carefully didn't rush to leave so as not to cause offence.

Once the door slid closed behind her, Alan let out a groan.

"Alan Shaw, menace to the public, strikes again," he muttered, shaking his head. "Add indecent exposure to pleasant bath house attendants to your offences, Alan. For God's sake."

He reached over the bath's side to a small table, which had appeared as he slept, and took up the foam tin and brush. Lathering his face felt like a little slice of civilisation, and each stroke of the straight razor that followed seemed to scratch away a foul moment from the last few days.

Skrrrrit, no more dusty temple.

Skrrrrit, no more Jiang Shi nightmare.

Skrrrrit, no more smug Mister Rook.

By the time he was done, Alan's mind felt as smooth as his face.

He sluiced the rest of the foam with a splash of water and went to place his tools back on the little table when he finally noticed that the stack of letters, which had been hidden in his coat, were sat waiting for him. The attendant had folded his clothes on the chair, and must have found the letters there. Being unhelpfully helpful, she'd left them within reach.

"Buggering balls," he muttered. Dabbing his hands dry on a towel, he snatched the stack of envelopes and snapped the string holding them together before tossing it over the bath's side. Some of the envelopes were worn and tattered at the corners, some even yellowed or crinkled as if they'd been wet and dried time and again. The top one alone had several post stamps, some of them military, some of them civilian. It must have taken Rook a lot of hard work to get those letters to Alan. A huge part of him wished the spy-clerk hadn't bothered, but they were in his hand now, which made them a lot harder to ignore. As Alan thumbed through the pile, he could see several styles of handwriting, but one pervaded the others; the patient curlicues of his adoptive brother, Simon. The last time he'd seen Simon, Alan had been rushing out of the house after visiting for a matter of minutes. There'd been an adventure to be had; Alan's first Letter of Marque as a Privateer, and he hadn't been home since. Alan thought of the few weeks following that visit in a maelstrom of images that shifted uncontrollably from one dark memory to another. The Indian jungle, thick vines like hammocks hung in the dark, a crumbling temple, a crew of friends, the dark eyes of a bandit woman he'd loved and lost, the flash of his revolver's muzzle and the fading light in a man's eyes, melting into the expectant face of the small boy Alan had made fatherless.

Alan pinched the bridge of his nose and sat for a moment, letting the nausea of his memories subside. When he felt like the welling in his eyes wouldn't cause any tears to fall, he opened them and snatched one envelope from the top of the pile, tossing the others onto the little shaving table. He looked at it for a moment, turned it over in his fingers, rubbed the surface with his thumb. Then he tossed it over with the others, and sank under the bathwater.

One more day wouldn't make an ounce of difference.

4

FINGER-COMBING HIS WET hair into something approaching decent, with his duster still bearing stains he hadn't managed to quickly scratch off, Alan waited on the airfield. The hot Chinese wind had picked up considerably, managing to make him sweat and yet feel drier at the same time. Forcing his hands into the coat's deep pockets, he drew it around himself as a drone of approaching engines came in on the breeze.

The glider had a swollen steel belly, housing one large turbine flanked by the cockpit and a rear cabin. Propeller-tipped wings spread out in a smooth curve over a narrow chassis. Alan didn't move, but watched. His stomach drew into a tight little knot. It had been a long time since a Letter of Marque had demanded he be part of a team, even a two-man one. Alan wasn't sure he still knew how to play with others. But the pilot was good, at least. Even in the buffeting wind, the glider dipped expertly as it came to a fluttering stop on the airfield just a short distance away. The pilot hopped down, a small fellow, and made across the field toward Alan, lifting his goggles to sit on the leather flight cap.

"I'll be damned," Alan muttered to himself.

The girl couldn't have been long out of her teens, pale as a daisy, her blonde tresses drew into a complex knot at the nape of her neck apart, from two soft waves which framed her face. Her overalls were air corps issue, so she was official, although the belt which drew them into her waist, and thus drew attention to a set of powerful hips and neat little bosom, was outside of regulation. Alan drew his Letter of Marque from his pocket, flashing the official seal, and the pilot reached into the back pocket of her overalls for a more crumpled version of the same.

Alan approached.

Not so long ago, Alan would have admired the young woman's figure, the neat point of her pixie chin and eyes which could have made the most crass slur seem innocent. He would have thought up a line, at the very least, tested the water. But who approached this girl was another Alan, and so he merely admired her as a collector would a fine horse, although he no longer rode himself.

The pilot gave him a warm smile as they finally met.

"No salute?" he asked.

"You're not military," she said with curt amusement.

"Name?"

"Captain Meredith Rockett. Merry." She extended a gloved hand. Alan took it and noted the friendly, even grip.

"Rockett. Can't be your real name," he said.

"Orphan raised by the air corps. They have a sense of humour."

Without acknowledging the answer he hit the girl with

another verbal volley: "Merry sounds like a boy's name."

"That feels like a girl's handshake," she retorted.

Alan fought back a smirk as he released her from his grip. At least this could be a little fun. He decided to push again.

"Aren't you a little young for a pilot?"

"Aren't you a little old to be playing cowboys and Indians for the Empire?"

Merry grinned, and Alan tried to hold back the twitch of annoyance from his eye. Damn it. She hit a nerve so quickly. She didn't seem to notice, or hid it very well.

There's a little whirlwind in that girl, he thought.

"Shall we?" she asked, gesturing to the glider.

The vehicle was even more impressive close up. It was obviously of sturdy British military design; not a single rivet was wasted where it could be spared, and there wasn't a hint of character in the glider's royal blue paint job. Alan had seen the military transports of officers, complete with their chandeliers and plump upholstery. This wasn't one of those. The glider was a functional creature.

Merry slid back a door in the glider's side and Alan stepped up into the cabin behind the cockpit. A single upholstered bench lined the back wall, mirrored by storage lockers above. A pair of handles under the seat showed where a bed was likely stowed away. He wondered how long the job would take and what the arrangements would be. Glancing over his shoulder, he watched Merry climb up behind him. She had evidently caught him looking at the bed and was smirking to herself.

"Don't worry. I'm sure we'll work something out," she

said as she glided past him and into the cockpit. Whether the brush of her hand on his elbow was purposeful or not, he couldn't tell. Merry began to buckle herself in behind the controls.

She was pretty. *Balls.*

And easily as witty as him. *Double balls.*

Interesting women were always his downfall.

Dropping his duffle bag on the ground, he took a seat in the rear cabin, where he had an unparalleled view of the back of Merry's head and his back was to a nice safe wall, and strapped himself in with a lap belt. He tried to think back to India; to the look in Rani's eyes as she watched Delhi destroyed by the British Army. She had been so strong, staying behind when Alan couldn't stand to. The sickness he'd felt as he drove away into the jungle rose up again. He looked at the back of the young pilot's head.

Never again.

Merry called back to him, looking over her shoulder from the cockpit. "You going to sit back there all trip? I'm not your chauffeur, you know."

Alan shook himself. He thought about it for a silent second before unlocking his belt. She was right, he supposed. No point being uncivil. His damages weren't Merry's fault. He ducked through to the cockpit, taking the co-pilot's seat, and re-buckled himself in.

The console was full of gauges and switches. A control lever sat between his legs, the handle decorated with even more buttons. Alan took one look at it all and cranked the lever under his seat, sliding himself as far away as possible, which was nowhere near far enough.

"'Fraidy cat," Merry muttered so that he could hear, and continued to stab at the console in what may have been a completely random way as far as Alan knew. But things started to happen in the hum of the glider's engine, and he could feel the purr as his bottom and hands rested on the chair.

"Righty-o. Let's be off," Merry said. "Hope you're not airsick. We won't be making many stops."

The glider pitched forward to the command of Merry's steady hand on the control lever as if a giant were lifting its tail. Just as Alan thought they might flip over entirely, the glider drifted forward. They'd left the ground so smoothly that he hadn't even realised it. His eyebrows rose as he looked at the young pilot. She was very, very good.

They rose slowly for only a few feet before Merry teased the controls to the left and punched the accelerator with her foot. The glider responded with a happy *whoomph* of speed that threw Alan back in his chair. They hummed over the nearby rooftops, so close that they skimmed the glider's belly, so close that nearby washing lines and flagpoles were tugged into their slipstream. Alan grinned to himself; the speed lit up the little boy inside him like no other thing could. Merry caught his grin.

"Nippy, isn't she?"

"Is this all she can do?" he teased.

Merry smiled, flicked one switch on the console, turned a dial to the red, and hit the accelerator again. The world blurred and Alan let out a little laugh he hadn't heard since he was a boy.

"YOU SURE HAVE a lot of admirers," Merry said.

They had cut away from civilisation, heading directly west. Alan knew this because the old fashioned compass was only one dial on the glider's console he understood. He tucked a letter back in its envelope.

"Mostly just the one."

"Persistent, isn't she?" Merry asked.

"He," Alan corrected. "It's my brother. I haven't been home in a long time." He had continued to dig through his pile of letters as they talked, coming across a small square envelope made of sturdy brown cardboard. Peeking inside, he slid out a miniature recording disc about the size of his palm and held it up to the light. "I'll be damned."

"You've been on the other side of the planet too long," Merry said. "Everyone uses those now. Here," reaching across, she plucked the disc from Alan's fingers. Down between their seats was an upright metal cylinder that Alan had ignored as just another complex piece of flight equipment. Merry lifted its lid to reveal a thin metal peg, which received the disk. A pale green light winked to life beneath the disc, which began to turn, slowly picking up speed. Through a speaker hidden somewhere in the cockpit, what sounded like a wildcat's pained growls wound up in speed until it became a familiar voice.

"Bbbbbrrrrrrrrrrrooooooooowllisten to me, Alan. This is the last time I'm going to try. Lottie thinks I'm mad for even trying this long, but I know I can get through to you if only you'll listen to me. Whatever happened after you left that day—" Alan fumbled at the cylinder, but couldn't figure the damn thing out.

"Shut it off," he snapped. "How do you stop the damn thing?"

"—whatever made you not want to come home again, I don't care. I'm *asking* you to come home. We—I need you to come home."

Merry reached over and killed the connection. The green light under the disc died, and its revolutions wound to a stop. Alan didn't touch it. He just snatched the disc from its pin and huffily shoved it into its paper sleeve.

Merry checked the console's instruments, adjusted their course, and shuffled herself comfortable in her seat. When the clotted emotion in the air seemed to have dissipated somewhat, she dared to speak:

"How long exactly? Since you were home, that is." She talked while checking the ground below from her window, keeping her eyes diverted from Alan, and that somehow made it easier for him.

"About four years."

Merry whistled between her teeth. "A lot has changed. You might not recognise it."

"I'm sure it's still the same old hole," Alan said. He suddenly felt drained. This had to be the longest he'd thought about London in years, and it had exhausted him. "So, what does your Marque say?"

Merry shot him a raised eyebrow, but decided to let him steer the conversation his own way. "Didn't you read yours?" she asked.

"Not as such."

Merry rolled her eyes and made a show of sighing. "We're stealing a box of punch cards once owned by some

French hen who lost them to the Russians. They're algorithm cards for a new Analytical Engine. Not like those in an Automaton or the like, more like the big thinkers they have in London."

"What do they use them for?"

Merry shrugged. "I have no idea. It's all about maths when you get right down to it. I guess you won't have seen the Babbage Institute if you haven't been home in a while?"

"Never heard of it," Alan admitted.

Merry eased on the controls and the glider swooped up and over a small copse of trees, rounding a rise in the land. In the distance, Alan could already see foothills that would lead to the mountains.

"It's down by the Thames where Alsatia used to be," she continued. "One huge building just filled with Analytic Engines. All picking at the universe, they say, trying to figure out answers to the big questions. This Lovelace is a bit of a genius when it comes to writing algorithms for A.E's." Merry rolled her hand in the air, moving things along. "Blah blah blah. The short version is that she's done something that just about everyone wants a piece of."

"I was getting bored of the backstory anyway," Alan quipped. "When do we get to the fun part?"

"If you mean when do we sneak aboard a moving locomotive, outsmart any number of Russia's finest spies, steal the cards, and make a dastardly and daring escape into the night, then probably tomorrow. We'll fly through the night and reach Arunachal Pradesh where the railway starts, then we can start looking for the train." Merry looked over at him, the excitement causing her pleasantly shaped lips to stretch into a smile. Her exuberance certainly was infectious. Alan couldn't help but reciprocate. He felt his pulse gallop in anticipation of the action.

5

AFROZEN WALL of air hit Alan square in the face as he slid open the glider's door, turning to an icy fluid which managed to find the weak point in his quilted snowcoat, slither down his shirt collar, and knock the air out of him all at once. He tried very hard to curse but could only gasp.

Through the brass headset circling the back of his head with twin cups resting over his ears and ending in a small microphone by his left cheek, Alan swore he heard Merry chuckle.

He tried to find the ground but it was entirely obscured by the snowstorm which had hit as soon as they approached the eastern tip of the Himalayas. As far as he knew, they could have been a thousand feet in the air or hovering inches above the tundra. Now and then as the swirling flakes left a void, he saw iron rails stretching ahead like ink lines on crisp white paper; the Trans-Asian railway. The Russians had built it, as they did everything, Alan thought, with an overkill which he admired. The rails could have run along the tundra on the Nepalese side of the mountains and have it curve up into Kazakhstan before reaching Moscow, but no, instead they had cut right through thousands of miles of rock with high-gauge tri-rails that stayed functional even in the most severe weather conditions. He had just enough time to wonder what kind of locomotive might run on track like that before he saw its rear end appearing out of the storm.

Wide and low, each steel carriage looked something like the upper half of an oyster shell skimming over the snow, the smoke from various outlets whipped away by the storm as soon as it emerged. Alan could almost believe that the train itself was generating the storm; that would be just like the Russians. He took stock of the train's roof in particular; that speeding, impossibly smooth and surely ice-slick surface he was about to attempt a landing on.

"Why aren't *you* doing this?" Alan shouted into his headset.

"*Feel free to take the controls whenever you like,*" Merry's voice came into his head, tinny and fizzing. She must have taken her hands off the steering lever because the glider pitched violently, turbulence from the storm rattling Alan like a pea in can, and nearly throwing him out into the snow storm.

"You made your point," he grunted, and the glider righted itself.

"*Right then,*" Merry said, shooting him a wicked wink over her shoulder. "*Off you pop.*"

Checking the ties on his coat and hood, then wiggling his goggles until they were comfortable, Alan gave the crotch of his harness one last tug away from anything valuable and flung himself head-first into the storm. The high-pitched whirr of the cable drum, his life-line to the glider, was swiftly lost in the storm's tumult. His coat, which Merry swore was built for this kind of thing, may have kept him warm, but did nothing for the buffering of the wind or sheering force of the air on his face as he hurtled earthward. His duster would have been wholly ineffective, but he still missed it. The cable ran out with a jerk, and Alan let his body go completely flaccid in order to absorb the shock. The train's roof was perhaps ten feet below. Close for comfort. If Merry had taken a dip with the wind, he'd have gone splat. He managed to look upward and realised that the glider wasn't directly above him as he had assumed. Merry was accounting for the train's speed, the force of the storm, and Alan's pendulous weight all at once, so that the glider was actually out to the side of the train, and the cable ran diagonally, tugged sideways by the wind. Alan shook his head. He was suddenly glad that Merry's letter of Marque had put her on his team.

Her voice came in over his headset: "*Now comes the hard bit. Try not to die.*"

And he slowly moved downward, toward the train's rooftop, only occasionally spun by the wind. His boots dangled inches over the steel, and then he was down, crouched on the train against the storm. Cutting the cable loose, he threw himself flat. The cable whipped away, as did the dark shape of the glider in his peripheral vision, just as the mountainside swallowed the train whole.

A frustrated crackle came in over the headset, but no words. The rock had cut him off from Merry for the moment. Luckily, it had also cut off the storm. The air in the tunnel still felt fast enough to flay him, but at least he could see. He had to move quickly. Uncoupling a caged lamp from his harness, Alan activated it, letting his eyes adjust to the new light for a fraction of a second. Bathed in the greenish glow, he made an executive decision, slipping a small knife from his boot and cutting the ties on his coat in one deft sweep of the blade. The cumbersome garment rolled away, lost in the tunnel's darkness, and the train's slipstream tugged at him a little less. Rising into a half stand, he began to scuttle back along the train, moving with the motion rather than against it in odd goosey strides as the train moved faster than his feet would compensate for. He didn't know how long the tunnel was, but he needed to be between the carriages or preferably inside before it ended. There would be nothing more embarrassing than someone finding his corpse flash-frozen when the locomotive reached its destination.

The lantern made scuttling shadows on the tunnel's low ceiling and shimmering pools on the train's roof; a combination which left Alan feeling drunk and dazed. His eyes just didn't want to see both effects together.

Before he knew it, he had reached the rear of the carriage, and was just dropping beneath the parapet when the tunnel ended and the storm smashed into him. A short drop turned into a cacophonous barrel roll as the wind and snow and light came back all at once. The lantern was whipped from Alan's hand and smashed on the carriage's platform. Spun by the wind in mid-drop Alan twisted in the air and didn't contact the ground where he had planned. He threw out a hand and caught a slippery railing with a tenuous grip, his body continuing to fall until his stomach hit the edge of the platform and he bounced, legs flapping uselessly in the gap between the carriages, making the aches from his previous day's activities seem brand new again. His fingers began to peel from the railing, no longer able to halt the momentum of his body. He slapped the platform with his other arm, cast wide, fingers straining against freezing steel as he started to slide. With nothing else he could do, he screwed his eyes shut, as if that would help, and tried to think heavy, sticky thoughts.

The train seemed about to jettison him out into the fleeting tundra when Alan's flailing feet finally hit something solid. He didn't question it. His eyes snapped open and with every ounce of energy he could muster, he leapt from the unseen foothold, scrambling with his hands and letting his body roll onto the safety of the carriage's platform.

Looking back, he saw that the connection between the carriages was what his foot had come into contact with; a very narrow steel arrangement which he'd been incredibly lucky to have found. He took a moment to note the throb in his bones, the burning in his fingers, the sting of the cold, and was just convincing himself that his luck was natural skill when his headset crackled.

"*Are you dead?*"

"Yes," he managed.

"*I'm inconsolable.*"

"Weep at my funeral, won't you?" he muttered into his microphone as he dragged himself up into a seated position and hugged his ribs for a moment.

"*Probably not. But I'll pay some attractive women to throw themselves on your coffin before we bury you."*

Through the freezing numbness in his face, Alan thought he felt himself smile.

There was a moment of blessed, pain-filled silence before Merry chirped in again.

"Those cards aren't going to steal themselves."

Alan said something unsanitary under his breath, but hoisted himself to his feet anyway.

The locking wheel on the carriage door took a little persuasion, ice crystals cascading from it as Alan wrenched, but it finally opened and he ducked inside, banishing the storm behind him. Rubbing his hands together, he took a moment to catch his breath and see if any of his frost-bitten body would regain feeling, or possibly drop off. When he didn't hear anything thud onto the floor, he took that as a good sign and looked around the room. Tightly packed steel crates left only a small space for movement. Frosty light from the blizzard outside filtered in through small windows which, accompanied with the orange glow of caged light bulbs overhead, gave an odd grey/orange luminescence to the room.

But, more importantly, the carriage was occupied.

Four people stood in a tense tableau between the crates, a small army's worth of ordinance trained on each other. They stared at Alan for a moment, and then some intricate manoeuvring happened between them, and suddenly some of the guns were being pointed at Alan as well.

"Alan. What's going on? Have you found the cards?"

"I'll get back to you, Merry," Alan said. "This just got a bit complicated."

6

ALAN ADJUSTED HIS harness nonchalantly, then the set of his shoulder holster, and corrected where his shirt had become twisted in his fall. While he made a nice show of all that, he took in the carriage's other passengers through his peripheral vision.

He'd walked into the middle of a Mexican standoff. Ironically, without any Mexicans, but plenty of other nationalities. One man, slick, dark, stouter than Alan, was trying to own the whole room with a pair of oversized Colt pistols. American, then. A petite Asian woman in a high-collared black tunic and matching trousers embroidered with silver cherry blossoms seemed poised to fend off bullets with a slim katana; a number of other blades adorned her person. As Alan watched, she slowly reached for the holster at her hip, producing a naked sword hilt from which a blade flicked open like a switchblade.

That was pretty impressive.

The remaining two were Russians. No mistaking it. Stern mouthed with platinum hair and identical faces, both women dressed for the weather in long, black, fur-lined coats. They each had a revolver, and what looked like a short sword.

On a pedestal behind the Russians was a small mahogany box with a paper label pasted to the top. Even from where he stood, Alan could make out the vague Frenchness of the handwritten words. Not that he knew what they said.

"If you all leave now—" one of the Russians growled.

"—no more will be said of it," her sister finished.

Alan hoped they didn't always do that. It could get really annoying.

"Not on your life," the American muttered. "I've got you all right where I want you."

Alan sighed, and waited for the Asian woman to have her say. She maintained a dignified, violent silence.

"Russia, America, the East Asian Empire—" he began.

"—and an Englishman," interrupted the American. "The British Empire wants those cards too, huh?"

"I think you'll find the British Empire wants everything," Alan snarked. "But let's not talk politics. It's boring. Everyone here has a Letter of Marque, yes?"

With much shifting of eyes, the group agreed.

"Good, then we're all Privateers. We're all doing the same job, and none of us are really bothered about who gets those cards as long as we get paid. Stop me any time if I'm wrong."

"Alan, who are you talking to? Get out of there. The train is about to hit a long tunnel. I won't be able to get you out."

Alan tugged his headset down to hang around his neck so that Merry became a distant hiss.

"You are wrong, Englishman. We are here—"

"—for the good of Russia. No longer will your little country have a—"

"—monopoly on advanced technology."

"Hey," said the American. "We invented some stuff, too."

Alan rolled his eyes. "What I *mean* is that there's a really easy way to make sure we all get paid and leave here without any unnecessary bullet holes. Can anyone guess what it is?"

The EAP representative finally broke her silence: "We split the cards."

"And no one will be the wiser. Let the brains back home race each other if they want. We could all be a long way elsewhere by then," Alan nodded along as he spoke, willing the other Privateers to agree.

The silence was deafening. The tips of two katanas lowered slightly. The American moved his index fingers a fraction of an inch away from their respective triggers. The Russians exchanged a glance.

America: "The man has a point. Smart and rich is better than dead."

East Asian Empire: "Your philosophy is sound."

Lots of weapons began to look less threatening. Except the Russians. There was a flicker between the women, something Alan spotted but couldn't decode. He reached for his revolver just as one of the sisters grabbed the open box of punch cards, and they both bolted toward the carriage's furthest end, firing wildly behind them. The other Privateers dropped or leapt or rolled for cover.

The bullets made wild ricochets around the carriage's

steel interior, forcing Alan to stay down until the *shpang*s and *doing*s died away.

Then he was on his feet and in pursuit, doubled over and running behind a row of storage crates.

From the corner of his eye he could see a swift blur of motion. The American ran straight after the women at full speed, firing off random shots as he went while the dainty form sticking to the in the carriage's shadows was surely the Asian woman heading in the same direction, All three Privateers reached the door at the end of the carriage at the same time, almost slamming into each other. They all skidded to a halt.

"Alan Shaw. Three way split," Alan blurted.

"Wai Liling. A third is better than nothing."

"Harrison Stanhope. Ladies first."

Wai booted open the door with a placid smile, and disappeared through it. Alan jabbed his thumb at the door and followed the American as he barrelled through.

The storm was still raging outside. Wai had already jumped the gap between the carriages and was struggling with the locking wheel of the next door. Alan and Harrison cleared it together, Alan grabbing the American under his arm as he almost slipped on the ice, and dragging him to his feet.

"Steady on. No need to make me think Americans are clumsier than I already do," Alan shouted over the wind.

The American flashed him a sarcastic smile. "You're a hoot, Shaw."

Both men reached the door and, sliding Wai aside, put their backs to the locking wheel.

Nothing.

"Damn it. They must have it jammed," Harrison kicked the door with his boot.

Alan tried again, and again, with the same result each time. "Balls. Bloody balls."

"Say, where'd the girl go?" Harrison said. Alan spun around to see that they really were alone on the platform. Just as he was about to use a more severe curse, the door behind them creaked and swung inwards. There stood Wai with a smile on her face.

"So slow," she said, and then was gone into the gloom of the carriage's insides again.

"Do you get the feeling we're surplus to requirements?" Alan asked.

Harrison grunted and broke into a run.

They almost careened right through Wai where she stood in the walkway of the next carriage. It was unimaginatively similar to the first, stacked with crates at either side, small windows casting more shadows than light. The one stark difference was the pair of corpses on the ground.

Alan sidled closer, thumbing the hammer of his revolver. The dull click gave him a moment's comfort.

The Russians hadn't gone easily. Their lifeless faces were contorted into a fear without end, sweat still graced their rapidly cooling flesh, their pupils were black holes in the stark globes of their eyes. Wai knelt between the corpses, pressing a finger to their throats, and shook her head to confirm what they already knew. When she removed her fingers, a viscous grey fluid slicked her dainty gloves. Trying to shake it off, she failed, and wiped her hand as respectfully as possible on the nearest corpse's coat.

"You don't see that every day," Alan muttered.

"Hell, Shaw, who sees that *any* day?"

"Stick with me, it's more often than you'd think," Alan retorted.

Wai seemed just about to point out that the card box was missing when the carriage plunged into darkness.

"We've hit the tunnel—" Alan said, but stopped dead when he heard a rattle from the other end of the carriage. In the sudden dark it sounded louder than it should; the rattling of a locking wheel, perhaps; then a high-pitched screech of complaining metal.

"Light! Who has light?" Alan hissed, letting his revolver lead him into the darkness. A lance of pale luminescence cut over his shoulder bright enough to make him wince. Harrison stepped up beside him, stretching out his palm, which wore a device made of a single lens wrapped in wires trailing along his arm to a small contraption on his belt that he had to keep cranking to maintain voltage. Alan squinted into the shadows at the end of the carriage, where the steel door had been wrenched from its hinges and lay in halves on the ground.

"Did anyone's Marque mention anything incredibly strong, slimy and homicidal?" Alan asked.

"Unfortunately, no," Wai muttered.

"Investigate or retreat?" Harrison said. He looked to his fellow Privateers. There were more grins than sane people. He chuckled, "Yeah, that's what I figured."

They moved forward in unison, each climbing out

through the ruined door into the whistling darkness of the tunnel. The next carriage was a low, wide platform, clusters of steel cable along one edge to connect more cage lamps which shook in the wind, and pyramids of wooden logs at regular intervals.

And that was when Alan noticed what he'd been missing. Where were all the people? Even a freight train had some guards, the odd engineer. But they'd seen no one. He had the sinking feeling that there were a lot more corpses in front and behind him. It wasn't a nice feeling, but one he was oddly accustomed to.

It'd be just my luck to get blamed for all this, he thought.

He hopped the next gap to catch up to Harrison and Wai, who were both stood stock still in the dark. And Alan, who had to admit that he was having a slow day, finally saw why.

In the centre of the platform, with the tunnel's barrelling wind flapping at a long, high-collared coat, stood a dark figure. The platform's safety light did nothing to illuminate it. Harrison raised his torch slowly, revealing black boots with the punch card box set between them, leading up to grey uniform trousers beneath the double-breasted coat. The grey fluid ran from out of the coat's sleeves, slicking a pair of black leather gloves before dripping to the floor. Alan caught his breath as he spotted an insignia embroidered on the coat; the sun-eating wolf of the Ordo Fenriz.

Alan swallowed hard: "Oh God, no."

7

PERCHED BENEATH A black officer's hat, shadows clustered around two pinpricks of light, and ran like oil in the wrinkles around a pointed nose and impossibly wide, grinning mouth. The same grey fluid slicked the figure's teeth and lips as it hissed two words.

"Alan Shaw."

Harrison manage to tear his eyes away from the creature long enough to give Alan a stare. "You know this thing?"

"We're hardly pally," Alan managed to mutter.

The creature chuckled to itself; a deep, wet sound. Underneath the figure's long coat, something writhed, shifting the material in odd ways. Alan had sensed something off about Herr Volkert on their first meeting, especially when the villain had shrugged off a bullet, and now he could see what he'd always suspected. There was something paranormal about the leader of the Ordo Fenriz, and it seemed to be getting worse as the years passed. Now, he was more monster than man.

Alan took a deep breath.

"Volkert. You're looking like shit, actually."

The officer threw back its head, tossing laughter into the wind. Every hair on Alan's body did a Mexican wave.

"Oh, if only you knew. If only you knew," Volkert hissed.

"I don't suppose you're willing to hand over the cards so we can all be on our way?"

"Counter offer," Volkert's grin slithered even wider and Alan could see more teeth, more than were possible in a human head, "I murder you all."

Alan looked to Wai and then Harrison. "Any objections?"

Everything happened at once.

Harrison dropped his light, pitching them into relative darkness, drew his revolvers and began firing just as Alan did the same. In the muzzle flare, Volkert darted forward frame by frame, his feet startlingly fast in the darkness. He didn't even bother to dodge the bullets. Every one hit him with a wet thwack, and didn't slow him even a little. As his revolver ran dry, Alan saw Volkert's mouth yawn open. He gulped when he saw even more teeth, row upon row spreading down Volkert's throat, glistening with grey fluid, each set gnashing independently of each other as what had once been a man cleared the final steps toward Alan's throat.

Wai's switchblade katanas caught the creature in a snick-snack of blurred razor edges. Volkert screeched in the dark as Alan took retreating steps, fumbling with the bullets in his pocket in an attempt to reload. In the half-light of the carriage's safety lamps, Wai pressed the creature. Her feet were deft and blows certain, forcing Volkert to retreat and dodge and weave constantly. Glops of grey fluid leaked from the creature and flicked from the ends of Wai's whirling blades. As Volkert's uniform began to shred and tear, thick limbs could be seen beneath, like eels wrapped around his body. Alan tried desperately to forget as soon as he saw them.

Harrison tore off a few rounds, puncturing Volkert's shoulder and thigh. The creature didn't flinch.

A sound like thunder crashed over them, knocking Alan and Harrison on their backs. Even Wai had to brace herself against the concussion of light and wind as the train punched its way out of the mountainside. Cursing against his sudden blindness, Alan threw a hand over his eyes. They adjusted quick enough for him to see Volkert leap from the platform's edge. Alan scuttled forward, slipping on pools of slime, cursing the whole time and, grabbing a lamp's post, leaned out over the edge.

The tracks continued out over a gorge between the mountains on a viaduct which had to be a hundred feet high. Volkert was gone; not a sniff of a slither of him. There wasn't even a splash in the river below.

Alan span around to his fellow Privateers: "How were you getting off the train?"

"What the hell kind of monster was that?" Harrison retorted.

"Answer the question!"

"I would wait for Moscow and use stealth," Wai said, apparently unperturbed by coming face to face with Volkert. She was wiping her katana blades a little too calmly.

"Parachute," the American said.

"Better," Alan said. "Give it to me."

Harrison slid off the harness he wore over his shirt and tossed it over. "Great. Now what about me?"

Alan took off his headset as it began to crackle and hiss with the reconnection. "Her name is Merry. Tell her what happened."

"What *did* happen?" Harrison demanded.

But Alan had already thrown himself off of the platform and into the ravine below.

8

ALAN COUNTED IN his head as he struggled to shrug on the parachute mid-air. Luckily, this wasn't his first time. He actually began to wonder why someone would do it any other way. This was so *fun*.

Maybe a hundred feet, he thought to himself. *Don't wait long enough that Volkert has a good lead. But give yourself chance to slow down and not break your legs.*

That should do it.

His body lurched as the parachute caught the air and spread wide. Taking hold of the parachute's cords, he tried to steer the parachute away from the river. Either bank would do, but an icy bath would probably be the end of the chase.

The riverbank was a mixture of rocky outcrops and strangled trees. Sailing over the canopy, Alan tugged his feet up as naked, icy branches tried to snag his boots. There. Just ahead the river curved around the mountain and had cut a neat shale beach, which would be perfect for landing. Alan was upon it almost as soon as he'd seen it and his boots finally hit ground. He ran with the motion as the parachute tried to overtake him, and then jerked back when a nearby tree grabbed the complex network of cords and yanked him off his feet. His trousers did nothing to cushion the blow as his bottom hit the shale hard enough to knock him sick. Managing to eject the parachute before the wind could catch it and drag him along the beach and leave him shredded by the rocks, Alan rolled over and struggled to his feet. He took a deep breath to still the nausea, and set off along the riverbank at something pathetically less than his full speed, rubbing his behind with one hand.

Volkert had to have landed somewhere. Alan just had to find the signs.

But there was nothing. Stopping to search the ground, he couldn't see a single boot print or, he shuddered at the thought, slithery trail.

The damned Ordo Fenriz had slipped him again. As a boy, they'd sunk Alan's ship, drowned his friends, shot his brother, and escaped him every time. God only knew what had happened to Volkert since they'd last met eight years ago; the sickening grin was the same, but the grey goo and teeth were a new development. Alan kicked up a clump of shale in his frustration, sending it scuttling across the icy river. He'd had a chance to even the score and Volkert seemed to have slipped off the hook so easily.

Turning back toward the viaduct, fully prepared to scream with frustration, Alan saw that he had simply overshot Volkert by about ninety feet. The creature hadn't fallen. He'd swung beneath the viaduct with inhuman agility, and was now crawling into the cockpit of a contraption waiting in the protection of the great structure's eaves.

"I'll be damned."

As he watched, Volkert's machine disengaged from the viaduct's underbelly, dropping like a rock. There was a soft *whoomph* of engines and the machine unfolded wing-like prominences that pumped and stretched, making the machine bob and swoop. It skimmed the ground, cutting a ditch in the snow with the heat of its exhaust, and headed straight for Alan. Alan swore he could see Volkert behind the windscreen, grinning with those too-many teeth, salivating goo, eager for murder.

The glider scythed overhead as Alan hit the ground, arms over his head. He rolled, certain that his clothes were aflame from the exhaust, and realised that the snow had melted, leaving him in a puddle of slurry which chilled his bones but made sure he wasn't alight. Dragging himself to his feet, he winced at the crackle and tug of singed skin along his forearms as he tried to follow the glider's trajectory, but it was accelerating away, blurring with the speed. Alan span on the spot. He couldn't follow on foot. He was done. Volkert was gone and it could be years or never again when Alan saw him next.

The hum of engines grew in the valley between the mountains, rising from a whisper to a deafening drone as echoes surrounded him. Shielding his eyes against the blinding white of the snowy sky, Alan spotted a dot, which became the speeding shape of Merry's glider as it dipped underneath the viaduct's arches and headed toward him. Throwing his arms in the air, he waved the glider toward him, trying to convey urgency through mime.

Merry pulled the glider up short, effortlessly going from a hurtling dive to hovering a few feet above the tundra. The sliding doors were thrown back, and Harrison and Wai's hands extended down to drag Alan unceremoniously onto the cabin's floor.

"Follow that glider!" he yelled to Merry who, to her credit, didn't even ask why. The glider lurched, throwing Alan onto his back, and forcing Harrison and Wai to grab for anything they could to stay upright.

"Got away did he?" Harrison asked.

"Not bloody yet, he hasn't," Alan muttered as he dragged himself up and through to the cabin. "Merry, can you catch him?"

The pilot gave him a tired smile. "Please."

"Good. Someone needs a boot up his arse."

"Anyone I know?"

"Insane cult leader who leaks slime and may be transforming into some kind of tentacle beast."

Merry's eyebrows knotted, but she managed to quip anyway. "Doesn't ring any bells."

"Lucky you."

The glider swooped upward in a steep climb, cutting high over the trees and giving them a better vantage point. Merry's face lit with the green glow of the radar globe as she searched for their prey. Right at the edge of the globe a flicker of movement quickly disappeared. She made a sound of satisfaction in the back of her throat, and the glider swung about in pursuit of the signal.

"Is there a plan?" Harrison leaned through from the rear cabin onto the back of Alan's chair.

"Run in, shoot Volkert until he doesn't move anymore.

Possibly get Wai to cut him into pieces to make sure he's really dead."

"And get the punch cards so we can get paid, right?" asked the American.

"If you like." Alan was too preoccupied with searching the horizon for Volkert's glider.

"That's a rubbish plan, Alan," Merry offered.

"Ill-advised, perhaps," Wai offered from where she sat in the rear compartment, tending to her blades and other kit. "The Volkert creature appears to be formidable."

Alan spun in his seat so that he could address them all. "Does anyone have anything better?"

"Don't look at me; I'm just fine with the shooting," Harrison offered from behind raised palms.

"I might, actually," Merry offered. "Check under Wai's seat."

Harrison disappeared back into the cabin; a minute later, his voice carried back.

"I'll be damned."

Everyone except Merry craned their necks to see.

Alan reached into the satchel that Harrison returned with and plucked out a small glass sphere. Holding it up to the light, he tilted the sphere back and forth, letting the golden liquid inside slosh around.

"This isn't what I think it is."

"That depends what you think it is," Merry chuckled.

Harrison took one look at the sphere and suddenly held the bag as far away from himself as possible, as if it would do him any good.

"You have a bag of nitroglycerin in your glider?"

"Don't worry; it's diluted, and the glass is toughened.

Unless you really give it some welly, it should be fine."

"What if you crashed?" Harrison couldn't hide the disbelief from his voice as he searched for somewhere to put the bag that was far, far away, and came up with nothing.

"I'd probably be dead anyway," Merry said, matter-of-factly.

"The English are insane. This much nitro would turn you to soup."

"Best not drop it, then," said Alan as he carefully placed the sphere back in the satchel. Reaching into the storage above their seats, Alan took out his duster, feeling instantly better as he slid it on.

Throughout, Wai just sat and smiled to herself quietly.

"We've got him," Merry reported.

Just ahead, Volkert's glider came into view through a cloudy haze, bobbing and jerking its way through the sky. Alan grinned and dove toward the glider's side door.

"Give me one of those nitro-spheres. I've got some revenge coming my way."

"Do that and you'll blow the punchcards to kingdom come!" Harrison complained.

"Damn the punchcards. This is about more than money." The sentence was barely out before Alan contorted his face and muttered: "I can't believe I just said that."

"To hell with you, Shaw," Harrison said, moving the satchel out of Alan's reach. "I want to eat this week."

"Hush." Wai had stood up and was pointing past them both, through the cockpit's window. "The creature is not alone, it seems."

9

DESCENDING LAZILY FROM the cloud cover was the belly of an immense airship. If it landed on London, Alan thought, it would dwarf the Houses of Parliament. Thunderous turbines held its dark metal body aloft, from its broad nose fin to the fluted rear. Alan couldn't help seeing a giant air kraken, lacking of its tentacles. And, as he expected, a huge wolf's head eating a small red sun decorated the side.

"Subtle," Alan muttered, as he watched Volkert's glider head straight for the Ordo Fenriz airship.

Harrison was shaking his head in silent disbelief. "Forget it. It isn't worth it. I'll wash some dishes or mop a floor for my supper. Drop me off here."

"I am tempted to come with you," said Wai. "If it wasn't for another chance to meet that creature in combat—"

"We need a new plan," Merry said.

"Why is everyone so preoccupied with plans all of a sudden?" Alan threw up his hands. "They're overrated if you ask me. Merry, get us as close as you can. I'm going to blow something up. Then I'm going to shoot things. And when I run out of bullets, I'll punch something. Anyone who needs more of a plan than that can stay behind."

"Aye aye, Captain!" Merry said warily, taking the glider high before they could be spotted, withdrawing into the clouds. "They'll get us on radar but it's a lot harder to shoot us down if they can't see us."

"Fine. Then let's not mess around," Alan said as he checked his gear. "Get us as close as you can."

"Us? I haven't said I'm going yet."

"For the love of God, Harrison, stop whining. I'm not going to beg you, and I could frankly do without your hassle. Sit tight like a good boy and we'll drop you off on our way back. Unless you want to get off here, of course," Alan said as he pulled back the glider's door, letting a gust of freezing air into the cabin. "Wai, you ready?"

The Asian warrior set her toes to the edge of the cabin in answer, swaying in time with the breeze and the dip of the glider. She seemed more steady than Alan felt.

The glider hurtled onward, making the Ordo Fenriz airship loom larger and seem more impenetrable with every second. Merry took them upward, over the crest of the airship's hull, which looked quite a bit like a steel cliff face from so close. Then the airship was skudding below them. Merry scanned ahead from behind her goggles and finally found what she was looking for.

"Aha! Hold tight!"

Drastically decelerating, she swung the airship about and landed them right on the roof next to a glass viewing dome.

Alan's jaw dropped.

"You said close," she said. Slipping out of her seat, she

moved through to the cabin, buckled on a gun belt that she produced from a compartment above the cockpit, and shouldered the satchel of nitro-spheres. "Harrison, watch the bird."

And she was gone, hopping out onto the airship's roof, with Alan and Wai in her wake. Harrison sat for a moment, looking after them with his jaw desperately trying to connect with his knees.

As they ran toward the viewing globe, bent double against the wind, Alan caught up to Merry.

"You didn't have to come," he said.

"I might not have mentioned it, but this is my last job as an aircorp captain. I've officially done my term. I'll be damned if I'm going to spend it sat down the whole time. If nothing else, I want to see this thing you're all so dizzy over."

"Careful what you wish for, Merry."

As they reached the reinforced glass dome, Merry smiled at him, and plucked a nitro-sphere from her satchel. She tested the wind, something than Alan would have never thought of, circled the dome so that she was upwind of it, and yelled, "Open sesame!"

The nitro-sphere vapourised the dome, the violent wind tugging the explosion almost instantly into a comet tail before snuffing it completely. A smoking hole indicated where the dome had been. With Wai leading the way, the Privateers dropped down into the belly of the airship.

The décor was the exact opposite of what Alan had expected. Long tapestries lined the walls, half-lit by glass lamps made to look like fiery brands. The corridors that the three Privateers moved along were narrow and cold, carpeted down the centre in alternating dark reds, greys and black. If Alan ignored the hum of distant engines, which seemed to make every surface shiver, he could have been in any ancient castle across Europe. The ship was quiet, too. Every door was closed, every corridor empty. They passed vast, open rooms, which could have held banquets, devoid of any Ordo representatives. Alan started to get a twitchy.

"I don't like this. Something isn't right."

"Agreed. We should separate," said Wai.

"Take some of these, and see what damage you can do," said Merry, digging in her satchel.

"If I set them down correctly, I should only need to set off one when we're ready, and the rest will break as a consequence," Wai answered.

"Smart," Alan agreed. "I'm glad you came along, Wai."

Merry handed over a dozen nitro-spheres, which Wai stowed away in various pouches and pockets, and then the petite warrior vanished into the bowels of the ship.

Alan and Merry moved on, heading toward the fore of the airship where it seemed a control centre might be, and still, no resistance.

"Have you noticed—" Alan started.

"Yup," came Merry's reply.

"Not just me then."

And finally, through a winding, circuitous route, they came to a pair of metal doors, inlaid with various woodland creatures in an old Norse style, all bowing to (or possibly dying beneath) an overpowering sun at the tableau's peak. Alan noticed a distinct lack of wolf in the image, but was less disappointed when he eased the door open.

The chamber, backed by a huge steel-reinforced window which seemed to show the entire earth beyond, was exactly what Alan expected from a villain's lair. A deep red carpet, softer and richer than some Alan had seen in opulent homes, stretched from wall to distant wall. A series of consoles ran in a semi-circle at the room's furthest end where hooded cultists worked feverishly. But the ceiling was the real spectacle. The huge gaping maw of the Fenriz wolf stretched across the entire space, artfully carved in mahogany, the lolling tongue (which held a red-glass chandelier at its tip) reaching out to taste the intruder's flesh.

Alan felt every muscle tense as if his inner ancestral monkey was screaming for him to flee. He caught Merry's aghast expression in his peripheral vision. Good, at least he wasn't the only one.

"You are persistent as ever, I see."

Across the ocean of Ordo Fenriz soldiers that filled the hall, on a platform backed by an immense window, Volkert couldn't be grinning any more if he tried, and that was really something for a man who seemed to be more teeth than face. He stood before the console, totally at ease with himself. "Well, don't just stand there, welcome our guests."

Row upon row of Ordo Fenriz soldiers turned on their heels to face the Privateers; hundreds of grinning little wolves staring out of their uniforms.

Alan tried to think of something funny to say, but his heart wasn't in it.

10

AS IF THEY had just wandered into a friend's living room, Volkert waved them over "Come in, come in. Come see what we've made."

"We could leave," Alan whispered.

"Do you want to?"

"I'm a bit intrigued."

Volkert was still grinning, waiting patiently for them to decide.

"On a scale of yawning-kitten to Satan-with-a-headache, how evil is this cult?" Merry asked.

"If the Devil were here, he'd be taking notes," Alan said.

Both Privateers came to their conclusions at once, and set off across the room at a nonchalant pace, the Ordo soldiers parting for them. Alan nodded to a few, passing pleasantries that weren't reciprocated.

"—bit nippy out, isn't it?"

"—bet this place keeps the cleaners busy."

They climbed the few steps to Volkert's platform. Alan's skin began to tug at his bones as it tried desperately to crawl away from the Ordo leader. In a last ditch effort at self-preservation, Alan rounded the table at the dais' centre to stand directly opposite the grinning creature. Merry followed him. He spotted the punch card box on the table's edge by Volkert. Too far away for a quick smash and grab effort.

"Pretty isn't it?" Volkert hissed, gesturing to the table. In its hollow centre, a large gyroscope took up the space, with silver rails carrying spinning spheres of multi-coloured metal around a central golden globe. "Spinning, spinning, and we don't feel a thing."

"You've lost it, Herr."

Volkert gave a wet chuckle. "Perhaps. But I'm sure you didn't chase me this far for the sake of debate. What is it you want from me? Or have you come to be a nuisance?"

"The punch cards you stole. We want them back."

Volkert stroked the small wooden box with a gloved finger, leaving a streak of ooze across the lid. "Are they yours to demand such a thing? I think not. They were in the possession of those pleasant Russian ladies when they came to me."

Alan had a mental flash of the Russian Privateers' contorted corpses. "What the hell did you do to them, Volkert?"

The Ordo leader returned his attention to the planetary gyroscope. "You see how they spin, Mister Shaw? Like a great cosmic loom, pulling threads of the future into the present and leaving the tapestry of history behind. And we are all there, on this little planet." He traced the arc of a small blue sphere "Do you think that was luck? I don't. The Gods have left us here for a reason. My reason, Mister Shaw, is to play out the end of the Gods' story. The final flourish to an epic saga which has spanned the ages. I have the privilege of bringing all this to an end."

Alan rolled his eyes at Merry. "You get used to the ramblings after a while. I find it easier to just tune it out," he said.

The young pilot gave a shaky smile.

"Jokes and quips and mockery. They are all you have." Volkert sneered.

"I stopped you last time, didn't I? You had me outnumbered, outgunned, and outmanoeuvred. I still stopped you."

Volkert nodded. "I was most annoyed to find the amulet had been taken from the Hand of Glory. You played well with nothing but a handful of gypsy magic. But no, you didn't win. You were once a nuisance. Now, my destiny has surpassed the point where you might be significant."

Alan could feel the anger rising like hot mercury in his throat. He balled his fists tight, letting the feeling pass, and forced himself to relax again.

"The amulet was kept from me for a short time only." Volkert gestured to the cultists working behind him, their deep red hooded robes decorated with a black circle outlined with a white corona. With their hands pressed to the console's top, the cultists swayed in time. Alan swore he could hear muttering coming from each of them, but he couldn't make out the words. Looking closer at the console he could see that there were no buttons, no dials, nor gauges or levers, only a length of black marble with veins of a purple, shimmering mineral. The colour reminded him of an amulet his brother had once hidden in the British

Museum for safekeeping. He had the sinking feeling that those robed figures were somehow flying the airship. As with anything that he found vaguely disturbing, he ignored the hows and whys, and focussed on planning to blow it up.

"Alan, this is technomancy," Merry muttered, snapping him back to the present. Her eyebrows were knotted and she seemed to be fighting the urge to run away. "Cutting edge technology mixed with magic. The Empire outright forbids the practice while insisting it doesn't exist. They say there definitely isn't a secret government ministry studying it. At all."

Alan made a little sound in the back of his throat. The Ordo Fenriz were starting to make sense. It had only taken a decade or so.

"You don't seem very surprised," Merry continued.

"I've been around a bit. Seen some things." Alan tried to look nonplussed while the hairs on his neck tried to uproot themselves and run away. "Do you believe in this stuff?"

Merry nodded toward Volkert. "Crazy face over there does. And that's enough for me right now."

Volkert shuddered. Something beneath his uniform writhed and pulsed. Groaning, he gripped the edge of the table until indentations were left in the wood. "Your young friend is most astute." His smile never slipped, a long droplet of the grey slime slithered from his lip. "I could show you such things, Shaw. Things beyond our world that I have been blessed to witness. Such incomprehensible darkness—"

A thump of distant concussion shook the floor, throwing Volkert off balance, and the subsequent groan of straining steel battered their ears. The airship pitched violently. Through the huge viewing window Alan could see the smoke of a destroyed engine beginning to trail around them as the airship began to spin. The mountains, which they had been skirting to the east, loomed closer in one almighty lurch.

Alan span toward the assembled Ordo soldiers, who all seemed to think that raising their weapons would somehow stop their airship from crashing. He grinned.

"Hold on tight, everyone!"

Another punch of thunder and the right side of the hall exploded inward. Ordo uniforms with slack meaty fillings flew through the air. Merry grabbed Alan by the shirt and yanked him toward the door, tossing a nitro-sphere ahead of her. She screamed something at him but the next explosion drowned her out. Alan tried to follow but his legs wouldn't move. Looking back, he saw a thick black tentacle had wrapped around him from ankle to knee with an almighty grip. Merry jerked back when Alan proved immobile. Snapping her fingers from him, he pushed her away, yelling for her to run as another of Wai's distant explosions shook the airship. Alan fell to his hands and knees as the tentacle snaking up toward his groin gave another tug. Merry rocked on the spot for a moment, looking uncertainly between the door and Alan. He stared at her with every ounce of sincerity he could muster and screamed for her to run.

He saw her dart away, down from the dais and through the writhing mass of injured soldiers, and he turned back. The tentacle emanated some penetrating cold that made the bones in his leg ache. As the limb snaked around his lower stomach, Alan gasped, the icy slime stealing his breath. He tried to pry at the tentacle, to twist himself away, but its grip was absolute. At the other end of the ebony limb where it disappeared around the table's base, the face of Volkert came into view. His own limbs carried him crab-wise around the table, his joints twisted beyond their normal range, body hung low from the ground with more tentacles questing from the gaps in his uniform, cuffs and neckline. His mouth was open to reveal those rows of ooze-slicked teeth.

Alan tugged at his revolver, which came free on the second attempt, and emptied the chamber into Volkert's gnashing maw. The creature screeched and shook but continued to advance, just as the tentacle dragged Alan closer. Alan gripped the hot barrel of his revolver, wincing against the pain, and pistol-whipped Volkert across his distended jaw. The creature barely noticed. Alan thrashed and kicked with his free limbs, catching Volkert's wrist and knocking the creature to the ground momentarily, but there were too many other limbs and tentacles for it to slow his adversary for long. Alan's teeth gritted hard enough that his jaw ached, the tentacle's squeeze making his head pound as if the pressure might pop his skull. Volkert lunged, hungry for a fatal bite from Alan's throat. The Privateer jammed his revolver into Volkert's mouth, knocking out several teeth in the process but forcing it to stay open, and continued to punch the creature with everything he had until his arm and back and neck throbbed with the effort.

Against everything he expected, Alan began a tirade to fill his last moments, emphasising his words in time with his blows. "I was *only* supposed to be *stealing* a bloody *box*. And here *you* are, *ruining* everything with your *face* and your *stench* and your *stupid* plans. If I had a *pound* for every *bad* dream I've had about you, *you bastard*, I'd be *rich*. And now you're going to *kill* me. Well, I *hope* I give you *indigestion* you—"

Volkert screeched, rattling Alan's eardrums. The creature writhed, its legs a blur of motion as it tried desperately to turn itself around. Spotting the hilt of a katana jammed between Volkert's shoulder blades, Alan began to laugh hysterically. He twisted and pulled, but still couldn't move until Wai dropped down in front of him and severed the tentacle with one swipe of her remaining blade. He fell back as the limb went limp. Something grabbed him under each armpit and yanked. He kicked with his feet, gaining distance from the thrashing Volkert, and looked over his shoulder briefly to see Merry dragging him away.

"I told you to run," he said, as she helped him gain his feet.

"You never said I couldn't come back."

Alan turned to shout Wai over his shoulder, only to see the mountainside looming before the huge window. "Balls. Merry, hold on!"

The airship clipped the cliff in a shower of rock that shattered the airship's window as it rebounded, scraping along the mountainside. The ground beneath the Privateers' feet seemed to disappear and then slam into them all at once. Only Wai managed to stay upright. As the floor pitched forward, Volkert screeched and slid along the inverted ground toward the window and the yawning void beyond. Alan jammed his hand into Merry's uniform, fumbling desperately.

"Oy! This is hardly the time!" Merry yelled, but Alan had found what he was looking for, and hurled the nitro-sphere at Volkert's feet. Chunks of grey flesh and slime spattered the air, the rest of Volkert shooting straight out into space, hurled through the dissipating flame of the explosion with a silent scream, to disappear beneath the airship. Alan hoped for a shredding sound as Volkert hit one of the few remaining engines, but knew he wasn't that lucky. It had still felt good.

Using each other to stand, Merry and Alan headed for the door, ignoring the groaning Ordo Fenriz soldiers who lay strewn around the room. Out in the corridor, Wai caught up and shoved them ahead.

"Head for the port side! Hurry!"

Amid the death throes of the airship as it bounced along the mountainside, the Privateers wove their way onward, completely ignored by any Ordo Fenriz they came across.

"Here," Wai yelled. All three Privateers put their backs to the locking wheel of a bulkhead door, and it whipped away from them with the force of the wind, spewing light and snow into their faces. Alan and Merry peered out. It was a long drop and the airship was still moving quickly. Rolling tundra spread out below, but who knew how deep it would be.

"That's a long way down," Merry protested.

"You've jumped out of airships before, you're air corps."

"Usually with a parachute, though."

They both ducked as Wai shot out between them, and disappeared into the snow below.

Alan gestured to the door. "Off you pop."

Merry had just enough time to shoot him a snide smile before Alan shoved her out of the door and hurled himself after her.

11

THE SKY HAD cleared to an impressive blue, broken by infrequent eddies of snow crystals carried on the wind. Alan lay spread-eagled, watching the snow swirls and trying desperately to have some sort of inner existential epiphany, which he always felt he should at moments like these. But nothing would come. And so, when he heard the crunching footfalls of someone approaching, he sat up and looked around.

Trudging across the tundra toward him, Wai was a little travelling smudge of charcoal against the white. Alan managed to find his feet and dusted himself down before the snow could melt and wet him through. It was only when the next breeze caught him that he realised how cold he was. He waved to Wai, who came up toward him.

"Have you seen Merry?"

"I think she is farther down. There is a trail."

They cut across the mountainside. Although trying to avoid the deeper drifts, Alan plunged in up to his chest twice and Wai had to pull him out.

"This is getting really boring now," he mumbled.

As they reached an outcrop in the mountain they saw two things; one was the enormous hulk of the grounded airship, a great steel whale ran aground, half buried in the snow and smoke. There seemed to be no lights or movement from this distance. Not a solitary flicker of life. As they watched, a small avalanche slid down over the airship's prow, obscuring the sneer of the painted wolf.

"Do you think he is dead?" asked Wai.

"I'm not that lucky. But let's hope."

The second thing was a deep rut in the snow, beginning higher up the mountainside and heading down hill. At its lowest end they found Merry, stood with her hands cupped under each armpit, stamping her feet in the cold, blonde tresses flat to her head, ample lips pouting.

"I can't believe you threw me out of an airship," she chattered.

"Better than being in there." Alan jabbed a thumb toward the ruined Ordo airship. He stepped closer and began to rub some warmth into her upper arms. She didn't complain but didn't exactly snuggle into him like he half-hoped she would.

The familiar drone of engines echoed around the mountain, so none of the Privateers could tell which direction they came from. It was Merry who spotted the glider first. It came in less steady than if Merry were at the helm, but it landed successfully on a plateau not far from where they were. The side door slid open as they approached, and Harrison leaned out to greet them.

"Remind me never to invite you three to any parties. You made a real mess out here."

Merry strode straight up to him, punched him square in the chest and shoved past him. "If you've moved anything, I'll kill you."

Wai gave the American an appreciative nod.

Alan shot Harrison a wry smile. "Not bad. For an American."

The roar cut through each of them, on a soul-deep level where their base fears lived. Merry froze, her eyes widening at Alan who spun on the spot, revolver suddenly in hand and cocked. Harrison leaned out of the glider, hand extended to Wai.

"For the love of God, get in."

Wai ignored him, her remaining switchblade katana snapping into full length, but it didn't matter anyway. As Merry leaped into the glider's cockpit and began stabbing buttons, she looked up through the cockpit window as the writhing mass of Volkert approached.

He was snarling, those teeth seeming to take up the entire lower half of his head now. His hat was gone, and he walked barefoot, but the shreds of his coat remained, flared around him by the tentacles which spilled from every tear and cuff and collar, whipping like slimy cat tails. As he prowled toward the glider, small trails of smoke wisping up from him, he lurched forward, darting cheetah-like into an all-fours run, straight toward her. She had just enough time to scream as, tendrils bursting the uniform, Volkert slammed into the glider's side.

At the loud crack of steel and the crunch of snow as the glider rolled on its side toward them, Harrison dived forward, clearing tons of falling steel with a tight roll. Wai seemed to take no effort in dodging, calculating exactly where the glider's wing and tail would hit the ground, stopping its motion dead and managing to stand precisely on the spot where she'd be safe. Alan threw himself forward, toward the falling glider, and hit the ground where the hole left by the open door would be.

As the glider settled, he stood up, on a small square of snow and inside the now-sideways vehicle. He took no time in climbing up to the cockpit where he found Merry, who'd slipped out of her seat to sit on the snow-facing window in a crumpled heap. He leapt in, standing on the sideways dashboard. As he looked down at her, and she up at him, her eyes widened.

The window above him shattered as he curled his shoulders, glass peppering his back, falling past him, only his body shielding Merry from taking a thousand little cuts from the shards. Tendrils dripped down from the broken side window which was now above them, lashing around his arms and neck, and yanked him right off his feet. Merry shouted something that he couldn't hear as he was whipped up and out of the window—slicing his arms and back on the remaining spines of glass—and tossed into the air. There was no stopping or fighting it, a strength like that. All he could do was close his eyes and brace for the crunch as he twirled off-kilter over the tundra and waited to hit the ground.

Volkert roared atop the glider, arms thrown back and tendrils thrashing with rage.

The shuriken hit his chest in a neat triangle, burying themselves deeper than they should have been able to if he still had bones to stop them. He snarled, dropping into a crouch, and launched himself toward Wai, taking her in a full tackle that sent them both rolling across the snow. The scissoring of her blades was the only sound as she tried desperately to carve her way out of the knot of slithering limbs. But they were tightening, and soon a piercing scream erupted as Volkert began to squeeze the life from her.

A nitro-sphere hit his back dead-centre, sending him rocketing forward, his tentacles loosening so that Wai's body slipped free in the fall, landing face down in the snow as Volkert flew a further ten yards. Harrison's revolvers patiently followed the creature along its trajectory. And when Volkert stood up once more, with what remained of his long coat now long gone, the American opened fire. Knocked from his feet by Harrison's heavy ordinance, Volkert disappeared over a snow bank with a distant thud. Merry leapt down from her vantage point atop her glider as Alan rounded the vehicle's shattered prow, stumbling, soaked and grimacing.

"He can't take much more, can he?" she asked, producing another nitro-sphere in her hand. But as she drew back for the throw, Alan's fingers closed around her wrist.

"That won't do it." He slid the sphere from her fingers.

"What're you doing? We've got him on the run," Harrison snapped.

"Nothing will make this thing run. It's taken fire and bullets and a drop of God-knows how far into rocks and ice. Tossing another of these isn't enough. Wait here."

They traded uncertain looks as Alan stalked off across the tundra, all-but ignoring Wai as she stirred with an exhausted grunt. Alan walked right over to the dune that

Volkert had disappeared behind. Topping the ridge to see into the natural hollow below, he saw what was left of the creature; the various injuries and explosions had torn away what was left of Volkert's human skin, exposing slick, eel-like flesh beneath. The face was still recognisable, although made of the same oily substance as the rest of it. Only charred and smoking rags remained of the Ordo leader's uniform. The hat was long gone. The Volkert creature struggled to muster its limbs, to right itself, the tentacles laid sleepily around it, twitching here and there. With great effort, it swayed to its feet, its rheumy eyes clearing as it shook its head, coming to focus on its old adversary.

"Bloody hell. Barely a scratch on you," Alan muttered to himself.

He dropped to his arse without ceremony, sending himself scudding down the snowy slope, and slid clumsily back to standing but didn't miss a step on his way forward.

Volkert snarled. A tendril lashed out, but Alan bobbed away like a boxer. He had the knack of it now. Another snarl of frustration and Alan caught the next blow on his forearm. As the tentacle tried to take hold, he stabbed it with the blade he kept stored at the back of his belt. He couldn't tell if it was the tendril itself or Volkert that screeched, but it felt good all the same. He kept walking. He kept dodging. And all the while Volkert took his time to stand and straighten himself. Where the tentacles entered his body, the skin had turned the same mottled black so that only his face and one hand were truly himself any more. Alan could see the nexus of the tendrils now, where they exited his lower abdomen in a cluster and spread around him in those slick coils.

Alan shook his head.

"What have you done to yourself, Volkert?"

Alan stopped a few steps away.

"A blessing," the officer hissed. "From the darkest reaches of existence I have been given power older than the stars—"

Alan rolled his hand in the air. "My evil is the biggest baddest evil there ever was. Darker than dark, bigger than big, older than old. Blah blah. You're boring, men like you."

Volkert grinned, shivering. "Then let me entertain you."

The creature threw back its head, its many limbs finally awake once more, hands clawed and maw wider than a human skull could allow.

Alan leapt forward and slam-dunked the nitrosphere into Volkert's open mouth. The creature choked on it only once.

12

A SOFTENED *WHUPH* and a column of snow and grey slime erupted into the air. The other Privateers broke into a dead run despite their exhaustion, topping the rise to look down at the splattered grey blossom of goo slowly melting the snow with its warmth. At the centre of the flower, a charred chunk of meat gave off a thin whisper of smoke.

"Sweet Jesus," Harrison muttered.

Merry darted down the snowy slope, falling arse over head as she hit the bottom, but it didn't stop her scuttling forward in search of her teammate. She called his name, whipping her head around for any signs of movement. But there seemed nothing left to find. As she came across the tip of a tentacle or a section of serrated gullet, she kicked it away.

"For God's sake, Shaw, you'd better not be dead!" she screamed.

"Why? What'll you do if I am?"

She spun around and almost missed him again. Sat panting, covered from head to foot in grey ooze, spitting even more from his mouth and scraping it from his eyes and hair with a tired hand, was Alan.

"You bloody idiot!" She ran toward him as he dragged himself upright. "I don't know if I should give you a kicking or a kiss."

"It's up to you, but I'm kind of covered in this stuff." As he said that, he softly slapped a slimy hand across her lightly freckled face.

"*Ahk!*"

He had just enough energy to laugh.

WITH GREAT DIFFICULTY, they set the glider upright and swept the glass out of the seats. Despite its barrel roll in the snow, there were surprisingly few bumps and bruises on the glider's hide. Alan stretched his duster across the broken window to keep out the worst of the wind. Once Merry had wriggled some sensation into her hands they took off and cut south, moving toward warmer climes as quickly as possible. The snow fell away at the foot of the mountain and deep green valleys hugged the range's feet. The compass was broken but with the help of Harrison and a map the American had stowed away, they found a small railway which would carry him and Wai south to Kolkata, and anywhere they wanted after that.

The platform was a series of wooden planks set in the dirt with nothing but a tall steel pole to mark the spot. Alan had a deep sense of disbelief about waiting for a train in the wilderness, but the feeling proved unfounded when a rickety old locomotive did indeed stop next to them. Wai gave the others a curt nod and stepped aboard. Harrison stopped only a moment longer to shake hands and then was gone as well. Once inside, he slid down the carriage's window and leaned out.

"It's been a riot, boys and girls. Next time let's get paid, eh?"

Alan grinned back as Merry waved the train into the distance.

"A tragedy that they went away with nothing," Alan said.

"A real shame," Merry agreed.

There was a weighted silence as Merry regarded her nails and Alan tried to whistle and failed.

"So—"

"So—"

"How many did you get?" Alan asked.

Merry produced three punchcards from inside her flight suit. "You?"

Alan reached down and slid two from his boot.

They started to laugh, Alan leaning bodily on Merry as the waves of mirth overtook him. Merry grabbed him by his waist. With one hand she dragged his face down to hers and kissed him hard. He fought back—after a moment or two.

"What was that for?" he asked, although hardly caring.

"Celebrating," she said.

He shook his head with a smile. "Let's find the nearest embassy and cash these chips. There's a bottle of brain-melter with my name on it somewhere."

ALAN'S WHOLE BODY whip-cracked into consciousness, the nightmare fading, leaving him full of fear and adrenaline with nothing to show for it. He set the revolver back beside the bed, from where his sleeping brain had grabbed at it. Running a hand over his face with a heavy sigh, he tried not to remember what the dream had been about.

Merry was making little purring snores in her sleep. His feverish awakening hadn't stirred her. He'd apparently slept with his arm over his head because he had pins and needles in his hand. Wiping a little line of drool from his lip, he took note of exactly how sexy he was at that moment, and slid his other arm gently from underneath Merry's head.

The sheets were a tussled, churned mess on the glider's pull-out bunk, and Merry's pale thighs and shoulders were a sight to behold in the morning light. He tore himself away and, taking a moment to pick up his stack of letters, took them through to the cockpit where the cylindrophone accepted Simon's message record. Sliding the door to the cockpit closed behind him, Alan lowered the needle and waited for the crackles to turn into a familiar voice as he sorted through the letters.

They had landed as high on the hills as they could, and Alan listened to his brother's voice as the Burmese sunrise turned the river to bracelets of glowing yellow and gold, which cut between shards of forest and finally picked out the golden spires of the pagodas leading down to the waterside.

He listened and he read, determined to cover everything and have it done with. After a while, he heard waking sounds from Merry inside, and she eventually stepped up beside him.

She could see the letters strewn around his feet, and the hiss of the needle where it had run out of record but hadn't been removed.

"They thought I was dead, and I let them think it," Alan said. "Simon contacted someone official to retrieve my body and pestered the life out of them until they tracked me down, alive. He's good that way. Annoying. Relentless."

"Are you going home?" Merry asked.

"I'm not ready."

Merry ran her fingers over his chest where three long teardrops of scar tissue ran over his heart. "I've never seen anything like these. How did you get them?"

"Homicidal, mechanical tiger."

"You're joking. Who makes something like that?"

"No one. Not anymore." Alan turned to look up at her. She was so pretty. Young and vital and she made him feel human warmth for the first time since Delhi. "I can't love you," he said, possibly to himself.

"I know," She said. "Rani must have really been something."

Alan's jaw almost snapped off its hinges.

"You talk in your sleep, sweetie," she said. "A lot. But I never asked you to fall madly for me. I don't know what kind of woman you normally come across, but I'm not one of them."

Alan could suddenly see what she meant. Merry was different. And despite how they had spent a very fun night together, he didn't feel like he had to placate her, or explain, or be anything other than himself. They could have had a friendly meal and he'd feel the same way. Something that he'd kept left locked away creaked open, and a light feeling spilled out.

"I need a friend," he said, feeling less pitiful than he thought he would. Merry cradled his head to her chest, stroked his hair, and kissed the top of his head.

"Let's do that." Then she slapped his face, just enough to sting. "Now get your naked arse off of my seat."

Dear Simon,

I'm not sure what to say that will explain this properly, and so I have a story to tell. On the day I saw you last, which seems like a lifetime ago, I was picked up by a pair of Privateers and taken to India where we were contracted to hunt down an enemy of the British army, a Raj. A man called Major Sumner held the contract. To cut a story short, we found the Raj hidden in a disused temple in the jungle. He'd been making mechanical animals. You'd have loved to see it. Monkeys, crocodiles, and even a tiger. But he'd been using them to attack the British supply chains and so had to be stopped.

It was a terrible, terrible mistake. I had always thought I knew how the world worked and my place in it. But the things I saw, Simon. Delhi was completely destroyed, people and all. The British Army did it from a distance with machines, like cowards. I saw it for myself, and through the eyes of a woman I met while I was there. Her name was Rani. I'm not sure what we had but I've never had it before or since. She was incredible, Simon. Strong, smart, so loyal to her people and fierce. She was truly incredible. And I loved her. And I lost her.

We met the Raj. We talked. He was a good man,

trained in England under Professor Normen for a time, believe it or not. He had a family, Simon. A wife and small children. Sumner killed them all. He used us to track them down and then levelled the whole temple with us inside. Sumner cared no more for the lives of us Privateers than he did for the people of Delhi. But the Raj, that was my fault. I killed a man, Simon. It wasn't an accident. I knew what I was doing. But it was a mistake. He knew everything was lost, and he wanted me to save his son. I misread his intentions. I thought he wasn't going to let us leave. All I could think of was staying alive, of getting myself and Rani out of there. God help me, I shot him. He put his boy in my arms as his eyes went cold. If it wasn't for Rani calling my name, I'd have been buried in the rubble like the rest of them. Maybe I should have stayed. Let Rani take the boy. The look in his eyes haunts me. That small boy lost everything because of me. His family, his home, and even his country. The Raj could have stopped Sumner. But I stopped him first.

How was I supposed to come home after that? Sumner thought we were dead, so I let him think it. I walked away from the greatest blunder of my life, the greatest love of my life. And I still can't come home. I can't face you or Father or Lottie. Not with this hanging over me. I'm not who you think I am. I need to stay away, to atone, if such a thing is possible.

I'm sorry. For everything. I'll be in touch. Please don't look for me anymore.

Alan

Dear Alan,

Your letter says nothing that would make any of us think less of you. The decisions we make in a moment should never be speculated upon by others. I have no desire to judge you, and neither does Father or Lottie. Being out in the world is all well and good, but it seems a lot like you're running away. I've never known you run from anything.

Come home. Everything will be well. And I can show you how much people think of you here.

I speak often with Helen. She and Lottie have become fast friends. She will be glad to know that you finally answered my letters. I'm sure she would love to see you in person. Percy, however, remains himself. But if there were no bad things in the world, with what would we compare the good?

And speaking of good, I am aware that this letter seems to be a barely veiled list of reasons for you to come home, but I have news of special importance. You are to be an uncle. In less than a month, in fact. I have no clue how to raise a child but I have every confidence in Lottie's ability to rise to any challenge. Still, it would be good to have my brother's support, and for our small blessing to be accustomed to their uncle's face.

Just bloody well come home. As soon as you're able.

Yours sincerely,
Simon

Excerpt from a letter from a military outrider scout to Jung Bahadur Rana, Prime Minister of Nepal.

Translated from Nepali.

...rode into the town of Makalu in the shadow of the mountains, I find a most disturbing situation. The townsfolk are gone. All belongings have been left behind. A strange grey substance leaves trails on the ground, on the walls. I am headed into the mountains to investigate a large plume of smoke that can be seen over the horizon. Reports to follow.

Alan Shaw and the Wretched Revenge

1

Chicago, USA
July, 1862

A DRUM, A piano and a trombone held the bar's inhabitants rapt. Alan had never seen anything like it; a smattering of drinkers sat at varnished pine table and chairs, their heads nodding along with the intimate music. With his feet up on a chair opposite, he took a sip of the rich liquid in his glass, and licked away the cold when the chunk of ice touched his lip. The liquor tasted terrible, with nothing of the subtlety of scotch, but it was better than the American beer that still filled half a discarded bottle next to him.

The music merged from one song to the next, enticing the listeners in spirals of sound. It was a lot better than parlour music, he had to admit. What he'd first mistaken for a slow, droning beat accompanied by the lonely whine of the trumpet, all seemed to come together when the piano joined in and the three black musicians beside the stage seemed as lost in the music as their listeners. It could use a singer, Alan thought. A pretty one. Checking the triple dials of his wristwatch, then the door, Merry still didn't produce herself, so he drained the last of his glass and held it aloft. The bartender in his sleeve-cinchers and braces turned to the wall of shimmering glass receptacles and half-full bottles behind the bar. Alan checked his watch again. She had been gone over two hours. How long did it take to buy some clothes?

Popping down a cork coaster, the bartender delivered Alan's next drink and plucked the empties and undrinkables as the music changed. The drum picked up a slow, driving beat, almost tribal in its simplicity; *dum dum dum dum dah-dum dum dum dum*. Alan couldn't help but tap his fingers along. The trombone drew out a long, low note that rose to a mid-tempo drawling melody. An arc lamp cut a spotlight on the small bar's raised stage which reached out into the drinking area like the prow of a canoe, into which a stunning specimen stepped in her rich green corset, silk bloomers and tiny matching boots, with her chestnut hair piled high and pinned by a series of long turqoiuse feathers. She could have been a bird of paradise transformed into a woman. She dragged a wooden chair by its high back toward the tip of the stage and, watching the purposeful motion of her hips, Alan finally understood the drum's beat. Every movement she made was a step in the sultry dance; the rotation of her hips, the roll of her shoulder, the kick of her feet and delicate poise of her hands. Every man and woman in the room wished they were that chair. Alan realised his drink had paused half way to his mouth, which hung open. Taking a quick look around, he checked that no one had noticed, of course, and thank God. While his attention was momentarily broken from the breath-holding hypnotism of the burlesque, he spotted the immense brute who had just stepped into the bar, letting in a blast of noise and light from the street outside.

The thug was tall enough that he'd developed a hunch from shuffling through normal-sized doorways until his head, shaved to a prickly ginger finish, hung below his shoulders like a rhinoceros. His dusty black suit must have been fashioned from three others sown together. Alan noticed his hands were balled into fists already, as if he had doled out so many beatings it wasn't worth expending the energy to stretch his fingers. And, just as Alan's luck would have it, the brute took one look around and lumbered directly toward his table.

His voice was deep and rolling, like a cataclysm. "You Shaw?"

Alan took a sip of his drink. "Absolutely certain."

The brute either didn't get it, or didn't care. Alan saw the thug's muscles bunch as his thick fingers grabbed the table edge. He tried to stand, reaching for his revolver, but the furniture was already flying toward him, slamming into his arms, which he threw up at the last second. He flew backward to the sound of splintering wood and shattered glass. Someone screamed and there was a lot of foot-thunder as the bar cleared. Alan managed to open his eyes to regard the ceiling and dragged a breath into his lungs. His head took a moment to realise what had happened; just long enough for the thug to swagger forward and try to stomp a foot the size of a tombstone on his head. Alan rolled on reflex, grabbing the edge of his duster, which had fallen from the chair to lay trapped under the thug's boot. Rolling to his feet, Alan yanked hard, taking advantage of the thug's own weight.

Years of stitches, mends, patches and threadbare wear decided to take that moment to give in and, instead of throwing the thug to the ground, Alan's duster tore into two even parts. He stood for a moment, with only the collar and one arm of his favourite coat limp in his hands. A little lump rose in his throat. But the thug was a single minded bastard, and lunged forward with a freight train fist. The stage broke Alan's fall as he careened backward. Someone grabbed the arm of his shirt and he looked up to see the burlesque dancer's pretty hand, pretty arm and pretty face attached to the other end.

"You better move it, Mister," she said, and hauled him up by his shoulders. Alan kicked out, catching the thug square on the jaw and propelling himself up and back at the same time. A quick fumble of limbs and he was on his feet, on the stage, with the dancer tugging him toward the red curtains at the back.

The thug slammed his fists down onto the stage and roared. Alan just had time to catch the brute's thunderous look before disappearing back stage.

Back stage turned out to be a single room where crates of beer and bottles of liquor were stored. Someone had laid a lace blanket over one crate and propped up a small hand mirror to form a makeshift dressing room with a three-legged stool. The dancer led him down a short corridor to a large wooden door that slammed back onto the wall as they darted out into a Chicago alleyway. The dancer pulled up short so that Alan barrelled into her.

"Down the alley, take a left, and head straight on. You'll

be a block away before he makes it back here," she said matter-of-factly.

"Much appreciated," Alan said, and almost burst into a sprint. But, before he did, he turned back. "Did I mention it's my birthday?"

The burlesque dancer cocked her head to one side. "Really?"

"Well, if I'm being honest, I don't know when my birthday is. I just pick one day a year and celebrate it when I feel like it. So it might as well be today."

The dancer smirked, grabbed him by the front of his shirt and kissed him hard enough to rattle his teeth.

"Happy Birthday. Start running."

The grin on his face soon melted when he saw the thug round the corner of the building and enter the alleyway with a scowl.

"Bloody hell. He's faster than he looks."

2

THE THUG—THAT Alan had decided to name Brutus—was picking up speed as he ran down the alley. His tiny head was down, powerful arms pumping, unstoppable as a glacier. The burlesque dancer made a little squeak and darted back inside, slamming the bar's rear entrance behind her.

"Charming," Alan snorted. Vaulting the balustrade of the small steps which led down to the alley floor, he set off at an easy pace, testing Brutus' speed by checking over his shoulder and noting whether the distance had opened or closed. The thug was apparently moving at his fastest speed and so, instead of trying to get away, Alan found his stride and just maintained the distance. A man that size couldn't run for long, no matter how fit he was. It wasn't until Alan reached the corner where the alleyway met another that he skidded to a halt, almost barrelling into Merry.

They looked each other up and down; Alan was sweating, covered in liquor stains with bits of glass stuck in his shirt and trousers; Merry had apparently been shopping as she was wearing a completely new outfit than when he last saw her; pinstripe trousers with a bustle and neat little boots, her blouse was well cut to her figure and the sleeves were tipped in tan gloves. She was still wearing her aviator goggles on her head, using them as a headband to hold back her blonde waves.

Alan tried to say something nice but Merry cut off the attempt.

"Are you running from someone?"

"Yes. Coming?"

"Of course."

Alan grabbed her hand and they leapt into a sprint just as Brutus rolled around the corner. Merry checked over her shoulder.

"He's a big fellow, isn't he? What did you do?" she asked accusingly.

"Not sure yet. Ah—"

The end of the alleyway suddenly wasn't an option. A large, canvas-backed truck screeched to a halt, covering their exit, and spilled three new characters from its doors. Dressed in desert attire consisting of various bandanas over their mouths, wide-brimmed hats and mismatched leather, they each held ordnance of some shape or form. And finally, kicking out her skirts to avoid tripping, a young woman stepped daintily down from the cab. Her bonnet, lace-lined jacket and skirts were all of a matching blue cotton in the American style.

Alan saw her face.

"That explains it."

The desert warriors raised their weapons. Alan almost plucked Merry right off the floor. Throwing his arm around her waist, he propelled them both toward an open doorway to their right and they bundled inside.

A dark corridor lined with wheeled rails of clothes and rolls of cloth led to a small room with a tailor's table and then a larger room, which turned out to be a shop. A man stood on a box with arms spread. The tailor measuring him caught only a glance of the Privateers as they dodged through the shelves and darted out of the shop's front door, setting the bell above it dancing.

Where London had grown organically into a spiralling labyrinth of cobbles and facades from centuries of building, burning, falling down and rebuilding, Chicago had no such *lasseiz faire* attitude. It had spread fast and straight, fighting to grow as the population expanded. But still, when Merry and Alan stepped out into the chaos of Washington Street, every single person of the 120,000 strong population seemed hell-bent on cramming themselves onto one road. The blast of sound and smoke was physical. Horns blared and voices cursed. Trucks chugged and coughed and through a hundred steam-cabs wove cyclists and strolling pedestrians.

"Why build a pavement if no one uses it?" Alan said as he shoved his partner into the throng.

"You're so English, sometimes."

"Is that supposed to be an insult or a compliment?"

But Merry didn't answer. She pointed to their left, where a familiar truck was trying to pull onto the road in pursuit. The traffic stopped the truck dead, and the cab door opened, spilling two of the three armed individuals and Brutus, who ran to the back of the truck and started uncoupling something.

"Quick as you like, Merry," Alan said, and they ran on into the crowd.

Ducking and weaving between people and vehicles, Alan buried his face in the crook of his elbow to save from breathing the exhaust fumes that had created a noxious fog on the road. He couldn't help noticing that most of the locals wore some kind of cloth mask for the same reason. Merry ran along behind him until he stopped dead in the road.

"Here," he said, "up you go." And he made a step with his knotted fingers, propelling her up into the flat bed of a chugging lorry jammed in the traffic. He hauled himself in behind her and they lay still, listening for all the good it would do in the noise.

"This is cozy," Merry chuckled. "Want to tell me why we're being hunted?"

"Short version. I always had a thing for running away to America when I was a boy. So, when everyone thought I was dead, I figured it was the right time. I was here a few months before I needed money, so I picked up a Letter of Marque from the Marshall's office. They wanted a Privateer to infiltrate a gang of outlaws so they could be brought in. I found the Hemlock family in time to make myself useful at a bank robbery they were planning, and did a few more jobs to earn their trust. I was ready to take them out, one by one, and turn them in, when their sister, Patience, distracted me and I—"

"How exactly?"

Alan paused.

Merry rolled toward him so that he had to look at her,

her head rested on her gloved hand.

"How, Alan?" She was smiling.

"You just couldn't let it go could you?"

In the dark of the lorry's cover, Merry maintained her grin.

"Samuel Hemlock, the fellow with the cowboy hat, is their leader and Patience's oldest brother. Let's just say he came across us in a moment of intimacy. He tried to kill me and I got away. They must have spotted me around town somewhere."

"So you're saying all this trouble is because of a woman?"

"You'd be amazed how often ladies are the start of my troubles."

"I doubt I would," Merry snorted. "So they're a family, and they want your special bits on a wall. What about the fellow with the bull neck?"

Alan propped himself up on one elbow and slowly peeked over the truck's end gate. "Never seen him before. He must be new. I can't see them. Think they've had long enough to wander off. Let's go."

Sliding out of the lorry, they crept along the rows of stalled vehicles, mindful at every corner as they headed down toward lake Michigan with Merry leading the way.

"Where did you land the glider?" Alan spat. "New York?"

"Be quiet. You think it's easy to find a landing spot in a city like this? Should I have just put it on top of a building?"

"Yes!"

"Grumble grumble," Merry mocked.

The screaming started far off, back the way they had come. With vehicles blocking their view, neither Alan nor Merry could find the source. Soon people were rushing toward them. The truck doors were thrown open and drivers leapt out. People abandoned their bicycles and bags in the street. Alan and Merry pressed themselves to the side of a stationary (but still puttering) cab as a hundred people stampeded past, shoving and cursing and panting in fear.

At first, it was the rhythmic shaking of the road under their feet, then it was the hiss of steam which grew louder to accompany it. Soon they could hear footfalls; solid crunches as if something were churning the ground with each step. Then the vehicles around them began to bounce on their suspension springs, the rumbling was so great. Alan searched up and down the rows of traffic, but could see nothing. The Privateers exchanged a glance with a growing sense of foreboding. It wasn't until the little sunlight piercing the exhaust fog was blotted out completely that Alan thought to look upward. There, with its legs spread wide to straddle the space between two trucks, was the shadow of a machine like nothing he had ever seen; a gunmetal rhino that had learned to walk on two legs. There came a high-pitched whirring and the bipedal war engine expanded two new appendages from its chassis with a *clunk-click*. Alan yelled just as bullets tore through the fog toward them, ripping up the road into stone shards. Merry tried to grab Alan, and Alan tried to grab Merry, which ended in them both scrambling under the carriage of a nearby truck with the roar of Gatling guns behind them. The ground shook as the huge machine dropped down in pursuit. Metal screeched and the truck disappeared. The machine's huge three-fingered claws had torn into the truck and lifted it, exposing the Privateers like bugs under a rock.

3

"**G**ORDON BENNET," MERRY muttered.

Alan and Merry lay on their backs in the road, the war machine lifting the truck up on two wheels, and they finally got a good look at it. Made from gunmetal, it had been built for pure destruction. Its bulk was low and wide, hunched like a bipedal bull with Brutus nestled in its centre, his meaty hands gripping great control paddles and boots strapped to the pneumatic legs. His body was protected by a riveted plate and an attached metal skullcap seemed designed to help him aim the guns with the turn of his head.

Alan was muttering to himself. "Nuts. They're absolutely nuts."

"Christ alive, Alan. What did you *do* to his sister?" Merry wheezed.

"Things that normally encourage a positive response."

They scarpered. The machine may have been impossibly powerful, but it took Mecha-Brutus a moment to rearrange the gyros and pistons to drop the truck and turn in pursuit, which gave the Privateers a slight lead.

At times Alan was ahead, other times it was Merry, but they both knew they wanted to be as far from the murderous machine as fast as possible. Alan was panting a little by the time they reached the edge of the traffic and the pavement beyond, and sweat was becoming a ruling factor in his life. His boots hit the open walkway and he slammed himself into reverse. A few feet away, his rifle scanning left and right, Samuel Hemlock was waiting for them.

Alan muttered a curse and dragged his partner out of the way as a shell ricocheted from the lamppost next to them. "Back. Back. We were better off in there!"

Back into the traffic they ducked and weaved, taking as evasive a path as they could.

"What're the chances that other fellow is waiting on the other pavement?" Merry gasped.

"Joshua. Dead certainty. We're trapped."

With a hiss of pneumatics, Mecha-Brutus rounded the corner of a log-bearing vehicle, and Alan had an idea. Shoving Merry ahead, he ran to the cab-end of the lorry and made sure that Mecha-Brutus was following with its sprawling strides. With a grin, Alan hopped up behind the cab and tugged the truck's release mechanism. With the sound of enormous bowling pins, the logs began to roll toward Mecha-Brutus with a satisfying momentum, until the automaton threw out a powerful claw and stopped them dead. Shoving hard, Mecha-Brutus sent the logs toppling back on themselves and over the other side of the lorry. Alan groaned. Merry looked up at him, shaking her head.

"That was rubbish."

"Feel free to join in any time."

Another whir of Gatling barrels and the Privateers were treated to the sound of shredding metal and their own departing footfalls. From somewhere beyond the vehicles, the whoops and hollers from the Hemlock clan made Alan's blood run hot.

"They think they're winning," he said.

"They're right," Merry countered.

"'Leave your guns in the glider', she said. 'You're in a civilised city now', she said," Alan quipped.

"How was I supposed to know your trousers would get us into mortal danger?"

"You've met me, for starters."

Taking advantage of their bickering, Mecha-Brutus had gotten close again, building to running speed along the rows of vehicles and using them to bounce himself around corners like a murderous pinball. The Gatling guns roared, chunks of the road flew up in trails of hot lead. Hurdling a stack of fallen bicycles, they spotted their chance to escape.

Dragging the steam-cycle upright was harder than Alan thought. It was more than a simple velocipede. This was a streamlined beauty built for giddy excesses of speed. Alan liked it right away. Someone had just dropped it, probably unable to drive it in the initial rush of people. The muscles in Alan's arms screamed for a moment, but he managed to lift it and swing a leg over the leather saddle. It was a sleek beast, a man and a half long with wheels wide as Alan's shoulders. The handlebars were a little far forward, so the rider had to lay their belly on the engine block to reach. The steel and brass bodywork was scuffed from the fall but reassuringly solid. Alan grinned and waved for Merry to get on behind him.

She didn't move. "Really?"

Alan rolled his eyes and carefully slid himself back across the saddle while maintaining the bike's balance. Merry swung herself over, grasped the handlebars, the bustle of her trousers covering her dignity, and popped the starter crank with her boot. The steam-cycle responded immediately with a rumbling purr that sent waves of giggly pleasure through Alan.

Mecha-Brutus hurtled around the corner, battering a roofless automobile to a crumpled scrap pile in the process and threw itself toward them. Merry lowered her goggles and wound the steam-cycle's throttle as the machine closed the last few feet with Brutus' frustrated roars audible over his mount's deafening engines, and slammed its huge feet into the spot where they had just been.

Alan whirled his arms, barely managing to stay in the saddle. Wrapping his arms around Merry's waist, he grabbed handfuls of his own shirt in an effort to stay in place. Through his forearms he could feel his partner's stomach spasming as she used her weight to steer the cycle. Alan's bottom clenched time and again as Merry took them to more blinding speeds, carving her way through discarded vehicles, shopping baskets and disoriented people. As always, Merry had everything under control. With Brutus in the dust behind them, they punched out of the traffic and onto the quay road, where the air exploded with bullets.

4

THE HEMLOCKS HAD gotten around them. While the Privateers tackled Mecha-Brutus, the other outlaws had taken a circuitous route to cut them off. With the truck at their backs, Samuel and Joshua fired volley after volley from their rifles, right into the path of the steam-cycle. There was no avoiding it. Alan felt the cycle buck as one tyre exploded, and a sideways skid sent him airborne for a moment before he made a series of painful spirals across the hard ground, his shirt and trousers shredding as easily as the skin beneath.

There was no air in him at all. Half of his brain screamed to unbuckle the new armoured waistcoat he'd had made so he could take a deep breath, but he knew that would only make him much more likely to take a fatal bullet. He rolled instead. Pushing himself up onto his hands and knees, he crawled over to Merry who was staring at the sky in shock, hands clasped across her stomach.

"Merry, you alright?" he gasped.

"I don't think so," and she removed her hands. Her blood welled instantly, soaking through her new cotton blouse. Alan clasped her hands back down onto the wound, but it was no good. There was a swiftly expanding puddle of gore on the ground beneath her.

"They perforated me," she said, breathlessly.

Alan swallowed hard, and made sure his voice would be even when he spoke. "Stop complaining and keep pressing down. You're fine. I'm just going to make short work of these morons, and we're off to get you stitched up. A bunch of grapes and you'll be back on your feet."

"Alan I didn't want to mention this earlier—" She grabbed his sleeve with one bloody hand, he tore it away and pressed it back in place again.

"Quiet. You're wasting valuable villain-bashing time."

"No. You- you're wearing lipstick."

Alan swiped what remained of his sleeve over his mouth. The burlesque dancer had left her mark.

"You didn't think to mention this before?" he said.

"Couldn't have you villain-bashing with make-up on." That seemed to be all Merry had in the way of energy. She laid back and closed her eyes. Every breath must have been agony, but she kept each shuddering exhalation slow. Alan wasn't sure he could have been so calm in the same situation.

He stood up in one fluid motion, turning his back on his comrade, and stormed across the open space before the truck, straight for Samuel. Joshua started taking small sideways steps away from his older brother as Alan strode toward them. He could see the weapons, the scowl on Samuel's face. He knew Mecha-Brutus was behind and a hail of bullets was ahead. There was nothing to hide behind, nothing to fight with; Merry was injured. And so Alan surrendered in the only way he knew how. By making it sound like he wasn't.

"Right, Sam, here's how it's going to go. I'm taking my partner to a hospital. When I'm sure she's alright, you can have me. No fisticuffs."

"What's the catch?" Samuel drawled.

"You have to give us a lift."

Samuel spat on his gloved hand and extended it.

"Oh come on."

The outlaw held perfectly still.

Alan grimaced at the pain in his road-rashed palms as he shook.

ALAN TWITCHED ASIDE the drab hospital curtains. The sun was going down, shedding amber light that washed Chicago with sepia. From down in the street, Samuel Hemlock tugged the brim of his hat in salute. The truck was bearing low on its suspension, so Brutus' toy was stowed way again.

They have to have nicked it, Alan thought. Although God only knew from where. He had a sinking feeling that Chicago's notoriously corrupt police force would be spending a recent anonymous donation in a bar very far away from where the Hemlocks were at any given time. No help would arrive anytime soon.

He regarded the long room with its twin rows of beds, most of them filled with people wearing varying degrees of cotton bandaging. Merry's clothes were folded neatly on the steel stand by the nearest bed frame. Alan took a particularly uncomfortable chair, dragged it to the foot of the currently empty bed and propped his feet on the frame. Within minutes of folding his arms, his chin was on his chest and he emitted small snores.

He woke up twice in the night. Once, when the nurses slid Merry from the gurney to the bed. She was completely unconscious and her abdomen was wrapped in bandages, but other than a pale face and a fussing nurse, she looked to be stable.

The second time was to the sound of Merry's voice.

"You saved my life," she said, in the sweetest voice Alan had ever heard her use. Opening his eyes, he saw her reach out a limp hand to the dashing young doctor leaning over her, grab his collar, and drag him down into a toe-curling kiss. Alan smiled to himself, and drifted back off to sleep.

He jerked awake, the blinding morning sun bouncing from every sterile white and steel surface, the chronic rattle of a trolley, the chatter of the nurses and moans of the other patients all came to him at once. He had already been off balance on his chair and he only just managed to retract his feet from the bed frame and stop himself falling by sheer luck. Rubbing his eyes with the heel of each hand, he stretched, letting his vertebrae pop back into place, rubbed at a few knots and bruises, and decided he'd felt worse. Merry was propped up on her pillows, her left hand laid protectively on her abdomen. She was awake, and smiling weakly.

"Ask me how I feel and I'll kill you," she said in a dry rasp.

"I wasn't going to."

Merry coughed, wincing at the jarring action, and Alan

leaned over to pass her the small glass of water on the cabinet. She took a sip, swilled it around her mouth, and swallowed.

"Go on then. How did you get us away?"

Alan smiled at her. "Sheer genius. I'll tell you when you're better. Now you've stopped being melodramatic, I'm off for a hot bath."

Merry smiled at him and let him go.

Stepping through the ward's double doors, Alan gently took the sleeve of a passing Nurse.

"Meredith Rockett. Everything she needs comes out of this account," and he passed her a slip of paper.

"Sure thing sir. We'll look after her. Have a nice day."

"Oh, I doubt it," he said with a wry smile, and headed toward the elevator.

After sliding across the brass folding doors, Alan tugged the lever to the ground floor and the elevator juddered into action. He stretched himself again, making sure his shoulders were back, his spine straight, and that he was compensating for every ache which might show exactly how hurt he had been in the fall from the speeding cycle. As the elevator jolted to a stop on the ground floor, he was certain he could pull off a calm saunter, and practiced it on his way across the hospital's green-tiled lobby before stepping out onto the street.

Samuel Hemlock tipped up his hat, which had been shading his eyes from the sunrise, and slithered a grin. There was no sign of Patience, but Joshua sat behind the truck's steering wheel and Brutus hovered at the back of the vehicle.

"You made us wait, Al. Thought I'd have to come get

you," Samuel drawled.

"I'm worth it."

Alan rode in the back of the truck with Brutus, who insisted on popping his knuckles and snarling at every opportunity. The giant resting hulk of the war machine looked no less menacing while inert. Alan plastered an amused smile on his face for the trip, just in case he hadn't annoyed the mountainous man enough yet. The truck rumbled for almost fifteen minutes through a series of turns which Alan didn't bother to keep track of, and drew up with a gravelly crunch in the warehouse district beyond the curve of Lake Michigan's southern shore. The truck's cab door opened and slammed, and the tarpaulin which covered the truck's rear was yanked aside.

"Out you get," Samuel called.

Alan stepped down to find himself outside a series of low, dark warehouses on a pier which stretched out onto the lake. The air was chill, blowing down from the frozen forests in the North. Alan suppressed a shudder, and a pang of loss ran through him as his sundered duster rose in his mind. He turned to deliver some quip just as a rifle's butt slammed into the back of his head. He hit the ground and felt his hands being forced behind him. The rope burnt as it wrapped his wrists, and his shoulders throbbed when Brutus dragged him back to his feet and shoved him into a stumbling walk.

"No offence, Al. But I don't trust you one jot and I never knew a man who wouldn't try everything to avoid being tied up."

"You've gotten smarter," Alan mumbled. "That's

annoying."

The outlaw guffawed and prodded Alan onward with the barrel of his rifle.

5

INSIDE THE WAREHOUSE was exactly how Alan had expected. Cold and dank, with only the odd spear of light poking through the boarded walls and ceiling. He greeted the post at his back and the burn of the ropes around his wrists as old friends. It had been a while, but it turned out that being tied up at a villain's whim was a skill which, once learned, was never lost.

"You defiled my sister," Samuel's voice cut through the half-light. Alan could just make him out, without his leather coat and hat, leaning on the opposite wall as he took a long draw from a damp yellow cigarette.

"We're not even going to pass pleasantries?" Alan asked.

"You seduced her. And laid with her out of wedlock like a heathen."

"That's not how I remember it. The first part, at least."

Alan tugged at his restraints, just on the off-chance. But the Hemlocks were outlaws who took pride in their work. He was going nowhere.

Samuel took another draw of his cigarette, and laid it aside so the burning end hung over the edge of a packing crate. He strode over to Alan, took a sideways stance, and drew back his fist. Alan rolled his head with the blow, but it was little help. His skull rang. Samuel was pulling his punches, Alan knew. He evidently planned a lot more to come.

"And then," Samuel came in close so he was eye to eye with his captive. He prodded Alan in the chest to make sure he was listening. "After you run out like a kicked mutt, I find out you betrayed me, too. The Marshalls were all over our hideout by next morning, screeching their laws and waving their writs."

Perhaps this was even worse than Alan had anticipated.

"Ah. Mentioned me, did they?"

The next punch splattered inky stars across Alan's vision that drowned out whatever Samuel said next. Alan's ears whistled from the blow, his speeding pulse provided percussion and his adrenalin thrummed like a double bass. The band was all there. He spat blood, but it was right back in his mouth again seconds later. The gnawing agony of a loose tooth erupted when he tested the inside of his gums with his tongue.

"I hate dentists," Alan slurred.

Samuel rang Alan's skull again, just for good measure. This time, Alan felt certain that he could physically feel his cheek swelling. Samuel was rubbing his fist. That last one had cut both ways. Alan tried to smile and managed it with only half of his face. Hanging from his bonds, he let the aching cut of the rope on his wrists keep him conscious. He couldn't keep this up all day, but there was no way out. No loose ropes, no shards of broken metal or glass, no way to slide up or down the pole he was tied to. There had to be a way out. If only Samuel would shut up and let him think.

"The good book teaches us an eye for an eye. That's how I know I can beat on you with the good lord on my side," Samuel said.

"Will he be long? I wouldn't mind asking him a few things." Alan spoke slowly so that he could be understood.

"I *am* your answers, Shaw. This is your reward for living a life with no morals, no honour. Selling out your partners for money. You're a pirate."

Alan's temper flared. "That's it," he growled. "I can take a lot of things, but stupidity is one thing I can't stand. You're a bloody robber, Sam. You steal things. Go on, give me one of your crackpot explanations for that."

"We tithe over half of everything we take to the poor!" At some point, Joshua had sashayed in, and had managed to stay quiet this long. The whine in his voice gave away his young age. Alan tried to remember exactly how old the younger brother was. Perhaps sixteen now. "We only take from those who hoard their money. The undeservin', the cruel—"

Samuel whipped his brother a sharp look. Joshua's lips clapped shut. "I don't need to justify myself to you, Shaw," Samuel snarled. "You got that poor girl of yours shot up. *You* did. If it weren't for your covetin' my sister, she'd be healthy right now. But you put other folks in harm's way. How many have been hurt because of you draggin' them into things that ain't their business? How many women are widows and kiddies are orphans?"

Alan had never told Sam about India. It wasn't

something he liked to spread around. Samuel, stretching for insults, had managed to hit a raw spot by sheer luck. Still, the face of a young Indian boy made fatherless by Alan's revolver rose in his mind, doing more damage than any punch.

He found himself with nothing to say.

Samuel snorted, gave Alan a slap across the stricken side of his face, just enough to set everything bleeding again. Counting off his injuries brought him almost into a state of meditation. His cheek bone, his lip, and his eyebrow felt split, too. Putting his weight against the post, breathing deeply, he let them hurt.

Samuel was shrugging on his coat.

"What are you doing, brother?" Joshua asked. The kid sounded almost disappointed. "You said he would be punished."

"I'm taking a leaf from the good book, Joshua, and making his torment eternal. Or at least as eternal as I can. We're in no rush. Let him rest and we'll continue his lesson tomorrow."

Alan waited until the warehouse door banged shut before he unlocked his knees and slid to the ground. By the time his legs splayed out and his bottom hit the floor, he was unconscious.

6

ALAN'S FIRST THOUGHT was how there should be a law against being woken against your will. Trying to roll over, he realised that there was nowhere to roll to; he was still held upright by his bonds. After attempting to open his eyes, and realising that only one would obey his commands, Patience Hemlock swam into view. She was wearing that pretty cotton dress again. As always, she seemed too clean, too pure to be in the company of her brothers. Her hair was tied with a blue ribbon into two strawberry blonde pigtails. Despite being only a year younger than Samuel, they still dressed her like a girl. Alan couldn't help but notice the patent leather shoes poking out from under her skirt as she hunkered down before him. In a villainous flash of memory, he remembered how she had shivered when she undressed, an arm laid across her stomach to grasp the opposite forearm. How had she put it?

"I'm lonely." That was it.

Patience didn't say a word now; there was the sound of water dribbling into a tin bowl and a wet rag stung his many cuts and bruises. Wincing, he fought the urge to pull away.

She took her time. Soon his face felt cooler, and the crusted blood which had been aggravating his wounds was cleaned away. She went from one cut to another with a small dropper of iodine. He rolled his eyes, but refused to groan. When she was done, Patience took her bowl and small bottle of pain, and left the warehouse without a word.

"That's that, then," Alan whispered, if only to test his voice which came out in a rasp. He cleared his throat and tried again. "The most kindness I'll be having today." Much better. He was ready to quip once more.

It was some time before Alan saw anyone else. Time spent feeling slightly sick, which passed, then listening to his stomach growl, which he thought was hilarious for all of five seconds. Then he took a few minutes to rotate his shoulders, move his neck back and forth, and generally loosen himself up as much as his ropes would allow. Skooching his feet up under him, he brought himself to standing, and allowed the post to hold him up when his head span. Just as the nausea subsided, the warehouse door creaked and slammed.

"If that's room service, I could really use a drink. Even water would do at this point."

But he got more than he bargained for. It was Brutus.

"Hello there, big fellow. I don't suppose you've come to let me go have you? I'm pretty sure I have a lot of painful stitches to be put into my face, so what do you say we call it a day?"

Brutus smiled, which looked a lot like a mountain snarling, and started to roll up his cuffs.

"That's right. Untying rope is a dirty job. Better roll up those sleeves," Alan said, as his heart sank. "Why do I even bother?"

The first punch hit Alan's stomach hard enough to make him vomit. Luckily his stomach was empty, unluckily his body tried anyway. Through the dry heaves and streaming eyes, Alan fought for breath. He took great gulps of air, every one insubstantial. It felt like drowning. For the first time, he actively struggled against his bonds, shaking the ropes ineffectually.

Brutus was winding up again. Alan felt the rib crack in a sparkler of agony. The bonds were no longer enough to hold him up. His knees hit the ground. Brutus' palm wrapped around Alan's face, easy as plucking an apple from a bowl, and he was hoisted up by his head. When his legs wouldn't hold him up on the first attempt, Brutus pulled him up by his shirt. But Alan's limbs were slack rope. Brutus grunted, and let his punch bag go. Alan hit the floor, barely able to breathe and wracked with agony. He'd lasted two punches.

He wheezed. "Finish me off, you bastard. Or are you worried I could have you?"

Brutus spun around and stalked back across the warehouse, but a familiar voice stopped him dead.

"Not yet," Samuel came in with a small sack slung over one shoulder. "We are going to do this the old fashioned way."

Setting down the sack and plucking something from inside, Samuel waved for Brutus to get out of the way. The mountain stepped aside. Alan could just make out Samuel tossing something from hand to hand; a small, sharp rock. That sack had to be full of them.

The first stone hit Alan in the chest. It felt like being

stabbed, and he should know. Turning his body sharply, setting his cracked rib afire as he did, Alan caught the second stone on his shoulder. By the third shot, Samuel had refined his aim. It hit Alan in the forehead, slicing as much as it bludgeoned. Blood poured down Alan's face instantly, filling his one good eye with sticky gore. The warmth spread down his face, into his mouth, and down the collar of his shirt. Trying desperately to concentrate on something other than the searing pain, or the fear, or the futile anger that welled up inside him, Alan began to pant hard. Breathing was good. Breathing meant there was still time.

"Leave him be."

Alan didn't even have the energy to lift his eyelids any more, but he knew Patience's voice when he heard it. Quiet, sweet like a breeze and clear as a stream. He felt something brush across his shirt front.

"Out of the way, girl," Samuel drawled.

"You will call me woman if you must call me anything at all," she barked. "Because that is what I am. No thanks to you, who would keep me as father did. I am as guilty as Alan. More so. If you would stone him, then I accept my punishment as well."

Samuel's voice grew closer.

"You're on dangerous ground, Patience."

"And you are living your life by the wrong testament, Samuel. God sent his son to guide us away from the wrath of the old God and toward compassion. Now you've had your revenge. Don't take it so far as murder."

There was a pause in which Alan could only hear his own rasping breath. Voices squawked somewhere beyond his pounding head, but he paid them no attention. He was hardly cut out for a theological debate on a good day, never mind as he was now.

Just as he started to slip into a grateful unconsciousness, the ropes slackened at his back and, before he could hit the ground, he was hoisted off his feet completely.

Time was impossible to keep track of. A door slammed, there was the rumble of road, and all of a sudden Alan was splayed on cold ground as tires screeched away. Someone screamed, there was a lot of commotion, and then the little light that he could make out through his burning eyelids was blocked by someone leaning over him.

Alan found it hard to care anymore. There was just too much sleep to be had.

7

STRIPES OF BLINDING light cut across Alan's vision as he tried to open his eyes. Blinking away the sleepy fog with his one good eye, he saw that it was the sunlight coming through the hospital ward's narrow windows. The mattress was an inch thick and well-worn, which made his aches and pains sing out. Trying to shuffle comfortable, he instantly regretted it when his cracked ribs roared into life. He groaned, his teeth gritted hard enough to give him lockjaw. There was a mirror by his bed. What it showed wasn't pretty. The left side of his face was a swollen mass all held together by a lattice of burning gashes stitched up until he looked like a lumpy old sack. The swelling would go down, but only time would tell with regards to the scars.

Merry's voice drifted into his consciousness. Alan turned his head, carefully, to see the same young doctor stood by the next bed. Merry must have requested that her and Alan be put together. The doctor shuffled away, a little red of cheek, and smiling. Alan watched him until he walked to the end of the ward and out of sight.

"I suppose you'll be staying around for a while," he said,

realising that his voice was not only croaky but hindered by the swelling in his face. It was a familiar sensation.

"I think so," Merry said. "Are you?"

"I might. I guess I have some things to—" he shuffled again in search of comfort and found only new pains. His next word was laced with a groan "—heal up. Plus, my pilot is going to be busy."

Merry smiled. She looked well. Rested. Or maybe anyone would look good compared to Alan. "Maybe you could find a little company for yourself. Someone to help the healing process."

Alan stared at the peeling ceiling, the only thing that didn't hurt to do, and sighed.

"People I get close to get hurt, Merry. I'm a walking curse. Maybe I pissed off a gypsy. I wouldn't be surprised with my record. How's the bullet wound?"

"Turns out it was shrapnel. The bullet must have hit the bike, shredded and peppered me with the remains of the casing. They found three bits in there. Lucky really. A bullet would have been much worse."

"Did they get it all out?"

"Probably. But I won't be hugging any magnets to find out. Now stop trying to change the subject, you stubborn pillock, and admit that sometimes you need to reward yourself."

When Alan spoke, he annoyed himself by realising he was paraphrasing Samuel Hemlock: "For what? Nearly getting you killed? Making someone angry enough to unleash a giant automaton on a busy street in Chicago? Oh yes, I deserve a medal. Where's the mayor when you need him?"

Merry ignored the sarcasm. "I wanted to be a Privateer. I knew what that meant; the adventure, the excitement, and the danger. You might be teaching me, Alan, but you're not my Dad. And I know what you did to get me here, how you got into the state you're in. If you think that's anything less than heroic, there's something wrong with you."

"You have a warped view of me, Merry."

"You have a warped view of yourself, Alan. Get some sleep, you miserable sod."

But he didn't. He couldn't. The nurses came and went and Alan barely spoke. He just kept staring at the ceiling, trying not to move, with his mind whirring. He couldn't decide if he'd taken his comeuppance like a man and should let the whole thing go, or whether the attack on the Chicago street meant he now owed the Hemlocks retribution of his own. The first meant he should walk away. The second meant there was work to be done. Simon would say let it lie. Merry would have him act like the hero he wasn't. Take the hit to his pride or take them down. Patience: revenge.

By the time the moon rose in the windows, Merry was making her gentle snoring sounds, and Alan had made up his mind.

Rolling to his good side, he kicked his feet out of bed and lowered them to where his boots laid waiting. With one arm wrapped around his chest, he dressed quietly, clumsily, leaving the buttons of his shirt but managing his belt, and slipped on his boots. His armoured waistcoat slid onto his shoulders and he loosely buckled the fastenings before diving beneath his mattress for his stash. Five little glass vials of morphine, a dose in each, lay in hiding, palmed from the nurse's tray who had brought him his doses throughout the day. It worked, this sweet liquid, edging his vision with a clear haze as the pain sank away. With some amusement, he slid four vials into the bullet slots of his belt, and cracked open the lid of the fifth. Knocking back the sweet poppy juice, Alan swayed a little, letting it sink in, before cinching his waistcoat buckles as tight as he could bear. Coloured spots flared in his vision, setting the dark ward alight with fireworks. Biting his lip, he gripped the bed end as tight as he could until the pain sank away. Eventually, he could stand again and he took a tentative breath. It was bearable. He checked his belt. He would need those other four vials if he was to finish the night's work.

Leaving the ward, Alan didn't bother to sneak. He walked with certainty toward the doors and straight out without looking around or back. Within a minute, he had stepped out onto the street and up to the curb, hailed a steam-cab and was rolling away into the night.

He had to make two stops, and then there would be a reckoning.

8

WITH HIS VOICE muffled by the chunk of chewing tobacco wadded in his mouth, the cab driver called back through from the vehicle's cockpit: "You look like hell, if you don't mind me saying so, sir."

Alan stared out of the window at fleeting Chicago. Bars spilled light and sound, groups of people wandered the streets in laughing groups. There was a celebration going on. A big one. American flags were strung over the street and snatches of the national anthem could be heard over every other noise. The mix of moon and lamplight shifted uneasily over his lumpy face.

"I've felt better."

"Say, you're from England, right?"

"I'm from a bit of everywhere."

"A man of mystery, huh? So how come you're slipping out of hospital in the dead of night and it isn't to join any of these parties?" The cabby was bloody incessant, but Alan found himself less angry than he would usually be. Maybe it was the morphine.

"I have a job to finish before I can rest."

"You say 'job' like God gave it to you himself."

"That would be ironic."

"So how come you're so hell-bent? Wouldn't be a lady would it?"

"A friend. She sees something in me that I don't. Call it an experiment to see if she's right."

"Folks don't pluck these things out of the air, sir."

"Let's hope the advice of a Chicago cabby is as good as they say."

The driver laughed, and didn't probe any further. Alan was glad. The conversation had drained him. Laying his head back against the seat, he tried to rest for as long as he could as the steam-cab rolled away from the hubbub of the inner city, down toward the lake where the roads became rougher, followed by the familiar sound of tyres on gravel that Alan had heard the night before. As a fenced complex of warehouses emerged from the dark, Alan had the cabby pull over. Paying over the odds to avoid conversation, he walked away before the cabby could even blink, one arm still wrapped across his aching chest. The wooden laths of the fence were well cared for, so the main gate was the only way in. Luckily, a small door had been cut into the larger gate, which was left unlocked. Alan slipped inside the compound and, hugging the shadows like a lover, skulked between the warehouses and down toward the lake. The soft lapping of water under the piers, accompanied by strumming insects, leant a peace to the night which made Alan uneasy. Silence was hard to maintain. Even the smallest sound would be heard from a distance tonight, and he was feeling nowhere near stealthy enough for the task at hand. Peering around the corner of a low, wooden shed, he spotted the Hemlocks' truck. There were no hints of embers in the truck's furnace grate; it had been idle for some time. The chassis was also low on the suspensions springs, which meant that Brutus' toy was still inside. Alan smirked to himself in the shadows. This could turn out to be fun. Plucking another morphine phial from his belt, he cracked the seal with his thumb, tossed back the clear fluid, and waited. Within a second or two, the warm glow of the opium filled his stomach, radiating to his cheeks and limbs, washing away the pain as it went. Alan sighed, enjoying the feel of breathing without the stabbing agony, and stepped out from his hiding place. He was halfway to the truck before the morphine's other effect came into play. His eyesight tunnelled, the world seeming to push away from him, and before he knew it, Alan was leaning on the truck, his face pressed against the chassis, taking exaggerated breaths to steady himself. Apparently there was a reason the nurses were careful with the frequency of the drug. He stood for a moment with his nose pinched between finger and thumb. The vertigo subsided like descending an elevator back into his body, and he was left with a foggy buzz which felt nothing short of amazing. Alan giggled despite himself.

Sweeping around the back of the truck, he climbed up into the rear and circled the folded hulk of Brutus' slumbering war engine. Finding footholds cut into the bodywork, he climbed up and popped the cockpit's lid. Taking one look at the gyroscopic levers, buttons, pedals and dials, Alan shook his head and climbed back down. Even on a clear head with an instruction manual there was no way the engine would have been useful to him. That was more Merry's style, anyway. Instead, he ducked underneath the machine. Where two large steel rings sank into its underbelly, the remnants of two broken chains still hung. The Hemlocks had stolen the machine alright. But be damned if he knew from where. Yanking out as many pipes and wires as he could find, black and amber fluids tumbled into the truck's bed. Finding an oily rag in the truck's toolbox he tore it in two and used it to block the war machine's exhausts. Satisfied with this piece of childish mayhem, he headed to the warehouse.

There didn't seem to be any movement inside as Alan pressed his ear to the door. The Hemlocks were either sleeping or not there at all. The latter thought left Alan feeling more nervous than the former. What if he'd come all this way and the outlaws were somewhere else?

Taking his time to quietly pry open the warehouse door, Alan muttered to himself: "Then I'll bloody well wait for them to come back."

But he wasn't disappointed. There, seated with his back to the very post that Alan had briefly called home, was the snoring bulk of Brutus.

Alan checked his trouser pocket for the small bottle he'd picked up from an all-night pharmacy on one of his stops. No, that was too good for Brutus. Instead, he crept crabwise, inching his way toward the immense human who had broken his ribs. On the way, Alan plucked a discarded shovel from the ground and tested its weight. Brutus never moved, but snorted in his sleep and adjusted his position. Alan stepped up close, hefting the shovel, and kicked the outlaw's outstretched boot. Giving Brutus just enough time to wake, see him, and widen his eyes into a look of terror, Alan swung the shovel with a satisfying *shpang*.

"Sweet dreams, Chuckles," Alan sneered.

If Alan knew the Hemlocks, and he did, they would be all together somewhere. Creeping on into the dark warehouse, avoiding the pools of moonlight as best he could, it didn't take long for him to spot them. Where a set of rickety stairs led to a mezzanine office which overlooked the warehouse floor, Alan spotted the flicker of an oil lamp behind the office's window. He took his time, tiptoeing on the outer edge of each step to avoid creaking, supporting himself on the iron stair rail. By the time he was at the top, he was out of breath, and aching again. He had lost all sense of time between the dark and the adrenalin. Surely he was due another dose. Cracking open his third phial of morphine, he let the pain fade away, the dizziness come and go, and the giddy light-headed nirvana lay over him. He smiled in the dark and, feeling immortal, made for the door. But the opium wasn't done yet. This time, it took Alan's feet, making them into old tin cans. He could barely walk. And after a light trip built momentum, Alan went hurtling through the office door, arms over his face, and hit the ground in the middle of the Hemlock's circle of bed rolls.

The outlaws were up in an instant, much faster than Alan could organize his limbs through the opiate haze, and Joshua was straddling him, landing light but swift blows down on Alan's head with his juvenile fists. Alan fended him off sluggishly with one arm while reaching into his pocket for the chloroform and, swinging the bottle, smashed it over

Joshua's head in a shower of shards and sweet ether-scented liquid. Joshua hit the ground, unconscious.

Alan was about to deliver a witticism, maybe something about the chloroform being more effective that way, but he couldn't arrange his thoughts before Samuel's boot swung down toward him. The outlaw hit Alan's already broken ribs, and one side of his body burst aflame, burning the air from his lungs until he was gasping for breath. He rolled and scrambled, anything to get away from the pain again, and managed to kick the outlaws' oil lamp with his flailing boot. It shattered, killing the soft light and replacing it with a swiftly expanding puddle of liquid flame. In the seconds it took Samuel's eyes to adjust to the new light, Alan was on his feet and hurtling toward him. Ignoring every variety of agony in his own body, Alan cannoned into the outlaw, knocking him bodily against the wooden office wall. The whole room shook. Samuel swung a neat right hook, which Alan swayed to avoid, only to bring his own fist lancing into the outlaw's jaw. Samuel took the hit, but wasn't ready for the next one, with Alan employing his favourite tactic of swift, precise blows taught by an aging boxer in the London fighting pits. Samuel didn't stand a chance and was soon sat on the ground, arms crossed over his head and screaming for mercy.

Perhaps it was the morphine. Perhaps it was the pain and the adrenalin. That's certainly what Alan told himself later. But when Samuel was down and begging for mercy, Alan just saw red. Scooping a tin cup from the ground, Alan swept Samuel's defensive arms aside and beat the snot out of him with it.

He only stopped because Patience screamed.

The fire had spread quickly across the office's dry old boards, and Patience stood beyond them, her back to the wall, hemmed in by the conflagration. Alan looked down at Samuel, whose breath stuttered in and out, and dropped the cup.

"Patience, you have to jump over it. There—" Alan pointed to the fire's narrowest point.

"I can't," she screamed.

"Don't be an idiot, Patience. Quickly!"

But the girl laid still, staring at the smoke-wreathed ceiling. The only sign of life was her shallow panting. Alan reached for something, anything that he might use, and came up with a personal favourite. Manipulation.

"Stupid *girl!*"

Patience's eyes snapped to his. He had her.

"Stood there like some pointless doll in your pretty skirt and pigtails. You're going to die, girl. You'll follow your stupid father to the grave and leave these idiot boys to rot in jail. Just stand there, then, and burn. That's all you're good for, anyway."

Patience's face tightened into a ball of hatred. She screamed and, instead of circling the fire, shot right over it, hitting Alan full in the chest. They fell together, with Patience screaming madness, unleashing years of frustration on Alan as she beat at him with her bare hands. Alan rolled, trying to get control of her while avoiding the fire himself, but Patience was a whirling mass of gnashing teeth and fuming anger. In the end, he slapped her hard, knocking her down for a second. But she soon started to scream.

"My legs! My legs!" With horror, Alan scuttled for the hem of her dress, which had set aflame in the scuffle, fire licking hungrily at Patience's lower limbs. He ripped the flaming cotton clean away and tossed it aside, but not before sustaining stinging burns of his own.

Now the office was a fireball with the window of escape swiftly narrowing. Alan had no idea how a simple "knock them out and tie them up" plan could go so awry, but he needed help now.

"Joshua! Get up!" Scrambling over to the youngest outlaw, Alan shook him roughly by the shirt. The boy roused, rubbing his eyes with his fist. Alan jabbed a finger at the fire.

"Get your brother and get out. Go!"

It took only a second for the danger to register on the boy's face before he was scuttling toward Samuel and dragging him to his feet.

Alan scampered back to Patience. The girl lay weeping, her pale, thin legs looking somehow forlorn in the way they tangled together. Alan tried to scoop her up, but his concoction of injuries wouldn't let him. The heat in the room was burning the energy out of him; smoky air rasp in his lungs, his eyes felt like weeping balls of hot lead.

Sliding his hands under her arms, he softened his voice as much as possible: "Patience, you have to help me. Get up."

The girl made a weak effort, but it was enough. Alan slid her arm over his shoulder and propelled her forward, through the encroaching smoke and out through the fiery ring that was the office door. They met the other Hemlocks on the ground floor, just in time to hear the office groan and crash in a rumbling fireball. As a group they hobbled, limped, groaned and stumbled out of the warehouse to find Brutus already there, held down by a squad of Chicago policemen. In the commotion, no one had heard the klaxons and rumbling engines of the police vehicles' approach. Alan sat Patience on the ground, which she accepted without complaint, and stalked over to the police officer with the most stripes on his arm.

"The place is on fire. You might want to sort that," he said.

The officer waved to two nearby minions who scuttled away to gather buckets and water from the lake. He popped a shining gold pocket watch from his pocket, checked the dial and clicked it closed again.

"New watch?" Alan asked.

"Got it today," the officer bragged, greasy with pride.

"Very nice it is, too."

"You did a good job," the officer drawled through his expansive moustache. He watched the flames spreading through the warehouse. "A bit thorough, though. Ever thought of being a policeman, son?"

"I did once. Then I came to my senses," Alan said.

The officer nodded. "Well, you helped nab a family of outlaws. That's good work for a civilian. And, as promised, I'll ask no questions as to how you knew where they were."

"Then I won't mention how you ignored a giant war machine rampaging through your city for half an hour yesterday."

The officer's moustache twitched.

Alan walked away, one hand hugging his ribs, the other dipping into his trouser pocket to stow a shiny new pocket watch.

9

ERRY WOKE NEXT morning to an odd scent. She rolled over, amazed at how the pain was already reducing in her injuries. Alan was sprawled on the next bed, fully clothed. Soot dirtied his shirt and trousers, his boots were still on, and his armoured waistcoat was splayed open to reveal the bandages beneath. She finally recognised the smell. Burning hair. Two empty phials of morphine lay on the cabinet beside him.

Slipping out of bed, she took her blanket and spread it over him where he lay in a crumpled mess.

"Told you so," she said.

THE NEXT DAY, after a few hours of teasing the young nurses about a sponge bath, Alan was bored enough to discharge himself, much to the Matron's stamping fury. But that was cut short when he donated an expensive gold watch to the hospital.

"Wait, I'll come too," Merry said, sitting up with some difficulty.

"Don't be stupid, Merry. What are you going to do if

one of those stitches pops while you're walking around? Plus there's a young doctor here who I'm sure will agree that you should stick around a little longer."

"Lucian. He's sexy," Merry grinned.

"That he is," Alan chuckled. "So lay back down. One of us has to get some action in this damn town to make up for all the shit."

Laying back, she held out a hand to him, which he took. "Come visit me."

"I'll be here every damned day." With a peck on her fingers, he strode out of the room as confidently as he could. By the time he hit the street, the pain had grown to a breath-taking throb. He popped another morphine vial and held it up to the sky. Light refracted a rainbow onto his face, which was all but swallowed by the spread of purple across his cheek.

"Sod it," he said, and tossed it into the gutter where it shattered. "What I need is a scotch."

With a few extra stitches, stiff from bruising, and without his duster, Alan found his way back to the very bar, and the very table, at which his Chicago experience had begun. Swirling his liquor around its glass, he let the music envelop him. A few drinks later, the lights lowered, and the long rasp of the trombone summoned the burlesque dancer to her spotlight. Alan made sure to catch her eye during the performance, tipping a little salute with his glass. Her brow creased briefly at his damaged appearance, but those heavy, dewdrop eyelids fluttered as she gave him a smile which set off fireworks in his mind. As the music thrummed a sensual beat, and the dancer's confident movements propelled her around the stage, Alan took out the notepaper and pen he'd bought on his way over, and started to write.

Dear Simon,

I write to you from a scruffy bar in Chicago. You know the kind I like. I don't think I've mentioned in my letters that I made it to America while I've been away. I suppose nothing would surprise you at this point. It wasn't what I imagined. I'm sure the wilderness filled with eagles and bears and natives is somewhere, but I'm yet to see it. There's either dusty nothing filled with rattlesnakes and bandits or steaming cities just like home. It's so different to how I pictured it. Life, that is. Growing up. Being an adult. I never really thought about what I wanted to be, not like you did, just where I wanted to be. All I wanted was to escape, and escape I did. But for what purpose? You can't run away from yourself. That's what I've realised.

Friends are starting to get hurt, Simon, because of things I've done. I've told myself that I can make up for it. But what if something happens that I can't take back?

I'll be in Chicago for a week or more, I think. My partner has been injured and needs some rest. Truth be told, so do I. But nothing you need worry about. I'll put the return address on the envelope for you. I hope you can reply by the time I have to leave.

The bartender plucked Alan's empty glass from the table. He had been a handsome youth, but a few extra pounds and a taste for his own wares had given him rudimentary jowls and yellowing eyes. Thick, black, slicked back hair seemed painted onto his head.

"Another?"

"Please. I don't suppose you could put some ice in a towel for me could you?"

The bartender took this as an invitation to inspect Alan's battered face.

"Saw you in here the other day. That big fella get a hold of you did he?"

"Well I didn't do this shaving."

"You deserve it?"

Alan thought for a second. "No. But maybe I needed it."

The bartender nodded solemnly, releasing an *mmm-hmm* of understanding. Alan wished he understood as well as the bartender did. A few moments later a glass of amber liquid sat on the table and Alan sank the ice pack onto his face. As the burlesque ended to generous applause, he hesitated before signing his letter—

Love to you all.

Alan

—and tucked it inside his waistcoat.

Dear Alan,

I hope this letter finds you swiftly. I think you're talking about responsibility. I never thought I'd say this, but I think you're growing up. Hell's bells. I've learnt a lot about responsibility in the last few months. Jasper is growing like a weed. Every day he becomes more and more aware of the world, and he watches my every move. He's learning from me and it has made me so much more aware of the way I behave. I see Lottie in him, of course, and nothing but good can come of that. But what of myself? What do I have to give to this child in way of advice or experiences? I am now so aware of the repercussions of my actions. I think perhaps we're having the same experience in very different ways. Who knew we would be men with responsibilities one day?

You walk through a dangerous world, Alan. One more dangerous, perhaps, than everyone else. From what your previous letters have told me, you have also seen more unearthly things than any mortal should ever have to withstand. I'm not giving you an excuse to ignore your responsibilities. Far from it. Instead, I suggest that you accept these dilemmas as an occupational hazard and have confidence in yourself to make the difficult decisions when necessary.

I hope my advice helps.

Stay safe.

Simon and family

Alan Shaw and the Vault of Hsekiu

1

Malta
August, 1863

STRIPPED TO HIS braces with sleeves rolled to the elbow, Alan basked in the Mediterranean heat. His new coat, shorter than his duster and made of tan leather, lay on the chair beside him. It was far too hot to wear it, but all of the extra pockets were useful and it had his revolver holster attached to the inside; a great way to keep it concealed but close. A pair of cloudy lemonades perspired on the little café's table and a light breeze licked the island of Malta, making the heat more bearable. Olive-skinned fishermen in short trousers and wide hats ran brimming lobster cages from the shoreline to the markets only yards away and the scent of rich, fresh seafood filled the air. Alan wondered how they did that; oblivious in their little lives, immune to the dark and danger, carrying on as of the sun never set. If he ever had a wish, perhaps he would ask for ignorance. To unlearn what he knew. Then, perhaps, he'd get a good night's sleep.

Taking a sip from his glass, he shaded his eyes as he followed the market's slope down to a pebble beach. Small ships came and went under full, triangular sails. He watched his partner, her overalls rolled up at the knees and the arms knotted around her waist, paddling in the warm sea. She gave a wave, which he returned, and she took a steady scramble back to their table.

"You're missing out, old man. That water is about the most succulent thing I've ever felt."

"That's encouraging," Alan smirked. She shot him a sarcastic smile. "And less of the old, please. I'm only thirty-two. Give or take a little bit."

Merry shook her head. "How do you go through life not really knowing your age? Did you never want to know for sure?"

"Is it important?" Alan took another sip of his lemonade. "What does your age actually do for you other than make you think, 'I shouldn't be doing this, I'm too old' or 'by this point in my life I should be doing so-and-so'. Age is pressure. I do what I feel like, free of the worry."

Merry wrinkled her nose: "You're still a crotchety old man."

"Don't make me send you to your room."

They sat and bathed in the sun for a while longer, ordering two more drinks when the first round ran dry. Alan kept an eye on the town's clock tower, an ancient stone pillar with a new mechanism attached.

"He's late," Alan huffed. Merry had her head buried in a book. From what Alan could tell it was full of schematics. She made a small sound while turning the page. "Which is annoying," he continued.

Merry didn't reply.

Beating out a rhythm on the table for a second, Alan stretched his spine and arms as far as his wicker seat would allow, then flopped back with a great sigh.

"Any advances from that doctor of yours? Still sending love notes?"

Merry exhaled pointedly, snapped her book shut, and glared at him.

"Yes. He's very nice. His name is Lucian as you well know, and yes, we are still in contact."

"Doctor Lucian West," Alan rolled the sounds around his mouth—"and his wife Mrs. Meredith West. I still prefer Rockett."

"Lucky for you he hasn't proposed, then."

"He will."

"So certain, Shaw?"

"Enough to put money on it."

Merry extended her hand over the table and Alan took it firmly. "By the end of the year," he said.

"You're on," Merry shook it firmly, but didn't let go. "And no cheating! Don't you go egging him on or anything."

"Perish the thought," Alan chuckled.

It was then that a gentleman wove his way across the square toward them. Standing a good head above everyone else in the market, he wasn't hard to miss. Hefting a pile of paper binders, he seemed strong and sure; definitely not what Alan would expect from a professor. For starters, there wasn't a hint of tweed.

"Miss Rockett and Mister Shaw?" the professor began, not waiting to drop the files on the café's little table.

Alan offered his hand, not bothering to stand. The Professor took it with a grip firmer than he'd expected. Merry gave the professor a single wave and a smile, which he returned.

"Thank you both for coming," the Professor said with a strong cadence, which must have served him well in lectures. "I'm so sorry to be late. I got wrapped up in what files to bring along."

"I can think of worse places to be kept waiting," Alan said with a smile.

The professor looked around at the sunlit square, the gentle undulation of the sea, the bustle of local life, and took his seat at their table. "Yes, a pleasant spot, isn't it?"

Waving to the café's barman, the Professor ordered more lemonades, including one for himself, and finally sat down. Alan took him in, from boots to sun-bleached hair flecked with grey at the temples. Unlike the pale examples he'd seen in London, Professor Lorne Anchorage was well tanned, his shirt open to the second button, forearms wide and hands strong. Archaeology evidently attracted more sturdy specimens than other academic pursuits.

"Shall we get on then?" Anchorage clapped his hands and reached for the folders before him. "Lots to get through. I'll try to make it as interesting as possible."

"You're paying for our time, Professor, you can be as boring as you like," Alan quipped.

"All the same, I'll keep my exposition to a minimum," Anchorage said, opening the folder. "And please, call me Anchorage. Everyone does. Professor was thrust upon me when I took up research and I never forgave my mother for naming me Lorne."

Alan couldn't help but smile. "If we're being friendly, I think you should call us Alan and Merry."

Anchorage nodded. "To the matter at hand, then. Have either of you heard the name Hsekiu?"

The Privateers gave him nothing but blank silence.

"Good. Let's start there." Flipping through his binders, he found a series of photographs, which he handed to Merry. She angled them so Alan could see. They were much clearer than the daguerreotypes he had known from his boyhood. They appeared to be aerial shots of sand dotted with bands of vegetation and silvery streams. Other than that, Alan had no clue what he was looking at. Anchorage continued: "Doesn't look like much there, I'll admit. But what you can see is the proposed site of a tomb from Predynastic Egypt.

"I can see by your face, Alan, that you're wondering what the whoopdeedoo is amazing about that. Well, I'll tell you. This tomb could be from the first terrestrial pharaoh ever to rule Egypt; the earliest, we believe, *not* to be a completely mythical figure. And I can still see that you aren't following. Let me show you—"

Leaning down, Anchorage hoisted another file and flipped it open to reveal photographs of the walls inside an Egyptian tomb.

Alan took a quick look at the photos and took up his glass of lemonade, nearly draining the whole thing in anticipation that he would be leaving very soon.

Anchorage seemed to spot the signs of flight, as he began to speak faster: "You see, Egypt's history has several phases, the earliest of which is considered entirely mythical where the gods, such as Ra and the like, were actual pharaohs who built the civilisation. After that, humans took over running Egypt on their own. Hsekiu could be the first of those pharaohs, the first human ruler of Egypt around whom the mythology grew."

"So you could learn an awful lot from studying this fellow's tomb?" Merry chimed.

Anchorage nodded excitedly: "We could finally have an insight into how the earliest human cultures came to create and believe in their deities. From there, it could lead to realisations about all the other major religions on the planet. That's my field of study, you see: Crypto-theology."

"So you don't believe in all that God stuff?" Alan asked.

Anchorage sipped on his drink. "Every human civilisation has its own creation myths and belief systems. I think that tells us more about how humans work than it proves the existence of celestial beings."

Alan slid the photographs back across the table towards himself and tried to ignore the excited gleam of Merry's eyes. "So we're looking to dig up a dead man, possibly a God, hidden under sand that has a habit of moving when you aren't looking. Based on a rumour."

Anchorage gave a curt nod. "Sounds like fun, doesn't it?"

2

THE DAY ROLLED on a little further until the sun started to scorch. The fish market packed away until only empty wooden stalls and puddles of melted ice remained. As the locals retreated to their homes to wait out the hottest part of the day, Anchorage led the Privateers to a small room above the tackle shop serving as his office, where heavy blinds would protect them from the worst of the midday heat. The shelves were lined with specimens which towed the line between artefacts and uninteresting lumps of rock as far as Alan could tell. Where there were no rocks, there were books. A large rug covered the room's terracotta tiles, on which perched a small desk brimming with stacks of paper and surrounded by a few cheap chairs. Alan sat in one of them, across from Merry, shaking his head.

"So religion is utter balls," Alan snorted. "I knew it."

Merry punched him on the arm.

"Come on, Merry, you don't believe that stuff anyway," he said, rubbing his bicep.

"That doesn't give you the right to get your smirk on," Merry chided. "Let people believe what they want."

"I have to agree with Alan, for the most part," Anchorage interjected from behind his desk. "What we know of the Gods people still worship to this day comes from ancient sources, badly translated, one source often paraphrasing another until you could justify any old bunkum."

Alan made a mute see-what-I-mean gesture. Merry ignored him.

"So why are you bothering to find this Pharaoh?" Merry said.

Anchorage waved a delighted finger. "It's fun," he said. "And whether I personally believe it or not doesn't mean I can't be interested."

Anchorage shuffled a map from his binder and, weighing it against the breeze from the open window with his glass, he began to point to places marked on the page.

"This is the Nile Delta, once known as Lower Egypt. Some kind of stone mound was spotted protruding from the sand following a recent sandstorm. It was marked with a hieroglyph of twin falcons, the glyph for Hsekiu. Now, as Alan rightly pointed out, the desert is a fickle creature and the tomb has since been lost again. But we know that it was somewhere on the western bank of the Nile, where the delta turns into desert."

"Miles and miles of parched nothingness to search," Merry muttered.

"Just talking about it makes me thirsty," Alan muttered, and got up to search the few bottles in the office for whatever liquor could be found. Merry and Anchorage huddled together.

"But it *is* there," Anchorage continued.

Alan poured some unidentified brown liquid from carafe to glass and took a sip. His mind instantly felt clearer. "Where are your researchers and bookworms? Why aren't they helping you?"

"For precisely that reason. They are researchers." Anchorage stabbed the map with his forefinger. "This is an adventure."

"Alan, we have to go," Merry sang with excitement.

"Never said I *wasn't* going to go. Just can't *believe* I'm going."

3

THE HARBOUR WAS a small, local-built affair that swayed underfoot, surrounded by a host of narrow rowing boats stacked with frayed fishing nets. Alan couldn't see anything that might resemble an archaeologist's vessel. If he was honest, if Anchorage didn't turn up at all, he wouldn't be so bothered. He liked the professor enough, but the chances of excitement seemed a little low for his liking. Maybe he'd get lucky and be captured by desert bandits or have to fend off some crocodiles. Until then, he was feeling grumpy.

"If we've been brought along to row all the way to Egypt, Anchorage can think again," he muttered.

"He's obviously not here yet, and we're still waiting on the other team member, anyway," Merry chided. "Patience is a virtue."

"I don't think I have any of those." Alan's face stretched into a grin as he spoke. "But never mind that. I think I see him. Ernest bloody Sledge!"

A thin fellow in an immaculate blue suit approached from a nearby street, frock coat folded over one arm and a large leather bag in his hand. He shook his head as he approached.

"You're looking well for a dead man, Alan."

"Thanks Ernie. I do try."

"And who is this dazzling young lady on your arm?"

"I'm not on his arm, Mister—Sledge was it? I bring him along on expeditions to make my tea."

"Now you know that can't be true," Alan said to Ernest.

"Yes, he makes a terrible brew," Ernest whispered to Merry.

Merry chuckled while Ernest set down his bag and shook Alan's hand.

"Good to see you, old boy. I demand you tell me everything about your adventures since we last met. Your demise was obviously exaggerated but I'd love to know what happened."

"As long as you keep it out of print." Alan winked.

"No promises," Ernest said, patting the pocket of his waistcoat where a notebook and pencil stuck out.

"You've changed, Ernie. You're more- confident."

"Being Editor of the Illustrated Times will do that to you. Sink or swim."

"It suits you," Alan said.

"How nice of you to say. Ah. Our chariot awaits."

Shading their eyes against the sun, the Privateers watched a small airship descend toward them. Ernest slapped a hand onto his hat to keep it in place, and Merry lowered her tinted goggles to better see their transport against the blinding blue; a huge steel clam turned on its edge with turbines on either side. The ship's hull hovered ten feet above their heads, dwarfing the rowboats around it, and a ladder of steel rungs on tensile wire dropped into their midst. Alan couldn't see Anchorage with the glare of the sun on the airship's steel, but he heard his clear voice over the powerful engines.

"Welcome aboard the *Aphrodite.*"

ALTHOUGH AIRSHIP TECHNOLOGY had come a long way, the archaeological vessel was a little cramped for Alan's liking. With corridors narrow enough for his sleeves to brush either wall, and the stark tesla lamps emitting their headache-inducing sham light, it took Alan a little while to adjust to the falseness of it all. Even Merry's little glider, which she had liberated from an air corps engineer in a game of cards, seemed roomy by comparison. Merry, on the other hand, was ridiculously excited at being on a new ship.

Anchorage led them to the bridge, where an upholstered leather seat sat behind the controls. Anchorage saw Merry's child-like grin, and opened a palm toward the console.

"I trust you won't have any problems, Miss Rockett?"

"Are you kidding?"

"What's the point of having a pilot on board if she isn't going to use her expertise?" Anchorage cooed.

Merry was almost squealing when she threw herself into the pilot seat and began stabbing buttons, turning dials and muttering to herself with delight.

"We can leave her to it," Alan said. "She wouldn't hear us even if we tried."

"In that case, gentlemen, let me show you to a more comfortable spot where you can experience the journey."

Anchorage gestured for them to follow and they ducked back into the narrow tunnels. Anchorage set his boots on a ladder leading downward, and disappeared below as he talked. "I'll be in my quarters reviewing the plan for when we find Hsekiu's tomb. But you should be quite comfortable here for the time being."

Ernest smirked at Alan, who rolled his eyes. He could almost see the reporter vibrating with excitement.

At the bottom of the ladder was a room which, by its curved floor, must have been the airship's lowest area. Alan stepped down gingerly at first, as the floor and walls were made of such clear glass that he swore he was going to fall to his death. He stepped aside so that Ernest could follow him in. Beneath them, people scuttled across the quay.

"Astounding," Ernest gasped.

Anchorage gave a proud smile and gestured toward the pair of chairs he'd set up at the ship's fore so that the men could watch their journey.

"If you need anything at all, don't hesitate to find me. The kitchen is in the aft. There aren't many more rooms in our little ship so I'm sure you can find it."

Neither Alan nor Ernest said anything as the archaeologist left. Merry had teased the engines to a low hum and the airship was moving out across the harbour. Alan sank into his chair to enjoy the view.

ONCE THEY HAD gotten over their initial amazement of watching the sea scud beneath their feet, Ernest struck up conversation. Eventually, they were both chattering as if they were sat in a café on the Strand rather than flying above the sea.

"So how come you didn't send some snotty young journalist on this escapade, Ernie?"

The reporter sat with his bowler on his knee, tapping a merry beat with his long fingers. He was smiling, and hadn't stopped since he'd set eyes on Alan in the harbour.

"And miss out?" he said "Not likely. This was the perfect opportunity to get out of the office. The Illustrated Times has been swamped with stories of pathetic little wars, scaremongering tales of the East Asian Alliance spreading their influence, and tattle-tale exposes of British politicians."

"You wanted a little adventure, didn't you?"

"I might have heard whispers of a name, a Privateer who would be on the team. And I thought, 'If Alan Shaw is there, insanity will be close at hand.'"

"You just summed up my life in a sentence."

"It's what I do," Ernest chuckled. After a moment's introspection, the journalist narrowed his eyes at his old friend. "And so, Mister Shaw, what made you disappear from the world?"

"That's scary," Alan muttered.

"What's that?"

"The way your voice just changed. Is that your interview voice? Because it's horrible," Alan remarked, mimicking a shudder.

Ernest laughed. "Must be force of habit."

"Well force it away again. I'm not telling you anything. There are people who probably don't know I'm alive that I don't want getting wind of it."

"Like?"

Alan shot him a raised eyebrow.

"My pad is in my pocket, and it shall remain there until you say otherwise," Ernest said.

Alan sucked air through his teeth for a moment. "His name was Sumner. A Major in the British Forces stationed outside Delhi."

"The revolution?"

Alan sighed and, despite his better judgement, told his story: how he'd lost respect for the Empire when he'd seen Delhi demolished without reason or remorse, how Major Sumner had sent a small team of Privateers to do his dirty work, only to follow them and raze a stone palace with them still inside, and how Alan had decided to stay dead rather than be hunted by the British army for what he knew about their underhanded dealings. God help him, with a hand over his eyes, he even told the parts about Rani and the Raj's son. Ernest's jaw hung loose on its hinges. Sat forward in his seat, as he had been for the past hour, he finally flopped back and took a deep breath.

"Dear God," the reporter sighed.

Alan looked out across the glassy sea to where the northern coast of Africa was a rising cliff of amber, and nodded. "I hated the Empire. I hated what it stood for. But I had to take more letters of Marque to get by. The last thing I wanted was to find Rani again and for her to see me working for a tyranny we both hated. But I couldn't get away. Getting into trouble is all I know how to do, Ernie, and Privateer means you work for who pays. The Empire pays."

"That's an amazing story, Alan. You know, I'm just

thinking off the top of my head here—"

"Don't start, Ernie," Alan grunted. "I'm not beyond tossing you out of this airship."

Ernest spread his hands wide. "Listen just for a minute and, if you say no, I'll never mention it again. Word as my bond."

Sitting back in his chair, Alan wished he had something alcoholic to swirl.

"I'm listening."

"The Illustrated Times—no, *I* have been looking for something like this for a long time. The British public are becoming jaded, and it's starting to show. People are angry, disillusioned. We used to have stories of discovery and excitement; Great Britain was the jewel of the world. And now what are we? Tyrants and usurpers. Our politicians are crooked and our name sullied. People have forgotten the heroes, the adventurers and inventors who discovered lost civilisations and created mechanical wonders. The British public feel it most of all. There's no pride left, Alan."

"That was an impressive speech. You should have written it down," Alan said.

Ernest physically deflated. "But nothing I said was untrue. I've been looking for something inspirational, and instead I've found some*one*."

Alan sank further into his chair, resting his chin on his hand; the airship was ascending now, passing through a bank of cloud which cast uneasy shadows across his face. For the first time, Ernest noticed the darkness in his friend's smile. The strain of it was causing early wrinkles around his eyes and mouth.

"You haven't found anything, Ernie. Didn't you hear what I said about India? I killed a man and orphaned his son. You think I could face Simon and Lottie after that? Just drop myself into their perfect little life." Alan shook his head. "I've done too much wrong. When I was a boy I avoided the low life as much as I could. It would have been easier not to, but I always stayed away from the really bad kinds of trouble. Since leaving London I've done nothing but steal and kill and fight and run. If that's what people think of as a hero, then Britain really is broken."

Ernest shook his head in disbelief. "Your problem, my friend, is that you think everything is about you. It isn't. And by extension, not everything can be your fault. There are millions of people in this world of ours, all taking their own path. You can't account for them all. You couldn't even account for *me* turning up, so how can you be responsible for anything that happens as a consequence of my choices?"

Alan opened his mouth, but found nothing to retaliate with.

"You've done good, Alan. People still remember you as the boy who saved London. Twice!"

"That was a bloody long time ago, Ernie. And both times I did it for myself."

Ernest popped his bowler on the floor and, leaning forward, stared at his friend with a sobering sincerity.

"What I propose is this: let me write your adventures for you. If there are any parts that you want left out, then we leave them out."

Alan snorted. "Lie, you mean."

"Not at all. More like names and such. We simply show

the heart of the story. Do you remember those Graphical Adventures we used to read as children?"

"I remember. Titus Gladstone was my hero."

"Oh my, yes. Beat the baddie, get the girl," Ernest chuckled.

"It isn't like that out here, Ernest. Out here it's back stabbing and double crossing. It's dangers on a level that would make Gladstone wet himself."

"Agreed. So let your stories show that. We'll show the tales from the perspective of a man outside the Empire and be damned to those who oppose it."

Alan's lips tightened.

"I'll think about it if you shut up."

"That is a deal to drink to."

Alan snorted. "If there was anything worth drinking on this bucket."

Arid wastes whizzed beneath the airship; a golden canvas stretching as far as Alan could see. With Ernest gone to seek food, he was alone and, unless he was vastly mistaken, quite at peace. It was an unusual feeling, and he found himself wishing it would go away.

In time, the motion of the rushing land below drew him down into a fitful sleep with his head resting on the wing of his chair.

Fingers slick with grey slime grasp at his waistcoat. The feeling of soil pouring down his collar as he's dragged into the earth. What had been earth was now inky black water. Needle teeth descend from the darkness, drawing into a grinning face surrounded by tentacles cold to the touch, consuming every ounce of fight in him, dragging him down. And he's falling into the darkness now, the water gone. He knows what he will find at the bottom is worse, so much worse. He tries to scream but there's nothing in his lungs—

His arse hitting the glass floor was what finally woke him. Bleary eyed, he whipped his head left to right, convinced that he had woken in freefall before he remembered the glass room he'd fallen asleep in. As his heart pounded and the senseless images scattered back into the shadows of his mind, Alan's gaze fell upon a dark shape hovering off to the airship's port side.

He exhaled gratefully; an addict taking his first dose of danger in days and, pulling himself up with the help of the chair he'd slid from, all thoughts of his nightmare pushed away. He rubbed the sleep from his eyes, and with one final shiver, scampered up the ladder and along the corridor, where he found Merry still happily piloting the vessel. Apparently the novelty would never wear off.

"Have you seen them?" he asked.

"They've been on the globe for a while, just keeping pace."

"That's what I figured." Alan grabbed a speaking tube from the wall and whistled into it. The other end crackled before Anchorage spoke.

"Yes?"

"Anchorage, does anyone else know about your work out here?"

A hiss, and then an answer: "My plans for an expedition weren't a secret."

"And I imagine anything we find would be worth a fair bit to the right people?" Alan pressed.

"Some scoundrels would rather keep valuable historical artefacts to themselves than share them. Why do you ask?"

"I think we're being followed by some scoundrels."

4

"**C**AN WE LOSE them?" Alan asked as he leant over the back of Merry's chair. The other vessel was still lurking in view. Merry looked below where the Nile split into a hundred silver worms leading down to the sea, dense foliage packing the fertile delta in green fingers.

"Out here? Not a chance. There's nowhere to go," the young pilot huffed. "Not even a cloud to hide behind. Bloody perfect bloody weather."

"Rook offered us the manhunt Marque in Scotland. Lots of clouds there. But you said, 'no, let's get some sun'," Alan chuckled.

Alan turned to Ernest and Anchorage who had joined them, and both stood huddled over the radar globe. "Ideas, boys?"

"What could they possibly want?" Ernest grumbled.

"Probably Raiders," Alan said, peering at the shadowing vessel.

"Grave robbers with their own airship," Merry added.

Alan *humph*ed. "Very good grave robbers, then. Bugger. Let's say hello. Knock on their door, Merry."

Merry smirked as she swept the airship around, heading straight for the other vessel.

"You can't be serious," Ernest said.

"Now, Mister Sledge, this is the kind of thing I anticipated might happen. That's why Alan and Merry are here in the first place. Archaeology isn't a safe science by any stretch of the imagination," Anchorage interjected.

"Dangerous expeditions call for dangerous men," Ernest said, as if reading his own headline.

Alan waggled his eyebrows. "That would be me, then. Come on."

Ernest gave a little sound of half-excitement, half-fear, and scurried after his friend. They made two stops on the way down to the main hatch where Alan spun the locking wheel and a gust of hot air swept into the narrow corridor. He had procured a bottle of whisky from the kitchen and an oily rag from the engine room, and was stuffing one into the neck of the other. He gave the bottle a shake and patted his waistcoat pocket to find the oil lighter hidden inside.

"Alan, that isn't going to work."

Beyond the open hatch, the scoundrel's airship was swooping close. They had stopped dead and were hovering, clearly unused to their prey being so bold, and Merry wasn't messing around. As Merry swung them into position facing the robbers' cockpit window, Alan spotted the name of the vessel painted sloppily on the side.

The Sellsword.

That, actually, was—kind of brilliant. He almost felt bad about burning the thing out of the sky.

"Watch and learn how we do things out in the big

world, Ernie."

IN THE RAIDER'S cockpit, the pilot squinted at their quarry's airship.

"Would you look at that? They're coming right at us. Are they mad?" he muttered, sweeping his shaggy grey mane back from his forehead before bringing his vessel to a cautious hover. His long-haired partner peered over his shoulder.

"They must be." Reaching for the hailing horn, he whistled and then spoke into it. "Look lively, boys, these idiots are making a move."

By the time he'd hooked the horn back in place, the *Aphrodite* was hovering dangerously close to their cockpit window. A hatch flew open in the airship's side and they saw the blonde Privateer for the first time, his stance wide, a revolver in one hand, a flaming Molotov in the other. But it was the grin that made the pilot shudder.

The firebomb shattered on the cockpit window, a sheath of flame lighting the Raiders' shocked faces in blistering orange as liquid fire spread across the glass. The altitude swallowed the flames quickly but the Privateer had brought his revolver to bear and was firing wild shots that sent black streaks across the glass.

"Sweet baby Jesus!" the pilot spat, hauling on the controls. As the *Aphrodite* slid from view, he fought the violent spiral he'd steered into, his view obscured by sooty streaks from the Molotov. "Clear the bloody screen, Thom!"

His partner darted across the console to a lever by the window's edge and began to pump it. Water jets squirted across the screen, followed by a high-pitched squeak as a brass arm swept down from above to clean the glass. On the third pass the arm was successful and the pilot was just in time to see the delta's canopy hurtling toward them.

"Oh."

THE RAIDER'S VESSEL was just entering a tailspin when Alan threw a wry grin toward Ernest.

"You were saying?" he said, the locked hatch cutting out the sound of the Raider's struggling engines.

Ernest regarded his friend with concerned disbelief.

"Darwinism," he muttered.

"How's that?" Alan asked, cocking his head.

"A theory."

Alan turned away, heading back toward the cockpit. "I know what it is, Ernie."

"You have an inherent talent for mischief. Darwin might suggest that your urchin upbringing in a frequently deadly environment such as London has caused you to evolve a most diabolical skill set."

"And you got all that from a Molotov?" Alan smirked as he stepped into the cockpit where Merry and Anchorage were chattering. "Hey team, Ernest thinks I'm evolved."

Merry snorted. "Evolved for trouble, maybe."

"My point exactly!" Ernest nodded enthusiastically.

Alan threw up his arms. "I'm stood right here!"

"We are only animals," Anchorage mused. "It stands to reason that being brought up in an age of danger, surrounded by constant threats and doing what it takes to survive would create a certain kind of person. With Alan's very specific life experiences, he's evolved into the equivalent of a ruthlessly clever apex predator."

Alan grinned wider than he had in some time.

"Now *that* I like the sound of!"

WITHOUT THE RAIDERS in pursuit, the *Aphrodite* swept across the Nile delta until a band of blistering amber began to fill the horizon, which in turn began to ripple in a sea of dunes. Under Anchorage's instruction, Merry eased the airship to swoop over the boundary where the delta melted into sand and stiff grasses came in clumps out of the arid earth. This was where the stone markers had been spotted and the desert's fickle shifting had since reabsorbed them. Several passes over a five-mile stretch led to no signs for the naked eye.

"There's nothing for it," Anchorage sighed, already strapping on a long pair of soft leather boots. "We'll have to go on foot."

"Of course we bloody will," Alan muttered.

"Don't worry, I'm sure there'll be something else to shoot at soon enough," Merry snarked.

Alan winked at his partner. "If I get sand anywhere unmentionable, I like it to be for a bloody good reason."

She gave him that devilish grin from behind her innocent eyes. "Ask nice and see what you get."

"I'm not begging!" Alan retorted.

"No, but I am," Ernest interrupted. His face was a beetroot shade. "Please stop it, you two."

Alan and Merry were still snickering between themselves when the *Aphrodite's* landing gear had settled on the soft

Egyptian sand.

Whipped up by the desert breeze, grit filled Alan's mouth as he took his first breath of Egyptian air, a bad omen for his visit if there ever was. Trying to spit out the debris, he found the arid land guzzled his saliva instantly. He took a swig from the canteen at his hip instead, flushing out his mouth and spitting the water out onto sand what gobbled it.

"This place needs a good old-fashioned English springtime to sort it out," he muttered.

"They wouldn't know what to do with that much rain out here," Ernest said, slapping his friend on the shoulder.

Putting their backs against the large crate which Anchorage had brought along, the Privateers slid it from the *Aphrodite's* belly and down the slope onto the sand. With a deft pop, Anchorage crowbarred the sides until packing straw and wood lay strewn on the ground with a pedestal-like machine in the centre.

Anchorage unfurled a reel of cable from the machine and fed it back to the *Aphrodite* where the engines were still running.

"If only we could store energy and have done with all these engines and cables."

"I'm certain that if it were possible, someone would have by now," Ernest said. He had tucked a handkerchief into the back of his bowler to create a protective skirt and produced a pair of tinted spectacles. In his pinstripe suit and shiny black shoes, beside the other Privateers in rolled sleeves and open collars, he managed to look completely out of place, unprepared and yet refused to sweat a single drop.

As Anchorage and Ernest set up the machine, Alan and

Merry began pitching the large canvas tent that the professor had brought along with them.

"Look at this, our first home," Merry chuckled.

"You've got a feel for nesting haven't you? You'll be getting squishy feelings at the sight of other people's children next."

Merry hefted a coil of thick rope onto her shoulder as Alan hammered a curved wooden peg into the ground. She tossed the loop of the rope over the anchor and pulled it tight, one side of the tent behind rising into place as she did so.

"I think it's you who's getting broody," she said, swiping sand from her brow. She licked her sun-dried lips. "You're obsessed with me getting wed and dropping sprogs, but I think you're projecting. You ready to settle down old boy?"

Alan shot her a disbelieving look. "You're kidding. There's no settling for me. I'm better on the move. I just— never mind."

Merry looked down at him, hands on her hips, as he hammered another peg with a little more force than before.

"Go on."

He looked up at her, feigning that the sun was in his eyes so he didn't have to look right at her.

"I'd like to see you be happy, that's all. People who do this too long, they forget how to stop. I don't want you ending up like them."

"Like you?"

He shot her a dark look but she ignored it. Ruffling his hair as she went for another rope, she said:

"Don't fret about me."

He thought of saying something, but she was out of earshot, and he wouldn't have been able to say it right anyway. He grunted to himself instead, and hit the peg one more time.

The tent was up and the crates and folding furniture put away by the time Anchorage called them over.

"Alright, everyone, your assistance please!"

Handing a long metal cylinder to each of his teammates, Anchorage gave instructions for them to spread themselves evenly at least ten feet from the machine. With a twist and a pop, the cylinders extended feet at one end and glowing crowns of light at the other. The machine gave a hoot of recognition, reciprocated by a pip from each cylinder. Apparently, something was happening, even if Alan had no idea what.

"Now, if everyone will remain quite still." Anchorage turned a dial and the centre of the machine rose slowly, and dropped, thudding into the sand. It repeated the process several times. Anchorage gathered them around as a high pitched trill issued from the machine, accompanied by a ream of paper.

Dark shapes peppered the print-out's otherwise white page.

"These marks are our feet, those small ones being Merry's," Anchorage said with a wink toward the young pilot. Alan held back a quip as the professor carried on. "These are the *Aphrodite's* landing gear, trees and such—ah!" His finger stabbed the page where a symmetrical shape spread across the page much larger than anything else.

Alan looked at the page then across the desert to where

the large shape should have been and there was only a stretch of naked sand.

"I'll be damned. Guess we should break out the shovels."

5

THE MOUTH OF the tomb lay open in the valley of sand they had created. Shovels lay exhausted in a pile. Ernest and Merry were sharing a water canteen, Alan wiped his brow and wondered how much water could possibly leak out of a person's face before they die. Panting, Anchorage stood before the rectangle shadow leading down into the tomb, and his neon light tube winked to life in his shaking hand. Without even looking back at his team, he set off into the dark.

"Looks like rest time is over. Anchorage is on automatic. Come on, you two," Alan said, lighting his own neon by shaking the glowworm liquid inside, and using it to beckon to the others.

Venturing inside, an aura of pale green light travelled with them, exposing the hieroglyphed walls and hay-strewn floor of the stone corridor, a steady slope which led them down into the earth where the heat of the desert evaporated into a stony chill. Stale air and dust were the odours of choice. Alan wasn't sure whether he wanted to cover his mouth or take larger gulps to counteract the thickness of it in his lungs. Catching up to Anchorage, they found him muttering to himself as he traced his fingers along the walls, reading as he went, pulling them deeper into the tomb.

Finally, the professor spoke.

"Here. This is it."

A painting of a man in two dimensions, wearing a high white hat with a curled tongue reaching out of the crown, an ornate throne beneath him, with other figures prostrate at his feet. Alan snorted. Even he could have figured that was the pharaoh.

"This cartouche. We've found him. It's Hsekiu." Anchorage straddled the boundary between laughter and tears. Ignoring his team, he took off down the corridor with Ernest in tow.

Merry looked over her shoulder to where Alan had been on rear guard.

He was gone.

"Oh bloody hell."

Retracing her steps, she soon found him working by the light of his glow tube with a small blade, picking at the tomb wall.

"What are you up to?"

He shot her that disarming smile, full of charm and mischief. "Take a look."

In the sandstone, Alan had made a crude carving; four stick figures, one tall, one small, one in a bowler hat and one who appeared much more strapping than the others.

"Someone thinks highly of themselves," Merry said. "And my breasts aren't that big."

"Artistic licence," Alan chuckled. Stepping back to his

work, he quickly carved the date beneath their names.

"You're one of the first people to step into a sealed tomb of an Egyptian king in a few thousand years and the first thing you do is graffiti your own name on it." Merry shook her head.

Alan just smiled at her. "You don't like it?"

"Don't give up your day job. Come on. If Anchorage gets any more excited, he'll soil himself." Grabbing him by his shirt sleeve, Merry dragged Alan after the others.

They found them where the corridor opened up into a long chamber. Lining either side of a central aisle, offerings in marble and gold reflected their light. Dormant torches lay in their wall mounts. Alan made his way across to one and took the liquid oil lighter from his trouser pocket. The torch *whoomph*ed into life, and a hidden gutter behind the bracket caught the flame, carrying a thin line of fire which licked around the room with the faint huff of ignition coming from each torch in turn. Finally, a bark of flame lit the centre of the room, revealing a stone sepulchre.

Anchorage was already moving down the aisle, taking little notice of the painted pots and priceless statues standing around knee height, golden mockeries of servants and animals. The Privateers followed, surrounded by the sound of crackling flames and Ernest's constant muttering as he scribbled in his notebook. Even Alan knew that the sale of just one artefact could set him up for life. Maybe in a penthouse in Paris. French girls loved him. Keeping an eye on the rest of his team, he knelt beside a golden ox laden with a cart full of trinkets. Dipping his hand inside, Alan pulled out an amulet of gold and sapphire, which fit nicely in his palm, and a few golden medallions.

"Oy." Merry stood a little way off, the look beneath her raised eyebrow burning into him.

"I was just looking," he said. The medallions chinked back into their place. The amulet, however, never made it home. Dusting off his hands, Alan snorted at Merry as he stalked past her. "There's no trust in the world anymore."

He felt something slide from his pocket and turned to see Merry brandishing the amulet. With a flick of her wrist, she sent it arching through the air, back where it had come from.

"Can't think why," she said, and gave him a shove. "You go first."

Alan pouted at her, but decided not to argue.

Anchorage set his trembling palms against the sepulchre's lid and heaved. Not an inch of movement. Alan stepped up beside him when the thing wouldn't budge and, between them, they managed to create a gap. A cough of ancient air assaulted them and Alan reeled back, hand over his mouth and nose.

"Bloody hell. That's impressive," he coughed.

The Professor didn't seem to notice the stench, shoving on the lid until it slid all the way to the floor with a crash.

There, carved in wood and painted with pigments of white and gold and blue, was the death mask of Hsekiu.

"He's real," Anchorage said to his companions. "I knew it!"

"And he'll bring a real price, too."

The new voice cut across the room, sure and calm.

The Privateers turned slowly as the Raiders raised their

various weapons.

Their leader, the pilot, continued: "And, thanks to you, most of that will be spent on repairing my ship. Hell, maybe I'll just buy a new one."

Alan looked right into the barrel of the lead Raider's gun, saw light glint on the tip of the bullet, and raised his hands.

6

THE RAIDERS WERE a mismatched, hotchpotch group. Their leader seemed only a little older than Alan despite his cluster of curly grey hair. His red waistcoat over baggy trousers tucked into knee-length galoshes managed to look dangerous and dapper in a way that Alan appreciated. Leader's keen eyes regarded Alan unhurriedly, just as Alan stared right back.

The second raider leaned forward to whisper in Leader's ear. He was taller by a head, with a long brown ponytail and dusty old coat. Alan was reminded of a highwayman. Maybe Dick Turpin. When Dick was done whispering, Leader nodded and turned his attention back to the Privateers.

"Let's keep this simple. My associate thinks we should shoot you. I don't. Does anyone want to express a preference?"

The Privateers looked at each other.

"So," Leader continued, "You understand the nature of a rhetorical question. Good. Now turn around, hands behind your heads and stay very, very still. I haven't had a cup of tea since my airship took a nosedive into the desert and my trigger finger is twitchy."

The Privateers did as they were bid, and even Alan decided not to push his luck just yet. Leader seemed a little too intelligent for his liking, and he didn't fancy Dick finding an excuse to riddle him with bullets either; in the heat, he'd left his armoured waistcoat on the *Aphrodite*.

"Now, I have a proposition for you all," continued Leader. "Professor Anchorage—please don't look surprised, it's insulting—you will stay here and tell us exactly what in this room is worth what. Without our airship we have to be picky, and you're going to help us choose. The rest of you, outside."

"Please." Anchorage piped. "The work would go a lot faster if you'd let me keep my assistant with me."

Leader cocked an eyebrow. "And that would be?"

"Him," Anchorage said, nodding toward Alan.

Leader stepped close enough to Anchorage that he could have bitten off the professor's nose. "Insult my intelligence again and I might just put a bullet in you for the sake of it. You can keep the girl. Bowler Hat and the Pyromaniac, outside."

In short order, another raider, lanky with a dark beard, corralled them back out into the desert where Alan realised what a poor substitute torchlight was for the true power of the sun. Even in London at the height of summer, the sun filtered through a thick haze of cloud and smoke, making shadows easy to find. But not here. Here the sun ruled supreme and Alan felt his skin beginning to prickle uncomfortably as they sat trussed in the sand, watching the raiders raise a canvas tent they dragged from the back of a small quad-truck.

Beardy shoved them to their knees in the sand.

"Alan? What do we do?" Ernest hissed.

"Why do you always ask me?"

"Because you usually have an answer?" Ernest shrugged.

Alan shook his head at his friend. "I sometimes have ideas. They're hardly answers. I make it all up as I go along."

"But you always seem so convinced," Ernest said with a smirk. "I say, the wind is picking up a little isn't it?"

The desert was stirring. Sand slid down the dunes, eddies scuttling on the rising wind. The dry palm leaves began to rustle as their trunks swayed and bowed to some unheard music. Alan caught a mouthful of grit and spat it out as the breeze increased to a bluster.

"What the shitting hell? I come all the way to the desert to get caught up in a storm?"

But, looking upward, he saw only a clear blue sky.

He grunted. "That's pretty odd. Even by my standards."

"Alan…" Ernest gestured with his chin toward the tomb's threshold, from which the wind was now bellowing hard enough to clear a rivet in the sand before it.

Alan cursed. "Why does everything have to get so complicated?"

FOR WHAT IT was worth, the Raiders were taking good care of Hsekiu's artefacts, and once he settled into the realisation that they weren't a band of casual vandals, Anchorage relaxed a little. Leader even seemed quite interested in what the professor had to say as they made their way around the chamber with Merry in tow, who tried to give off an air of archaeological intelligence—whatever that looked like—while planning the best time to kick someone in the gut and steal a weapon.

"These are offerings of the lower classes," Anchorage gestured to a small golden cart pulled by a gilded ox. "I think you'll find that most of the gems are made of paste and glass."

Merry wished she'd let Alan keep one just to see his face.

"If you're looking for easy money, you'll want the jewels in the larger coffer by the sarcophagus."

"If you think tracking down renowned archaeologists and trailing them into the desert is an easy way to make money, Professor, you're sorely mistaken," Leader said, and gestured with his rifle for the Privateers to walk ahead of him. "Boys, take that chest there, the whole thing. We'll sort it out later."

Dick and another Raider hefted the coffer between them, putting it onto a cart. The raider with long blonde hair and a baby face grunted and complained as he pulled it up the tunnel to ground level.

"Then why do it?" Merry asked.

"If you're trying to make me see the error of my ways, you're wasting your breath," Leader smirked.

Merry huffed.

"You're just like Alan," she said. "Too smooth for your own good."

"The maniac who tried to set fire to my ship mid-air? I can see the darkness on that man's face sure as the freckles on yours. We're nothing alike. What about this?" Leader leant down into Hsekiu's sarcophagus and brought out a gleaming golden rod as tall as himself, with a beryl orb set into the ornate housing at its tip.

"That… actually I don't know what that is." Anchorage stepped forward and plucked the staff from Leader's unresisting hand. He inspected it from tip to tip, especially the orb, which reflected the room in fisheye perfection. "Amazing craftsmanship. No markings except decoration around the orb. Usually you would expect some kind of maker's mark at the least, or a cartouche of the owner, who was presumably Hsekiu himself. Curious."

Even Merry had to admit that the staff felt different to every other artefact in the room. And then she realised she had thought *felt* rather than *looked* and wondered why she chose that particular word. She pondered it for a few seconds before a stirring in the room interrupted her. It started with a faint jingling of disturbed pots knocking together, and rose as the sand on the tomb floor began to shift in a breeze that had no right being so far beneath the earth. Before she knew it, she stood at the centre of a windstorm, shading her eyes from flying sand, and spitting out her hair, which had come loose in the gust.

"What the f—"

"FIDDLESTICKS!" ERNEST COUGHED as he fell over onto a dune and regretted it when grit filled his mouth. He tried desperately not to breathe in since every lungful filled his nose with more wayward grains.

Alan was trying desperately to shake the sand from his eyes, to peer through the rising maelstrom, but the visibility was becoming more occluded by the second.

"Oy! Don't just leave us out here, you shit!"

But Blondey was taking shelter in the cab of the truck and seemed unmoved to help, and Beardy was nowhere to be seen. Alan and rolled toward his friend, trying not to taste sand as he shouted:

"Ernest, we have to move. Let's go."

Using each other, they struggled upright and Alan led them through the now impenetrable sandstorm.

"Alan, where are we going?"

"Somewhere else. Any-bloody-where else."

STUMBLING ALONG THE tomb's corridor, Merry fought against the gale that hurtled behind her, strong enough to take her right off her feet. Her clothing whip cracked around her and speeding sand burned her skin. The goggles she normally used to hold back her hair were down over her eyes and she could feel Anchorage's large hand on her belt as she led him blindly out of the tomb.

From behind them came the sounds of Leader and Dick cursing at each other, shattering pots and toppling statues as they fell over in the blinding maelstrom. Merry chuckled.

Reaching the entrance, they nearly fell over Alan and Ernest, huddled in the tomb's entrance.

"Either of you know what's going on?" she screamed over the storm.

Alan shook his head, a cloud of sand erupting from his hair, which had formed into a blonde tidal wave. He stabbed a thumb toward the outdoors and shook his head again, then patted his hands in the air. Merry got the point and led Anchorage into a seated position against one wall.

It looked like they would have to wait it out.

7

EYES AND MOUTHS crusted with sand, like moving parts of the desert itself, the Privateers stumbled out of the tomb's entrance. Running fingers through his hair and shaking out his clothes, Alan swore he donated at least a ton of golden grains back to the earth. Shading his eyes, he looked around.

The large canvas tent still stood, if only because the wind had been able to whip through it. But the *Aphrodite* had taken a beating. She sat lopsided, sand piled high against one side, and her landing gear swallowed by the desert. As they made their way over in silence, Alan could see that the sandstorm had blasted every piece of glass to an impenetrable cataract. They wouldn't be flying anywhere for a long while.

As they inspected the airship, the Raider's truck doors popped open and Blondey appeared unscathed. As he surveyed the carnage around him, Leader and Dick came sputtering out of the tomb entrance.

"You!" Dick roared, making his way over, the loose sand sapping the power from his stomping. "You're a curse!

We've had nothing but trouble since we came across you—"

Alan stormed forward until he was nose to nose with the Raider.

"Intent to cause an affray and loitering, which counts even in the air, you were justly punished. Hostage taking and causing bodily harm, you were justly punished. Getting in my face—" Alan's fist hooked around like a comet, smashing Dick to the ground. "Justly bloody punished. Get out of my sight before I give you a good kicking."

Dick reached for the revolver in his belt. But there was something bullet-proof about Alan's stare, the sure set of his jaw, the slight snarl on his lips as he stared down at him. The Raider took a tally of every scar on Alan's face and made a decision. Dragging himself to his feet, Dick limped back to his group where Leader stood with his arms folded. Although they had all been watching, none of the Raiders decided to say a word. Dick snapped an order and they set to work. The back of the truck was secured, and two Raiders removed the truck's sand-blasted windscreen.

Merry stood aghast. "Where did that come from?"

"I told you, my adopted father was a policeman. You pick things up. Doubt he'd agree with how I dealt with it, though. He's more of a by-the-book man."

"Actually, I happen to know he's rather proud of you."

"Ernie, don't. The thought of vomiting sand isn't worth thinking about."

Across the sand, Leader tossed something into the back of the truck and, as angrily as possible, opened the truck door and jumped inside. Piling back into their vehicle like circus clowns, the truck shuddered, started and, slowly at first, made its way across the desert.

"What? No goodbye?" Alan said.

Ernest sniggered.

"We have a lot of work to do," Anchorage piped up. "I'll see if there is anything left to salvage from the tomb."

"I'll see what the storm has left lying around," Ernest offered, and they trotted off in different directions.

"That leaves us to deal with this, then," Alan dropped his arm around his friend's shoulder as they regarded the half-buried airship. "Any ideas?"

"Since the shovels we had earlier are buried god-knows-where under this damned desert, I'd say no. I have no idea."

"What're the chances of us just taking off?"

Merry sucked her teeth. "With all the sand the ship is under and lack of being able to see, I'd say between nought and nothing."

"That's a shame. Although I meant just me and you sodding off and leaving this whole thing behind. Possibly never speaking of it again."

Merry raised him an eyebrow. "You can't fool me, Shaw. You'd never do that."

"I suppose leaving Ernie in the desert would be a pretty god-awful thing to do. Right then, you go tell the others we're on foot. I'll check the tent."

"Why me?"

Alan smirked. "Your legs are younger than mine."

"Ugh," merry snorted.

Merry made off toward the tomb, but not before Alan gave her a playful slap on her behind. Over her shoulder, she showed him her tongue. Still chuckling to himself, Alan climbed inside the *Aphrodite* for a moment, and reappeared shrugging on his shoulder holster.

Be damned if I'll be caught out again.

Alan had to admit that he and Merry had set the tent up well. Not a single guide rope had come loose despite the sandstorm. Pulling back the flap covering the entrance, he saw that the inside was relatively untouched despite a coating of sand. The hammocks still swung between the upright posts and a small table and chairs stood against the tent's far wall. Oddly, they were still upright, and a flame flickered under the camping teapot.

Alan's hand slowly moved toward his hip.

"Who's there?"

In the shade of the tent's far wall, where the sun wouldn't reach as it poured through the doorway, an unfamiliar figure shifted its weight in one of the canvas backed chairs.

"Before I answer, I urge you to open your mind a little. What I'm about to tell you may sound odd."

"Strange is my bread and butter," Alan snarked.

The oil lamp on the table leapt to life, casting a warm glow over the figure.

Alan's eyebrows shot upward. "*Huh.*"

Hsekiu's dessicated face spread into what should have been a warm smile if it had teeth rather than a gaping black hole. His eye sockets regarded Alan civilly.

"You aren't going to raise your weapon?" Hsekiu asked in perfectly enunciated English.

"I've learnt not to shoot unless I know who it is I'm aiming at."

"A wise lesson to learn."

"It was learned the hard way." Alan gestured toward the tent's other chair. "Mind if I sit down?"

"Please do. Tea?" The mummy leant forward with an audible creak and manoeuvred elegantly around the tea tray as Alan lowered himself into the opposite chair.

"You know how to make tea," Alan said with realisation rather than question in his voice.

"Tea is much older than you think, young man. The practice appears to have changed very little. What is this?"

"Milk."

"In tea? Why?"

"I wish I knew. I have mine black."

Hsekiu finished the task and slid a steaming cup toward Alan's side of the table with his twig of a finger.

"You aren't having one?" Alan said, suspiciously.

"I don't have the stomach for it, I'm afraid."

Ignoring the joke, Alan took up his cup. Once he spotted the fine powdering of bandage dust and ancient grime floating on the tea, he set it back down. Hsekiu didn't seem to notice.

"So what's it like being dead?"

"Quiet, mostly. I used to listen to the Gods while I slept. But they went quiet. It was lonely for a while. Until recently when I began to pick up your modern radio signals. A fascinating world you live in."

Alan had long since ceased to be amazed by casual occult obscurities, and so carried on the conversation politely.

"That's one word for it." Alan let the silence descend. Hsekiu didn't disappoint by remaining quiet for long.

"And so to a more pertinent subject," the pharaoh began. If possible, his face became even more grave. "Something has been taken from my tomb—"

"Ah," Alan interjected. "That's actually nothing to do with us. We're here to find your tomb to prove you're real. The others are more your lets-take-souvenirs type."

It was the pharaoh's turn to raise his eyebrows.

"Why wouldn't I be real?"

"Some things just get lost," Alan said.

"And you're the kind of man who finds them?"

"I have trouble finding myself some days. No, I'm with some very smart people. For what it's worth, I'm sorry you've lost things."

"As I'm sure you can imagine, death provides you with a certain perspective. What they took were trinkets of no value to me. Let them have them. Except for one thing. A sceptre. It must be returned."

"Is that why you caused the storm?"

"Me? Oh no no. My magic is limited to staying upright. Even my reception of radio signals is a feature of my tomb's construction. The storm was caused by the sceptre. Just a small example of why it must be returned."

"How dangerous is it?"

"If given the chance, it will raise the dead of Egypt and a plague of sand will sweep across the earth."

"So, quite dangerous then."

"The staff is an heirloom of Wadjet, passed from the Goddess to men when they were deemed fit to rule Egypt on their own. But we never knew how to use it and, quite frankly, it scared the willies out of us. So they buried it with me, and set a curse that would wake me to warn the world if it was ever stolen. It's all right there in the hieroglyphs on my tomb."

"I don't read many ancient languages," Alan said.

"Indeed? A shame," Hsekiu shrugged, dislodging a beetle from somewhere in his rib cage, which dropped to the ground and scuttled away. "Suffice to say the staff is old magic. Old to me, so positively prehistoric to yourself. Old and dark and raw. It doesn't have a mind, and will unleash its power at random without someone of strength to wield it. It was actually made so that if Egypt ever fell, the invaders would unleash an unholy horde. I suppose no one thought that the ancient world would just…evolve. Gods are rather short sighted for all-powerful beings, don't you think?"

"I suppose I'll be off sharpish, then, before we have a serious undead problem. No offence," Alan said, standing from his chair and giving a stretch.

Hsekiu gave another cavernous smile. "None taken. Good luck, and please be swift."

Alan gave the mummy an encouraging smile and strode outside.

8

MERRY WAS JUST rolling a small steam-trike from the bowels of the *Aphrodite* as Alan made his way across to her.

"That looks useful," he said. "Guess who has a new mission?"

"Go on," Merry said, inquisitively.

But they were interrupted by Anchorage, who came hurtling out of the tomb with gazelle-like strides as Ernest made his way from his scavenger hunt, still clamping his damn bowler to his head with one hand.

"Hsekiu. He's gone!" Anchorage seethed.

"And I found one of the Raiders. Quite dead. Poor chap got swallowed up in the storm. Just one hand sticking out of the sand like a boot scraper." Ernest shook his head. "Terrible business."

Alan gestured to the tent. "It's alright, Anchorage. He's in there."

The professor's face clustered in confusion.

"Just go take a look. Ernest, go with him. I think you're both in for a treat."

Now it was Merry's turn to look confused as their companions set off toward the tent, chuntering between themselves.

Alan turned to her, hands on hips. "Undead mummy says a magic staff will unleash the hordes of hell unless we can get it back from those Raiders."

Merry nodded as if the sentence made perfect sense. "Gotcha. Let's fire this thing up then."

"I love that you're so unfazed."

"If I wasn't used to this craziness by now, Alan, I'd have gone crazy myself." She stood up, looking thoughtful. "Unless we're both insane. Maybe we're inmates in Bedlam, sat next to each other dribbling and making up stories."

"At least we're having fun."

Merry laughed. "Get on, Crazy Al."

Steering the steam-trike across the crest of the sand dunes with slow, easy power on the throttle, Merry's complete control of the vehicle no longer surprised Alan. There were still deep rivets where the Raiders' truck had passed, making easy work of following them. They had headed back toward their airship, it seemed, as the tracks entered the delta's jungle, flattening the vegetation to a lush green carpet. The trike bumped up onto the firmer land, and Merry took off at a fair lick, the palm trunks and grasses rocking in their wake. She had to brake fiercely only minutes later.

The trike skidded on the freshly-crushed vegetation, almost throwing Alan over Merry's shoulder as they jerked to a stop.

"What is it?" he asked. But he soon saw what Merry had

stopped for. Where the truck had passed, a section of the road had collapsed, filling with water from some jungle stream and turning to a thick mud. Alan hopped off the trike for a closer look at the torn earth, trampled grasses and muddy boot prints. Circling the site, he dipped down into the overgrowth and plucked out a hefty gold bracelet.

"Looks like the boys had some trouble," Alan said. "They must have got stuck. Any chance we can go around?"

Merry considered the ditch and nodded confidently.

With care, they picked their way around and followed the track a little more carefully than before. But it wasn't long before they stopped again. Alan cocked his revolver.

"Wait with the trike, just in case."

With Merry on the chugging trike, Alan made his way toward the Raiders' truck, sat in the undergrowth with one wheel in the air. With as little stealth as possible, he strode confidently over to where the rear wheel sat at odd angles from the chassis, a piece of the broken axle still attached.

"These boys get all the bad luck."

The back of the truck lay open and a long score in the earth showed that something had been dragged away into the jungle. The Raiders had gone on foot, it seemed. But, just in case, Alan looped around and took a look inside the truck's cab.

He really wished he hadn't.

The driver's seat was still occupied. And it would remain that way for quite some time as far as he could tell. Where the engine block had hit a tree, Blondey's legs had been pinned inside the cab. The rest of him had carried on, and was now sprawled in a bloody mess beyond the trees.

Alan stepped away, very slowly. With a shudder, he headed back to Merry.

"Damned luck I can believe," he said. "I think this is something else."

"What did you find?"

"Pieces," Alan muttered as he swung himself back onto the trike.

Merry's face lost all colour, even through her blossoming tan. "Oh God."

"Possibly. And a not very nice one at that."

The going became much slower. Where the truck had made a wide path to follow, the Raiders on foot were no such help and the trike was constantly snagged on grasses and lurching over branches. Alan grumbled and cursed with every tilt and roll, his mood growing worse as he considered what they might find next. The occult held no more fear for him than a regular bullet or beating, but usually there was something to fight against, something large and snarling that he could shoot or trick. Here there was nothing. Just a thing, an object. If he couldn't kill it, what else was there? Before he had time to think up an alternative, his day got worse. Merry slowed to a crawl.

"Don't suppose there's any chance we could go pick up the others and run like hell is there?" Merry said. The fact that her voice quivered set Alan even more on edge. He'd never seen her afraid before. The trike rumbled forward, painfully slow, until Alan spotted where the coffer lay discarded on its side, golden contents spilled onto the ground. Blood slicked the gilded box. Alan was very close to agreeing with her. Very, very close.

"These boys are dropping like flies." He gave his friend's shoulder a little squeeze. "Let's get this over with, Merry. And be careful. If we find anyone still alive, they'll be petrified and twitchy."

She cast her wavering blue eyes back at him. "What makes you say that?"

"Because *I'm* petrified and twitchy." He took a deep breath, and one last look over his shoulder as Merry eased them on into the jungle.

9

THERE SEEMED TO be no reason to it, Alan thought, how the occult managed to stay hidden from almost everyone. As far as he was concerned, it was infuriatingly common. Merry's comment had snagged in his mind; what if he *was* insane? Maybe he'd been hit on the head one too many times. It would certainly explain a lot. Like how he continuously got himself into these scrapes. No one he'd heard of had ever been asked a favour by a mummified pharaoh, or seen an army of plant-men running a circus, or come face to face with whatever the hell Volkert had been. And yet his life was filled with it. Why couldn't he just come across a normal villain for once? A garden variety lunatic, just for the change of pace?

He was seriously considering professional help as the land beneath the huffing trike began to rise. Alan and Merry leaned into the slope, letting the trike do its work, but even the machine laboured as they wove through the undergrowth. Alan wasn't sure when he became aware of it, but the boughs of the jungle were beginning to creak above them. The canopy danced frantically, the noise growing as they climbed, rising to a tumult that made Alan's ears ache.

Cresting the top of the hill, the trike shot up on two wheels. There was a moment of unsure balance before they fell together, Alan dragging Merry with him to roll free of the machine. Without the jungle to hold it back, the wind on the hilltop clearing had built to a surging tempest strong enough to knock the Privateers clear off their vehicle.

From behind the arm he'd thrown across his face, Alan saw the jungle around the hilltop had been torn from its moorings, trees laid like dominoes by the power of the storm. There were still no clouds above, but the air was dark, as if the shadows had lost all fear of the sun. Shredded leaves and vines whirled in a green tornado, at the centre of which were the two remaining Raiders.

Leader sprawled on the grass, raised up on one elbow, and was screaming something to his companion who was the only thing still managing to stay upright. Alan saw why, and his heart sank. No matter how the storm raged around him, Dick could have been regarding the sky on a calm summer day. He stood at the storm's eye, Wadjet's sceptre raised over his head, its beryl orb giving off a deep purple glow.

Pain lanced across Alan's face as speeding foliage slashed his cheek. Merry let out a yelp. Grabbing at the grass with her gloved hands, her whole body was sliding across the ground. Eyes widening, the wind got beneath her and rolled her once, twice, and finally sent her spinning up off the ground, arms and legs threw out in a vain effort to control her flight.

An arm lashed around her waist, snapping her to a stop and bringing her crashing back down.

Alan hugged her close, using his own weight to keep her grounded.

"Put on some weight, will you?" He muttered into her ear.

She laughed, a shuddering fear-giggle.

With one hand latched to his companion's overalls, Alan dragged himself toward the centre of the storm. Both of them were careful to keep their bellies in contact with the ground. He struggled to make out the shapes of the Raiders ahead as the wind streaked cold tears down his face until the whole world existed the other side of a shimmering puddle. Several times he had to stop as his breath was snatched from him, or a high-velocity rock bounced from his back. He felt a tug on his shirt. Merry was shaking her head at him. She mouthed words that could have been, *too slow*, or possibly *you go*. Either way, she whipped off her goggles, eyes screwed shut against the wind, and thrust them at him. There would be no arguments.

Dragging on her goggles, the straps far too tight for comfort, Alan wondered for the thousandth time how she could have such faith, especially in him. His eyes dried quickly beneath the heavy lenses and he saw his friend sprawled out, stretching her small frame across as much ground as possible, prepared to weather the storm, to wait for him.

She could die there, he thought. *If I didn't come back for her, she'd lay there and die, still thinking I'd save her.*

What had been the stakes? The World. That's what Hsekiu had laid in his hands. But until that moment, Alan hadn't considered what that meant. The world was a terrible one, if he was any judge, hardly worth saving except to say that you had. Looking back toward his friend, his Merry, as she struggled to stay alive in the face of an ancient danger, he knew what was really at risk. The world was where he kept all his favourite things.

And so he pushed himself up from the ground. His boots finding purchase on the fickle ground, Alan fought his way into the maelstrom, so that he had something worth coming back to.

The goggles made movement through the storm easier, at least from a sensory perspective. Now Alan could use his arms to fight the wind, rather than to protect his face. He'd never been particularly strong, not like some Privateers he'd known who spent their off hours bench-pressing cattle, but a life of danger kept him lean. Still, no matter how many parapets he'd vaulted, how many midnight rooftop chases he'd performed, Alan was struggling. The tempest made every movement a herculean effort. Even his mind was straining as he willed himself forward, pushing his muscles to do more than he should reasonably expect.

Striking with an invisible fist, the storm spun him. Losing purchase on the slick grass, the ground rose up and slammed into him, shoulder first. The muscles in his neck and shoulder erupted in gritty pain as they tore. Alan felt his jaw go slack. A familiar sensation swayed toward him under full sails, billowing smoky darkness that filled the edges of his vision.

He rolled over, face pressed against the earth where the wind was lowest, and took shuddering breaths. If he passed out now, there would be no one to save his world.

Get up, you pansy. Delicate flower, laid out by a breeze. Get. Up.

He tried. But his right arm dangled uselessly, the fingers stubbornly flaccid. As he raised himself on the other, the sheerest pain rocked him onto his back where he laid gasping with the steamroller storm battering him.

That shoulder was dislocated for sure. He'd seen it in others, but never imagined it could be so painful. There was no way he could put it back in without risking blacking out. It would have to wait. With tears fogging the inside of his goggles, he yanked off his belt, stuffing his revolver into his trouser pocket, and clumsily pulled it over his head, drawing it tight enough to strap his useless arm flat to his side. It hurt like hell and it was barely doing the job, but it would have to do.

Once more, he raised himself on his good arm, waiting for a brief break between gusts before shoving upward. The pain served to keep him focussed despite the wind.

All his rolling and crawling and falling had brought him right to the edge of the storm's eye where the Raiders seemed unmoved. Alan could see Leader's wound now, the crimson slick and spilling out across the ground where something sharp had punched through his shirt and then his body. Dick was unmoved, but red laced his hands, the sceptre's lower tip a scarlet spike.

"Stop what you're doing, and put that thing down," Alan spat, his useless arm hitting his thigh as he stepped forward into the storm's eye.

Dick's head cranked around, painfully slow, and Alan realised that the Raider couldn't obey if he wanted to. His eyes were pleading and pained, the skin around them cracked like old paint to show bloody muscle beneath. Dick tried to say something; the muscles strained to move, but he couldn't. Motes of crackling skin peeled off in the wind. Leader didn't seem to be moving. Nothing alive laid in such a discarded a way; even unconscious, the human body would only make certain positions. Leader was long gone. Alan stepped over the corpse, one hand clasping his dangling arm, and stopped a companionable distance in front of Dick.

"Got yourself into a mess here, haven't you?" Alan asked the Raider.

Nothing but those pleading eyes.

"For the record, I don't know how to stop this," he sighed, looking deep into the only part of Dick's face which still seemed to be his own. Right into his eyes. "I could shoot you, if you like. But there's no guarantees that would work. I was talking to a dead man only an hour ago. Nothing's certain—"

The leg of Alan's trousers snapped taught, almost dragging him down. He let out a bark of surprise, fighting to keep his footing, and dropped to one knee. A pale hand latched onto his shirt as he fell, and the gaping face of a creature that had once been human, once been alive, dragged itself toward him. Alan fell back, the slack maw of Leader's animated corpse releasing a mournful groan as the eyes widened to reveal two rolling white orbs.

Alan made an incomprehensible sound and lashed out with his good hand, catching the corpse across the face. Its eyes never flinched, even when its head snapped to the side, those pale orbs still roved toward Alan as if magnetised. He tried to shove himself away but the corpse's weight was on his legs and his good arm just couldn't take the load. Instead, he dropped onto his back, fumbling at his trousers as the corpse slithered itself over him, drool stalagmites growing by the second. One of the corpse's hands had found his shoulder, the other clasped on the top of his head, dragging Alan down and itself up. The gaping hole of Leader's mouth was inches from his face, the droplets of saliva dappling his cheek.

Alan pressed his lips tight, turned his head as if those scant millimetres would help at all.

The revolver's retort sent a splatter of grey and red into the air.

Leader's corpse buckled.

Alan flopped back onto the grass and dragged a hand down his face in an attempt to wipe off even a little of the gore. It didn't do much good.

Kicking the corpse away, he got himself to his feet and stared out through the storm. Beyond the trees, a wall of swirling amber rolled over the top of the jungle's furthest edge, moving closer. What was that? It was the colour of sunrise but with none of the glow. And then it hit him, as he watched the wall of sand come tumbling over itself. Closer still, around the hilltop's shifting perimeter, there was movement in the trees. Alan could barely take it all in. Crawling, striding and dragging, more risen corpses were arriving on the hilltop. A few he even recognised as the former Raiders.

"Storm. Check. Undead. Check. This is getting bad."

Dick's eyes strained to see, but his head still wouldn't

turn.

"Trust me, you're better off not seeing."

Panic hit him. He couldn't see Merry.

Darting out into the storm, he stopped only at the very edge of the eye as the wind shoved him backward. He might as well have hit a brick wall. Frantic, he screamed her name, uncertain whether she would even hear him. She was gone.

Yanking his bad arm back under the belt made him yelp, but he was past caring. Running back to Dick, he made a deft leap. Easy as picking an apple, he snatched the sceptre right out of the Raider's hand. It felt like grabbing a snake. Firm and cold and very much alive. Dick hit the ground in a heap beside his former companion. By the time Alan's feet met the ground again, he could already feel invisible vines of crackling power crawling down his good arm. Without stopping, he spun around. Alan thrust the sceptre up into the air, the beryl orb pointing straight at whatever deity might be watching.

Raising his voice, he made damn sure they could hear him.

"That's *enough*."

The world seemed to fall through space by several feet as everything dropped. The roar of the wind gave way so quickly that Alan's voice rang out across the hilltop and echoed back to him. He'd never heard himself like that before, such roaring determination. He felt a pang of fear usually reserved for monsters.

It's only you, you fool.

Maintaining that fire inside was harder than he thought. The cold creep of the sceptre was cramping his bicep now, the first few tendrils of energy creeping into his chest. He didn't have long. He set out across the hilltop, back the way he came. The dead had fallen, too, returning to whatever uncertain rest they could get in a world where gods and monsters plotted under every bed, in every cellar and shadow. Alan pushed it out of his mind for now. Some things were too big to consider and it took everything he had to control the sceptre. Keeping hold of it was easy, he had the feeling that letting go would be the hard part, but controlling that slow tiptoe of unearthly power through his body wasn't so simple.

Making the edge of the hilltop, muttering angrily to himself about damned luck and supernatural bastards of every kind, he rounded the tipped bulk of the trike and stopped dead. Huddled in the well between the seat and the pedals, arms wrapped around her knees, Merry looked up at him. Relief. For a moment the freezing fingers of the sceptre's power seemed miles away. Without her goggles, her hair had been whipped into a towering blonde knot above her little face, pale as stone, and the lay of her mouth and wide eyes, so innocent and fraught, Alan couldn't hold back a snort of laughter.

"What do you look like?"

"You have the stick?" she asked, wiping her face and hair in one sweep of her hands.

"I have the stick."

"Should you be touching it?" She tried to stand up but had to use the trike as a handhold. How long had she been huddled there? Long enough to seize up.

"I don't have much of a choice. We need to get it back.

Quickly."

"I can drive."

"Merry, you're exhausted."

"I can drive." Setting her shoulder to the trike, she managed to shove it over onto its wheels and in a moment she had it purring again. "Come on. Let's get you back."

No longer fighting against the slope, the trike hurtled through the jungle, which was now peppered with disconcerting amounts of limbs and slack faces in the undergrowth, mounds of torn rags, swaddled bodies, fallen branches and loose vines. What the hell had almost happened, and how easy would it be for them to get back up if he lost control of the writhing artefact in his fist? It was all he could think about. That, and the sensation that he should stop, turn around. It was easier.

Merry breathed heavily; keeping her eyes forward and head up was making the muscles in the back of her neck quiver before Alan's eyes.

"Merry—" He had to say her name twice more before she slowed the trike. Still, she didn't turn around. "I need to stop. Wait."

Alan hopped off and stumbled toward the bushes. The sceptre thrust out at his side as if the distance would help, he dropped to his knees and heaved into the long grass. When he came back, Merry's face had fallen.

"You look like death."

"Better hurry or we might find out if you're right." But getting back into that saddle was a chore. Leaving seemed like the very worst idea he could possibly have. Luckily, Alan was used to throwing himself at bad ideas on a daily basis.

Like knowing you had a parachute and ignoring the cord, Alan struggled back onto the trike behind Merry. Unable to sit upright any more, he slumped over his friend, using all the strength he had to keep the sceptre tucked up under his arm, and his own mind firmly in his skull.

The trike revved harder, scatting dirt as it hurtled forward with frenzied urgency.

Alan came to as the wheels dropped hard from the relative firm ground of the jungle and hit the more uncertain terrain of the dunes. He made to ask how far they had to go, but groaned instead. The cold was everywhere now. What had started as a creep was a stampede. His mind had started to cloud over, to be pushed to the side. The pain in his stricken arm flared as the trike hit a bump, clearing his senses. Whatever was coming through the sceptre, it didn't like that very much.

Merry called back to him: "Almost there. Hold on tight."

The trike skidded to a stop and he was falling. The sensation snapped him awake.

When did I pass out?

The sand caught his crumpled form when he was unable to put out a hand to slow himself. There was barely enough air in him to cough. Hands rolled him and a voice yelled. Yet more hands, under his arms, around his body, and he was lifted to his feet, which pitter-pattered out of habit. He was moving, but he couldn't tell where or how. The sceptre's song was rampant in his head, and other voices were lost in the fog of his mind. The world became darker around him and the toes of his boots scraped on stone as his knees stopped working altogether.

Then came the fighting. Surrounded by the hazy glow of torches, with an ancient scent in his nostrils, the sounds of muffled cries came to him as if blown inland from a distant sea. Alan felt his body invigorated. The crack and slap of flesh, the hum of adrenaline, and then only the sceptre screaming to him as he flew, was carried, not even feeling the ground any more.

Alan's vision reeled into focus so suddenly that he tried to step back. But there was something behind him. Anchorage. The large man had his arms locked under Alan's and hands clasped on his neck in a firm hold. Alan found stepping away, in any direction, would be impossible. Ernie gripped his forearm with both pale hands, keeping his arm and therefore the sceptre, held out before him. Blood streamed from Ernest's nose, once neat, now a lightning bolt of bone. His friend was pleading with him, although he didn't know what he was pleading for. And then there was Merry, her hands pressed to either side of his face. She was screaming at him, her eyes filled with tears. She kept looking over his shoulder, the knot of fear tightening between her brows, and then coming back to him. Tears ran down her face and into her mouth, her lips twisted as she cried for him to—

Alan's hand snapped open.

He had been shoving backward, and Anchorage braced against him so much, that when his body went slack, both men fell forward until Alan was doubled over the sarcophagus' edge, face to face with the body of Hsekiu. The pharaoh was sleeping. Alan liked that idea, that much he knew. Looking down, he saw the mummy's hand on the sceptre's handle, Hsekiu's obsidian visage slid into the faintest of smiles.

Alan's legs finally gave up on him and he slid to the ground like a wet rag.

He had no idea how long he sat there, but when his muscles became his own again, he took in the sight of Ernest, Anchorage and Merry, all sprawled around the burial chamber, tending wounds and heaving great exhausted sighs.

Anchorage noticed him first.

"You're back?" the professor said, his voice a haunted whisper.

"Did I go somewhere?" Alan winced as his throat sparkled with pain, his voice a wheeze. Had he been screaming?

"Best you don't remember, perhaps."

10

ALAN SLUMPED IN the corner of the *Aphrodite's* cockpit, head propped on one hand as the other Privateers bustled around. Merry was clasping the pilot's headset to one ear and twiddling dials. Alan occasionally opened his eyes to check on her. Just in case she blew away again. Anchorage had carefully catalogued and photographed every aspect of Hsekiu's tomb, with the help of Ernest's note taking, and then put everything carefully back where he'd found it. If there was one thing he'd learnt from the expedition, it was that things which had been buried should remain that way. Alan had always thought there was something ghoulish about the display of artefacts for people to wander by half-heartedly in some museum a continent away. But people wanted them so very badly. And where was the line? How long dead did you have to be before some busybody came along and dug you back up, put you on a shelf and you had groups of children pointing and gurning at your gaping corpse?

Shuffling his arm comfortable in its sling, he wondered how his perspective could have changed so drastically. He'd been the one happy to permanently borrow anything at all. Could it be he was learning his lesson, too? He hoped not. That set a dangerous precedent.

Perhaps his thoughts were just a little dark right now, but he'd had an experience which had shaken him. If the power of a God was what he'd experienced, then there would be others. Sitting on high, judging everything, waiting for you to die so they could get their clutches on you for eternity. That meant a potential pantheon of deities that Alan had to show two fingers to. That kind of commitment could be tiring.

Merry spun in her chair. "Looks like everything is in working order. Once we get the vents cleared and the landing gear free, all we need is a new window. I've radioed ahead to Cairo and the embassy are going to send someone out. It could take a while, since everyone's frantic after the sandstorm."

"Don't suppose they mentioned walking corpses?" Alan muttered. Even talking was an effort. That damn sceptre had drained him more than a debaucherous Parisian weekend ever could.

"No signs of them. It must have just been local."

"We get all the fun as usual." His legs didn't want to, but he managed to make them take his weight so he could stand. "I think I need some sleep. Shout me if you need me."

He was asleep before he hit the bunk. For once, there were no dreams.

WAKING TO THE hum of the *Aphrodite's* engines, Alan pressed a hand to the wall, reading the vibrations. They were flying already, the engines putting in some serious effort. He looked out of the porthole to confirm that Egypt was indeed whisking below them.

"—someone with strength enough." Anchorage stopped dead when Alan came into the cockpit.

"What are we talking about?"

"You, for a change," Merry snarked. "We're debating how bloody stupid you are, grabbing that thing."

"You're welcome," Alan sighed, and plonked down next to Ernest, who had a white dressing on his face two sizes larger than his actual nose. "And how are you, old mate?"

Ernest smiled from behind his pair of black eyes. "I have enough story to intrigue London for a couple of months at least." Alan patted his knee with a weak smile. "I don't suppose you've thought about our literary venture any further?"

"As a matter of fact, I have, just now. Do it, Ernie. Just as we said. No lies, but nothing that would incriminate anyone. I'll tell you every story I've got." That sentence almost seemed to tire him more than the previous day's events. "When we get back to Malta, I'm not going anywhere for at least a week. You can pick my brains all you like. As long as you're buying the drinks."

Ernest laid a hand on his shoulder. "You have a deal."

Dear Simon,

Apologies for my handwriting. My shoulder was dislocated and it's still a little sore.

This job has been like no other. I can't even describe to you what we've all been through, but I think it has changed me somehow. Ghouls and ghosts I can take in my stride. There's something about that kind of thing that is still down to earth, no matter how weird. But this job, this one has made me wonder if there's more out there. I know you're not a God-fearing man. But maybe you should be. I still don't think there's one bearded almighty watching over us. The idea seems too much like a bed-time story. But I know for a fact that there is something bigger, darker, and crazier than you can imagine. How are we supposed to contend with that? Are we even supposed to? Maybe that's why people tell themselves the bedtime story. We all need to sleep at night.

You may find something on your doorstep in a month or so, courtesy of our old friend, Ernest Sledge. I suppose you know all about his promotion at the paper, but it was news to me (sorry for the pun). I think it will amuse you to read it, anyway. And there's more where that came from.

I hope all is well with the Carpenters. Say hello to father for me.

Alan

Dear Alan,

I know that you worry about my delicate sensibilities, but I assure you I can take any story you wish to share. This one, in particular, sounds like the kind that requires alcohol and a dark room, however. I worry about you, Alan.

In case you were wondering, I don't share my

letters with father. He knows we are in correspondence, of course, and I have even urged him to write to you himself. But he won't. He doesn't know what to say. I don't want to make you feel bad, Alan, but I don't think he will get over your leaving as easily as I can. I understand your motives. But you know father. He thinks only in straight lines, as do many Policemen. Maybe you should write to him first? But that is only a suggestion, of course.

All is well here. Jasper continues to grow faster every day. He is a real little person now. He's using words and stumbling around like a mad drunk. It's quite heart-warming to see. Lottie is in her element. She still organises the west-end suffragette's group and manages to corral Jasper at the same time. It really is like herding cats, sometimes. The other day I sat him down with a book while I nipped to make the tea. When I came back he was sat in the same spot but almost every cushion on every chair was around him, including a few more books and a clock from the table (Lord only knows how he got that). He seemed quite comfortable in his little nest with a doily on his head, but I swear I was only gone for a moment. He's a whirlwind. I'd swear he takes after you if I didn't know better. I think you're going to get on very well.

Please get some much-needed rest. We look forward to your letters, and to seeing you in the near-future.

Simon and family

Alan Shaw and the Blood Curse

1

Yorkshire, England
July, 1864

"**D**EARLY BELOVED, WE are gathered here today in the eyes of the Lord to witness the blissful matrimony of Doctor Lucian West to Captain Meredith Catherine Rockett—"

THE AUTOMOBILE BOUNCED off the road, its suspension barely taking the beating with a loud *glonk* that made Alan's teeth clench. He checked his watch for the hundredth time: he would never make it. But he had to *try*. His eyes were off the road for only a second, but the sheep didn't seem to care. Alan slammed on the brakes, the automobile fishtailing in the mud as it skidded to a halt. A solid cluster of bleating stubbornness, the sheep stood in the road and regarded Alan with disinterest.

"Get out the bloody way!"

"—DESPITE ALL THE weddings over which I have presided, it never ceases to strike me that there are moments in a person's life when the hope and majesty of God's love cannot be denied. A new birth, the comfort given to those in their last moments, and when two young people come together to dedicate themselves to each other for the rest of their lives—"

The gunshot rang out across the fields, followed by a cacophony of bleating. The sheep broke their ranks in an instant, flowing away like bath foam. Sticking his arm back into the cab, tossing his revolver to the passenger seat, Alan gunned the engine, the *phutphutphut* rising in urgency as the automobile shot forward. Through the fogged window, the shepherd could make out only the wild visage of some madman before he was gone.

Hunched over the steering wheel, Alan was vaguely aware of a throb of tension in his neck and back. His muscles were so tight that when he rounded the next corner on two wheels and hit the pothole he actively left his seat, slamming his head into the cab above, and then the door as the automobile landed off kilter.

"Bugger it!"

"THEREFORE A MAN shall leave his father and his mother and hold fast to his wife, and the two shall become one flesh. What therefore God has joined together, let not man separate."

THERE HAD BEEN no way of getting out of the cab without having to wade, and so Alan stood on the grassy bank, his new suit soaked to the knee, his flimsy dress shoes water-logged, and regarded the shattered axle of the automobile with misery.

There were no curses strong enough, and so he simply slapped his forehead and spun around. There, only a few minutes' run away, was a farmhouse with a dilapidated roof and lopsided barn. He was already moving, sliding in the mud, his shoes flicking an unseen shower of dirt up the back of his suit jacket.

The farmer's wife answered his pounding fist on her door with a sheepish look. In three or four panting sentences, he managed to convey enough of his situation that the old maid grabbed his hand and dragged him around the side of the farmhouse. There was his salvation. His only chance.

A horse.

"This is a bloody wind up."

"AND DO YOU, Meredith Catherine Rockett, take this man to be your wedded husband? To have and to hold from this day forward; for better or for worse; for richer, for poorer; in sickness and in health; to love and to cherish from this day forward until death do you part?"

"I do."

IF HE GRITTED his teeth any more they would shatter. Alan gripped the horse's reins until his fingernails dug into the palms. His head was low over the beast's neck. The beat of every hoof shook him close to potential death. His thighs screamed as he gripped the saddle for all he was worth.

But there was the old stone church, just the other side of a stream which cut across the road and down to the lakeside.

He was close. He could make it.

"IF ANYONE KNOWS of any reason why these two should not be joined in holy matrimony, let them speak now, or forever hold their peace."

The door exploded inward. The entire congregation whipped around to regard the silhouette of Alan Shaw. Each of his footsteps squelched as he trod slick mud down the aisle's flagstones. His suit was thoroughly sodden and dripping. If a comb had seen his hair that morning, its work was entirely undone. Running a hand down his face streaked only more slop. Every head turned to watch him pass. For what it was worth, he tried to straighten his tie, his jacket, and flicked a little mud from his waistcoat before giving up.

With a curt nod to the priest, Alan stepped behind Merry.

"You're a little late," she chided, looking him up and not bothering to go back down.

"Auto trouble. You look nice."

"Nice? It's my wedding day."

"Very nice?"

"*Caw*," she sighed. Turning back to the priest, she gave him a pretty smile. "Sorry, Father, my friend is… challenged." She also mouthed *sorry* to Lucian, who gave a jovial shake of the head to greet Alan's boyish shrug.

"Then I now pronounce you, man and wife."

The congregation all stood to applaud, Alan took a step back so that clapping his dirty hands wouldn't spray more mud.

THE PARTY WAS in full swing by the time Alan made it back. He'd returned the horse and the old Farmer had insisted on him bathing before he returned. She'd cleaned his suit, but it was still damp despite a good mangling.

In the old stone barn which stood behind the church, someone had strung fizzing electrical bulbs around the hayloft and the steam-generator's gurgling chug was mostly masked by the fiddle and drum band at one end of the room. Merry and Lucian were already dancing, arms locked together at the elbow, round and round. Alan couldn't help but grin. Merry had already hitched up her dress using a pair of old braces and her army issue boots, the same that had trodden ground on many adventures with him, were stomping the ground in time with the music beneath the crinoline.

Spotting the sodden mess in the doorway, she waved him over. He obliged, but stopped at the edge of the wooden planks that had been laid for a dance floor.

"You know I don't dance," he called over the music.

"Remove that broom handle from your arse. It's my bloody wedding day, Shaw." Alan couldn't help but notice Lucian's face twitch at the bad language.

Get used to it, Pal.

"Is that your excuse for everything today?" he chuckled.

"Yes. Do it."

With a shudder for what was about to occur, snatching a bottle of unknown spirit from a passing servant, Alan went to dance.

ROLLING OVER TO the crinkle of hay beneath him, Alan

cursed the Yorkshire sun as a shaft caught him straight in the face, for surely it was a special kind of painful sun that only rose after consuming bottles of whiskey. He rolled back into the darkness to groan for a while. It wasn't until the scent of cooking eggs and bacon rose up to him that he decided to move. He didn't remember climbing the ladder to the loft, and so he had a good excuse for how shakily he climbed down. He turned around to be greeted by a hundred strange faces, and he was the only one still wearing clothes from the night before.

A mix of Americans and English sat at the trestle tables where a party had once been. Some of the men Merry had known in the Air Corps were still raucous in one corner. Lucian's family were chatting loud enough to ring the hangover bell in Alan's head. Locals were bringing in platefuls of expertly balanced food. He eventually caught sight of Merry and Lucian, huddled in one corner, eating breakfast together, their fingers locked on the tabletop. Alan found an empty seat and plonked himself at the end of a table of strangers, snagging a plate of breakfast for himself in the process. It went down easily, and then threatened to come back, but Alan kept it in check as he wandered outside to find a trough to douse himself in. It was just as he swept the freezing water from his face and hair that a small local boy arrived. Alan saw him talking to the farmer's wife who pointed in Alan's direction.

"Excuse me, sir. But I have a letter for a Mister Alan Shaw." The boy thrust the envelope forward with great pride.

"That's me. Just a sec," Alan dried his hands before

taking the letter. Fumbling in his pocket, there was a single one-pound note crumpled right at the bottom. He gave it to the boy anyway, whose eyes expanded far wider than they should have been able. "Don't spend it all on sugar and toys, you hear me?"

But the boy was off in some fantasy, grasping the note by its very edges in wonder as he wandered off.

Shaking the letter down, Alan tore off the end of the envelope and delved inside.

He read slowly. Then read it again. Then he sat down heavily on the trough's edge.

BY THE TIME Alan came back inside, the breakfasters were dissipating, some still groaning and clutching their heads. At least one person had darted for the barn door to make wet noises outside. Merry and Lucian were still seated, fingers entwined. With a deep breath, Alan stepped forward.

"Time for me to be off, then."

Merry stood up, placing one hand on his arm. "What are you in a rush for?"

Alan shrugged as if she we were crazy. "Nothing. Just no point hanging around watching people recover. There'll be some trouble somewhere I could be getting into."

Narrowing her eyes at him, she poked him in the chest. "You better not be fibbing to me, Shaw."

From out of his facial toolkit, he pulled a smile he'd used a thousand times before, the one to set people at ease, the one that melted maidens' hearts, oozing lopsided boyish charm.

"Don't turn that on me," Merry grunted, and Alan

realised who he was trying to use it on.

Balls.

With all other options expended, he would have to be honest. Taking her biceps gently, he looked earnestly into his dearest friend.

"Your next adventure is right here, Merry. For you and Lucian. I've never been one to sit and watch. I need to be moving, finding my own trouble." He gave her a long hug, her hair tickling his chest through his half open shirt. She still smelled vaguely of her wedding perfume as if she wanted the scent to linger forever. Something he couldn't do. "You look after him."

From the crush of his arms, Merry mumble something. He gave her a little room.

"What was that?"

"I said, 'be careful'."

"I always am." With one last squeeze, he stepped away, gave Lucian a companionable nod, and made the fastest exit of his life.

Dressed and back out on the road, a thin rain pattered against his coat. The lake faded away, letting him know that the barn would be out of sight, too. And so he stopped for a minute. The letter crinkled in his hand, both buried deep in his coat pocket. He regretted not telling Merry, but she would have only wanted to come, and that was impossible. She had to go her own way.

He took out the letter and read his brother's handwriting again. There wasn't much to it, but what there was gave his insides the shivers.

Dear Alan,

I hate bearing this news to you, brother, but there's no other way. Father is gone. Taken in the line of duty, as he would have wanted, but sooner than any of us could have prepared for. Ernest was injured in the same attack and lays in a dire state, a man made of bandages and black silk stitches. He has woken only once in the last three days, and it was your name he uttered.

There is a deep wrong in this city, Alan. London has surely become the most fearful place on earth. Everyone walks a little faster on their way home, and never alone where it can be helped. Markets and businesses will only open after sunrise and don't wait for nightfall. The police are only ever seen in groups. I have never known the like.

Come home, Alan. You must.

Simon

Crumpling the letter back into his coat with one hand, Alan held out the other to a green, mud-dappled truck, which laboured along the dirt road in the direction of town. When it pulled over, he threw his duffle bag and then himself into the rear bed with the hay, and banged on the cab. The truck set off once more.

There was nothing for it this time. No excuses. London had done everything in its power to draw him back over the years but now it had won. He was going home. Back to hell.

2

STEPPING ONTO THE Hyde Park docking pylon, Alan pulled up the collar of his coat and tucked his scarf tighter around him. The same thin rain seemed to have followed him from Yorkshire for the specific purpose of soaking him through on his home turf. Pushing from behind, his fellow travellers forced him onward. He stepped out of the crush, toward the railing. Below, Hyde Park itself was barren of people. To his surprise, the old roads had been widened and multiplied, eating away until the grass was an afterthought. The days he'd spent as a boy, pestering young lovers on those lawns, using the ladies' sympathy and the gentleman's purse for a shilling or two. He doubted anyone came to the park now. Not unless they were taking a dirigible or airship.

"Pardon me, Sir. But you can't linger here. The docking levels will be realigning soon and it's quite dangerous." The pylon engineer's voice had a calmness that counteracted the pounding in Alan's chest. Why was he so nervous? This was his town. He'd saved it from uncertain destruction. Twice. He'd once known every dank inch of the North bank. And here he was feeling like he was attending school for the first time. For a moment he remembered Simon's hand in his on that day long past, his eagerness to share the experience with a well-scrubbed urchin that had become his friend, his brother. And now Simon needed him. Perhaps that was why Alan's nerves were as they were. He owed a lot of debts here, and the feeling was upon him that it was time to collect. He just hoped he had enough in him.

Turning to the pylon engineer, he flashed a smile, which turned to pleasant surprise.

"You've worked here a long time, haven't you?" Alan offered. Surely enough, the engineer was older, the years of high winds on the pylon's upper levels had leathered his face, but stood in that same grey and red uniform, the same peaked cap and ear muffs, was the engineer that had seen Alan onto an airship the last time he'd been home.

"Almost eight years, Sir. Wait. I remember you. I put you on that rickety barge. Your name's Shaw isn't it, sir?"

Alan's eyebrow climbed his forehead. "That's in incredible memory you have."

"Not really, Sir," said the engineer, guiding him over to the elevator cage. "You were in the newspapers. The lad who saved London. They said you died in India, and I remembered I'd put you on a rusty old scuffler headed that way. Glad you ain't dead, sir. Have you not been home since?"

"Seven years," Alan muttered, letting it sink in.

"Well, for what it's worth, Mister Shaw, it's good to have you back. London needs a fellow of good calibre right now."

"If I find one, I'll let you know."

The engineer ignored him. "If I might make a suggestion for your visit, you might want to head to Covent Garden. Do you know the florist's arcade, around back?"

Alan nodded. After escaping the workhouse, it had been his regular haunt.

"Just drop by if you have the chance," the engineer said with a wink.

Alan gave a curt nod as the elevator's concertina door slid closed and the whole cage gave a shudder before descending.

HE CUT ACROSS the park, following the banks of the Serpentine before veering away to take the shortest route out of the park. He could have stayed there for longer, and then to St James' on his way to his old home, but part of him was aching to see London cobbles and curb stones, to sink into the streets he'd known, to get a feel for the place again. Reaching the road, he waited beside the brass hulk of the old Mark II automaton which stood there, a full head taller than him, its body dappled with welding spots from years of repair. After its allotted waiting time, the automaton let out an almighty clatter of its klaxon and stepped out into the road with its arms stretched wide. The traffic puttered to the briefest of stops at the machine's command. Alan crossed with the other humans and dived into the city beyond.

If London had changed, it was for the worse. The muddy browns and red bricks of his childhood had faded to a uniform grey. From sky to foundation, the city was a slate crush with only smoke and smog finding any room between the bitter crowds. New electrical streetlights hummed in their globes, a constant backing to the blare of machines and bodies. Now and then a spark of electricity would shower splinters of light from an overhead cable. From the lettering over shop fronts to the lay of the roads, everything about his home seemed hell-bent on making him ill at ease. Several times on his way from Hyde Park to his old home, he was turned around by a road which had once been and now wasn't. After a frustrating hour of diversions and refusing to ask anyone for directions, Alan took a right into a familiar alleyway. Suddenly everything was right with the world. There, exactly as he remembered, was a smattering of bins, overflowing gutters, and a ladder. With his hands greeting the rungs like old friends, although the rungs were now steel where they had once been wood, he headed upward to a place where London could never surprise him. For the first time since the airship brought him home, Alan could breathe. Apart from a few exceptions, London's rooftops were exactly the same. Or near enough that, if he didn't concentrate too hard on the details, he could fool himself. He felt better. There was his old home, the bastard that it was. There was the vista of smoking slate, the plumes of startled pigeons, the whistle of the roof rat children calling to each other where the noise of the city didn't reach. He'd hidden up here so many times, letting bruises heal, distracting himself from the pangs of hunger, escaping the brutal hands and voice of the old barman Callas. And here he was again, distracting himself from the fact that there was one less good man in the throng below. Better to let the tears come now, he thought. Better to let the knot choke him here than in front of strangers elsewhere. Better to consider the unpayable debt that he owed Jonathan Carpenter among the chimney stacks where he was safe.

He waited.

The clot in his throat was there, the weight in his chest, but nothing else would come. Maybe he was just tougher than he thought. Or maybe Merry was right and he'd spent so long chaining his box of emotions closed, he'd lost all the keys. Checking the dials of his wristwatch, Alan took a deep breath. He had his bearings now. The house wasn't far away.

Back to the streets, he crossed Piccadilly at another klaxon call and made his way between the gentleman's clubs which lined James Street, taking a left and stopping dead.

There, in front of the old house, were Simon, Lottie, and their son, Jasper. Simon was fussing with the door, which had stuck in the jamb as long as he could remember. Lottie bent down to the boy, straightening his entire persona one item of clothing at a time. Simon joined them on the street. Linking his arm with Lottie's, he gave her a weak smile, his body heaved a breath, and they set off along the road, away from Alan. He didn't know he'd been tense until he relaxed. After waiting for them to turn the corner, Alan made his way to the old red door and, fumbling in his pocket, found the old key. He had no idea what he was doing or why he had the urge to see inside his old home. What confused him further was why he had waited for Simon to leave.

Ruminating on how he always seemed to be the last to know his own thoughts, Alan actively missed Merry for the first time. He had thought about her very little, with his head being full of old London ghosts and new layers of guilt and regret to add to his existing collection. But as the key clunked and refused to turn in the new lock, Alan would have gone right back to Yorkshire and stolen his friend away if he could.

"She'd know what to do," he grumbled, and turned to follow his brother only to find a familiar policeman smiling up at him from the foot of the steps. In full dress uniform, Sergeant Jennings looked strapping. He'd aged, although he'd done it well, retaining the fitness of his youth and gaining a few wrinkles of wisdom around the eyes.

"I hope you're not breaking and entering, Mister Shaw."

"Don't worry, Jennings, I have a key. At least I used to." Alan made his way down to the street and clasped his old friend's hand firmly. "It's good to see you."

Jennings clasped his shoulder and set him under a gaze which Alan had known since he was a boy. It was hard not to like Jennings' earnest, calm demeanour.

"I'm sorry about your father, Alan. I—"

"If that's going to be some foolish excuse for not being there, I'll slap you. No one can be everywhere, Jennings. And you know as well as I do that no one would have stopped Jonathan Carpenter from doing as he damn well pleased. Not even you."

Jennings' lips drew tight, but he nodded.

"Want some company?" he said, after swallowing the lump in his throat a few times.

"I think I probably need it," Alan replied.

AT THE OTHER end of the grave, the priest droned

platitudes to a dismal crowd of drab figures and the smattering of hunched ravens on the nearby mausoleums and gravestones of Highgate cemetery. Jennings' eulogy had been appropriate for a copper, full of praise and utterly droll. Alan could tell that the sergeant wanted to say more. He paused too long at the end of the speech, looking down at his notes as if the words weren't there at all. But his voice was breaking, and it wouldn't do for a copper to weep at the lectern, so Jennings had returned to the black-clad constables as they bowed their heads beside the grave into which they had just lowered Jonathan Carpenter's coffin, and tugged his helmet down a little over his eyes.

Simon stood with one arm around Lottie's shoulder, the other on the head of a small boy with rain-slicked spectacles. He didn't seem to hear a word anyone said. Lottie would remember it for him. Alan stood across from them. Standing by his brother, right now, this late, seemed wrong.

It was funny, but Alan could only think of his own, future death. Confining. To be in one place for all eternity. How small that coffin was. His father, it might suit. He was always the immovable man, the line not to be crossed. It would be just like him to be the last thing in this cemetery when the world ended and the earth fell apart. Alan saw himself more of a river, always passing through on his way elsewhere. Everywhere was a phase to him. Except this damn city, entirely without morals, using his brother's pain to tempt him back.

WITH THE SERVICE over, Simon, Lottie and Jasper were making their way toward Alan on their way out of the plot.

Simon's face was drawn in charcoal shades as he looked up at his brother.

Alan tried to smile but just stretched his face instead.

"Don't worry," he said. "You don't have to tell me not to run off again. I'm sticking around for a while."

Lottie gave him a half smile and a nod. Simon lunged. Alan was certain he was about to get a pasting, and lifted his chin to take the hit. But Simon grabbed the lapel of his coat, drawing himself in close as if he might need to be caught. Grief had turned to bloodshot fury and, when Simon raised those deep-set eyes to his brother, Alan wondered if he hadn't gone mad since he saw him last.

"No. You go. You go and catch this mad bastard and don't you dare bring him to justice. You end him, Protector of London. End him. I know you can."

"Simon, I—"

His brother's face might as well have been aflame for all the heat he gave off. Lottie slid her hand under his arm and drew him away. "Enough, my love. Alan will do what he can. Won't you, Alan?"

He could only nod and his eyes came to rest on the young boy at Lottie's side who stared right back as if petrified of him. What had he done to deserve that? Maybe Jasper could see the colour of his uncle's soul. The boy looked back as his family trudged away, but Alan couldn't bring himself to wave or smile. Better the boy not grow accustomed to him, perhaps. Once this thing was done, Alan couldn't see himself fitting in or sticking around, no matter what he'd said.

Jennings drifted by, giving Alan's shoulder a squeeze,

but saying nothing.

Out of the crowd came a familiar face. She was running toward him, not caring for the spectres she jostled, blonde curls floating behind her, unrestrained. And she was wearing a pale blue dress. Alan couldn't help but smile. Not a damn thing could dampen Helen Harrigan's force of spirit. She slammed into him, throwing her arms around him without a care for the stares of those around her. The same summer-fresh scent wafted, unchanged in all the years he'd known her. At age eleven he'd fallen in fiery, boyish love with a girl called Helen Normen, a love which had grown into a fiendish friendship between a young lady and a bad influence of a boy who she clearly adored. But Alan had kept a promise to himself and left the city as soon as he was able, and had returned to find he'd lost his chance.

The man that had changed her name strode up behind her, a rakish Naval Captain with a mean little moustache.

Alan nodded to him. "Percy."

"Shaw," the Captain spat.

But Helen had taken his face in her hands and he couldn't look away from those eyes, no matter who was watching. The tears were there, but they were for him, Alan knew. Helen always knew what he was feeling. She would have loved to meet Merry. The two of them would skip away, because Helen had skipped or ran everywhere she went ever since childhood, and Merry would never deny anyone their fun. And then they'd talk about him, and come back with some conspiracy to marry him off to one of Helen's friends, he was sure. On reflection, thank God that Merry hadn't come.

"My poor, dear Alan. You can't know how happy I am to see you. I was lost when I heard about India."

Alan pulled away from her.

"Heard what?" he snapped.

Seeing her face fade into concern, he realised what he'd done. She hadn't meant *that*.

"That you were lost to us. I thought you were gone."

Everything relaxed. A deep sigh escaped him.

He smiled at her, and she took the bait. "You should know I'm harder to get rid of than that."

From behind, Percy snorted.

"Come for lunch. Please. Not today, of course. But come."

He agreed, shooting a look at Percy over her shoulder as she hugged him again. Hungry tigers snarled less than that man. As he passed, Percy made sure to brush shoulders with Alan.

"I'm watching you, Shaw."

"And here I thought you didn't like me."

"One mistake. Just make one mistake and I'll—"

"Have a nice day, Percival."

The Captain swivelled away and stalked after his wife.

The gravediggers stood sharing a wrinkled, yellow cigarette. Alan gave them a nod as he drifted away from his father's resting place, back through the promenades of ivy and cherub faces, until he reached the road and turned toward the city centre and the hospital where his friend was currently a guest.

ALAN HAD BEEN to St George's hospital before, many years

ago. He'd been on the hunt then, too. This time he only needed to find Ernest. A gruff nurse, stiff as her starched pinafore, showed him the way to a long room, which looked identical to any other hospital he'd ever seen. Two rows of cold steel frames with thin mattresses, separated by wheeled screens. A well-suited doctor chuffed on his pipe as he visited each bed, a fetching young nurse wheeling a tall contraption behind him, clacking at the keys of the recording machine's cylinder with insane speed.

The stiff nurse gestured to a screen and left Alan to his own devices.

Simon had only hinted at what had happened to Ernest, and his father. When pressed, before the funeral, he was clearly not in the right frame of mind for an interrogation. I would be up to Ernest to fill him in on the circumstances of his father's death. It wasn't until he pulled the screen aside that he realised that that, too, was going to be difficult. Alan looked over his shoulder at the disappearing nurse. There had to be some kind of mistake. In the bed was a mass of ragged bandages held together by a pair of crisp pinstripe pyjamas. Alan could see splotches of purple under the bindings, nothing like the colour of human flesh. As he watched, one of the purple areas creaked open to reveal a shimmering eye and other bandages beneath shifted into some semblance of a smile. A hand, swollen beyond belief, came out from beneath the covers and extended toward him.

"Alan," the creature rasped, but could manage no more.

Alan took it all in as his brain screamed for him to run from this thing. This thing that wasn't his friend. It couldn't be. Instead of recoiling, he stepped forward, taking the hand as lightly as he could, and sat on the edge of bed.

"You know, I've seen real undead mummies that look better than you, Ernie."

Ernie chuckled, and regretted it when his body shook with pain.

"Can I get you anything?" Alan had never felt pity so deeply. "Some pain killers? Maybe that young nurse I just saw in here?"

Ernest chuckled again and the pain came stronger than before. Alan hung on to his friend's hand.

"Sorry. Sorry. I can't help it, you know. What do you need?"

Sliding his thick purple hand from Alan's, Ernest gestured to the table beside his bed where a well-worn folder waited patiently for attention. Alan cracked it open.

Ernest tried to lean forward, to speak, but Alan put a gentle hand on his chest.

"Rest while I read. I'll still be here when you wake up."

Ernest laid back with a pained grunt, but his one good eye refused to close.

"Alright, you stubborn sod. But don't go talking too much."

The folder was ordered chronologically starting on January seventh. Grainy photographs of an alleyway in Whitechapel, the lower part of a pale leg protruding from the shadows. Closer photographs of the neat pile of body parts which had once been a middle-aged seamstress by the name of Grace Jones.

"Jesus," Alan muttered. "What is this, Ernie?"

Ernest tapped the folder. *Keep reading.*

Twentieth of January. The disappearance of a young heiress to the Rowton estate; a sixteen-year-old girl by the name of Hannah. Last seen outside Fenchurch Street station on her way to meet her father at his workhouse in Whitechapel. She disappeared while under the supervision of her matron, Eliza North.

Second of February. Another photograph. A neat pile of body parts, carefully washed, almost no blood present. Found on the doorstep of the Rowton workhouse at midday. Later discovered to be the remains of young Hannah Rowton.

"And absolutely no witnesses. This is starting to give me the willies, Ernie."

"February- twenty—"

"—fifth. I know. Be quiet," Alan chastised. As he read on, the young nurse came with a steel tray filled with small paper pots and helped Ernest to take his medication. Alan couldn't help noticing that not all of them could have been for pain of the physical kind. Within minutes, Ernest was noticeably less responsive. At least he could rest. Despite Alan's attempt to angle the folder away, the nurse saw the contents. Her face flushed violently.

"A nasty business," she offered, pronouncing it 'naarsty' as Alan himself would. "Are you a policeman, sir?"

"Something like that," he replied, not looking up.

"Poor Mister Sledge has seen some things. Terrible things. I hope you catch the bastard, if you don't mind my language."

Alan finally looked up into the pale, freckled face of the nurse. She was pretty, and would have been prettier if she wasn't so trapped by starch and cotton. A single curl of vibrant orange hair fell from her cap, which she tucked back when his eyes fell on her.

"He's already dead," Alan said. He looked down at his friend, and conjured the image of his father at the same time. "He's been dead since the day he did this. You don't send a policeman to look for a monster like this. You send me."

Startled into silence, the young nurse scuttled away, casting a fearful glance behind her.

Good. Best people be afraid, Alan thought. *Best that the word gets out that I'm back. Let there be rumours and hearsay. Let this monster know my intentions. And just let him try to hide.*

Without thinking, he took a spare piece of paper from the back of the folder and began to write. The letter was short and when he read it back, the hairs on his own neck stood on end. Was that what he sounded like when he was angry? He almost felt bad. Despite his constant protests to the contrary, his schooling had obviously paid off.

Back to the folder. The letter could be delivered later.

Twenty-fifth of February. The matron, Eliza North, was found on the pavement of Fieldgate Street after leaping from the roof of her former employer's workhouse. A note pinned to her dress spoke of her guilt at having lost her young charge. Upon later inspection at the morgue, her body had also been dismembered where it had previously been whole. Violent questioning of the mortuary staff brought nothing to light. The villain had crept in past them to finish his work. Alan knew the signature on all of the interrogation reports. His father had done it personally. Having been interrogated many times by the same man when he was a boy, Alan had complete confidence in the reports. The mortuary staff would have no clues for him. But, in Alan's mind, this villain became even more insane and cunning.

First of March, a young market stallholder found drained of blood and left in pieces.

Good Friday, another male, slightly older, found in a pile. This time the heart was missing.

Twenty-first of April, another female disappearance and the finding of her dissected corpse nine days later.

Then nothing. Until the twenty-first of June when a pair of constables attended an abandoned house in Whitechapel after reports of screams. Nothing unusual for Whitechapel, so the constables were in no rush to attend. The house was once again abandoned, but someone had certainly been there. Every internal wall not necessary for holding the house aloft had been knocked down to create one large area where a wooden dais had been built and was piled high with more body parts, a mix of male and female, and some animal. Great swathes of black cloth adorned the walls, every floor covered with congealed blood decorated with uncountable naked footprints later determined to be made by dancing.

Despite his usual strong constitution, Alan started to feel ill. He found himself giving only cursory glances to the photographs, and only half-reading words such as 'dismembered' and 'naked' and 'blood'. No wonder London had been in such a state of abject terror. Even with Ernie keeping the finer details out of the papers, this case was still soul-wrenchingly disturbing.

Finally, he could take no more and he skipped to the last report. Twentieth of July. Two constables were witness to the abduction of a young woman after following the sound of her screams into Goodman's Fields. Ten constables were eventually involved in the chase, and a runner was sent to bring Superintendent Carpenter. By the time Advisor Ernest Sledge of the Illustrated Times arrived with Police, the hunt was over. The culprit escaped. A night-long search of the area turned up nothing of lasting use. Everything seemed to have gone quiet until Superintendent Carpenter and Mister Sledge were making one last sweep of St Mary's cemetery, where they were set upon. Reportedly, five assailants were involved, and one more figure who simply watched. In the attack, Superintendent Carpenter was killed outright—

And the rest Alan could see laid next to him.

Setting the file down by his feet, Alan settled into the cheap wooden back of the hospital chair sat by the bed as Ernest's breathing took on the heaviness of sleep. Normally he would have shot out of the chair as a greyhound from a trap, but there was too much in his head, too many images and feelings weighing him to the spot. Pinching the bridge of his nose, he felt weariness take him. His head dipped for a moment and snapped back up. His watch told him that it was officially thirty-six hours since he'd slept. He should try, at least. But where could he go? Not Simon's house. Just imagining his brother's bloodshot orbs turning on him was too much, never mind being in their actual presence. Plus, descending on their home, being fed by Lottie, watching the nephew he didn't know playing by the fire; that brought a mix of odd emotions which he wasn't sure he could handle right now. Guilt, perhaps? Certainly some kind of discomfort. God, was his emotional range really so stunted?

These thoughts lulled him into an uneasy sleep in the hospital chair, his legs stretched out in front and boots crossed at the ankles.

His dreams arrived in bloody, whirling storms.

3

THE CHAIR SCRAPED on the hospital tiles, snapping Alan into consciousness with a rude jerk. His body shot out in all directions to catch himself, making him into an odd starfish when he didn't fall from his chair at all. The stiff nurse stared down at him with a look of utter disdain.

"Once. Just once, I'd like to wake up to birdsong and a beautiful young woman." The nurse's face didn't move an inch. "Used to happen all the time."

"Things change," the nurse snapped. "You can't sleep here. Stay awake or get sick."

"Charming."

Snatching the file from the floor, he dragged himself up. His watch showed he'd been asleep for a solid half an hour. With one last look at Ernest he squeezed past the nurse, who simply spun on the spot to keep her eye on him, and strode out of the hospital rubbing the ache from his neck.

Alan climbed the steel steps to the Hyde Park Corner monorail station outside the hospital, and waited only a few minutes for the whistling tube of brass and glass to arrive. He cranked the lever to slide back the doors and stepped aboard before scrutinising the faded monorail map above the door.

Now, where to? Whitechapel, he supposed. Change at the Regent Square terminal and head there right away. But why? What could he see there that hadn't already been seen? There seemed no point to him in going where the police had already scuffed the tracks. The Whitechapel trail was too cold. No, he had to think like himself, like a child of London's darker corners. Like a criminal. A nagging curiosity told him to take the pylon engineer's advice. He'd get off at Regent instead, and walk into Covent Garden. There would be no sleep for him, maybe until this thing was done, so food was probably the next best thing. And nowhere sold street-nosh like Covent Garden.

Walking into his old stomping ground was a trip into his childhood. Whereas a lot of London seemed to have been changed for the sake of progress, to allow for new pipes, new wires, new rails and new roads, the area around Covent Garden didn't seem to have changed at all. His relief was palpable. He took a slightly longer route to pass the Alhambra, currently buried in scaffolding, and then by St Martin's Workhouse, which had entirely vanished. What had once been the working prison of hundreds of London's lost and poorest, and then Professor Normen's laboratory, had outlived its usefulness and now there stood only a single spike of glistening steel with three rotating tiers climbing its length, all the way up to the sky. The rear of the Royal Academy looked like it might have been the power generator for half of London all on its own. Either that, or it was very pretty for the sake of the tourists, and did very little. *That would be just like London.*

Still, the pangs of old fear he'd been expecting at the workhouse were banished by the construct. The night that changed his life when he took to his heels with a small group of lads, the greatest decision he'd ever made, had been dismantled and taken away. The old workhouse bricks might be someone's home now, or a school. For all he knew, they were used to build toilet blocks for tramps. Still, Alan let the feeling sink in that even a little of London's, and his own, dark past had been wiped from the earth. If only the whole city would be levelled, maybe he could rest easy.

Onward into the market itself, Alan overpaid a portly Scottish woman for a sausage wrapped in newspaper and savoured the mix of grease and ink that coated his tongue. There might be all manner of blood and danger on the horizon but, right at that moment, he allowed himself to feel a little joy at being home again. Weaving through the throngs of the market, Alan noticed how easy it was as an adult. He'd once been a boy of below-average stature, battered by the legs of the Garden's patrons. Now, they flowed around him. The sounds and smells were just the same. The faces were different. He saw no-one he'd once known behind those stalls. But the overall feel of the place hadn't changed a jot. It wasn't until he turned the corner, heading toward the floral arcade, that he spotted it: standing head and shoulders above the crowd, a form cast in bronze.

Alan approached, letting the remainder of his meal fall to the ground. He didn't even finish chewing, but stood there, aghast, with a half-chewed mass in his mouth.

The statue was of a boy, stood in front of a man. Both

likenesses were incredible. Him. As a boy and as a young man. The plaque read:

In memoriam of Alan Shaw
Protector of London

"a tenebris ad magnum"

Commissioned on the suggestion
of Scotland Yard
for his services to the city.

His legs abandoned him. Pigeons scattered as Alan fell to his knees at the foot of his own memorial, dark blots spreading on the stone steps at its base as his tears finally came.

His father had done this, he knew. Jonathan Carpenter had lost a son, or so he'd thought. And his first consideration had been to make sure that not a single person in the capital forgot his face. And even though Alan was very much alive, that statue remained. A reminder, perhaps, that even the lowest of London's children could rise to do great things.

Alan could have let the tears come until they wore a hole through stone and earth. Now he'd started he could see no end to it. No one interrupted. In fact, as he slumped on the statue's steps, the space around him grew wider and wider as people avoided him. His hands were slick with tears as he tried desperately to cover his face. But it made no difference. They saw him. And for what it was worth, no one seemed to care.

A small hand tugged at the cuff of his coat.

Alan lowered his hands to reveal a streaked face.

A small boy stood before him, ragged and dirty, with a concerned expression. "You alright, Mister?"

"No," Alan managed. "Not at all."

"Well, cheer up, eh?" the boy offered.

Alan couldn't help but smile through his pain. "Do you know where to find the Illustrated Times?"

The boy nodded.

"Good. Here's a pound, and a letter. The first you can keep if the second makes it to the newspapers in the next hour."

Alan stood, wiping his face as the boy shot off across the cobbles, holding his cap on with one hand. He took another look at the statue, and heaved a deep breath to stop the clot in his throat tightening again.

"That's it," he said. "No more of that. I'm back and some bastard has got a dose of me coming to them."

4

IN A MOMENT of clarity, Alan had realised that he'd have to find somewhere to stay if he was going to be in London for any length of time. A swift visit to The Telegraph Bank on Fleet Street and Alan's Privateer funds were transferred from his last account access in Marrakesh. He had never felt the urge to check exactly how much was in there, but always had his payments into the same account and only withdrew what he needed to stay clothed, fed and comfortable. At some point, he presumed, it would run out. But it had never happened. Now, back home and in need of somewhere to stay, Alan felt the need to know what he had to spend. Apparently his Privateering adventures were more lucrative than he thought. There were several zeroes to the balance of his account, and that was several more than he'd expected. Had he ever asked exactly what the pay was for one single job?

"Bloody hell, Alan, you slack sod."

His head spinning with financial jargon he'd all-but ignored, he left the bank. His feet took him back toward the Strand, on a tour of his old haunts, up through Covent

Garden and out the other side, almost heading back to his adoptive family's home. He stopped dead where Broad met Berwick Street. The clatter of the rail station was just over the rooftops, and a monorail shuttle hummed its way out of the Piccadilly station in the other direction. A good amount of traffic honked and whizzed along the road and the smell from a bakery on the corner sent stomach-flipping scents floating toward him. It was there on the corner that he saw a vacancy sign in the bay window of a narrow brick five-storey house. Without much more thought than the few things his hind-brain had noticed, he stepped up to the door and knocked. A tall, older gentleman, well-dressed and turned out, answered the door.

"You have a room for rent?" Alan knew he was being terse, but his toils and travels, both physical and emotional, had exhausted him free of his manners.

"I do," the gentleman said, apparently unperturbed by Alan's demeanour. He took in Alan's sagging shoulders, his coat and scarf, and the duffle bag which Alan himself had almost forgot he'd been carrying. The gentleman seemed to sum all of these things carefully with a twitch of a thin grey moustache.

"I'd like to rent it," Alan said.

The gentleman's eyebrow raised. "Just like that?"

"Just like that."

"You should come in, then."

Alan stepped into a narrow hallway, papered with green and black flock. A mahogany sideboard held a stack of crumpled fliers that had been rammed through the letterbox. Several doors led away down the corridor and a carpeted staircase rose before him. Cheap little portrait paintings lined the walls, turning to photographs at the distant end. In those pictures, a young man gained a copper's uniform, and then a suit and a wife. He grew old, children turned to adults, the wife stopped appearing. In the last photograph, the man shook hands with a younger one, a certificate was exchanged, and Alan could see that that man had become the one stood before him.

"You're a copper," Alan offered.

As he set his foot on the staircase, the gentleman looked back at the young Privateer.

"Bother you somehow?"

Alan leaked a smile. "My father was a copper."

The gentleman led him upstairs. "I might know him."

"You might."

Neither man pursued further.

They passed the first two floors, which evidently belonged to the landlord. The fourth floor's single door led to a series of inner rooms and one bathroom.

Barren of furnishings, with dust in the corners and between the floorboards, it seemed nothing special. Alan reached into his pocket.

"Who lives above?" Alan asked, jabbing a thumb upward.

"No one. It's storage. There's some space if you need it."

"Cleaning?"

"Done by a young lass, she's regular and trustworthy."

"Food?"

"The kitchen is downstairs, you'll have a shelf in the larder."

"I'll take it." Alan scribbled on a book of slips the bank had given him and scrawled his name.

The gentleman took the note as he asked: "How long for—" stopping dead when he saw the cheque he'd be handed. "This is too much. You could buy the place for this."

"I snore," Alan said, as his duffle bag hit the ground.

For the first time, the gentleman seemed flustered.

"A- at least I won't have to chase you for rent. I'll start on the ownership paperwork straight away. When would you like to bring your things?"

"I just did," Alan said. "Now, if there's nothing else you need to know, Mister—"

"Forsythe."

"—Mister Forsythe. I'm desperate for sleep."

Forsythe stepped out of the room, his mouth making motions with no sound as he stared, confused, at the paper in his hand.

If Alan had fallen asleep any faster, he'd have injured himself. Laid on top of crumpled clothes from his duffle with the bag itself tucked under his head, he slept through the night, his mind too tired to react to any nightmares that might have visited.

He woke to the sound of the newspaper landing outside his door.

In the same clothes and bare feet, with the newspaper tucked under his arm, Alan entered Forsythe's kitchen for the first time. The door swung open to the smell of bacon. Forsythe stood at the range oven, sleeves rolled, apron strings tied behind him. From his movements, he was frying the bacon. Alan pulled out a seat, the older gentleman not even flinching at the sound, and sat down to read. The front cover was a photograph of his own letter. Apparently printing the words just wasn't good enough in the modern age:

To my Prey.

This letter addresses the murderer of Grace Jones, Hannah Rowton, Jonathan Carpenter and the other innocents of London. The Madman who haunts London's streets.

I am the protector of this city. Every cobble and slate. And you are not welcome here. I have been away for a long time, but I'm back, even from death, for you. I will find you. And there is a hellish price to pay for your crimes. Do not take this letter lightly. This is no idle threat. This is a promise that I weigh against my soul. I am neither a policeman nor a good man. When I find you, Mercy will not be arriving with me.

Yours sincerely,
Alan Shaw

In time, Forsythe sat across from him with a plate of eggs and bacon, a single slice of bread and steaming tea. Alan nodded to him over the top of his newspaper.

"There are two rashers in the pan and the tea's hot," the older man said.

Alan had to swallow before he spoke, his mouth watering at the smell alone. "Much appreciated." He retrieved the offerings, ignoring a plate in favour of eating the bacon with his fingers, and gulped the first cup of tea before taking a second.

"You've made quite the stir since you got home, Mister Shaw. That letter is on the cover of every news sheet and penny paper in the city. I figured you'd want a copy." Forsythe gestured to the newspaper's cover with a piece of eggy bread. When Alan looked a little surprised, the gentleman smiled. "You signed your cheque. A little digging in the old files—" he tapped his head "—and a little asking around, I remembered you alright."

"You were a copper," Alan nodded.

"For many years." There was a moment's silence as both men eyed each other in the politest way possible. "Your Father was a good man. Damn shame. You out to get the one who did it?"

Alan nodded.

"You planning on behaving while doing so?"

Alan shook his head.

"And no one knows where you're staying?"

"I didn't know myself until I knocked on your door last night."

"Till this thing's done, I'd appreciate if it stayed that way." Forsythe said, his tone heavily suggesting there would be no negotiation.

"You have my word," Alan said. "And if you want me out before then—"

"Don't worry. You'll know."

Both men turned back to their breakfasts. When Alan was done reading the conjecture about himself, most of which was fairly accurate, he slid the folded newspaper across the table to his new landlord and made to leave.

"Water's hot in the tap, your key is on the table by the door."

Alan nodded.

Back in his barren rooms, Alan stripped to his underwear as he wondered how he'd go about bringing his things out of storage. Over the last seven years he hadn't had something as fancy as a room to put anything in, but he had accrued some odds and ends, mostly mementoes and souvenirs of his adventures, things given to him or things he'd found. It had been his way of scrapbooking, he supposed. And those trinkets were scattered across a few places across the globe in storage units he paid a little to maintain each month. That seemed useless now, since he'd bought himself a place outright. When this thing was done, he'd have it all shipped, he supposed. And buy furniture. One comfy chair and an even comfier bed. That actually appealed to him. To have those things waiting, even if he didn't visit so often.

The water was, indeed, hot. In the fog of his bathroom, Alan cursed as the skin almost peeled from his hands on dipping them into the sink. Once he was used to it, though, the feeling was exquisite. He washed himself slowly, enjoying the heat on his sore muscles, and took a long look at himself. He needed a shave. 'Stache or beard never really suited him. His hair was a week or so too long and had started to whip up in places, making him look overgrown. Now he had a decision to make. He had a tin of 'Browning', a cheap boot polish which, when watered down, could be applied to make him look like a soiled beggar or sailor or some such. They were his default disguises. But, popping the lid, he paused and looked at himself again. Was that the way to go? Disguise had worked for him before. But this was different. The letter to the newspaper had changed the game. When did the predator hide from the prey? People needed to see him around town to perpetuate the rumours, to let the villain know he was unafraid and hot in pursuit. The lid went back on the Browning and he went to find the least-crumpled clothing he could. It didn't matter too much; his armoured waistcoat covered the shirt anyway. Even an English summer was too warm for his scarf and coat, and so he left them behind, but strapped his old revolver holster around his shoulders. A clock somewhere down the street chimed the hour and he checked the dials of his watch before sliding on his comfortable old boots, and stepping out into the city once more.

Something was different.

London didn't seem so blatant today. Perhaps he was acclimatizing, or focussing on the things that had survived the years, rather than those that had changed. The noise, the smell (which actually seemed to have worsened), the ignorance of everyone he rubbed his elbows with. He found himself almost smiling as a rotund gentleman banged into him and rumbled away without a word. He was definitely home. This was his territory. He had reclaimed it. And he had a job to do. Without stopping, he swerved a course toward Alsatia, where even the police feared to tread.

Or they had. Alsatia was no more. One of the darkest corners of London's north bank was utterly gone. Alan stood by the road, staring at the spot where there had once been densely knotted streets filled with all manner of little deaths for you to come across. Now there stood a white marble façade, even larger than the British Institute of Trafalgar Square. Its pillars and domed roof dwarfed every other building it neighboured. A large marble slab read: The Ministry of Analytic Engineering. Alan vaguely remembered Merry mentioning such a thing, but he'd assumed she was exaggerating.

He stared at the building quite some time, pondering his next move. The Gentleman's Consortium had always run out of Alsatia, and now it was gone. But that didn't mean *they* would be gone, too. The largest syndicate of cutthroats, burglars, muggers and worse wouldn't have just laid down and died. He had to find the next best place they might be hiding. So he rode the monorail to Whitechapel.

WHITECHAPEL HADN'T CHANGED a bit. The buildings had always been close, every wall plastered with mouldering playbills, wet newspapers and other rubbish clogging the gutters, redirecting rivulets of green sludge across the dark cobbles. The smell of rotten vegetables was rife. Feral animals and the odd child scuttled between the too-deep shadows. Lost souls in ragged shawls and frayed hats dragged themselves along the streets. Every now and then Alan found a cluster of market stalls as he wandered through the rookeries, brothels and chop shops, watched by the hollow-eyed denizens who never raised their voices above a whisper. There was a low murmuring about the place, a white noise which he barely noticed at first. Nothing like the calls and buzz of Covent Garden. Alan felt he might be swimming in some murky pond rather than walking. It seemed simply wrong that this was the last place his father had seen. He should have been an old man, falling asleep by the fire, passing quietly surrounded by his family. Not this place. Not these people. Not this stench in his lungs as he breathed his last.

A shudder shook Alan as he watched the gloomy shapes in the alleyways and alcoves. He needed criminals right now, and this was the place to find some. The tap of his revolver on his ribs was reassuring, at least. Holding his breath, as if it would help the smell, he took the most deserted side road he could find. A familiar sensation scratched at the hairs on his neck, knowing he was alone and yet knowing he wasn't. It was a feeling he had in the dark as a boy, a feeling he had in the jungle when night fell. Glancing over his shoulder, he swore he caught the flash of a familiar face behind him. Blonde hair, thin moustache. But he was gone in an instant. And why would Percy be in a place like Whitechapel?

Turning into Dorset Street off the main road, he spotted a pub bearing a sign with a boy in long blue coat. The bleak frontage was coal black, every window blanked from the inside. If he hadn't seen people coming and going, Alan would have been sure the place was burnt out. He had to move a small board leaning against the door, hand painted with "Rooms for rent", so he could duck inside. He took one more look at the street, but saw no-one he recognised.

It threw him back to his days at Harker's Tavern. The floor was strewn with straw, congealed in places with all manner of dark substances. Grizzled men huddled over their pint pots. No one looked each other in the eye. The sound of half-heard whispers rolled like dark water. He strode toward the bar and slapped down some change. Without a word, the barman slid a rough ceramic jar across the bar. It tasted like acid, but Alan drank it anyway. No wonder everyone looked so miserable.

"I'm looking for a man by the name of Dick Whitsun."

The barman froze in the middle of wiping the bar.

"My name's Ala—"

"Don't much care, Gov. Be on your way," the barman grumbled.

"I'm not leaving until I get what I need."

He became aware of movement behind him. Pint pots were set on tables, and a few chairs scraped on the floor.

"I think you might be wrong about that, Gov," the barman replied.

After years of these kind of interactions, Alan had developed an odd sixth sense, a tingle he felt when he was about to be knocked unconscious.

It tingled now.

He spun, catching the first cudgel on his shoulder as he threw up an arm to protect his head. The assailant lost his balance, and Alan's right hook slammed his head down toward the bar with a crack. A leather cosh whooshed down between his shoulders. Fists up by his temples, Alan pivoted, darting into the man rather than away, surprising him with a flurry of blows that sent the ragged mugger stumbling into a table behind him. The table's inhabitants scattered, jeering, but weren't put out enough to get involved. The third mugger lunged with small knife, the blade still wet with the juices of the apple he held in the other hand. Alan knocked the clumsy strike aside, scooped his pint pot from the bar and slammed it into the back of the mugger's head. Like all good tavern crockery, the pot broke second.

Alan made a show of dusting off his shirtsleeves as he addressed the bartender.

"Sorry, you were saying?"

"Wait here," the barman grumbled.

5

THE BARTENDER LED Alan up the back stairs into a squalid hole he called accommodation. There were rooms for rent, certainly, but there had to be twenty or more people to each. Slumbering bodies littered the floors, the bunks, a few hammocks, and spilled out into the corridors. Laudanum bottles littered the bare floorboards where they'd slipped from slumbering fingers. There were even a few well-dressed gentlemen among the bodies, the bright colours of their coats like emeralds in the dirt. Taking a casual glance over his shoulder, Alan noted a gruff individual trailing them. The thug was only a shade taller than Alan, older by a decade at least, and his long fur-collared coat bulged over all manner of unpleasant weapons. At least he was keeping his distance for now.

Through another door, a few small windows showed that the next corridor was actually a bridge connecting the pub to an old warehouse.

Pausing at the next door, Alan peered into what should have been a smelly, rat infested old warehouse heaped with disease. Instead there was a long, low room with floorboards scrubbed clean and laid even, and walls plastered and painted—albeit in a lifeless grey-brown. Actual electric lights fizzed in their cages above.

A large hand shoved him forward. Alan shot a grim look at the grizzled thug who had drawn up behind him. His revolver itched by his side, but he left it where it was. He was deep in the den now, and there were more criminals than he had bullets. So he used his other weapon:

"Ugly bastard, aintcha."

The man shot him a grin of brown stumps.

"You'll hurt his feelings." A familiar voice, although distant.

Alan drifted forward warily, his boots like doom-laden drum beats on the wooden floor. In an old leather armchair at the end of the room sat a man with slick dark hair, and scars along his cheek and bare forearms. Buried somewhere under all that was a boy Alan had once known. He recognised his old friend immediately.

"Dick. You've done well for yourself."

"Could say the same about you. Not being dead suits you." His accent was thicker than Alan's, deeper and more dangerous. He didn't rise from his chair but motioned to another across from him and, with the weight of a mortician, said, "Welcome to the Gentleman's Consortium, old mate."

"Still hanging around with this lot then?" Alan crossed his legs as if he were sitting in a cosy living room rather than a criminal's hideout.

"I don't hang nothing, I run it," Dick answered.

"I figured," Alan said.

Reaching to the table beside him, Dick filled his own glass and another. "And it still beats the workhouse."

"Everything beats the bloody workhouse. I see they knocked it down."

"I might have had a hand in that."

Alan took the offered glass and clinked it with Dick's.

"To good riddance."

They both took a sip, eyes trained on each other. After a moment, they even swallowed.

"That enough chat?" Dick said. "It's good to see you, Al. I'm glad you're not toast. But I'm busy. And, to be frank, I don't have what you want."

"And what would that be?" Alan asked. Dick shot Alan a withering look. He chuckled. "Alright, alright. I guess you read the papers. Or have them read to you, at any rate. I'll take anything you've got. This nutter can't be one of yours. You want him gone, and now so do I. So let's have him gone."

Dick shook his head. "My people are calling him Mister Slay. Thieves like names. And they haven't seen a damn thing."

Alan eyed his old friend. "Not a thing?"

"Nothing that makes any sense."

"Well that's a different thing entirely."

Dick sighed, leaning forward until his elbows were on his knees. As he looked up through his eyebrows, Alan could see fear there. "They say this Slay character isn't like normal men. Anyone who's seen him don't see him for long. They say he disappears. They say he walks through shadows and can appear anywhere he wants. They say they've seen him in our tunnels more than once, and not one of the worst bastards in London dares approach him. I know men who would flay you if they forgot their coat that morning, Al. People who would slap the Queen—"

Dick took a drink.

"—He's the devil, is Mister Slay. There's no other way about it. We've looked into the folks he killed. They were nobodies. He's a particular kind of man that just likes what he does. And you can't catch him. Even your dad, Al, god rest him and I'm sorry for that, but not even your dad could catch him and he's put more of my Consortium boys away than any other. Mister Slay is a damned shadow. You shouldn't be hunting him down, you should be praying that nothing brings him your way."

"I hear what you're saying, Dick. You know I'm not going to let this go, though."

"I know. But when you're buried at least I can say I tried." Dick sat back.

"Are you going to let me see the tunnels he's been in?"

Dick sucked his gums for a second and beckoned to Browntooth in the doorway.

"Show him," he said.

Browntooth's face fell. He looked from his master to Alan, a bead of sweat appearing at his temple. Dick caught sight of it, just as Alan did. "You show him, Jack. And you come right back. My friend here will do what he likes. He's mad that way, and probably destined for death. But I know him like I know myself and, if anyone is going to end Mister Slay, it's him."

"That was bloody heart-warming," Alan said as he got to

his feet.

Dick couldn't help but smile. "Don't push your luck, Al. You'll need all you can get.

Descending through the warehouse, Browntooth Jack led Alan past more rooms. Some were filled with clerks on clacking machines, others with gruff men eating at long banquet tables. The surprise came at the lower floors, where he found a single open space. Browntooth Jack led the way past small groups of children, all learning the craft of the criminal from an older expert. Alan paused to watch a cutthroat lead a team of young boys through the strokes of a knife fight, another demonstrated the finer art of pickpocketing. And be damned if there wasn't a mock-up of a London street right there, with criminals simulating the crowd as the children practiced their new skills. Alan looked to Browntooth Jack who was waiting patiently.

"I'll be damned!" he muttered to himself, and managed to tear his eyes away only as they took more stairs downward.

Alan had always suspected the Gentleman's Consortium had some way around the city, but he'd never had it confirmed. The tunnels beneath London must have gone on for miles. Every few feet, it seemed, there was another offshoot leading Lord-knew-where. But Browntooth Jack knew his way around, making a succession of turns too quick for Alan to keep track of, walking with a lolloping gait which belied his actual speed.

"Have you seen him, Jack?"

As Alan spoke, the man stopped short with a half turn. He actually looked up to the curved brick ceiling as he said:

"Thanks be to God, I have not."

"How far to where he was seen?"

"Not far." And with that he headed on.

He was right. When Browntooth Jack drew to a stop Alan's watch showed only fifteen minutes or so had passed, although the darkness and silence would have made him think it was longer. They stood at a junction of three tunnels, including the one they'd come along. A slimy ladder reached down to shin-level.

"So what's up there?"

"Churchyard."

Alan looked up. "That makes sense. I'm going for a look. What are the chances you'll be waiting for me when I get back?"

"Mister Whitsun says I show you around, I show you around."

Alan set his foot on the ladder. "Fair enough. Back in a jiffy."

The thug leaned back on the tunnel wall and crossed his arms to wait.

The sewer cover slammed back on its hinges as Alan shouldered it open and climbed out. The back of St Mary's church faced him on one side, its spire towering over the littering of trees around it. He could hear the chug of traffic on Whitechapel Road just beyond and, beyond the railings, he could see people milling around. When he'd pictured the place his father had been brutally beaten to death, Alan had imagined something quieter, something isolated. This smattering of sloping stone tablets was right by the damn road. But did it really surprise him? As he meandered through the gravestones he thought of every time he'd heard a scream or a curse, the begging voice of a woman beyond a wall or down an alley, every slap of wood on flesh as he'd grown up in this hellhole city.

"Apathy is perhaps London's greatest sin," Simon had once told him, and Alan had laughed. It was dog-eat-dog on London's streets; it always had been. Except a pack of them had taken someone close to Alan, and now he was the one wondering why no one had put a stop to it. From sadness to pride, Alan switched in a moment, shoving those feelings down to the compost heap, burying those that came before in the mouldering pile. He didn't need any help. No one was going to end Mister Slay but him.

HIS BOOTS CLANKED on the ladder as he took it back down to the tunnels. There had been nothing there to see, really, but the urge to look at the last place his father took a breath had been too strong to ignore. He met stone at the bottom and searched around for his brown-toothed guide. He was alone. His stomach lurched. At the edge of the light spilling from above, the bloody boot of Browncoat Jack stretched out of the darkness. Alan took a single step forward, reaching under his arm for his revolver. As his eyes adjusted to the darkness once more, he could see the mess of torn flesh which had once been Browntooth Jack's chest and neck. The thug hadn't even had time to draw one of his many weapons.

A sing-song voice cut through Alan like an icy wind.

"It only takes a jiffy. It only takes a tick. For Mister Slay to do his work, and make his hands all slick."

Alan spun, his revolver swooping from side to side as a diabolical cackle echoed out of the darkness.

"Balls. Bloody buggering bollocks," he spat.

Another cackle swam around him as he spun on the spot, staring down each dark tunnel in turn. There. It had to be that one. He rushed after the sound of fiendish laughter.

His footsteps on the stone floor were too loud; his pulse hammered in his ears. Every now and again Alan stopped dead, straining to hear any sound. *There.* Footsteps retreating, but he could have been chasing ten men for all the echoes that rattled around those stone walls. He took a right turn, not knowing where he was or how he would get out if he became lost, but his mind was trained with inhuman focus on his quarry. If there was ever a chance of catching Mister Slay it was here and now.

Sliding to a halt at the foot of another ladder, he stared upward as a sound caught his ear. The trailing of some dark cloth, the tails of a coat, perhaps, slid over the edge of the hole and was gone. This time there was no sunlight, only a lighter patch of darkness where there must have been a room beyond. As Alan looked up, the shape of a man's head and shoulders appeared, silhouetted only barely.

Alan unleashed a shot from his revolver, firing straight up. As his ears stopped ringing from the echoing retort, that sing-song voice came fluttering down.

"Hoo-*hoo*. You nearly got me, you nearly had me there. But Alan is a tortoise, and Mister Slay the hare."

Alan started up the ladder with a snarl, revolver still in hand, just in case.

The stone edge of the drain was slimy, but Alan hoisted

himself out, being neither careful nor caring who might be waiting. A cellar. Stone-walled, cold and utterly empty but for the shrouds of cobweb slung across high letter-box windows which let in only a sliver of light.

There was only one door. Pressing his shoulder to the frame, Alan peaked around. Nothing. Only those footsteps, always moving away. Alan maintained his pursuit, revolver leading the way, not bothering to check around corners as he barrelled on. Until he darted out into another damn cellar. This one was filled with barrels and crates, making perfect hiding places for fleeing lunatics. Alan stayed very still. His breaths steadied, his pulse recovered. Even in the gloom, he closed his eyes. A rat scuttled across his foot, but he ignored it.

There was movement somewhere close by, but he couldn't pin it down. The sound of soft-stepping shoes on the gritty floor. A click. Alan's head snapped to the right. Silence, and then the squeak of a hinge.

Alan's muscles bunched. The bastard was heading out of a door.

"Stop where you are, Shaw!"

Alan half-turned in his sprint to see Percy Harrigan stood behind him, revolver trained on his back. The Captain didn't give another warning before firing. Alan flung himself to the side. One bullet slammed into a crate, shattering whatever glassware was inside, the other found its mark. Alan felt it punch into his side, and a gout of hot blood slither down his body. Hitting the ground, Alan was already fumbling at his back in a panic.

T-tink-ink

The smoking bullet bounced along the ground. He stared at it, picked it up, and instantly regretted it as it was still damn hot. He dropped it into a pocket, feeling it grow warm there. Sucking his fingers, he laughed. He was alright. His armoured waistcoat had taken the brunt of the blow and there was only a little oozing indentation rather than a gaping hole in his right flank. Relief soon turned to anger.

"Percy, you idiot! Stop shooting at me!"

"This is a citizen's arrest, Shaw. Throw out your revolver and then yourself, hands on your head."

"You're bloody nuts. I'm not coming out so you can shoot me again. Holster it so I can get back to chasing Slay."

There was silence.

"Percy?"

Nothing.

Alan leaned carefully around the crate he was slumped against. Percy was gone. Alan darted to his feet. What if Slay had gotten to him like Browntooth Jack?

"You can't talk your way out of this one, Shaw."

Just for a second, as Percy stepped out from behind him, Alan wished the lunatic *had* stabbed his adversary. He raised his hands very slowly.

"I've followed you ever since the funeral. I know you visited Ernest Sledge, and then you came to Whitechapel. I lost you when you disappeared into that hellhole public house but I figured you'd go back to the graveyard at some point and so I waited there. Blow me if I wasn't right, and you popped right up. So I followed you. Found your latest victim. I suppose he caught you slinking around. Then you ran, and I followed you all the way here."

"Percy, you pillock, I'm turning around." He did so very, very slowly. "You're talking drivel as always. I didn't kill anyone. I was chasing Mister Slay, who killed the poor bugger you found. You shot me. Luckily you're rubbish. And now he's probably long gone."

Percy stepped forward into what passed for light in that dank cellar. Alan felt his throat tighten. Percy's perfect pencil moustache was stretched into a hideous shape by his sneer. His eyes were red hot and unblinking. Alan had seen madness before, and this looked pretty damn close.

"Why does everyone have to lose their mind when I'm around?" Alan muttered.

Percy paid no attention. The tip of his revolver shook as he began to recite:

"1857. Alan Shaw fakes his own death. His family and friends mourn a hero. A statue is raised in his honour. His adopted brother, loyal idiot that he is, attempts to retrieve his body only to find that there's no body at all. Alan Shaw is very much alive and taking mercenary contracts in a truly staggering criminal career that spans the globe. 1861. Simon Carpenter finally gets word from his brother who refuses to return home. In his communiques, Shaw admits to murder, and professes his guilt as being the reason he won't return home—"

"How did you know about that, you shifty—"

"The letters continue. The crimes continue. Shaw is linked to frequent acts of violence, destruction and lawlessness. 1864. Alan Shaw returns home. But not when everyone thinks he does. In an attempt to secure a hero's homecoming, Shaw murders several innocents in truly disturbing displays of lunacy in order to set the stage for his return. While doing so, he is captured by his adopted father, Jonathan Carpenter, and supposed friend, Ernest Sledge. In an attempt to save his hide, he murders the man who loved him as a son. But he makes the mistake of not quite killing off Mister Sledge."

Alan couldn't stop shaking his head. "You're certifiable, Percy, certifiable."

Percy thumbed back the hammer on his weapon as he stepped forward, spitting his words, his eyes begging Alan to give him any excuse to take another shot.

"In London all along, you pretend to arrive home just in time for your father's funeral. Not an ounce of remorse on your soulless peasant face. You dare embrace my wife with the same hands that have been smeared with the blood of all those people. You visit the hospital to find out what Ernest remembers. Lucky him, he gets to live because you beat the memory of your face from his head. Then you start to look for the killer. How long were you going to string that out before you killed some other innocent, pegged him as your Mister Slay and talked your way through the rest? Well too bad for you, because I've been on to you for years. And now I finally get to show everyone what you really are."

Alan panted, his gums ached from the clenching of his teeth. He shook his head to clear his thoughts, but a mist of rage had taken him. The pain in his side throbbed, stoking his anger.

Percy didn't seem to notice, or to care. "—a parasite. Feeding on those better than you since birth, charming your way into the home and wallets of your betters only to slaughter them and everything good they stood for. You sicken me. Just like every other vagrant on these streets—"

Alan surged forward, fists eager for battle. Percy's revolver barked. Blinding flashes lit the cellar in time with each retort.

Percy's back slammed into the crate before he realised he was retreating. Opening his eyes, he stared around the room. He was safe. He was alright.

Alan Shaw lay dead on the ground before him.

6

BEHIND HIS HANDS, Simon was muttering to himself. He was shaking, and it showed in his voice.

"Why? Why is this happening?"

Knelt by his side, Lottie hushed him.

Percy leant on the mantelpiece, staring at the carriage clock's second hand as it spun on into eternity. He'd told his tale and the room had fallen silent. There was nothing more for him to do but wait for the praise coming his way. He'd caught the most diabolical villain ever known to the city, singlehanded.

"I don't believe it," Helen said.

He smiled at her. "I didn't want to believe it myself," he lied.

"No, I mean I don't believe *you*," she continued. "I always knew you hated him, Percy, but this is too far. You've lost your mind."

Percy turned to regard her, his eyes wide. "I beg your pardon?"

Helen was on her feet. She roved around the room, arms tight to her sides, fists clenched.

"This is Alan we're talking about. Our Alan. The same boy who saved my father's automatons."

"We only have his word that—"

Helen's finger lanced out. "*Shut up, Percy.*"

His mouth snapped closed with an audible chomp.

"He *saved* this city. He was a hero. Now I know what happened in India—and I don't blame you for not telling us, Simon—and it doesn't make a damned bit of difference. I know he was a good man. I know that. And no matter what he did as a Privateer, I know that he would never hurt an innocent person on purpose. He might be hot headed, and rash, and sometimes blindingly selfish, but my God, he isn't evil. I don't believe it."

She finally stood still, her hair a golden halo around her as the light spilled in through the bay window.

"Luckily, we agree."

Heads swivelled toward the door as Jennings stepped in, helmet tucked under one arm, and Alan tucked under the other.

Simon was across the room in a moment, taking Alan's other arm across his shoulder.

"Set him down, set him down."

Alan slumped into one of the wing-backed chairs beside the fireplace, Simon and Helen stooped beside him.

"Jennings," he wheezed. His finger gestured, exhausted toward Percy. "Shoot him for me."

Jennings smirked. "If I could, Alan," his smirk fell as he regarded Percy, "I would."

"I think it's only fair," Alan groaned.

"That's not funny," Simon chided.

"I'll do it then." Helen span around. When she realised she didn't have a gun, she grunted in frustration and turned her fury into words instead. "You get out of my sight. Get out of my sight, this house, and then the city. I swear, Percy, if I see you before I say so, there will be hell to pay."

His face slack, mouth open, Percy looked from person to person for some kind of response.

"Lottie, surely you're the voice of reason. You know what these people are like." He gestured to Alan, who was too bruised to do anything. "They're pests. Leeches. He's a lunatic."

Lottie moved along the fireplace toward him without a word.

With her face hard as steel, she reached up above the mantelpiece and took down her shotgun. Her eyes still fixed on Percy, she broke it open and reached behind the clock, producing a pair of shells, and very pointedly began loading.

"Mrs Carpenter—" Jennings warned.

But she wasn't listening.

Percy looked from woman to policeman, and realisation hit. He almost barged right through Jennings on his way to the door, which slammed behind him.

Lottie slid the shells back out of her weapon and pocketed them.

Alan was chuckling, even though it hurt like hell.

Lottie gave him a wink.

"It turns out that Percy is a rubbish shot," Jennings offered. "The ones that did hit, Alan's waistcoat took the brunt of. The bruising will be a thing to behold, I reckon," Jennings offered. "I'm thinking of having some made for the force, actually. Damn handy thing."

"Where the hell would you buy such a thing?" Simon asked.

"You don't know half my stories, Simon." Alan tried to pat his brother on the cheek, but his heavy arms turned it into a light slap.

"Ouch."

"Sorry."

"Off to bed with you," Simon ordered. "You must be in agony."

Alan was hoisted to his feet.

"Nothing three spritely women and a bottle of scotch won't fix," he said as he was borne away between brother and sister-in-law, leaving Helen and Jennings alone.

"Alan almost had him, didn't he?" said Helen.

"Damned close, by all accounts. Damn close."

"Whoever dies next is on Percy's conscience, then."

"I daresay he won't need reminding, if it comes to that."

7

"CAN WE TALK about this some other time?" Simon tried to derail the conversation as they sat before the fire in their living room. But his wife wasn't willing to follow. In the shifting firelight, she looked afraid. He'd seen this woman hunt, shoot, and fight, all while maintaining a graceful dignity. That she shivered now made Simon wary.

"When else is there, Simon? What do we do about this?" Lottie stabbed a finger at the newspaper.

"I'd usually say ask Alan."

"And usually I'd agree. But your brother—" she pointed to the ceiling, beyond which Alan snored his way through a laudanum slumber. "—is in a bad way and there's already been another of these, dare I say it, offerings? This is far from over, Simon, and we have the one man who these people want dead laying in a bed in our house. The same house where our son eats his breakfast."

Simon took off his glasses to polish them furiously.

"What do you suggest? Because if you'll remember, the last time we were wrapped up in Alan's adventures I was shot and we were both nearly killed by an insane cult in a gypsy circus." Despite himself, a smile crept across his lips. "You were very sweet in caring for me afterward."

Lottie tried to maintain her gruff exterior, but failed. "You were very sweet helping your brother, although you were so far out of your depth. It's one of the many reasons I fell in love with you."

Leaning forward, Simon took her hands in his and, when that wasn't enough, dropped to his knees on the carpet so that he could hug her.

"Send Jasper to visit your father. He'll enjoy the train ride. Explain as little as we can. Once he's safe—then we let these lunatics come if that's how it's to be."

Lottie pulled away. She looked up at Simon with the same proud beauty that he'd fallen for years before and said: "I'll buy more shells on my way home from dropping off Jasper. Maybe pick up something nice for our tea."

With loving disbelief, Simon shook his head.

A MAP OF Whitechapel lay across the Carpenters' kitchen table, an aerial photograph with the roads and important buildings highlighted in primary colours. Alan couldn't stop looking at Jennings. He'd always assumed the man had only uniforms to wear, but there he now sat in brown trousers and a roll-sleeved shirt, a long coat slung over the back of his chair. Alan could see his wrists. Jennings had wrists. Who knew?

"What's with this?" Alan said, gesturing to his friend's outfit.

"Uniforms don't catch men like Slay. It makes us too easy to spot. I don't want this lunatic knowing I'm there until my foot's on his neck. Then, I might just show him a badge. I might bloody not as well."

Alan smirked.

Simon carefully marked Mister Slay's victims on the map with sugar cubes.

"Couldn't you find something a little more appropriate?" Alan jibed his brother. His chest ached fiercely, but he'd be damned if he'd let them know.

Simon spied him over his glasses. "Such as?"

"Raisins?"

Simon rolled his eyes.

Jennings placed a new sugar cube: "Here's the latest, just yesterday. Another pile of a person left right on the steps of the police station. And it had a note." He slid it across the table. Everyone leaned in to read.

> *Mister Shaw chased Mister Slay.*
> *But clever Slay, he got away.*
> *Shaw can never find his lair.*
> *Mister Slay is everywhere.*

"Ack. He's even annoying on paper." Alan said. "Who's the victim?"

Jennings gave Lottie and Simon a sideways glimpse. Simon nodded.

"A street urchin," Jennings began. "Unnamed. Blonde hair. Couldn't be older than eleven."

Alan's face hardened. Leaning his elbows on the table, his eyes burned into the map as if a tiny Mister Slay might be found there, looking back at him.

"So that's how it is." Ignoring the throb of his ribs, he

scooped up his gun and headed for the door.

"Is there any point—" Jennings began.

"Not in the slightest. Come on, boys." Lottie's chair scraped back from the table and she headed out after Alan, draping a shawl over her shoulders.

They rode the monorail in silence, skimming over and through the rooftops of London on their way to the East End and alighting where Hannah Rowton had ended her final journey. When the shuttle doors slid back, the throng moved in a crushing stream toward the exit archway. Alan went with it, letting himself be carried along with his friends behind him. The sun had crested over London that morning with the sole purpose of frying every living thing that lay below it. Even the smog clouds had been burned away to reveal the blue beyond. In retaliation, the stench of the streets rose up. The drifting scents of flower sellers were nothing before the clouds of hot refuse. The Londoners barely seemed to notice.

Alan drew his accomplices aside as Whitechapel seethed around them.

"Lottie and Simon, stay together. Jennings, carry on doing non-copper things. Spot everything, do nothing. Wander and watch. We'll meet back here in a couple of hours."

"What are we looking for?" Simon asked.

"I don't know. Signs. People. Slay pops up and disappears here. He has to have somewhere to go. And that can't be any old room in any old hotel. The man cuts people into bits and ships them around. I don't care how sneaky he is, Londoners are too damn nosey."

"Londoners are also experts in looking the other way," Lottie offered.

"Not with this. Everyone is scared. Men and women, crooks and kids. I don't know anyone who doesn't want Slay gone."

"And what are you going to do?"

"Follow my feet. They usually get me into trouble all on their own."

Lottie and Simon sauntered away, arm in arm, pretending they had all the time in the world. Jennings turned up the collar of his coat despite the heat and lurched off with a convincing limp.

Alan stood for a moment longer. He let himself breathe a little freer now that no one was there to see the wince that accompanied each breath. Up until then, he'd been playing it calm. But now his mind raced. His blood ran hot at the thought of Slay's last victim, chosen specifically because of the likeness to Alan's younger self. That was a personal taunt, a message, maybe even a trap to dull his mind with anger. Was Slay suggesting that Alan would be as easy to kill, perhaps? That he was a child in Slay's eyes? Arrogance. That would be Slay's downfall. With that, Alan set off along the pavement.

WITH A LARGE glass display-window and a single open door, the police station looked like it could have been a shop at some point. But after a previous riot, the window had been reinforced with a hash of metal bars and the steps led up to a giant steel door where policemen came and went, delivering villains to her majesty's cells. Alan stood for a moment to regard the stairs where the boy's remains had been found. The stone steps were probably the cleanest they had been in a long time. Still, the boy's blood had seeped into the dirt between the slabs, and the cracks in their surface.

Alan turned slowly on the spot, checking up and down the street, spying the windows of the buildings opposite for vantage points. He couldn't imagine that Slay would just leave his offerings and wander away without wanting to see the reactions of those who found them. He was a housecat, proud of his kill, and would want to witness the horror they caused. There were alleyways, of course. London was nothing but a single, murky alleyway with buildings getting in the way. Slay could stay out of the sunlight and eyesight for as long as he pleased, just as Alan had once crossed the city without ever having to set foot on the ground. London had layers; the city that people could see, hemmed by sewers, alleys, rooftops, all existing and overlapping. Ecosystems. That's what Simon would call it. Just thinking of the word made Alan feel a little dirty, but it also brought the warm sensation that his brother might just have rubbed off on him.

His feet led the way. As usual, they took him down one of the many alleys that he'd been thinking about. *The simplest answer is usually the right one.* The alley itself was quite tidy. The tin bins were still upright, with the refuse that wouldn't fit inside piled neatly beside them. Green slime slicked the gutters and tiny feet scuttled in the half-light, but there was no point expecting miracles. Testing a sewer cover in the middle of the cobbles, Alan found it firmly sealed. So he hadn't gone that way. Around the back of the station he stalked through a chicane of dark walkways with nothing catching his eye, until he reached a parallel street full of bustle. Instinct turned him right, where stopped dead. The building he'd rounded directly behind the station was a church. A damned old church. If there had been grounds to it, they had been swallowed up by the city. It crumbled on the spot, ignored by everyone who rushed and sauntered by, not even important enough to be knocked down. Alan wondered if he was the first person to look directly at it in a very long time. The hairs on the back of his neck stood to attention. What better place than there? If he'd wanted to stick one to the police in the most royal way, wouldn't Slay make his lair right behind the damned station? And wouldn't a church be the perfect place to do the devil's work?

Alan circled the building, since the peeling old doors were barred and boarded. In a neighbouring alley, a trapdoor led down to cellar level. Thumbing the hammer of his revolver, he checked the entrance. Unlocked, and with the hinges oiled.

He paused. His revolver seemed to squirm in his hand. The ache in his chest increased to a crush. When was the last time he had paused before a confrontation? Had he ever? All the ancient dangers and modern strife he'd been through and his pulse had never faltered. But a dread stench seemed to emanate from the darkness he stared down into. His senses were stifled by it. Fear. Slay actually had him afraid.

"Balls to that," he muttered, and set his foot on the first step downward.

THE CELLAR REMINDED him of one he'd been shot in recently. Dingy, piled with crates, and cobwebs hung like harem curtains. Except as he crept along, he passed a low door which led to a long dark crypt lined with stone coffins. The creeps which had infected him before he'd even entered the cellar decided to dance a jig down his spine. Death surrounded him, and Slay was a master of it. On his home turf or not, Alan felt as if he was stepping into another domain entirely; the closest thing to hell that London had to offer.

There seemed to be no-one around. But Alan knew that his prey was a man of darkness, and the sun was up. Not that it made much difference here. As he took a few stone steps upward, Alan found himself in the church's main hall. Litter had flown in through the broken windows to pile in drifts in the corners. The few remaining stained-glass panes were dirty to the point of concealing whatever story they told. Broken pews had been moved into a large circle at the hall's centre and the stone altar, which had once lain at one end of the church, stood in their midst. From the far end of the room, the lectern still looked down on it all, draped with black cloth. Mister Slay leaned forward from behind it, an eager grin slashed across his face.

"Well?" Alan said, as he moved across the room.

"Well, well, welcome!" Slay screeched, throwing his arms outward. His cackle reverberated, making Alan twitch involuntarily. "Thank you for joining us, Alan. You are a man of your word, indeed. You found me, as you said you would."

Closer to the altar, now, Alan could see herbs had been

scattered across its surface, a candle lit at each corner. The pit of his stomach lurched.

"Just in time for a party," he said, spotting movement at the sides of the room. Memories of photographs he'd seen. Naked footprints, dancing around and around, making sickening curlicues in the blood. "Friends of yours, Slay?"

"Ladies and gentlemen, meet Mister Alan Shaw, Protector of London, raised from the dead." That cackle. Damn him. "Let's put him back where he belongs."

Alan turned slowly, taking stock of the men and women who surrounded him, utterly naked apart from deep red markings painted in spirals down their limbs. Trying to meet their gaze, Alan found it almost impossible; there was something in their glares that he didn't want to see. They were each panting heavily, wolves with a faltering quarry. Just as Alan saw a flash of himself as a pile of dismembered parts, the first of the cultists leapt forward. Alan caught him in the forehead with his first shot and the man's body slid to a halt at his feet. Blood pooled around his boots. The others let out an almighty scream of exultation which shook the remaining windows. Behind him, Slay yelled words Alan didn't understand, and everything happened at once.

8

IT WAS A dance that he'd done a thousand times. Alan knew every step, every dip. As the naked men and women lunged and screeched, Alan spun and ducked. His hands were a flurry of neat blows, his revolver taking the odd shot to finish what his strikes had started.

Their keen little blades kissed his skin, sapping his blood one drop at a time, crimson dewdrops flying to decorate the floor, the altar. Alan took a handful of brunette hair, dragging the woman's head back, and punched her in the throat without hesitation. As her body hit the ground, a pair of powerful arms wrapped around him and hefted him right off his feet. Jerking his head backward, he was satisfied with the crunch he caused, but the man didn't let go, even though Alan could feel his foe's blood streaking down the back of his neck. Alan slammed down onto the altar, chest first. Cold stone and pain stole his breath. He wrestled as the cultist struggled to hold him down, managing to worm one arm backward, and took a handful of what no man could ignore. A wail erupted as Alan snapped his hand into a twist. Dropping from the altar to a crouch, he threw his hands up as an opponent's knee shot toward his face. Scuttling to his feet, his last bullet only grazed the woman's arm. Switching grips on his revolver, he smashed her across the jaw with it. She fell across the altar, her blood mixing with any number of others as her face hit the stone and she slid off, unconscious.

And then silence. Panting. This time it was his own. His knuckles ached, pain seeped out of a hundred little places. But he looked down at the slumped forms of the naked cultists, the victor. Spitting blood, he turned back to Slay. The lectern was empty. Alan began to panic, eyes rushing around every corner of the room.

Mister Slay hadn't gone far. He stood quite still at the end of the room, hands raised in submission, but that nauseating grin still streaked across his face.

"Looks like you're done, Slay."

"I am indeed. Thank you, Mister Shaw. The orgy of pain has been satisfied by your eager hands. The blood of London flows through you and those that have come before you, even through those you've laid at your feet. And so it now flows through my Master. It flows through him and into me, for I am his agent—"

"For Christ sake. You're going on a bit aren't you?" Alan said.

Slay chuckled. "Perhaps, perhaps. I'm a man with passion, Alan. You know what that's like, to have passions. It drives you, flogs you into exhaustion. And you let it because it is your love. Some people have a cause, some wrap the world in words and trap it on paper. Some drink until they can't walk, some fight and spill blood."

"And yours is murdering to pay debts to the Devil?"

"Oh Lord, no." Slay's tone was convincingly sociable. "Satan himself is only a follower of the greater chaos. I sew its seeds for the love of the thing. What era of men hasn't had a great adversary? Empires always fall, Alan. Always. This empire has created so much. And so I destroy. To remind them that although their machines can touch the sky and plumb the depths, men are still just squishy bags of meat and water. That's what chaos does, it humbles. It reminds people that their petty efforts are ultimately in vain because they have no control. It's about balance, you see."

Alan paced back and forth, his fists clenching.

"I've heard some drivel in my time, Slay, but you take the biscuit. You think murdering a few innocent people can bring down the British Empire? You're more of a loony than I gave you credit for."

"The Empire is a great avatar of order, crushing everything else to its will, until everyone stands in the same lines, in the same clothes, with the same thoughts. Why were automatons created? To succeed where religion had failed. To take the will right out of a person, leaving only a useful worker husk behind.

"What maintains the Empire, Alan? I'll tell you. That no one can stand against it when met head on. How do you bring such a creature to its knees? You shake it from within. Order can never understand chaos because chaos cannot be controlled. There *is* no agenda, there *is* no plan… and so there is no fighting it."

Slay seemed to change gears, his zealous rattle subsiding. That unnerved Alan even more. A ranting lunatic he could handle. With a monster, he knew where he stood. But as Slay swept back his long coat to pop his hands into his pockets, he started to look like a person.

"We share a common ancestry, Alan. Did you know? Not of family, of course. Neither of us know where we came from. But a trial we endured. A certain workhouse, in fact. And an escape. Yourself and Dick Whitsun. And a few other boys. All streaking off into the night to seek your destinies. I sought my destiny that night, just as you did—"

Alan's jaw had almost unhinged. "You're lying," he managed. But the man stood across from him smiled, and Alan saw not a mad demon, but a man. He thought of a young Slay losing teeth as a boy and probing the gap with his tongue. He thought of him reading a newspaper. He thought of him brushing his hair and buttoning his shirt in the morning. Slay couldn't have been any older than Alan. He had the same damned accent. And he knew Dick's name.

"—myself and one other boy, we hid under a broken gutter pipe, soaked through and shivering. The alley was blind. They had us bang to rights. They would have taken us both back. Oh the beatings we'd have endured. Like nothing we could imagine, and we had already experienced so much. I would do *anything* to not go back, Alan. And I proved it. I killed the boy I was with. Whatever his name was. Do you remember the others?"

Alan scanned his memory. What *had* been their names? Himself and Dick, and four others. He and Dick had taken off together, never giving the other boys a second thought as they scattered in the dark.

Slay waved a dismissive hand. "Of course not. I don't

blame you. Me and that boy, we wrestled in the dark. We fought like dogs as the footsteps grew closer and even as the enforcer's torchlight spread into the alleyway. But I ended him. I left him for them to find. Their faces. Such fear." He took a deep sigh, like a man drinking the day's first cup of tea. Alan shuddered. "That seed of chaos that I left in their path turned them away from me. Chaos saved me just as the order of the workhouse had shackled me and worked me bloody.

"I visited Dick just before you did. I read your letter in the newspapers—quite rousing, by the way—and knew you would be seeking out as many old friends as you could muster. We talked about you. The boy from the papers. The Protector of London. Fated to be my adversary. I told him to help you, to set you on my trail. An obstacle is Chaos' will, and I welcome any of its gifts." Slay's hands moved in his pockets. He smiled, long and slow. As he spoke, he began to pace, in a mockery of Alan's own movements the other side of the altar. Back and forth they went together, baring their teeth; one with a snarl, one with an insane grin. "Me, in London, gathering followers and honing my skills in the dark; you, carousing across the world and staying alive against all odds. All that and we both still end up here, together, as we started." Slay shook his head. "Fate, perhaps, is what binds order and chaos together."

Alan's revolver whirled through the air, end over end, smashing into Slay's forehead with a solid *thunk*.

"Bored," Alan barked.

The cultist took a step back in shock, hands pressed to the gush of crimson from his face, reeling as Alan vaulted the altar and covered the intervening space at a sprint until he was face-to-bleeding-face with his adversary.

"There's no great purpose to *any* of this, Slay," Alan said, grabbing the villain by the forelock of his coat, the other hand bunching into a pale-knuckled hammer. "It might be armies of thousands or a few, they might use magic, or bullets. It might just be two men in an old church. But it boils down to this: There's men like you. And men like me. Just people following their nature against each other. Over and over, as far back as time goes." Alan paused, suddenly calm. His own words made such sense that he'd surprised himself. He stood before a villain, as thousands had done before him, and he recognised his place in the world for the first time; this place that he had made for himself, building with the bricks his father and brother had given to him, mortared with his own pride and spirit. He smiled. "Today is just our day."

Behind his hands, Slay grinned. From somewhere in his sleeve, a blade appeared in his nimble fingers, slender and night-black. Alan grabbed for the villain's wrist as he backed away, but Slay was fast. The blade dipped, seeming to trail a wisp of dark smoke, drawing a long line across Alan's stomach in what could have been a deadly slash, but for his trained reflexes. Slay sniggered, ramming his shoulder into Alan hard enough to send him sprawling against the altar behind. Slay advanced, blade held high, muttering to himself through that hellish grin of his. The blade darted down. Alan twisted and lashed out with his foot. A hot shard of pain lanced down his leg. His back arched and he let out a ripping scream. He'd been stabbed before. This was nothing like those times. He looked to the source, where Slay's blade had torn through his right thigh. Freezing cold spread through him from the waist down, like being dunked in an ice bath. He could feel his legs going slack and unrepsonsive. Unleashing a growl, he lunged while he still could. His hand hooked over, smashing Slay square in the nose, sending the lunatic reeling backward once more. Alan managed to catch himself as he slid from the altar, but his legs just wouldn't lift him. On his knees, he panted against the pain, marvelling at such agony as he'd never known before. Dropping to his stomach, he began to crawl, his arms doing all the work, toward the revolver laying open on the ground not a few feet away. He could hear Slay moving behind him, but there was no point turning around. Another clean strike with that knife and he was done for. His fingers wrapped around the warm sandalwood grip and he fumbled in his pocket for bullets.

Footsteps. Slow, but approaching. Slay was taking his time. That laugh echoed around the church's naked insides and Alan swore he felt a spasm in his legs as if they heard it, too.

"I would teach you your final lesson, Alan. Something for you to think on, wherever you end up. Just because I'm mad—" the blade plumed black smoke and an icicle of pain wrenched Alan's limbs "—doesn't mean I'm not right." Slay knelt beside him as if he might help him up just as easily as end him. "You're a man of blood. I respect that. If only you had gone left rather than right that night outside the workhouse. We could have been brothers." Slay shook his head and raised the knife.

Alan rolled. The shots splashed hot red into the air, each higher than the last, crawling up the front of Slay's waistcoat until his throat exploded backward in a crimson gout. With the blade still over his head, Mister Slay slumped backward, already cooling when he hit the ground. The sound of the blade skittering across the flagstones was the sign for Alan to slump back himself. Dropping his revolver, he tore at the leg of his trousers. But there was no pain, only lots and lots of blood. Assessing the damage, his eyes widened as he saw the wound through his torn trousers. The flesh around it was already black, fading to deep purple threads under his skin which moved even as he watched. From a pouch in his waistcoat, his emergency kit, he cast aside a coil of twine, a needle, and took the strip of rubber that he found, applying the tourniquet just above the wound. He let out an involuntary whimper when he felt no pain at all. He was already sweating profusely.

The numbness in his lower limbs meant walking out of here was impossible. He would have to drag himself. Arm over arm, away from the corpse of Mister Slay, Alan headed for the dilapidated doors of the church. It was unbelievable how heavy he was, how slow his progress. But eventually his shoulders sagged against the church door.

And now what?

With a lick of his chapped lips, he considered his only option.

"Help," he said, testing the word. "*Somebody help me!*"

9

EVERY SURFACE OF the room was patterned in some way. The walls were a repetition of sepia woodland scenes framed in climbing vines. The curtains and lampshades, mint green and edged with cream lace. Lace doilies protected mahogany surfaces from vases and clocks. The dark, varnished bed frame was a stark contrast to the rest of the room.

A clock poured leaden beats. Alan thrashed in the clean linens, his skin a clammy grey, his brow a persistent shimmer of sweat. His fingers grabbed at the sheets in the throes of his nightmare as he fought off god-only-knew-what.

"How long is this going to last?" Simon muttered, shaking his head. He looked almost as bad as Alan. "What kind of fever lasts for weeks on end?"

"No one knows, my love." Lottie laid a hand on her husband's shoulder. The skirts of her dress rustled as she moved. "But if anyone is stubborn enough to fight off whatever this is, it's Alan."

"I was horrible to him, Lottie. Was it really worth it?

Who am I to tell him what he should and shouldn't do? If he wants to run around the world on adventures, then why shouldn't he?"

"He's also been a selfish prat," Lottie offered. "Running off, letting us think he was dead. No matter what happened in India, no decent person does that."

"He had his reasons, I'm sure."

"And you say you were mean to him? You're the only person I know who still makes excuses for him."

Simon looked up at his wife, who was smiling knowingly. He nodded.

"How do you do that? Twist it around until I've talked myself out of my own argument?"

She kissed his forehead. "Talent." Making for the door, she said, "And I'm also right about you eating something. Come get your breakfast."

"I will. Just one more minute."

The door clicked into the jamb and Simon leaned back in his chair. He slid the velvet wrapping from his trouser pocket and uncovered the knife once more. The only thing they'd found in the church along with Alan, an altar and a host of corpses. Simon had matched it to the wounds on his brother with ease. But the nature of the thing still baffled him. Tests on the weapon showed no poison or unusual property to the metal. So why this fever?

Standing over his brother, Simon tugged back the covers from the metal frame which kept them from resting on his legs. The colour of the limbs was better, at least. The left leg was no longer affected at all and the purple threads had reduced to within only an inch of the actual wound in his brother's right thigh. The oozing from between the stitches had subsided as well. He looked back to the knife. Alan had always gotten mixed up in the most obscure adventures. Simon had been present at events that he would have passed off as absurdities had he not witnessed them himself. His scientific mind had come up with nothing regarding the weapon.

Wrapping the knife, he pocketed it again, and went for breakfast.

As the door clicked to the jamb for the second time, and Simon's footsteps retreated along the hallway, Alan's eyes creaked open. The room coalesced as if rising through murky water. He knew this room, he thought. At least he had once. The furnishings were different; the bed was certainly new. But that old fireplace, the window which looked just like the one an Irish villain had slipped through with murder on his mind. Alan was back in the first bedroom he'd ever known; one he'd shared with Simon when he had first left the streets. Trying to lift his head, he soon realised that it just wasn't on the cards, so he slid his lead-weight hand over the covers to feel his thigh. There was pain there. That was good. He wiggled his toes on both feet. Only the left obeyed. That wasn't so good. Part of him was glad that he couldn't lift the covers. The last view he'd had of his leg was something he'd rather not see again. That gruesome marvel could wait until he felt better.

There was no telling how long passed between Alan's fleeting moments of consciousness. People appeared and disappeared by his bed. Simon, Lottie, Jennings, and Ernest in his wheelchair, still bruised around the edges but smiling as always. The only way he could tell the time was by the change of their clothes or the dying of the light through his window. He could no longer tell the difference between dreams and waking. He would fade into awareness, only to find the room filled with inky swirls that burst apart as people passed through. Or he would rouse with a shudder, certain this time that he was awake only to wake again moments later. This time, all he knew was that Simon had just left to eat breakfast. So it was a new day.

MISTER SLAY POPPED himself down on the edge of the bed, hands folded in his lap.

"And how are we feeling today?" he said, companionably.

Alan jolted, a lance of pain shooting down his affected leg, but his body wouldn't obey when he tried to scuttle up the bed and away from the lunatic.

"Rest now. You've had quite a time of it. To be frank, Alan, you look like hell." Slay unleashed that awful cackle as loud as his lungs would allow. Alan darted his eyes to the door. Surely they heard that.

His mouth barely forming the words, Alan stuttered: "How are you—I killed you."

"Yes. It hurt rather a lot."

Alan could do nothing but slowly shake his head.

"But fear not," Mister Slay continued. "You haven't lost me yet. I'm thinking of sticking around for some time."

With that, the bedroom's door opened a sliver, making hushing noises on the rich carpet Slay and Alan turned in unison to see a small hand wrap around the door's edge and

Jasper's spectacled face peer around. The boy crept in, a small metal train clutched in one hand, and padded his way toward the bed in stocking feet.

Alan darted his eyes from the lunatic to the boy, he tried to speak but realised he couldn't.

Slay was perfectly still, his face filled with curiosity as Jasper climbed up onto his father's chair, leaned over, and put the train onto the bed. When it almost slid from the covers, his face scrunched in a way that was all his father. The boy lifted Alan's unresisting hand and placed it over the train. Satisfied that it would no longer slip and break, the boy made his way over to the window and cracked it open a little, then padded back out of the room as the curtains began to gently waft.

It was Slay who broke the silence: "How sweet."

"How—" Alan began.

Slay shushed him like a mother. "Quiet now. I'll be off. Your fever is about to give you another moment of excruciating pain and I'd hate to distract you from it."

Alan's whole body locked into a single iron rod of heat and agony, lifting his spine off the bed. As his eyes rolled back, Slay was gone again. There was only the searing of his muscles, and the metal of the toy train digging into his palm.

BOTH OF ALAN'S most frequent visitors were in the room. Simon sat by his bed, turning his son's toy train this way and that, his eyes as distant as his thoughts. Slay stood by the window, eyes closed as the sun bathed his dark self.

"You're missing out, Alan. The summer is out there.

Days are slipping away," he said.

"Sod off, Slay," Alan muttered.

"Alan?" Simon leant over him in an instant. "Can you hear me, old boy?"

"I can hear both of you."

Simon's brow furrowed. "We're alone, Alan."

"You're alone, Alan," Slay chuckled.

Alan groaned.

A hand slid down Alan's back, making him shiver as he felt the river of old sweat that ran there, and pillow after pillow lurched him forward. He had to admit, it felt good to be a little more vertical.

"You need to drink something," Simon said, offering a small crystal glass to Alan's lips.

"Scotch," Alan managed to mutter, and took a sip anyway.

Simon laughed. "Scotch we can drink until we fall over when you're well."

Alan's mind rewound and his eyes finally took on focus. When he went to grab Simon's shirt, he found that his hand finally did as it was told. He pulled his brother closer, Simon recoiling slightly at the cloud of fevered breath.

"Simon. Slay. He's right there."

Despite himself, Simon searched the corners of the room.

"Now, now, sit back. I assure you there's no-one here but me."

Alan flopped back, the energy expended in grabbing his brother was far too much. Before his eyes closed once more, Slay wiggled his fingers coyly at him from across the room.

LOTTIE AND SIMON pottered quietly around the bedroom as Alan slumbered. With fresh flowers and a water jug on the dresser, and the curtains drawn back to let in the daylight, they danced back out like wraiths. The door was closed for only a few seconds before Alan opened his eyes to darkness. Inky swirls danced at the edge of his vision for a second, and then dissipated to reveal the noon sun.

For the first time, he actively sought the room for Slay.

"Alright, Slay, where are you?"

There was no reply.

"You can't have a social life, you're dead. So I know you're here."

The sickly sweet song crept out of the air right by Alan's ear, freezing him stiff.

"There's no need to be that way. He's your friend is Mister Slay. And best friends are never far away."

Alan swallowed the lump that rose in his throat and forced himself up on one elbow. He took a little pride in the fact that it was getting easier. "Enough of that you evil shit. It's time you talked. I don't know if you're here or not, if you're real or a dream or a ghost or all three. But I've got an idea that you stabbing me with that knife means you get to stick around and if you're here, you'll make yourself useful or so help me—"

A slow, sarcastic clap filled the room.

Alan snapped his head around to see Slay sat in the window, one foot on the sill.

"There's the Alan we know and love. Good to see you awake for a change. Although, sitting in on your dreams has taught me so much about you. You are a mess, old pal."

"Shut it. This thing isn't over until you're gone. Tell me how I get rid of you."

"Oh, since you put it that way, of *course*. Let me explain *everything* to you in *great* detail, including locations and dates, and I'll hold your hand while we skip along and banish me from existence." The cackle rang out, shaking Alan's bones. Between Alan's blinks, Slay went from the window to kneeling by the bed, his face close enough that Alan jerked back. "Or perhaps not. I am, as you put it, sticking around. You amuse me. All those inadequacies, all that guilt. Such beautiful nightmares. You're made of rags and spit aren't you? If you are the hero of our tale, Alan, you can surely figure it out for yourself."

"You're a hallucination," Alan said, he jerked his chin toward the window. "If you were real, you'd be out there. More people would be dead."

"I'm as real as I need to be." Quick as he'd been with his blade, Slay bopped Alan on the nose with his forefinger. Alan recoiled from the sensation, his eyes wide.

Another blink and Slay was across the room, beside the bedroom door with his arms folded.

"I'll make you a deal, Alan. You walk over here, and I'll give you a clue."

Alan sneered. "What do you get out of that?"

"I get to watch you in pain, floundering and failing," Slay chuckled. "I'm already dead, so there's no rush."

Using the edge of the bed to lever himself over, Alan slid his legs across the cotton sheets, letting the weight of his feet pull him to sitting when they dropped from the edge. He could feel the floorboards with his left foot. The other felt as if it were sending signals from a great distance. Trying to wiggle some life into the afflicted toes still produced no movement at all.

"You don't need your little piggies to dance anyway," Slay quipped.

"Shut it."

Bracing himself between the bedpost and the mattress, Alan levered himself upright. To his surprise, vertical was the easy part. Then again, he wasn't putting any weight through his right leg yet. Carefully, he shifted his balance, and that was when the pain came, lancing into his thigh as if Slay had stabbed him anew. He sucked air through his teeth, his knuckles paling on the bedpost. But be damned if he'd yell out with Slay lapping up every ounce of his agony. Instead, Alan set his glare on the shadowy bastard by the door and grinned as wide as he could. Even when the beads of sweat began to pour down his spine, even when his stomach began to shake with the effort.

"P-Piece of cake," he stammered.

"Then step forward, brave warrior, and claim your prize."

It was as though there had been no intervening time. There was Slay's grin, and then the floorboards hit him. The thud must have been as loud as it was painful because seconds later, footfalls hammered up the stairs. The door burst open and Simon's shoes reflected Alan's grey visage back at him for the briefest of moments before they advanced.

"You idiot!" Simon said as he rolled Alan's slack form toward him.

"Didn't hurt a bit. Thanks for asking," Alan snorted.

"You never learn—"

Lottie came in, her apron splattered with things soon to be tasty, covered in flour to the wrists with one white streak across her temple where she'd brushed back her hair.

"Oh God, is he alright?" she asked, making white handprints on her skirt as she leant down to look at them both.

"Just wanted a change of scenery—"

"He's fine," Simon interrupted.

"Well if you wouldn't mind not bruising my floorboards, that would be kind of you," Lottie said with a smile. And then, more earnestly: "It's good to see you have your sense of humour back."

Alan smiled up at her.

"Simon, I'm stealing your wife from you with immediate effect."

The tension diffused a little as they laughed together, albeit haltingly in Alan's case as he held his stricken leg. But the pain didn't subside. Alan felt a rush of cold, like ice injected into this bloodstream. His body shook once.

Oh god. Not this again.

Simon looked down at him.

"Alan? Are you alright?"

But his eyes were already rolling back into his head. His body snapped straight, and then continued, his spine ratcheted backward, limbs drawn into cruel mockeries of movement. He was vaguely aware of a keening animal sound which, as it grew, he knew was coming from himself. The shadows lurched in, dropping the curtain on his mind.

BACK IN BED with a dose of laudanum warming his soul, Alan felt better. His brother and sister-in-law smiled at him from the doorway before stepping out. He did his best to smile back. They seemed fooled because they left him alone, Simon pointing to his eye and then Alan before leaving.

He addressed the silent room: "Before you say anything, shut up."

A low chuckle emanated from somewhere in the shadows.

ALAN'S CRUTCHES THUMPED on the carpet in little circles as he tried to balance himself, his right foot still held off the ground.

"This isn't as easy as I'm making it look," he said.

Simon *humph*ed beside him. "I'm still not sure you should even be up."

"I'm not sure I need your negativity, right now, Matron."

With a wry smile, Simon let go of his brother's shoulders. Alan started pitching forward before Simon clamped him again, and set him straight.

"You've gotten cruel in your old age," Alan scowled.

"And yet you refuse to change at all."

Alan set his brother with a deep gaze as he said: "I've changed plenty. You don't do my job without it changing you. Just ask Mister Slay."

Simon cast his eyes down.

"I should never have said what I did at father's funeral."

With no way to drop a witty line and walk away, Alan was stuck in the conversation for good or ill.

"It needed saying. And Slay needed ending. He wasn't the kind of lunatic you can just lock up. Not after what he did. I'm glad you weren't there, Simon. There was a terrible darkness in that man, and I've seen some dark things, so I'd know. He wasn't going to let me out of there alive. He nearly didn't. But don't think for a second that his death is on your conscience just because of some grief-stricken comment you made. It was all on me. *My* bullets cut him down. And so help me, I'd do it again."

With that, he looked up from his brother to the dark figure sat with its boots on the bed.

"Now let's try this again. I'm making it to that landing today if it kills me."

A FLURRY OF faces, gun flashes and silent screaming ended with Alan jerking awake. The sheets were freezing with his sweat. As he sat up, a stab of pain had him grabbing his thigh and breathing deeply.

"Why don't you just piss off," he muttered at his leg.

Scanning the room, he found Slay at his favourite post, perched on the frame of the open window.

Just one shove, Alan thought. *Not that it'd make any difference. But it would feel good.*

A warm summer breeze wafted around the room, reducing the stifling temperatures of the day to a bearable level. Even now, in the deepest hours of the night, the hum of traffic and the sound of shoes on the pavement continued.

Slay turned to him. There wasn't a flash of emotion in him now, only the pale slash of a face in the dark.

"Go back to sleep," he said.

Alan did as he was told.

THE CARPENTERS, ALAN and Jennings sat in the sunlit living room. As Alan stared out into the street from the window seat, his bad leg stretched out for the little comfort it gave him, he spotted Mister Slay. He was following people up and down the street outside, pretending to tip a hat to them or exchange pleasantries. Of course, no one reacted.

Jennings turned his helmet in his hands. Simon slurped his tea, looking sheepish when Lottie gave him a withering look.

"This has all been a little far-fetched, even for London," Jennings said. "Why is it that all the crazy people seem to come here?"

"The rest of the world has its share of lunatics," Alan chipped in between slurps of his scotch. Every now and then he shifted his weight in the window seat, which did nothing at all to alleviate the dull ache in his leg. The laudanum, however, was starting to kick in.

"Not like Mister Slay, surely?"

"It's a funny old world. And by funny old world, I mean a constant rolling heap of craziness."

"Do you think killing him did any good?" Simon asked. "There aren't any more of them, you don't think?"

"Made me feel better," Alan chipped. "And no. There'd be more bodies by now."

Jennings addressed the room. "We've made detailed autopsies of the cultists. Tried to figure out this writing they're covered with. Maybe we'll find a clue as to what was going on. But I think Alan got all of them in one spot."

From behind teacups and glasses and leaning hands, everyone cast a doubtful look in his direction.

"Yes. You're probably right, Alan." Jennings slapped his knees as he stood. "I don't suppose any of you would accept protective custody for a while so I won't offer. I will say this, though, and I'm talking to you, Alan. If there are any of Slay's cronies left, do not chase them. If only because you're in no shape. What's done is done. Let's try to get people back to normal. This particular case is over."

Alan saluted with his half-empty glass. He was going to say something smart but the laudanum had given his gums a rosy numbness and he was happy settling back into the glow.

Jennings left and there was some muttering by the door. Alan realised that his eyes had closed only when they snapped open again. Simon and Lottie were conspiring by the fire.

"What's the plan?" He asked.

"We were going to ask you the same thing," Lottie replied. "How do you normally go about recovering from these things?"

"To be honest—" Alan slid from the window seat onto his good leg and joined them by the fire with his remaining crutch. When he dropped into the armchair Lottie slid a stool toward his numb foot and he took it gladly. "—I have no idea. I'd normally have another job by now. Merry would be picking me up in the glider and we'd be whisking away somewhere exotic to do something stupid." He chuckled childishly. "I liked Merry."

Simon gave his brother a loving look.

"I think that laudanum is working. Come on, old boy.

Back to bed with you."

Alan shuffled down in his chair. "Actually, I think I'll stay here. The fire is warm, the scotch is at hand. And, to be honest, the thought of climbing those stairs right now is torture in itself."

Bidding him goodnight, the Carpenters retired upstairs. He could hear them moving around for a while, setting furniture straight, and then peace.

As the fire died down, bathing the room in a deep ember glow, Slay sat in the opposite chair. But he didn't seem talkative. His face drew open at the mouth, his teeth grinning in the dark.

Alan felt the jolt hit his stomach first. Hard enough to jar him in his seat, his stricken leg hit the ground heel-first and a shard of pain shot into him. He could feel it rising through him, what was about to come. The shadows clustered around his vision, drawing in until there was only Slay's intent face.

Pushing it back, Alan managed to make the shadows subside. It was getting easier, he knew, but the spasms that lanced through his leg were getting no better.

"God, I hate you."

Slay didn't move a muscle.

10

ALAN'S ROOMS ON Cecil Street were exactly as he had left them; completely deserted. His duffle bag was still in the corner where he'd tossed it. The only new addition was a package, pedestal-shaped and waist high, wrapped in paper and twine and left in the middle of the room.

"Let me know if you need anything," Mister Forsythe offered. Alan nodded as the old man closed the door behind him.

Alan made his way over to the package, his crutch striking the floorboards at odds with the softer sound of his boot and the light tap of his stricken foot as he forced himself to put at least a little weight through it. Leaning the crutch against himself so that it would be in reach, Alan untied the string and peeled back the paper to reveal the cover of a magazine, printed in full colour with a bold font that screamed excitement:

The Adventures of Alan Shaw

He stared down at himself, albeit a more rakish version, holding a beautiful woman under one arm, his revolver held dynamically in the other, while crocodiles and jungle snakes crowded the border around him. He flicked down through the pile, those same words with differing images each issue. Some were close enough to reality that they sparked a memory instantly, others were not so close. Those, he knew, were where Ernest had changed details for Alan's sake or that of someone else. Merry, for instance, was absent from all of the adventures they had worked together. Her anonymity had been one stipulation of his agreement.

He couldn't help wondering how many children read these adventures, under their blankets before sleep so that their dreams were of swashbuckling and danger, and how many children read the old soggy copies they found in bins and gutters, never knowing the end when the pages were torn or too stained. How many nights had *he* spent sleeping in hay lofts and under tavern tables, a damaged copy of Titus Gladstone clutched carefully so as not to tear it any further, looking at the pictures and the nonsensical hieroglyphs around them? He never knew what it was like to read a copy, never mind a new one, until Simon had shared his full and pristine collection, teaching Alan to read by lamplight before bed each night.

With one hand massaging the deadened muscles in his right thigh, Alan leaned heavily on his history. A hot stone pulsed between his ribs, a choking, swelling blockage that wouldn't go away. His mind wouldn't stop reeling in images of faces long gone and faces he couldn't get rid of. He could feel the city beyond the room, sense the world turning ever onward, and he had no idea how it could when so much was so wrong. He felt the core of his being turn to pure sorrow.

A wave of grief and disappointment and doubt swept through him. The first few tears hit the magazine's cover and spread, soaking in. He let them fall.

By the window, the slender shadow of Mister Slay looked out on the street below, at the lives humming by, grinning at the movement and the noise. Turning his gaunt mask toward the barren rooms, taking in the bare boards, the empty fireplace, the dusty windows, and the man with heaving shoulders stood at their centre, an inhuman smile severed his face.

About the Author

Beginning his career with short stories in 2008, Craig's tales have graced the pages of the British Fantasy Society, Misanthrope Press, Pill Hill Press, and Murky Depths. He has managed to avoid winning a single award in this whole time and has decided to take that as an accolade in itself, whenever the tears stop falling.

He likes to think that his books are about real people who live in impossible worlds. Whether his books are Fantasy, Horror, Steampunk, or Sci-fi, Craig loves to go wherever the stories may take him.

Find the author via his website:
craighallam.wordpress.com

Or tweet at him:
@craighallam84

More From This Author

Greaveburn

From the crumbling Belfry to the Citadel's stained-glass eye, across acres of cobbles streets and knotted alleyways that never see daylight, Greaveburn is a city with darkness at its core. Gothic spires battle for height, overlapping each other until the skyline is a jagged mass of thorns.

Under the cobbled streets lurk the Broken Folk, deformed rebels led by the hideously scarred Darrant, a man who once swore to protect the city. And in a darkened laboratory, the devious Professor Loosestrife builds a contraption known only as The Womb.

With Greaveburn being torn apart around her, can Abrasia avenge her father's murder before the Archduke's letter spells her doom?

Paperback ISBN: 978-1-908600-12-7
eBook ISBN: 978-1-908600-13-4

Not Before Bed

A collection of tales to tingle your spine and goose your bumps. Enter worlds filled with tentacle pods, bogeymen, dark gods; vamps zombies, werewolves, and things with no name. 'Not Before Bed' isn't just a title…it's a warning.

Paperback ISBN: 978-1-908600-34-9
eBook ISBN: 978-1-908600-35-6

Available from all major online and offline outlets.

Lightning Source UK Ltd.
Milton Keynes UK
UKHW041045010319
338103UK00001B/29/P

9 781908 600714

Derbyshire Stained Glass

by

Joyce Critchlow

ISBN 1-874754-98-5

2001

The Derbyshire Heritage Series

Walk & Write Ltd.,
Unit 1, Molyneux Business Park,
Whitworth Road, Darley Dale,
Matlock, Derbyshire.
England.
DE4 2HJ

Walk & Write Ltd.,
Unit 1,
Molyneux Business Park,
Whitworth Road, Darley Dale,
Matlock, Derbyshire
DE4 2HJ
Tel/Fax 01629 - 735911

First Published - March 1997
Reprinted - October 2001.

ISBN 1-874754-98-5

British Library Cataloguing-in-Publication Data. A catalogue record of this book is available from the British Library.

Typeset and designed in Avant Garde - bold, italic, and plain 10pt. 12pt, 14pt and 18pt. by John N. Merrill.

Cover design © Walk & Write Ltd 2001.
Photo - Stained glass window in Tissinton Church, by John N. Merrill © 2001.

Contents

Page No.

Introduction 5

Chapter One - Ancient and Heraldic Glass 7

Chapter Two - Designers and their art 13

Chapter Three - The Bible in glass 21

Chapter Four - Saints and Martyrs of the Late Church....26

Chapter Five - Stories in Glass...32

Chapter Six - Natural History, Symbols and Strange Things in Glass..39

Chapter Seven - Twentieth-Century Glass..........................42

Books by John N. Merrill 46

The Derbyshire History Series 48

Introduction.

More properly, I suppose this book should be called "*Stained Glass in Derbyshire*", since many of the glassmakers and designers have not been Derbyshire born and bred: in fact, our county's churches, as will be seen, have a fair sprinkling of Continental glass.

In the early days, pictures on glass enabled illiterate worshippers to familiarise themselves with the stories and saints of the Bible and the Church. Some ascetics, like Bernard of Clairvaux, looked askance at brightly-coloured glass, but accepted the pale yellow-and -white (often grey) of grisaille. This type of window, dating from the late thirteenth century, had many diamond-shaped panes, and sometimes instead of figures consisted of geometrical designs.

The Reformation saw the destruction of much beautiful glass; but there has also been a less religiously motivated danger, from architects and others seeking to replace the traditional with new ideas of their own: notably at Salisbury Cathedral, where Wyatt in the eighteenth century took out the old glass to lighten the nave, sold the lead for scrap, and used the glass pieces to provide drainage for the waterlogged cathedral close!.

Coloured glass can be entirely stained - that is, the colouring matter having been melded in from the start of its manufacture; partially stained, where "white" glass is mingled with the stained; or painted, where the colouring is applied externally to one surface of the glass.

These chapters on stained glass in Derbyshire by no means exhaust the great variety our churches (and, in a few cases, large houses) have to offer; but they are meant to whet the reader's appetite to explore the subject further. Now and then, we step a few miles across the diocesan boundary: why not? for, after all, art knows no bounds.

This little book, if nothing else, may encourage readers to explore towns and villages new to them; and also underline the welcome fact that the art of stained glass - though hit hard after the Reformation - is now very much alive and flourishing, as we head towards the twenty-first century.

In these hallowed places, where the beauty of the designer's and glazier's art is so manifest, take time to give thanks for them and their work, each in his or her day and generation; to praise the Lord who gave them the talent; and to reflect on the glimpse which St. John the Divine gives us, of the coloured foundations of New Jerusalem:

> "The building of the wall was of jasper:
> and the city was pure gold, like unto
> clear glass. And the foundations of the
> wall of the city were garnished with all
> manner of precious stones. The first foun-
> dation was jasper; the second, sapphire;
> the third, a chalcedony; the fourth, an emerald;
> the fifth, sardonyx; the sixth, sardius;
> the seventh, chrysolite; the eighth, beryl;
> the ninth, a topaz; the tenth, a chrysoprasus;
> the eleventh, a jacinth; the twelfth, an
> amethyst. And the twelve gates were twelve
> pearls; every several gate was of one pearl:
> and the street of the city was pure gold, as it
> were transparent glass." (Rev. 21:18 - 21)

Joyce Critchlow.

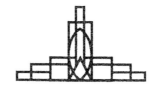

Chapter One.

ANCIENT AND
HERALDIC GLASS.

Grisaille.

Derbyshire churches are relatively well endowed with the ancient glass known as grisaille, popular in the thirteenth and fourteenth centuries. This was essentially a white glass on which was painted or stained, often in grey monochrome, armorial bearings, leaves, flowers or geometrical designs. The largest surviving collection of grisaille is at SS. Mary & Barlok, Norbury, where coats of arms from the nobles of the House of Lancaster are portrayed, together with lozenges, frets, flowers and a variety of circles. One of the flower-designs is thought to be unique to Norbury (see Ch.6). The chancel is a virtual "lantern", with its eight large side windows almost complete with the grisaille glass with which they were glazed prior to 1348. Their coats of arms, including those of the local Fitzherberts, are practically intact. Norbury's patterned grisaille glass has greatly influenced the windows in North Carolina's Duke University memorial chapel, to Washington Duke and his sons.

Several grisaille fragments from St. Edmund, Fenny Bentley, are now in the window of the Boothby Chapel, St. Oswald, Ashbourne. They form a pattern to a broad band of shields and disconnected pieces across the window. Here, again, we find the Norbury Fitzherbert arms, together with those of de Warrenne, Cokayne, Longford, Earl of Surrey, Stopford and Bradbourne. Among the designs on this old glass is a head of St. Christopher, a head of St. Modwena, and Christ in benediction.

Portions of fourteenth-century geometric grisaille glass can be seen at St. Wilfrid, Egginton; and the east window in the south aisle at St. John the Baptist, Ault Hucknall contains some stained grisaille and yellow glass, of 1527, installed by Sir John Savage. Above the figures of

Elizabeth Savage, her daughter and two sons, are remains of the figures of Jesus and His Mother, and two saints. Below the window is the grave of Thomas Hobbes, the philosopher (1588-1679).

There are two grisaille medallions at St. Giles' Chapel, Caldwell (see Ch.2), and fragments at All Saints, Risley, and St. Matthew, Morley (see Ch. 5).

But grisaille is not the oldest glass in Derbyshire: a lancet window depicting St. Michael, at All Saints, Dalbury, for long assigned to the thirteenth century, has by the art historian Dr.P.A. Newton, been dated early twelfth century. Carefully restored by the York Glaziers' Trust in 1980, it no longer qualifies for Pevsner's description as "blackened". If Newton's date is correct, this stands to be the county's most ancient surviving glass. St. Michael is depicted in the "orans" Romanesque style, winged, with hands palm-outwards, and large staring eyes.

Prior to this, the thirteenth-century lancet at St. Oswald, Ashbourne, with its five medallions, had held seniority. The five Nativity scenes depicted are 1) the Angel appearing to the Shepherds, 2) the visit of the Magi to Herod, 3) the Adoration of the Magi, 4) Christ's Presentation in the Temple, and 5) Herod's massacre of the Innocents. The glass was well restored in 1879.

Holy Cross, Upper Langwith, has a medallion of old glass; and three roundels in the chancel windows at St. John the Baptist, Dronfield, depict musicians of the thirteenth or fourteenth century. Dronfield, as were many other Derbyshire churches, was considerably richer in heraldic glass before the Reformation.

Old glass abounds in St. Nicholas Chapel, Haddon Hall: four lancets date from the time of Henry II (1133-1189); the lower west window of the nave is fourteenth-century, but other glass of the period was stolen in 1828. There is good fifteenth-century glass in the chancel, still bearing its Black-Letter inscription, that it was given to the chapel by Richard Vernon and his wife Benedicta: Orate pro animabus Riccardi Vernon et Benedicte uxoris eius qui fecerunt anno d(omi)ni 1427.

Pieces of ancient glass can be seen in the rear window of the clergy vestry at St. Cuthbert, Doveridge; a fourteenth-century east window at St. Mary the Virgin, Denby, with scenes of Christ's Baptism, Crucifixion, Resurrection and Ascension; and stained glass of the same date at St. Andrew, Cubley, showing in the chancel windows St. Catherine with her wheel, and a kneeling saint.

St. Peter, Hope, has beautiful glass of the fifteenth century in its aisle and clerestories, two windows containing glass after Leonardo's Annunciation in the Galleria Uffizi, Firenze. St. Giles, Hartington, has a rose among its fragments of old glass.

St. Matthew, Morley, Has a wealth of fifteenth-century glass from Dale Abbey, depicting the story of Robert of Knaresborough (with a small amount of later glass); the Invention of the True Cross; and St. Ursula and her virgins (see Ch. 5). In Dale Abbey Church today there are fragments of the fifteenth century in a couple of windows. All Saints, Bradbourne, has pieces from this period in a window of the chancel, which include the Arms of Edensor. Other fragments can be seen at St. Mary, Mappleton and St. Mary, Sutton Scarsdale.

Heraldic Glass.

Mediaeval glass was rich in heraldry: St. Oswald, Ashbourne, has twenty coats of arms on old painted glass (now incorporated with modern glass) commemorating leading families. Prominent are the Arms of John of Gaunt, Duke of Lancaster (d.1399), harking back to the time when Ashbourne in the Honor of Tutbury was part of the Duchy of Lancaster. There are also the Arms of Knyveton: Henry de Kniveton gave this glass c.1399, to commemorate his family's founding of a chantry in 1392. At Kniveton itself, in St. Michael & All Angels, the family arms are again portrayed in old glass, in a chancel window.

Norbury's Lady Chapel has, in the lower part of its east window, the Arms of Nicholas Fitzherbert and his first wife Alice Bothe. Nicholas is shown with the eight sons this marriage produced, and Alice with their five daughters.

Arms of the Blounts, Gresleys and Wastneys are all that remain of an original eight, in the east windows of All Saints, Mugginton. Of the same period, in the south window of the chancel, is a lozenge pane depicting a ciborium, (a box for the consecrated bread).

One of the windows at St. Peter, Netherseal, has fragments of old heraldic glass. More can be found in St. Peter, Hope; and at St. Chad, Longford, are some small heraldic shields in old stained glass, which used to be in the nearby hall.

Long gone, is the elaborate coat of arms in the east window at St. James, Norton, noted by Bassano when he visited the church c. 1710. At St. Michael, South Normanton, Bassano attributed a coat of arms to

Banaster, which exercised the minds of later historians, since the Banaster family had no known connections with either the church or manor of Normanton. Possibly, since the Leighs of Adlington bore the same arms, this glass was a commemoration of the time when they were patrons of St. Michael's

The armorial windows commemorating Sir Thomas and John Fitzherbert, in Padley Chapel, are a reminder of a time in history of which Protestants can feel justly ashamed (see Chs. 4 and 5).

At St. Mary. Sutton Scarsdale, the fifteenth-century John Leake enriched the church with stained glass, of which only a few fragments remain, while the Arms of the Leakes and their marriages are preserved on the roof-bosses.

The old glass in All Saints, Wingerworth, is white and yellow, with a crown-and-diamond pattern. Compare these with the yellow-and white diamonds of old glass showing a pattern of fleur-de-lis and trefoils, in a nave window at St. Giles, Killamarsh. A window in the south chancel here has a fifteenth-century crowned Virgin with sceptre, the Child Jesus holding a ringlet of her hair. Bassano, on his travels here c.1710, noted a coat of arms in the east window of the chancel, of the Whittington family, lords of the manor adjacent.

The Devonshire coat of arms can be found in a south chancel window at St. Michael (C. of E.), Hathersage; and beautiful glass of a more recent date in memory of Lord Frederick Charles Cavendish, murdered in 1882 in Phoenix Park, Dublin, is in the east window of the Cavendish Chapel at St. Peter, Edensor. Lord Frederick is also commemorated in the east window at Charles, King & Martyr, Peak Forest, together with Lord Edward Cavendish, who in 1876 stood most of the cost (£6,000) of the present church. The window shows Christ as Saviour of the World, and is interesting in its impact, being the central light of the five-light window, flanked by four clear lights.

Mediaeval heraldic glass in SS. Peter & Paul, Eckington, has been cleaned and restored by the York Glaziers' Trust, though in earlier centuries this church was considerably richer in heraldry; only fragments remain today of the earlier abundance of Darcy arms - John, Lord Darcy, having been granted the manor of Eckington by Edward III in 1340.

The case of St. John the Baptist, Dethick, is worse: nothing now remains of the glass of which J.C.Cox (1875) remarked: "It was formerly well supplied, although much mutilated at an early date" J.C.Cox, Churches

10

of Derbyshire, Vol.I (1875), p.45. arms including Ferrers, Babington, Sacheverell, Walton, Leche and Dethick.

Prior to the late sixteenth century, St. Mary & All Saints, Chesterfield, was rich in heraldic glass, which had all but disappeared by the time of the 1843 restoration. Cox said, critically, of a few remaining fragments of the Plantagenet arms, preserved in the upper tracery of the south window of the Foljambe Chapel: "They have been there inserted by an ignorant hand, for the arms of Wake are inverted and resting on the top of Plantagenet. In the same place may also be seen two more of the old shields, gu., a cross moline, arg., and arg., a cross moline, gu., and this is all that·now remains of the ancient heraldic glazing of All Saints', Chesterfield, whose windows once shone with the many coloured record of generation after generation of its time-honoured families", Ibid., p. 161.

At St. Peter, Alstonefield, portions of old heraldic glass came to light in a hole in the wall near the chancel door, and now grace the east window of the north aisle. They once formed part of the Arms of Mundy. Vincent Mundy was the local Lord of the Manor, c. 1570. The six-hundred-year-old armorial bearings of Munday can be seen in a window at All Saints, Mackworth, above an alabaster tomb of Edward Munday, the grandson of a sixteenth-century Lord Mayor of London.

The Turbutts, Lords of the Manor of Ogston, have a commemorative east window in Holy Cross, Morton. It is an exact replica of the window which stood in the old church (1850). Some fragments of old glass have been preserved in the tower.

The vivid east window in St. Mary the Virgin, Wirksworth, resplendent with reds and blues, and designed by Henry Isaac Stevens of Derby, was made in 1855 by William Warrington of London, to commemorate Francis Edward Hurt of Alderwasley (d. 1854). It incorporates the arms of the Lowe and Fawne families, together with the Hurt bearings.

Lords of the local manor, the Gells of Hopton Hall, are commemorated in glass at St. Margaret, Carsington. Squire Philip Lyttelton Gell is portrayed with a halo, together with his supposed forebear, the Roman soldier Gellius, St. Helena, St. John, St. Margaret, St. Giles and St. Philip. The women of the Gell family from 1452 to 1862, and their men from 1404 to 1926, are also listed.

Perhaps the most famous glazier of the late seventeenth century, Henry Gyles of York, was responsible for the glass commemorating John, Lord Frecheville, in St. John the Baptist, Staveley. In 1676, an excess of

Protestant zeal had all but eliminated the staining of glass for churches; the scarce examples of this time were produced by giving the glass a succession of yellow enamelling, varying the resultant colours from yellow to a rich red.

Gyles is thought to have imported his glass from France, and used much heraldry around the central figure of John, Lord Frecheville: arms including those of Monboucher, Darcy, Leake, Findern, Babington, Dethick and Grey, in addition to those of Frecheville - against an elaborate background of flowers and cherubim. John (d.1682) by all accounts was an extrovert: last of his line and the one and only peer in the family, he allied himself with the Royalists; decorated by Charles II, he was made Governor of York, and so met Henry Gyles the master-glazier.

Pieces of sixteenth-century glass can be seen at a number of other Derbyshire churches, including St. Anne, Ambergate and All Saints, Ockbrook; but for our last example of heraldic glass in this chapter, we come to more recent times. In All Saints, Trusley is memorial glass to the Coke family, of nineteen- and twentieth - century date; but near the door is a glass screen etched by David Peace, given by Mrs. Frances Coke-Steel in memory of her husband Ronald (1901-1963). The arms depicted are largely those of the old Coke family but with the canton charged with a caltrap: the cessation of the male line of the family came with the death in 1944 of John and Edward Coke. Frances, heiress to the family arms, and her husband Mr. Ronald Steel, then took the name Coke-Steel, and so the arms were altered. The steel caltrap was a four-spiked weapon thrown in mediaeval times in the path of enemy cavalry, to baffle their advance.

The inscription on the screen is timeless:

> "He honoured the past,
> rejoiced in the present,
> and built for the future".

Take time to observe the crucial position of this beautiful screen: on entering the church, the motto is easily read; on leaving, it is masked with the patterning. The sun and crescents, largely engraved with a high-rev carborundum, seem to pick up light from the door nearby.

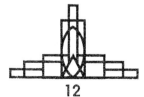

12

Chapter Two.

DESIGNERS AND THEIR ART.

In the fourteenth century a school of glaziers based in Lenton was responsible for much work in Nottinghamshire and adjacent counties. Derbyshire examples of the "Lenton School" still extant include grotesques at St. Peter, Netherseal; fragments at St. John the Baptist, Staveley; a border in the east windows at St. Lawrence, Whitwell; and border pieces in the south chancel windows, St. John the Baptist, Dronfield: the latter show baboons and quaint figures for which the School was noted, but also saints and angels, among whom is St. John the Baptist, and St. Cecilia at her organ.

Two brothers, Abraham and Bernard van Linge, came to England from Holland around 1621; both glaziers, Abraham stayed until 1641, or thereabouts, Bernard returning to his homeland in 1628. Some authorities believe that one of the windows in St. Chad, Wilne, is a van Linge.

William Warrington (1796-1869), a London glazier until 1866, has a Virgin and Child window (1845) in the south chancel at St. Giles, Killamarsh; a south-west lancet at St. Oswald, Ashbourne (1857), and work in the Lady Chapel and St. Katherine's Chapel, St. Mary, Chesterfield. He also did much restoration work in 1847 of the c.1480 Dale Abbey glass, purchased in 1539 after the Dissolution and transferred to St. Matthew, Morley (see Chs. 4 and 5).

The Belgium glazier, Jean Baptiste Capronnier (1814-1891) worked in a wide range of vivid colours, and many of his windows can still be seen in Yorkshire churches. Those which have survived in Derbyshire include the three-light east window (in the style of Burne-Jones), in All Saints, Lullington, which he painted in Brussels; and one at St. Matthew, Pentrich.

Frederick Preedy (1820-1898), a Worcester architect and glazier, was responsible for the east window in St. John the Baptist, Bamford (1860).

Sir Edward Burne-Jones (1833-1898), a co-founder of the firm of Morris & Co. in 1875, has several surviving works in the county, and his distinctive style was copied by a number of contemporary and later artists. In St. Helen, Darley Dale, his south transept window illustrates the "Song of Songs"; nearby, All Saints, Matlock, has three lancets in the east wall of the chancel. All Saints, Youlgreave, has two of his works: one in the chancel south window (1894), and a beautiful Salvator Mundi (1876). There are also Burne-Jones windows in Thornbridge Hall, Great Longstone. Copies of his work are in Holy Trinity, Ashford-in-the-Water (showing St. John the Evangelist and Pope Gregory the Great); and two windows in the north wall of St. John the Baptist, Ault Hucknall, are in the Burne-Jones tradition.

In the north transept window at St. Mary, Wirksworth, set off by Sir George Gilbert Scott's delicate tracery of 1871/2, is glass from the Morris workshop, Burne-Jones' depicting Christ, saints and prophets; and Morris' own, angels.

William Morris (1834-1896), together with the designer Peter Paul Marshall and C.J. Faulkner, founded the London firm of Morris, Marshall & Faulkner in 1861. After a re-organisation and his teaming-up with Burne-Jones in 1875, the firm was known as Morris & Co.

St. Helen, Pinxton, has a south transept window from the earlier days (1870-1); but later examples, with unmistakable Burne-Jones influence, include All Saints, Youlgreave (1897), and a window in St. Bartholomew, Chesterfield (1915), as well as the work already mentioned at Darley Dale, Ashford-in-the-Water and Wirksworth.

In All Saints, Bakewell, is glass by the artist, writer and designer, Sir Henry Holiday (1839-1927). One of Holiday's contemporaries, Thomas F. Curtis (1845-1924), joined forces in 1883 with Thomas Ward (1808-1870) and Henry Hughes (1822-1883). This was a period when glass designers were moving from workshop to workshop, as businesses expanded or contracted according to supply and demand: Ward had already been a co-founder of Ward & Nixon, and had teamed up with Hughes to form Ward & Hughes, c.1850, prior to the latter's linking up with Curtis.

Work from this triumvirate can be seen in the north wall of the nave at Christ Church, King Sterndale: one, dated 1908, in memory of Harriet Hombersley (nee Pickford), 1820-1898, titled "Blessed are the Pure in Heart", shows St. Agnes with a lamb, above a gruesome cameo of the

14

saint kneeling before her executioner; the other window (1910), is in memory of Charles Hampden Pickford (1816-1882), and shows St. Peter with the Keys, above a cameo of a Galilean fishing scene.

A window in the north aisle of St. Helen, Darley Dale, shows Resurrection witnesses (1860), and is the work of the firm of James Powell & Sons, of Whitefriars. Founded in 1834 by James Powell (d. 1840), who was succeeded by Arthur Powell, it closed as recently as 1973.

The Birmingham firm of John Hardman & Co., founded in 1838 (for glass, in 1845), is responsible for the west window in St. John the Baptist, Tideswell; windows in All Saints, Bakewell (1859-1892); work in the west window and the south transept, St. Mary, Chesterfield (1875); and the south transept south window (1874) and the north transept north window (1877), St. Oswald, Ashbourne; and the south aisle east window, St. Peter, Edensor(1882).

The south transept south window in All Saints, Bakewell, is by W. Wailes, the Newcastle grocer-turned-glazier, who opened his stained glass business in 1839, improving his talent in the early 1840s by working with Augustus Pugin; Wailes became a prolific glazier, and many British churches have benefited from his characteristically vivid designs.

The London firm of Clayton & Bell was founded in 1855 by John Richard Clayton (1827-1913) and Alfred Bell (1832-1895). Some years prior to this, Bell had supplied James Powell & Sons with a number of designs. The west window in St. Anne, Derby, is from Clayton & Bell's workshops (1886).

In 1855, Francis P. Barraud (1824-1900) founded the firm of Lavers & Barraud with Nathaniel W. Lavers (1828-1911). Lavers prior to this (1852) had teamed up with Alfred Bell. In 1860 Barraud and Lavers were joined by the scholar-designer Nathaniel H.J. Westlake (1833-1921), who wrote The History of Design in Painted Glass. The tripartite firm made the fine east window in old St. Michael, Queen Street, Derby.

Another trio of glaziers founded the Covent Garden firm of Heaton, Butler & Bayne, in 1862: Clement Heaton (1824-1882), James Butler (1830-1913) and Robert T. Bayne (1837-1915) were responsible for the great east window in St. John the Baptist, Tideswell (1875); the west window in St. Giles, Great Longstone, in the same year (and other windows in St. Giles, see Ch.3); work on the north wall, St. Mary, Chesterfield (1890); and the chancel windows, All Saints, Matlock (1920). Just across the diocesan boundary, the east window in St. James, Taxal, was designed by Heaton, Butler & Bayne, and depicts three women at the Tomb of Christ.

In 1868, John Burlison (1843-1891) and Thomas J, Grylls (1845-1913), founded the London firm of Burlison & Grylls, which produced fine stained glass until 1953, among which is the west window in St Oswald, Ashbourne; and memorial windows to the sixth Lord Vernon in All Saints, Sudbury (1885).

But perhaps the artist who has impacted most on Derbyshire stained glass, is Charles Eamer Kempe (1834-1907), the founder, in 1869, of the London firm of Kempe & Co., which closed in 1934. Noted for the range of colours and designs, and no less for his "signature" of a sheaf of corn, and for incorporating peacock feather "eyes" in his angels' wings, Kempe's work - like that of Burne-Jones - also inspired many other designers.

The east window at St. Michael (C. of E.), Hathersage, which originally stood in Derwent Church, is his. In St. John the Baptist, Buxton, are two windows on the north side, each preserving Kempe's sheaf of corn, in the bottom left-hand corner. The east window here is of Kempe style, but there is no corn visible. There are peacock "eyes" on his angels' wings in the St. Peter window, in the south aisle at St. Peter, Hope (1879), and the chancel windows here have his sheaf of corn. Peacock "eyes" again feature in his winged angels in the east window, St. Oswald, Asbourne (1896), and in two other windows. At All Saints, Youlgreave, is a Kempe Nativity window of 1883, and a nave south window of 1893. In 1896, he made the north chancel window for St. Peter, Somersal Herbert. At St, James the Less, New Mills, are his Crucifixion (1880) and Four Evangelists' windows (1888).

More of his work can be seen at All Saints, Bakewell. A baptistery window, depicting the Nunc Dimittis, at St. Peter, Snelston (1907), was made by Kempe and his son-in-law, Walter Tower (1873-1955), chairman of the firm from 1907 until 1934. It is possible that Tower was responsible for the World War I commemorative window in St. John the Baptist, Buxton, which has peacock "eyes" in St. Michael's wings.

The Kempe-trained glazier and church designer, Sir J. Ninian Comper (1864-1960), made the east window of the Holy Cross Chapel, St. Mary, Chesterfield (1941), and also the St. Peter's Chapel window here (1943).

In Christopher Whall (1849-1924), we have not only a glazier of the highest rank, but also the leader of the "Arts & Crafts" movement, which was to impose its mark on stained glass in Britain for many years. One of his best windows can be seen in the south aisle at St. Oswald,

Ashbourne (1905), with a unique blend of colours. It commemorates two sisters, Monica and Dorothea Turnbull, who died in 1901 at the ages of 19 and 21 respectively, from burns received when the dress of one caught fire and the other went to her aid. St. Cecilia is in the centre of the window: she has fallen asleep at her organ, but an angel is at the keyboard, and his notes are taken up by other angels. Two saints at the side have the faces of the two sisters, and below these a path leads to the Heavenly City, through a lovely garden (see Ch.7).

Christopher Whall's daughter, Veronica (1887-1970), was a designer in her own right.

In St. John the Baptist, Matlock, the moulding of the semi-octagonal plaster ceiling, as well as some of the stained glass, was designed by a follower of Christopher Whall, Louis Davies (1861-1914), who is probably better known for his beautiful series of windows for Dunblane Cathedral, near Stirling.

Frederick C. Eden (1864-1955), who was an architect as well as a stained glass designer, was responsible for two windows in the Lady Chapel in St. Peter, Hope: the Annunciation (1914) and the Adoration of the Shepherds (1919).

St. Stephen, Borrowash (built 1890) has work by the founder of Bromsgrove Guild of Applied Arts (1906), Archibald J. Davies (1877-1953). In St. John the Baptist, Chelmorton, the east window is by the firm of Jones & Willis (1880).

Among the women stained glass designers and glaziers, Caroline Townshend (d.1944) was deservedly well known. A Fabian and Arts & Crafts glazier, she joined forces for a time with Joan Howson (1885-1964), to produce, among others, beautiful work for the Jesus Chapel in St. Mary, Prittlewell, Essex. In Derbyshire, Christ Church, King Sterndale, has five of her windows: the three lights at the east end, in memory of Mary Ada Pickford (1884-1934), showing the Good Shepherd flanked by the Sower, Reaper, Ruth the Gleaner and the Good Samaritan - above which are the Diocesan Arms of Lichfield, Southwell and Derby, commemorating the episcopal history of the church since its building in 1847. In the south wall of the nave are two more Townshend windows, one depicting in vivid reds and purples St. Thomas More, above a cameo of Chelsea Old Church; this is in memory of Sir William Pickford, Lord Sterndale (1848-1923) who, when in London, used to worship at that church. The adjacent window shows St. Anne, above a cameo of the Houses of Parliament; like the east windows, it is in memory of Mary Ada Pickford, who was one of the first women M.P.s, and respresented

North Hammersmith. Caroline Townshend's motif - a small bird with outstretched wings - is visible in the bottom right-hand corner of this window.

Martin Travers (1886-1948), studied under Sir Ninian Comper and subsequently taught at the Royal College of Art. An early example of his work is in the east window in St. Andrew, Swanwick. It is thought to have been made by Joseph E. Nuttgens (1893-1983), who in 1953 also made the west window here. Nuttgens had been a follower of Christopher Whall, and after Kempe is probably the best known glazier to students of Derbyshire churches - though many other examples of his work survive, notably his "Life of St. Francis" (1943) in Aldwick-le-Street Church, Yorkshire.

His signature, a nut in one corner, is not always present - as in the Annunciation window (1948) in the Blessed Sacrament Chapel, St. Peter, Snelston. Other Nuttgens windows are at St. Cuthbert, Doveridge; in the Lady Chapel, SS. Mary & Barlok, Norbury; the north and south windows of the sanctuary, St. Thomas, Derby; and a window of 1959 in St. Bartholomew, Chesterfield.

In St. Mary, Chesterfield, are three works of Christopher R. Webb (1886-1966), who, with his glazier-brother, Geoffrey (1879-1954), was a pupil of Kempe.

Margaret Aldrich Rope, a retired Arts & Crafts trained glazier, formerly of the Birmingham School of Art, has a window in the Arts & Crafts tradition in the St. Peter Chapel in St. Mary, Chesterfield.

Another contemporary glazier, Patrick Reyntiens, of Somerset, has work in Derby Cathedral, having installed two abstract windows by Ceri Richards (see Ch. 7).

From Gloucestershire, the contemporary glazier, Edward Payne, has work of 1968 in All Saints, Ockbrook (which also has an east window of c.1500 depicting the evangelists). Edward is the son of the glazier Henry Payne (1868-1940), who was a pupil of Christopher Whall.

St. Giles, Matlock, has an east window of 1969 by the contemporary glazier Lawrence Lee; and in 1971 a five-light window by the artist and stained glass designer Brian Clarke was installed at St. Michael, Birchover.

One could continue: Derbyshire is not only rich in its quantity of stained glass, but also in its range of designers and glaziers. Space here allows for only the briefest mention of Barber of York (the great east window in

St. Peter, Derby); R.B. Edmundson, the Manchester designer of the window to the left of the Blackwall memorial in the north choir aisle, St. Mary, Wirksworth; and Harold Gibbons, whose east window of the Lady Chapel, St. Mary, Chesterfield, shows the Nativity.

In St. Giles, Matlock and Christ Church, Burbage, can be seen "Light of the World" windows, after William Holman Hunt's best-known work.

Foreign Glass.

Mention has already been made of the Belgian glazier, Jean Baptiste Capronnier, but Derbyshire has a fair variety of foreign glass:

St. Anne, Amergate, is a relatively modern church (1897), but in the porch are two small windows containing pieces of old glass discovered in a box in a cottage. As well as English fragments, there are some Flemish. A few pieces are thought to be of fifteenth-century date; an Ascension panel, sixteenth century; a Crucifixion piece, eighteenth century; and a tiny roundel came from Shrewsbury Abbey.

Flemish glass can also be seen in the four-light east window of the south choir chapel at St. Michael, Kirk Langley. Dated "1631", it is signed "Jane Seye". In the north aisle is more Flemish glass.

"Probably Flemish" (Pevsner), is the seventeenth century stained glass in the Willoughby Chapel windows, St. Chad, Wilne. Brought over and restored after the Civil War, the glass largely survived a ferocious fire on 7th March 1917. It shows the Ascension; the Crucifixion (backed by a domed church and mediaeval fortified town); and the Nativity, where the faces of the worshippers are distincly Flemish.

In All Saints, Youlgreave, in the north aisle, is a window commemorating Rennie Crompton Waterhouse, of Lomberdale Hall, Middleton-by-Youlgreave, who was killed in 1915 at Gallipoli. It is made up of fragments inside wreaths of green, collected by his brother from the devastated Ypres Cathedral, and other Flanders churches.

Two medallions of c. 1400 glass in the west window at St. Giles, Caldwell, came from Nuremberg, and depict Joab's killing of Abner, and the Resurrection with Roman soldiers around Christ's tomb.

Beyond the county boundary, at Twycross, is twelfth - to sixteenth century glass (among the oldest stained glass in England), which originated from the Sainte Chapelle in Paris, and the Abbey Church of St. Denis a few miles outside the city. Again outside the county, but nearer home, visitors to St. Batholomew, Longnor, can see Venetian glass in the east window.

Rose Windows.

High in the west wall of St. John the Baptist, Bamford, is perhaps the most beautiful rose window in the diocese, in the Decorated style, and depicting the symbols of the evangelists.

The Rev. W.J. Stanton, godson to Juliana Bowyer Stanton, the local lady of the manor, gave the lovely rose window at the west end of St. Peter, Snelston.

Above the Burne-Jones lancets in the chancel at All Saints, Matlock, is another rose-window - while the one at St. Michael, Holbrook, commemorating the Rev. William M. Leake (vicar 1840-1877), was originally at the east end of the chancel, but was transferred to the west end when a new south aisle was added after a severe fire in 1907.

The large, elegant Decorated east window at St. James, Brassington, was replaced in the extensive restoration of 1879-1881, by a smaller rose window, in memory of William Knowles (d. 11th October, 1859), given by his family.

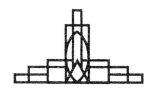

Chapter Three.

The Bible in Glass.

Old Testament Scenes.

These, naturally, are not as prevalent as those of the life of Christ, or even of later saints; but a pilgrimage round the Derbyshire churches in search of Old Testament windows can be both a rewarding and most enjoyable experience. You may in fact be surprised to discover that they are more numerous than expected. This chapter by no means exhausts the examples.

In Ch. 2, mention has been made of the Nuremberg glass in St. Giles, Caldwell, one roundel of which depicts the slaying of Abner by Joab, David's nephew and captain (II Sam. 3:27). Much younger (1856) is the Perpendicular west window in St. Michael (C. of E.), Hathersage, its richly coloured three lights given in memory of William and Mary Eyre showing Noah, Belshazzar and Job.

St. Giles, Great Longstone, also has a west window of Victorian glass (1875, Heaton & Co.), Commemorating George Eyre, it depicts David with his harp. In the south aisle the beautiful four-light window east of the south door has Naomi, Ruth, Dorcas and Lydia, thus spanning fourteen centuries or so of Bible history. Another Heaton window, it was installed in 1897 by the prime restorer of the church, G.T.Wright, in memory of his sister Emma who had died three years earlier; she was the widow of Longstone's vicar from 1877 to 1892, the Rev. John H. Bullivant.

The glass in the west window, St. Mary, Chesterfield, shows Joshua battling for the hill country of the Promised Land. He and his soldiery are under a canopy in a tented field, and over the battlefield itself the sun and the moon are stationary (Josh. 10: 12, 13).

We need to cross the diocesan boundary a little way, to enjoy the bounty of stained glass in the Church of the Holy Angels, Hoar Cross. Saints and martyrs, prophets and kings spanning around three millenia, are depicted in glass designed by G.F. Bodley and made by Burlison & Grylls (see Ch. 2): some have said, the finest of their art.

The north transept window depicts David and Isaiah; Jeremiah and Zechariah; St. Alban and St. Wilfred (b.634); St. Thomas Becket (b.1117); and St. Hugh of Lincoln (1146). It was given in memory of the Rev. Frederick Heathcote Sutton, Vicar of Brant Broughton, who had given great help to G.F. Bodley in the decoration of the church. Four biblical texts run beneath the figures: "They loved not their lives unto death" (Rev. 12:11); "The Lord is King for ever and ever" (Ps. 10:16); "The zeal of Thine house hath even me consumed" (Ps. 69:9); and "Blessed are the meek, for they shall inherit the earth" (Mt. 5:5).

A small pointed window in the south aisle features St. Peter and St. Andrew; but in the background, under a scroll with part of the Latin Credo, are Jeremiah and David (see Ch.4).

The brilliant Capronnier east window in All Saints, Lullington (see Ch.2), has scenes spanning the Old and New Testaments: Elijah's ascent to heaven; Shadrach, Meshach and Abednego in the burning fiery furnace; Daniel in the lions' den; Dives and Lazarus; the stoning of Stephen, the proto-martyr; Mary annointing the feet of Jesus; the Crucifixion and the Ascension.

The New Testament.

Examples of these windows are legion, and to mention them all would require several volumes. But linger first at the Church of the Holy Angels, Hoar Cross, where in the upper light of each window in both aisles, emblems of the Passion of Jesus are depicted: the pillar of scourging; the crown of thorns; the pierced Hands, Feet and Side; the handkerchief of St. Veronica, showing the "true image" (the veron ikon) of Jesus; the cockerel who reduced St. Peter to contrite tears; the reed and sponge; the soldiers' dice; and Judas' thirty pieces of silver.

A fine St. Peter window, on the east wall of the north aisle in St. Giles, Great Longstone, was given in memory of the Rev. G.H. Brown, vicar here from 1845 to 1847, and his brother Thomas. All four of the north aisle windows were installed at the time of the restoration of 1873: all are thought to be the work of Heaton, Butler & Bayne; the other three depict the Presentation of Christ in the Temple (for more of these Nunc Dimittis windows, see Ch.5); St. Giles, the patron saint of the church; and St. Paul.

In All Saints, Kedleston, are windows of the nine Marys, and one with St. George and the dragon. The Marys were designed by Frederick C. Eden (see Ch. 2), and executed by J. Fisher. They commemorate Lord Curzon's first wife, Mary Leiter.

Sixteenth-century representations of the Evangelists can be seen at All Saints, Ockbrook. Originally these windows stood in Wigston Hospital, Leicestershire, being brought to Ockbrook in the nineteenth century by a member of the Pares family, whose memorials can be found in the chancel.

At St. Andrew, Cubley, the east window is fourteenth century, showing in delicate colours the Nativity, Crucifixion, the Blessed Virgin Mary, and three Apostles. An unusual representation of the Virgin can be seen in SS. Mary & Barlok, Norbury, where in the Lady Chapel east window is St. Anne teaching the infant Mary to read. (For the later saints in this window, see Ch.4.).

The four Evangelists (Matthew, Mark, Luke and John) share two windows in the south aisle in St. Michael (C. of E.), Hathersage. They flank a memorial to Herbert Lander, a local G.P. at the turn of the century.

At the west end of All Saints, Mackworth, is a window of 1886 showing St. Peter's deliverance from prison; and in Charles, King & Martyr, Peak Forest, is a vivid window in the side chapel showing the Good Samaritan; it is in memory of Robert and Sarah Needham, and their two infant sons.

In St. Oswald, Ashbourne, the 1872 bapistery window by Burlison & Grylls shows in the upper level of the two side lights two angels, one with the affirmation "I acknowledge one Baptism", and the other with the completion of the article "For the remission of sins". The various panels depict Noah and the ark - imagery fulfilled in the text "The like figure whereunto even Baptism doth also now save us" (I Pet. 3:21); God's covenant with Abraham: "I will establish My covenant between Me and Thee" (Gen. 18:7); the Presentation of Christ in the temple: "Sanctify unto Me all the firstborn" (Ex. 13:2); Jesus' baptism: "This is My beloved Son" (Mt.3:7); Jesus blessing the children: "Suffer the little children to come unto Me" (Mt. 10:14); Jesus commissioning the disciples: "Go ye therefore, and teach all nations" (Mt.28:19); and Ananias baptising Paul: "Arise and be baptised, and wash away thy sins" (Acts 22:16).

Jesus' baptism features in the Capronnier windows at St. Matthew, Pentrich, together with scenes of the Last Supper, the Ascension, and Dorcas (Acts 9:36). As Christ the Good Shepherd. He is portrayed by

Powell, in the three-light window of the north wall at St. Wystan, Repton. Other Powell windows here show the Raising of the Widow's Son; the Annunciation: St. John the Evangelist, the Blessed Virgin and the Miracle at Cana; the Nunc Dimittis; an upper fragment of late fourteenth, or early fifteenth-century glass, depicting (it is thought) one of the kings of Mercia; Jesus commissioning St. Peter; and Jesus blessing the little children.

Not far over the diocesan boundary, Rocester Church has a beautiful window painted by de Morgan, showing two scenes from the life of Jesus.

Jesus' Birth, Baptism, Crucifixion, Resurrection and Ascension are depicted in the five windows of the apse in St. Chad, Derby. These commemorate the ministry of the first incumbent, the Rev Thomas Edwin Bradbury (1878-1886). Their cost was £183/15/-.

High in a clerestory window in St. Wilfrid, West Hallam, is James the Less, with a book and the club which brought about his martyrdom.

St. James the Great (Apostle, and brother of St. John) has, as one of his emblems, the scallop-shell. This can be seen in the upper lights of most of the nave windows in the church dedicated to him, at Taxal. Also here, the east window (by Heaton, Butler & Bayne) shows three women at Jesus' tomb - while the west window shows Jesus blessing the little children. The latter scene is also represented in a window in the south aisle of St. John the Baptist, Tibshelf. It was given by a teacher who saw four generations of local children pass through her school during her thirty five years' tenure. Tibshelf's east window has a lovely scene of the Resurrection.

At St. Michael and All Angels, Stanton-by-Dale, three vivid windows portray the Nativity, the Crucifixion, Jesus with His disciples, and SS. Luke and John. The Ascension can be seen in the east window at St. Margaret, Wormhill - a window commemorating the Bagshawes - for it was here that the "Apostle of the Peak", William Bagshawe, preached his first sermon.

In the east window at St. John, Alkmonton, are scenes of Jesus' Nativity, Resurrection and Ascension; while in the west wall are windows showing St. Paul and Lydia of Thyatira (Acts 16:14).

In memory of the Rev. Charles Bates, vicar 1817 -1853, the three-light east window of St. Edmund, Castleton, shows the Good Shepherd, Jesus' Charge to Peter, and Jesus preaching. On the south side of the

24

chancel are good modern windows showing St. Edmund and Dorcas.

Johnson memorial windows in St. Edmund, Allestree, depict the Annunciation, Nativity and Nunc Dimittis. Christ's Resurrection, and SS. Michael and Gabriel, can be seen in the fourteenth-century east window at St. Michael, Church Broughton. St. Gabriel's bringing of the Good News to Mary is part of a window in All Saints, Sawley, which also shows St. George. This window was given in memory of the Rev. Samuel Hey who was vicar here for forty-eight years until 1893. The Good Shepherd, resplendent in a brilliant red robe, is in a small lancet window in the same church; in the south aisle east window, Christ is seen blessing little children; and a modern window showing the "Communion of Saints". by Rosemary Everrett, is im memory of a churchwarden, Thomas Poyser.

Vivid red, gold and green brighten the "Good Shepherd" and "Christ with the Children" window, in All Saints, Bradley. More Gospel scenes are in St. Matthew, Hayfield: three triple-light windows are outstanding, and show respectively "Well done, good and faithful servant: enter thou into the joy of thy Lord"; the Nativity, Cricifixion and Ascension; and Jesus and the doctors, in the Jerusalem temple.

The east window in All Souls' Chapel, Church of the Holy Angels, Hoar Cross, shows Jesus as King of kings, with scenes of Calvary (copied from an Albert Dürer picture formerly at Temple Newsam), Gethsemane and in Joseph's garden.

St. Alkmund, Duffield, has windows spanning three mediaeval centuries, those in the chancel showing Jesus' last days in Jerusalem.

And in All Saints, Turnditch, can be seen a lovely west window in memory of the Rev. Francis Lambert Cursham, vicar here for forty years, who died in 1914. It depicts the Nunc Dimittis.

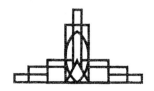

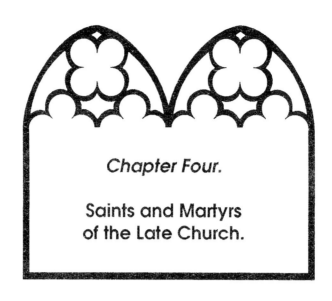

Chapter Four.

Saints and Martyrs
of the Late Church.

Before returning over the diocesan boundary, take a long look at the richness of Hoar Cross's stained glass hagiography and martyrology: here, in the east window, are St. Stephen the deacon, with a stone used in his martyrdom; St. Peter with his keys; the Virgin Mary; Archangel Michael; St. Paul, with the "sword of the Spirit" (Eph. 6:17); St. Laurence of Spain (c.A.D.258), with the gridiron on which he was martyred; St. Helena (A.D. 328), bearing her cross; St. Cecilia, patron saint of music; St. Mary Magdalene; the Virgin's mother, St. Anne; St. Catherine of Alexandria; St. Etheldreda (A.D. 679); St. Anselm of Canterbury; St. Edmund (A.D. 870), with a handful of arrows; St. Augustine, with a crucifixion banner; St. Chad, Bishop of Lichfield; St. Edward the Confessor (d.A.D. 1066); and St. Christopher. What a window!.

But turn now to the west window: in the centre is the Virgin and Child, with Joseph and the Magi; God Almighty, with arms wide in blessing; angels; St. Elizabeth and the Virgin; the Nunc Dimittis; Jesus in the temple with the doctors; prophetesses; SS. James and John; Isaiah and Zacharias; St. Bridget (A.D. 448) and St. Swithun; SS. Dorothy and Margaret; St. Thomas Aquinas (the "Schoolman", and author of Summa Theologiae, essential textbook for divinity students) and St. John Chrysostom, the "golden-tongued" preacher whose lot it was to fall foul of the Empress Eudoxia; in John's face the artist has shown a likeness of Dr. Liddon, one-time Canon of St. Paul's Cathedral, whose learning and preaching has been likened to the saint's.

In the south aisle's large transept window we have St. Chad again, with scenes of the Annunciation, and the virgin Mary with Jesus. Standing below, in rows of four, are St. Agnes (A.D. 304, see Christ Church, King Sterndale Ch.2); St. Francis of Assisi; St. Vincent (A.D. 304), with a book and palm; St. Margaret; the sceptre-holding St. Oswald; St. Elizabeth of Hungary (A.D. 1231), with a basket; St. Martin of Tours (c. A.D. 360); and St. Clare (A.D. 1253). Three smaller windows in this aisle portray St. Hubert (d. A.D. 737) and St. Louis (1214-1270); St. Aidan (A.D. 634) and St. Boniface (A.D. 755); St. Cyprian (A.D. 200-258) and St. Clement (A.D. 96).

The east window in the Chantry Chapel shows the Crucifixion, and the Last Words of Christ: Consummatum est (Jn. 12:30); while in the south window two warrior saints gaze out dispassionately: St. Adrian, Bishop of St. Andrews, and St. Maurice, the third-century patron saint of soldiers.

Four Western Church Fathers are in the north chancel window: St. Jerome (A.D. 342-420); St. Gregory the Great (A.D. 540); St. Augustine (A.D. 354-430); and St. Ambrose of Milan (A.D. 397). Opposite, in the south chancel window, are Eastern Church Fathers: St. John Chrysostom; St. Basil the Great (A.D. 379); St. Athanasius (c. A.D. 296); and St. Cyril, Bishop of Alexandria.

One may be forgiven for thinking such a plethora of Lichfield diocesan glass would be difficult to follow: but Derby Diocese more than meets the challenge! A nave window in St. Oswald, Ashbourne, shows St. Columba of Iona, St. Aidan and St. Chad again (for of course Lichfield Diocese once spread over land which now forms the Sees of Southwell (since 1884) and Derby (since 1927). In fact, the oldest fragments of glass in this church, in the north window of the Boothby Chapel, illustrate Jesus, with St. Christopher and St. Modwena.

SS. Mary & Barlok, Norbury, has more saints in the Lady Chapel east window: together with St. Anne (see Ch.3) are St. Sitha (Zita) of Lucca, with keys and a book; St. Winifred; and St. Edith (Otha), again with keys and a book. St. Barlok himself, the Irish abbot-bishop is in the centre panel of the chapel's south window, flanked by St. John the Baptist with a lamb, and St. Anthony with a pig around whose neck hangs a bell. This ancient glass has recently been restored (see Ch.6). The restoration of the fourteenth-century glass in the great east window (181/2' x 28') was only completed in 1983. Twelve apostles in the four outer lights (each with a scroll showing part of the Apostles' Creed in Latin) flank the central light which has St. Edward the Confessor; Bishop and Saint, Chad, with his crozier; the mitred St. Fabian; St. Margaret and St. Mary Magdalene.

In St. Matthew, Morley, the old glass of the north aisle's east window has the figure of St. Ursula, ascending to heaven with an angelic escort. In the south aisle, a window to the memory of John Sacheverell of Bosworth Field, has lovely old glass showing St. Elizabeth in blue and white, and a red-cloaked St. Peter.

Another portrait of St. Christopher, carrying the Child Jesus across a river, is in the chancel of St. Cuthbert, Doveridge. St. Nicholas, the patron saint of sailors, is featured in a second window here; sailing to the Holy Land, his prayers are said to have saved his ship from disaster: the vessel can be seen with the saint in this window.

Strangely, perhaps, since it is at the Lancashire end of Derbyshire, All Saints, Glossop, has a Lady Chapel window showing St. Hilda's founding of her monastery at Whitby.

A group of martyrs is shown in the window commemorating a brave sufferer, Jane Burns, in St. Lawrence, Heanor: St. Lawrence with his gridiron; St. Catherine and her wheel; St. Elizabeth with roses; St. Andrew and St. Martin.

The patron saint of St. Leonard's Church, Thorpe (just over the Derbyshire boundary), is shown in a small window high up on the wall, near the lectern. Leonard was also the patron saint of prisoners, and is seen here carrying the shackles which are his usual emblem. Scholars are divided as to whether this little window is a "squint" (i.e. for giving those outside a view of the altar), since it is now in the wrong position; nor could it ever have given access to a rood loft, on account of its tiny size.

Modern glass in St. Giles, Sandiacre, depicts St. Werburgh, St. Chad, St. Giles and St. Elizabeth, within a Decorated framework, in the south-east wall of the nave. St. Elizabeth, representing "Charity", is also seen in a north aisle window of All Saints, Mackworth, together with St. Borromeo ("Humility") and St. Agnes ("Innocence"). St. Chad (yet again), along with St. Wystan, St. Diuma and St. Guthlac, can be seen in a four-light window by Dudley Forsyth, in St. Wystan, Repton. This window, in memory of th Rev. A.A.MacMaster, Repton's vicar from 1898 to 1911, also shows, in the lower lights, the Arms of Mercia; St. Guthlac's reception to Repton Abbey by Abbess Aelfritha; Bishop Finan of Lindisfarne baptising Prince Peada; and the Diocesan Arms of Lichfield.

Arguably the finest of the stained glass in All Saints, Ashover, is the three-light "Lee" window in the south aisle, at the east end of the south wall. The patron saint of those who cross water, St. Christopher, is in the centre. On the left is St. Nicholas, patron saint of northern sailors; on the right, St. Elmo, patron of sailors south of the Mediterranean, and credited with inventing the light carried on a ship's masthead. Note the top pinnacle of the canopy, in the shape of a lantern.

We should expect to find St. Chad in the church dedicated to him at Barton Blount - and he is there, in the east window. And St. Edward, Confessor and Martyr, is seen again at St. Martin, Osmaston, in the richly-coloured east window, together with ten saints.

A doctor who served Baslow for many years, Lt. Col. Mervyn Wrench, is commemorated there in the Church of St. Anne, by a window showing the "beloved physician", St. Luke, and St. Martin. Dr. Wrench's tomb, in the churchyard, is a rare "gravestone sundial", a slender pillar surmounted by a leaning cross on which is the dial.

And at St. Michael (C. of E.) Hathersage, can be seen two rarely depicted saints, Alban and Barbara, in a window on the north side of the Lady Chapel in memory of members of the Shuttleworth family.

More Saintly Souls.

There is no ancient glass in Sr. Thomas a Becket, Chapel-en-le-Frith, but the most westerly window in the north aisle has in its centre light the church's patron saint, holding a model of Canterbury Cathedral. Flanking him are scenes of his life and martyrdom: the king desiring his knights to get rid of the "turbulent priest"; St. Thomas in the cathedral defending his integrity; his murder; and vignettes of penance. At the eastern end of this aisle are three lights depicting St. Aidan holding a Saxon church; the high priest of antiquity, Melchizedek, holding bread and wine; and the Venerable Bede with the tools of his trade, a book and quill pen.

St. Bartholomew, Whittington (1896) is rich in latter-day Christians, among whom are the Earl of Shaftesbury, Mr. Gladstone, Hugh Latimer, Thomas Cranmer and Bishop Ridding of Southwell, in the windows of the north aisle. In a lovely window given in memory of an old lady whose portrait is in a roundel, are John Milton and John Wesley.

In St. Lawrence, Walton-on-Trent, are vividly portrayed Sir Thomas More, who put honour before discretion; the Dovedale fisherman Izaak Walton; the grammarian Dr. Samuel Johnson; and William Wilberforce, the champion of slaves.

George Herbert, priest, poet and musician, is in the newest (c.1955) window, in Christ Church, King Sterndale. It was given in memory of the Rev. Robert Hall Main (1868-1953), vicar of the parish from 1927 to 1943, by his niece, Dorothy Henry. The Arms of Main are in the lower part of the strongly-coloured glass. I remember this window being unveiled and dedicated: a thrilling occasion. Herbert was chosen as the subject, since Main had also been a poet and musician, among much else.

A much earlier priest is portrayed in a fine window in St. Matthew, Morley, Roger, bishop of London (d. 1241), resplendent in red and white robes and bejewelled gloves.

Relatively few churches are dedicated to Charles, King and Martyr: and so it is fitting that his church in Peak Forest has a window depicting the unfortunate monarch. Poignantly, it gives the dates of his birth and coronation, as well as his beheading, in 1649. The bearded king is sombrely grand in steel-grey, his crown on a table to his left, the execution block and axe to his right.

In the south transept of St. Giles, Hartington, the east window honours Augustus Wirgman, vicar here from 1855 to 1874, a period which saw the thorough renovation of the building, a new parsonage, school and schoolhouse built - to all of which Wirgman contributed handsomely.

The west window commemorates James F. Redfern, a mid-nineteenth century sculptor whose work can still be seen in many cathedrals the world over. The ironwork in the baptistery here was made by Redfern's nephew, William Smith, Hartington-born and bred, who later travelled extensively with his famous uncle.

In St. Mary (R.C.) Derby, the stained glass is in the altdentschen style, by William Warrington (1796-1869), the London glazier who had had as his illustrious teacher a man who advertised himself modestly as "Stained glass artist to Queen Victoria", Thomas Willement. Here, in the Chapel of our Lady of Lourdes, several local martyrs are commemorated in glass, notably Nicholas Garlick and Robert Ludlam, apprehended at Padley in 1587, tried at Derby, and hung, drawn and quartered by the Protestants of St. Mary's Bridge. Here, too, are Richard Simpson and Ralph Sherwin, reminding us that if around three hundred Protestants were martyred under Mary, when Protestantism was restored at least as many Catholics met the same fate.

Padley Chapel stands today largely as a tribute to the dedication and restorative zeal of Mgr. Payne, who in 1933 when Vicar General of the Nottingham Diocese redeemed it from the cowshed into which it had been allowed to degenerate. Here in the chapel is the story, in beautiful stained glass, of the trauma which turned a peaceful place into a scene of tragedy in the sixteenth century. Over the altar a two-light window depicts Robert Ludlam and Nicholas Garlick kneeling before a crucifix; in another window, Richard Simpson holds a martyr's palm; in another are the shields of Ludlam and Garlick (the latter showing a garlic plant). Nicholas is celebrating Mass, with the young server at his side about to ring the Mass bell. Two little windows show the arrest at Padley and the Derby executions. Another has the discovery of the old altar-stone (mensa). with the mason and Mgr. Payne: the date, 24th August 1933. In another window, is the re-consecration of the stone, 12th May 1934. Other windows have heraldic designs, showing the Fitzherbert arms, and are in memory of Sir Thomas and John Fitzherbert.

A pilgrimage is made annually to the chapel, on the Thursday nearest 12th July: the day on which over four hundred years ago, man's inhumanity to man wrought such havoc in this peaceful place.

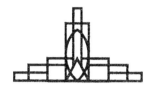

Chapter Five.

Stories in Glass.

From ancient glass to modern, Derbyshire churches have many stories to tell: some quaint, others tragic; some with particular local appeal, others universal; some legend, others factual; but all intriguing.

St. Robert and the Deer.

Originally lighting the cloister in Dale Abbey, the exquisitely-painted, fifteenth-century glass in three north aisle windows at St. Matthew, Morley, tells the story of St. Robert of Knaresborough and the deer who precociously ate his corn. The seven scenes are quaintly described:

    1) St. Robert shooteth the deere eating his corn.
    2) Whereat the keepers complayn to the kyng.
    3) Here he complayneth hym to the kyng.
    4) St. Robert catchyth the deere.
    5) The keepers inform the kyng who summons St. Robert.
    6) The kyng gyvyth hym the grounde.
    7) Here St. Robert plooyth wyth ye deere.

Legend has it that the king offered Robert as much land as he could plough round with the deer in a day (some records say, with a couple of deer).

Three of these scenes are in modern glass: at the Dissolution, Francis Pole brought much of the Dale Abbey glass to Morley, and this north aisle was built to accommodate it: but the masonry and glass was subsequently neglected, and a quantity of glass was lost; in the restoration of 1847, by William Warrington, patches of modern glass were needed to restore the sequence.

Another panel shows a monk, with chained hands, receiving penitential instruction from a fellow-brother.

The Invention of the Holy Cross.

Ten scenes of this legend are depicted in an adjacent window: again, there has been patching - this time, seven of the scenes are in modern glass. The Dale Abbey originals show

    1) Jesus on the Cross.
    2) The decapitation of Chosroes after he had removed the Cross at his capture of Jerusalem.
    3) The baptising of Chosroes' son.

While the combination of ancient and modern glass gives us these legends of St. Robert and the Invention in full, it is nevertheless a thousand pities that the old glass was not better preserved. In the early days of the Dissolution, when the north aisle was constructed, stout wooden shutters to the windows not only gave protection to the glass, but also allowed the Roman Mass to continue here, as and when priests were able to celebrate it. Time, however, saw the disintegration of the shutters, which were never replaced; further, according to a local record:

    ".... it was the custom of the friends and visitors
    at the village, at times of hospitality, such as
    Christmas and the Wakes, to show their regard for
    the church and its interesting objects, by pulling
    a bit of the stained glass out of the windows to take
    home as a relic, or as an object of amusement for
    children".

Small wonder, that around half of the Dale Abbey pieces have gone beyond the point of no return!

"Jesse" Windows.

These fascinating windows trace the ancestry of Jesus, a "Lion out of Judah, of the stem of Jesse". Perhaps the most intricate examples in England are both in Derbyshire. The first is the 1875 five-light east window in St. John the Baptist, Tideswell. The "tree" takes up the three inner lights, which are flanked by scenes from the life of the Baptist. Designed by C.G.S.Foljambe, whose family had been connected with Tideswell for centuries, it was made by Heaton, Butler & Bayne, and installed by J. Bower Brown.

The other Jesse window is at the west end of the nave in St. Oswald, Ashbourne, and commemorates the Rev. Francis Jourdain, vicar here from 1878 to 1898. Each figure along the genealogical tree is named: it is one of the finest Kempe windows in the county (see Ch.2).

Te Deum Windows.

The Te Deum ("We praise Thee, O God....") of the Book of Common Prayer's Morning Service, has become so well known and loved, that many worshippers accord it biblical status; but in fact its origin is still debated among scholars; some seeing vestiges of it in St. Cyprian's treatise "On the Mortality", which was afflicting his see of Carthage in 252 A.D. In its present form, it dates from the time of St. Hilary of Poitiers, 355 A.D. To confuse matters, it is often included as one of the four main "Canticles" (songs from the Bible other than from the Book of Psalms), the other three (all canonical) being the Benedictus (Lk.1:68-79), Magnificat (Lk.1:46- 55) and Nunc Dimittis (Lk. 2:29-32).

Te Deum windows can been seen in St. Matthew, Morley, among the old glass of the east window in the north aisle; the three scenes in the lower part of the window showing the "Church" as nine figures led by the Pope, the glorious company of the Apostles with St. Peter at their head, and the noble army of Martyrs.

The large window in the south wall of the south transept at St. Oswald, Ashbourne, has a Te Deum by Hardman & Co. (see Ch.2). Presented to the church in 1874 as a memorial to Canon Errington (vicar 1850-1872), it shows Jubal, the "father of all who play on strings" ; the prophetess Deborah; Moses; Barak; Miriam: Hannah; David; the Blessed Virgin; Solomon; the ill fated daugher of Jephthah; St. Cecilia, patron saint of musicians; Simeon; St. Ambrose, with a musical score of the Te Deum in his hand; and Zacharias. Angels of the heavenly host are praising God, in the spaces below the tracery.

A Benedictus window can be found in the north transept here. Again by Hardman & Co., it was given in 1877 by the Misses E. and F.G. Hartshorne of Ashbourne, to commemorate their parents. The colours are superb.

Nunc Dimittis Windows.

One of these, representing Mary and Joseph's presentation of Jesus in the temple, when Simeon sang as he held the Child (Nunc dimittis servum tuum, Domine, secundum verbum tuum in pace......), Lk. 2: 29-32, can be seen at the west end of Christ Church, King Sterndale in a

34

window appropriately entitled "Hope". It is in memory of Thomas Pickford (1778-1846).

Another example is at St. Peter, Snelston, in the baptistery. Made by Kempe and his son-in-law Tower (see Ch.2), it was given in 1907 in memory of Ellen Bowyer Harrison.

And in the north wall at St. Wystan, Repton, a two-light window by Powell, commemorating James and Ann Mugliston, shows the old lady Anna, and Simeon with the Infant Jesus.

These by no·means exhaust the Nunc Dimittis windows in Derbyshire; several others are briefly mentioned in other chapters.

Stories Old and New.

At St. Lawrence, Whitwell, the elegant four-light Decorated window at the east end, though filled with plain glass, has had an interesting history of survival. Reputedly, it was removed from the east window of Worksop Priory, at the Dissolution. Full marks to its preservers!

Three old medallions in the chancel windows at St. John the Baptist, Dronfield, show ancient musicians: a man with a primitive guitar; a monk with a clavichord; and a fiddler. There is an engraving of this fiddler in the Gentleman's Magazine (1757), accompanying an article on the age and use of English violins. The writer remarks: "this uncouth thing at Dronfield can be called no more than the rudiment of a violin. There is no neck, but it rests partly upon the performer's breast and partly upon his knee, and moreover was steadied, as I conceive, by a hand through a strap at the back. As there is no finger board, it could not be stopped, and with four strings could only produce four notes, which yet, I suppose, were sufficient at that time of day for expressing a chant or a psalm tune" (Vol. XXVII, p.560). St. Cecilia is shown with an organ, in a border around a collection of old fragments.

There is a similar figure to the Dronfield fiddler, at St. John the Baptist, Staveley. This strange old man, with an instrument as near as makes no matter to a hurdy-gurdy, is in one of two ancient yellow-and-white medallions in the east window. As he turns the handle of his quaint instrument, one can see the little fellow's turned-out, bare toes! What fun the artist must have had! One wonders whether in fact he was drawing from life, perhaps even a family friend, or a self-portrait: who knows?

35

From the amusing to the tragic: in All Saints (RC), Glossop, is a window to Sir Philip Howard, haled to the Tower by Elizabeth in 1584 for his Catholic faith, and dying there eleven years later.

On the county's borders, glass in St. Werburgh, Hanbury, commemorates the "largest explosion caused by conventional weapons in both the world wars" (as the notice at their nearby site proclaims). It occurred on 27th November 1944, when 3,500 tons of high explosives ignited by accident, causing a 300-foot deep crater 1/4 mile or so in diameter. Seventy people lost their lives, as the surrounding countryside was littered with fall-out from the crater.   Eighteen bodies were never recovered.

The window in St. Werburgh, of mellowed fourteenth-century stained glass, has been dedicated to all the casualties of the terrible explosion.

Mention has already been made, in Ch.4. of the window in St. Wystan, Repton, showing St. Guthlac being received into the Abbey by Abbess Aelfritha, in the south transept vestry window. In a lancet window, again by Dudley Forsyth, at the west end of the south aisle, is Aelfritha with an angel holding a shield charged with a drawing of the Abbey church, and the date "697 A.D." when St. Guthlac was received here. He was the son of a Mercian nobleman. However, a few years at Repton were enough to convince him that God was fitting him for the life of a hermit. He set out along the river in a simple boat without sail, rudder or oars, determined to settle where his vessel landed. The boat hove to at Croyland, where he lived in a tiny hut until his death in 714. Later, Croyland Abbey was built over Guthlac's shrine.

The story of Guthlac's life is beautifully illustrated in the windows of Repton School's library.

In 1949, Freda Rylatt, of Hathersage, lost her life on the mountain of Dinas Cromlech, and at St. Michael (C. of E.) is a window to her memory, in the Lady Chapel. It shows an excerpt from "Pilgrim's Progress". Look for the three small mammals and five birds, all to be found in the Peak District - and how the Benedicite omnia opera ("O all ye works of the Lord, bless ye the Lord") is portrayed in this lovely glass.

A window in St. Giles, Great Longstone, thought to be by Heaton & Co., shows Jesus with the children, and has the text from Mk. 10:14, "Suffer the little children to come unto me, and forbid them not : for of such is the kingdom of God". The window was given in memory of Joseph Scott, schoolmaster in the village for nearly fifty years. He died in 1887, aged 74. Another master, who founded West Hallam village school, is commemorated by a window in St. Wilfrid, West Hallam. His name was John Scargill.

St. Mary, Chesterfield, has a vividly coloured "Peace" window, depicting Jesus and four saints above three groups: (1) an old woman, a child and a widow kneeling at the town's peace memorial; (2) a nurse, sailor and soldier; and (3) workers on the home front: a clergyman, a man with a hammer, and a girl munition-maker. You will find this window in the south aisle.

Given to the same church by the townsfolk of Chesterfield, in 1984, another window, in the south nave aisle, commemorates the church's 750th anniversary. Scenes from Chesterfield's history are depicted, one panel illustrating the coming of steam power in the nineteenth century.

In St. Thomas, Derby, the stained glass figure of St. Christopher in one of the south aisle windows, originally stood in a church dedicated to St. Christopher near the Baseball Ground, closed earlier this century.

One-time Keeper of the Privy Purse, George Edward Anson, a native of Sudbury, has a window to his memory in All Saints' Church. At St. John the Baptist, Bamford, is a window to the "povider" of the church, one William Cameron Moore, a second-generation cotton-mill owner, who at a cost of around £7,000 in 1860 provided the village not only with a church but also a rectory.

A military man is commemorated in a window at St. Edmund, Fenny Bentley, showing the death of St. Edmund. He was Captain Hans Busk. Born in the year of Waterloo, Busk founded England's volunteer army. He wrote many books on rifle-shooting, and was an early pioneer of lifeboats. The window was given by his daughter. who married into the local Beresford family.

Other local benefactors are commemorated in lancet windows at St. John the Evangelist, Hazelwood: one to the Alleyne family, a member of whom carved the beautiful lectern; the other to the Strutts who did so much to put Belper on the map.

Thought to be the first stained glass in the country to show an aeroplane, is in the east window at St. Peter, Fairfield; it features a biplane, and commemorates the fallen of World War I.

No chapter on stained-glass stories in Derbyshire would be complete without mention of the Plague in the glass at St. Lawrence, Eyam. The window telling the tragic story was given in memory of her husband by

Mrs. C.M. Creswick in 1985, and was designed by Alfred Fisher, of the Chapel Studio, King's Langley. The central figure of the Rev. William Mompesson and his diminishing flock, is flanked by the present day church; George Viccars, the tailor, unwrapping the fateful bale of cloth; an early casualty, Edward Cooper; Viccars himself on his death-bed; the "Ring o' Roses" wreath, which was an early warning of the disease; the two clergymen, William Mompesson and Thomas Stanley, with the fated Catherine Mompesson in the background; and the lovers Emmott Siddall and Rowland Torre meeting in the Delph. Mompesson's Well, where food was left by outsiders; Eyam Cross; and the lonely Riley graves, are shown in the tracery above.

A happier story is told in the chancel window here: in memory of a rector who had hands-on experience with the church's restoration in the nineteenth-century. John Green is busy with his trowel, the workmen are busy on their scaffolding, and the architect is shown with his plans.

St. Martin, Alfreton, has a wealth of stained glass; but look for the window which records the bravery of a schoolboy who was drowned in at-tempting to save a young child. An angel is depicted raising him from the water, while a second angel rescues the little girl.

The window by the pulpit in St. Leonard, Thorpe, features Martha and Mary: but a red-haired Martha, which is not so common! This is because Emily Twigge, in whose memory and that of Mary her sister, the window was given, directed in her will that Martha's hair should be the colour of her own! A pelican - the heraldic symbol of the family - stands beside Martha in the window (and can also be seen carved on the cross-tombstones of the Twigge graves in the churchyard).

The naval window in St. Paul, Scropton, hides a story: it shows an angel and a man kneeling on the deck of a ship at sea. The figure represents Admiral Sir Arthur Cumming, who retired to Foston and was interred at Scropton in 1893. His life had been eventful, to say the least: active in the storming of Sidon at the age of 23, three years later while cruising off South America, he came upon a pirate ship with a cargo of slaves. Giving chase, Cumming shot the pirate captain, boarded the vessel with seven of his men and took on an opposition of thirty. The pirates were no match for the trained men, and Cumming soon had them chained in the hold, taking charge of the ship until his own came alongside.

Catherine, wife of Lord John Manners who became the Seventh Duke of Rutland, is commemorated by a beautiful window showing the life of St. Catherine, in St. Katherine, Rowsley. Dying at 23, as Lady Manners, Catherine did not live to take the rank of duchess.

Chapter Six.

Natural History, Symbols and Strange Things in Glass.

Morley"s deer and Thorpe's pelican have already been noted (Ch.5); but our churches are rich in natural history. Another pelican, in fact, can be seen in the Lady Chapel, St. Mary, Buxton. Over the glass illustrating "Suffer the little children to come unto Me", a lozenge-shaped window has a pelican on her nest. This motif of the mother-bird piercing her breast to feed her young with her life-blood, is a symbol of Jesus" sacrifice on the Cross. Given by Mrs. Pritchard after World War I, the glass is not only in memory of one son lost in the conflict, but a thanksgiving for a second son's safe return.

In a vivid window in the south wall at St. John the Baptist, Bamford, St. John is shown with a lamb, the whole framed by an exquisite border of oak leaves and acorns. The window was given by a former vicar of Hathersage, the Rev. Henry Cottingham. At. St. John the Baptist, Chelmorton, the saint's other symbol of a locust, can be seen.

In the side windows of the chancel at SS. Mary & Barlok, Norbury, the central intersections of the traceries carry a twelve-petalled flower, thought to be unique to Norbury. Dating from 1280, another window here shows foilage and fruit of vine, maple, ivy, oak and hawthorn, while the south window in the Lady Chapel has St. Anthony with a hog at his feet.

Green is the predominant colour in a two-light window at St. James, Whitfield, where the border consists of vine-leaves and grapes. Another window here portrays St. Francis. Derbyshire has a fair quota of St.

Francis windows (e.g. the lovely one in All Saints (R.C.), Hassop, some of which include animals and birds; the window in the north aisle at St. Peter, Parwich, is very new (1990), but in traditional style. It shows the saint with a horned Jacob sheep, and was given in memory of Sir John and Lady Crompton-Inglefield, late of Parwich Hall, Another St. Francis window (c.1923) is in St. Peter, Netherseal. The saint here is surrounded by many animals and birds, including a hare, squirrel, cat, dove, owl, pheasant, peregrine, swan, stork and woodpecker. Also in the scene is a swallowtail butterfly, fish and a dragonfly - together with a bat (an animal rarely found in stained glass).

A striking pair of windows in St. Mary, Wirksworth, illustrating the Benedicite, as has already been noted, shows snow (again, an unusual subject for stained glass), the moon and stars, a Christmas tree, a squirrel, and an old man warming himself by the fire. "O ye winter and summer, bless ye the Lord". Harvest-time is represented by an angel holding a cornucopia of fruit and a sheaf of corn. William Killer, in whose memory the windows were given, and that of his family, was a local man.

The fourth window of the south transept at Holy Trinity, Matlock Bath, is patterned geometrically, and full of symbols; but in addition to the INRI (Iesus Nazarenus Rex Iudeorum) and IHS (Iesus Hominum Salvator), we can see grapes and vine-leaves, lilies and a dove. More symbols are seen in the third window of the north transept, which shows the Visit of the Magi: the Greek Alpha and Omega, signifying Christ the First and Last (Rev. 21:6) stand out above the main lights. The window was given in memory of Edward Greenhough, who was churchwarden here for forty-two years. Geometry has also impacted on the east window of the south aisle in St. Mary, Weston-on-Trent; but here it is the tracery that is geometric, a feature thought to be unique in Derbyshire.

Six medallions in a small window of St. Mary, Pilsley, depict the Creation in beautiful glass: here are the sun, moon and stars; fishes and fowls; fruit and flowers; and the animals - which include an ox, lion, lamb and baby rabbit.

The fifteenth-century glass in the chancel at St. Wilfrid, West Hallam, shows a range of small birds; and in glass of the fourteenth century at St. Lawrence, Whitwell, are intriguing little pink squirrels and monkeys ringing handbells. What fun the mediaeval glaziers must have had with these!.

At Norbury's old Manor House, ancient glass includes six fifteenth-century medallions depicting the occupations of the months from January to June. Low-side windows can be found in St. Wilfrid, Barrowon-Trent (albeit blocked up, on the north side of the chancel); St. John the Baptist, Clowne; and (again blocked up) at All Saints, Aston-on-Trent.

A fragment of early glass at St. Helen, Etwall, mentioned by J.C.Cox but now missing, showed an emblematical representation of the Trinity. Perhaps the Norbury example, of the late fifteenth century, in the restored west window of SS. Mary & Barlok, is now the only such representation in the county. Between the knees of the crowned Father, is the Son on the Cross, while under the beard of the Father and above the halo of the Son, is the dove representing the Holy Ghost.

Unusual, too, is the window over the chancel arch, in St. Clement, Horsley - though this feature is common enough in the large Cotswold churches; and at St. Saviour, Foremark, in place of a rood there is a triangle of painted glass on the chancel screen, showing two kneeling angels, and a dove with its wings outstretched in a mandorla.

"Faith, Hope and Charity" (I Cor. 13:13) can be seen at SS. Peter & Paul, Old Brampton; St. Andrew, Radbourne; and St. Giles, Marston Montgomery.

An unusual feature of the Gothic tracery of the windows at St. Peter, Hartshorne, is that it is made of cast-iron.

In Streetley Chapel, the apse is beautifully lighted by three lancets of glass in a patchwork of rainbow-colours; while at Staveley, the west window has glass in "tongues of fire".

The great east window of St. Mary, Ilkeston, has an exquisite "wheel" in its tracery; it depicts the Good Shepherd, Jesus with the fishermen, and the Blessed Virgin. Long noted for its windows, it was said of St. Mary's by an architect of 1855, that "no church in England possesses any to equal them, and they can never be surpassed in the lightness and elegance of their tracery". Another lovely wheel can be seen in the east window at SS. Michael with Mary, Melbourne.

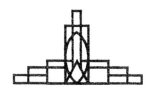

Chapter Seven.

Twentieth-Century Glass.

"We will remember them....."

Many Derbyshire churches were built, or restored, during Victoria's long reign, some of them "inheriting" glass from earlier buildings; but of the twentieth-century glass to be found in the diocese, a large proportion has been given in memory of the fallen in one or other of the World Wars - though Mr. Hitler's ironmongery scored a hit, mercifully, on only one Derbyshire church - St. Michael and All Angels, Earl Sterndale.

With Ceri Richards' abstract glass in Derby Cathedral, and Pope & Parr's, in All Saints, Wingerworth (1963-4), notable exceptions, much of the modern glass has been of traditional design, some of it being among the most beautiful in the diocese.

Among the windows commemorating the fallen, see the two-light window on the south side of the nave (c.1320), in St. Leonard, Thorpe. St. Bartholomew, Whittington, in its east window, remembers 172 local men who did not return in 1918. It shows St. Margaret, the Black Prince, King Alfred and St. George. Three windows in St. Anne, Ambergate, show St. Alban, St. Martin and St. George; and St. Michael and St. George can also be seen in the south transept memorial window, unveiled in 1920, in St. John the Baptist, Buxton.

Perhaps the most dazzling of these commemorative windows, is the one at the east end of Christ Church, Holloway - though some will no doubt still remember the beautiful peace window in old St. Alkmund, Derby, which showed the Crucifixion and saints, soldiers, a chaplain, nurse and sailor.

In All Saints, Breadsall, a pieta ("Our Lady of Pity") stands by the Haslam window commemorating an officer from Breadsall Priory killed in action on 27th April 1917, near Arras. A scroll, inscribed "Saint George", is portrayed over a crown and gun carriage.

Thirteen fallen are commemorated in a window at St. Anne, Beeley, showing Jesus and two soldiers with Beeley Church in the background. In Holy Trinity, Yeaveley, the east window honours twenty-four local men who fought (twenty-three of whom returned). St. George is shown, resplendent in red and purple, and St. Joan of France in blue and gold.

In St. Lawrence, North Wingfield, the eastern clerestory window in the north wall commemorates Captain H.C. Boden, the rector's son, killed in Flanders' fields at the age of nineteen, in 1915. It was given by his brother officers.

The east window in St. Peter, Chellaston, is a beautiful blend of strong and delicate colours; and in Christopher Whall's striking window at St. Matthew, Pentrich, in memory of a hero who fell at Ypres, are the warrior saints of England and France, with St. Michael Archangel.

The east window in St. Michael (C. of E.), Hathersage, was installed "as a thank-offering for the end of the War 1939-1945, and the safe return of relatives and friends".

Around and About.

Beautiful modern glass in the east window of St. Michael, Kirk Langley, complements the seventeenth-century Flemish glass in the south choir chapel (see Ch.2). In St. George, Ticknall, a vicar's forty-seven year ministry here, ending in 1885, is commemorated in a striking window.

On the south side of the nave aisle in St. Oswald, Ashbourne, the most easterly window commemorates the daughters of Mr and Mrs. Peveril Turnbull of Sandybrook Hall. Monica and Dorothea lost their lives in a fire in 1901 (See Ch.2). Designed by Christopher Whall in 1905, the virgin-martyr saints Cecilia, Barbara and Dorothea are depicted; and in the lower lights is a landscape garden in stained glass. More modern glass, in the only window of the Tudor clerestory on the west side, dates from 1933 and commemorates a local couple, Thomas and Mary Ann Foster. It shows the Good Shepherd.

Two windows in the south wall of SS. Peter & Paul, Old Brampton, commemorate Albert Barnes (d.1901) and Charlotte his wife (d.1905).

Albert's window depicts the Nunc Dimittis. In St. John the Baptist, Winster, a four-light window in which green predominates shows as its main scene the baptism of Christ. It is on the north side of the nave, and was given "In memory of the Rev. Herbert Milnes, Vicar of Winster 1865-1895, who died at Cheltenham, March 2nd 1909".

The Annunciation window above the altar in the Lady Chapel at St. Peter, Hope, was given in 1914 by Mr and Mrs. H. Freckingham, of Higher Hall, in memory of their daughter. Some old glass, bearing the arms of the Eyre family, has been incorporated at the bottom left in this window by Frederick Eden (see Chs. 1 and 2). The Annunciation scene is a copy of Leonardo da Vinci's painting (in the Uffizi Gallery, Florence). To the north of the Lady Chapel altar, is another F.C.Eden window, depicting the Adoration of the Shepherds. It was given in 1919, in memory of Mrs. Vincent, the vicar's mother. A window commemorating her son, the Rev.E.C.Vincent, is in the north aisle. It shows the young Jesus in the temple, and is the work of Miss D.M.Grant.

In St. Mary, Mappleton, the east window in memory of members of the Wheen family, is of good 1920s glass. The west window, in St. Leonard, Thorpe, designed in 1950 by Mr. A.F.Erridge, has as its text: "I am come that they might have life". And there are two modern windows in St. Cuthbert, Doveridge, given in 1954 by two parishioners in memory of their sons. The south window is the work of Mr. Gerald Smith, and shows the patron saint of the church with St. Ceadda (Chad, first Bishop of Lichfield, in which diocese St. Cuthbert's once stood).

In Holy Trinity, Ashford-in-the-Water, the windows on the north aisle wall are both modern: one shows St. Nicholas, patron saint of children (1951); the other, Mary and the Christ-Child (1960).

On either side of the altar in Derby Cathedral, are the windows designed by Ceri Richards and made in 1966 by Patrick Reyntiens. In vivid colours, they represent All Souls (on the left) and All Saints (on the right) - for the Cathedral, prior to its elevation in 1927, used to be the Parish Church of All Saints.

The east window at St. Giles, Matlock, by Lawrence Lee, was given in 1969, and represents God's love in the Incarnation of His Son.

Mention has already been made of David Peace's beautiful screen at All Saints, Trusley (Ch.1); there is more of his work in St. John the Baptist, Ault Hucknall, in a small window of clear glass with exquisite lettering. Another engraving - this time a glass screen depicting the story of Ruth - by Chapel-en-le-Frith parishioner David Pilkington, in 1992, can be seen in Mansfield Woodhouse church, just over the diocesan boundary.

And one of the most recently-installed windows- though not itself modern - is the east window in St. Michael and All Angels, Taddington. Brought from a church demolished near Birkenhead, in 1993, this was originally a six-light window, and the pieces have therefore needed some juxtapositioning to fit the mullions and tracery of Taddington's five lights. From left to right, the scenes are those of the Baptism of Jesus, the Cana marriage-feast, the Last Supper, the Resurrection and the Ascension.

As you visit Derbyshire's wealth of churches, imitate the ancient Romans and festina lente; hurry slowly, so as not to miss a single gem.

Joyce Critchlow, Brook House, Brandside, Nr. Buxton, Derbyshire. SK17 0SG.

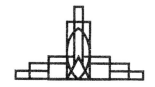

OTHER JOHN MERRILL WALK BOOKS

<u>CIRCULAR WALK GUIDES -</u>
SHORT CIRCULAR WALKS IN THE PEAK DISTRICT - Vol. 1,2 and 3
CIRCULAR WALKS IN WESTERN PEAKLAND
SHORT CIRCULAR WALKS IN THE STAFFORDSHIRE MOORLANDS
SHORT CIRCULAR WALKS - TOWNS & VILLAGES OF THE PEAK DISTRICT
SHORT CIRCULAR WALKS AROUND MATLOCK
SHORT CIRCULAR WALKS IN "PEAK PRACTICE COUNTRY."
SHORT CIRCULAR WALKS IN THE DUKERIES
SHORT CIRCULAR WALKS IN SOUTH YORKSHIRE
SHORT CIRCULAR WALKS IN SOUTH DERBYSHIRE
SHORT CIRCULAR WALKS AROUND BUXTON
SHORT CIRCULAR WALKS AROUND WIRKSWORTH
SHORT CIRCULAR WALKS IN THE HOPE VALLEY
40 SHORT CIRCULAR WALKS IN THE PEAK DISTRICT
CIRCULAR WALKS ON KINDER & BLEAKLOW
SHORT CIRCULAR WALKS IN SOUTH NOTTINGHAMSHIRE
SHIRT CIRCULAR WALKS IN CHESHIRE
SHORT CIRCULAR WALKS IN WEST YORKSHIRE
WHITE PEAK DISTRICT AIRCRAFT WRECKS
CIRCULAR WALKS IN THE DERBYSHIRE DALES
SHORT CIRCULAR WALKS FROM BAKEWELL
SHORT CIRCULAR WALKS IN LATHKILL DALE
CIRCULAR WALKS IN THE WHITE PEAK
SHORT CIRCULAR WALKS IN EAST DEVON
SHORT CIRCULAR WALKS AROUND HARROGATE
SHORT CIRCULAR WALKS IN CHARNWOOD FOREST
SHORT CIRCULAR WALKS AROUND CHESTERFIELD
SHORT CIRCULAR WALKS IN THE YORKS DALES - Vol 1 - Southern area.
SHORT CIRCULAR WALKS IN THE AMBER VALLEY (Derbyshire)
SHORT CIRCULAR WALKS IN THE LAKE DISTRICT
SHORT CIRCULAR WALKS IN THE NORTH YORKSHIRE MOORS
SHORT CIRCULAR WALKS IN EAST STAFFORDSHIRE
DRIVING TO WALK - 16 Short Circular walks south of London by Dr. Simon Archer Vol 1 and 2
LONG CIRCULAR WALKS IN THE PEAK DISTRICT - Vol.1,2 ,3 and 4.
DARK PEAK AIRCRAFT WRECK WALKS
LONG CIRCULAR WALKS IN THE STAFFORDSHIRE MOORLANDS
LONG CIRCULAR WALKS IN CHESHIRE
WALKING THE TISSINGTON TRAIL
WALKING THE HIGH PEAK TRAIL
WALKING THE MONSAL TRAIL & OTHER DERBYSHIRE TRAILS
40 WALKS WITH THE SHERWOOD FORESTER by Doug Harvey
PEAK DISTRICT WALKING - TEN "TEN MILER'S" - Vol One and Two
CLIMB THE PEAKS OF THE PEAK DISTRICT
PEAK DISTRICT WALK A MONTH Vol One,Two & Three.
TRAIN TO WALK - The Hope Valley Line
DERBYSHIRE LOST VILLAGE WALKS -Vol One and Two.
CIRCULAR WALKS IN DOVEDALE AND THE MANIFOLD VALLEY

<u>CANAL WALKS -</u>
VOL 1 - DERBYSHIRE & NOTTINGHAMSHIRE
VOL 2 - CHESHIRE & STAFFORDSHIRE
VOL 3 - STAFFORDSHIRE
VOL 4 - THE CHESHIRE RING
VOL 5 - LINCOLNSHIRE & NOTTINGHAMSHIRE
VOL 6 - SOUTH YORKSHIRE
VOL 7 - THE TRENT & MERSEY CANAL
VOL 8 - WALKING THE DERBY CANAL RING
VOL 9 - WALKING THE LLANGOLLEN CANAL

<u>JOHN MERRILL DAY CHALLENGE WALKS -</u>
WHITE PEAK CHALLENGE WALK
DARK PEAK CHALLENGE WALK
PEAK DISTRICT END TO END WALKS
STAFFORDSHIRE MOORLANDS CHALLENGE WALK
THE LITTLE JOHN CHALLENGE WALK
YORKSHIRE DALES CHALLENGE WALK

NORTH YORKSHIRE MOORS CHALLENGE WALK
LAKELAND CHALLENGE WALK
THE RUTLAND WATER CHALLENGE WALK
MALVERN HILLS CHALLENGE WALK
THE SALTER'S WAY
THE SNOWDON CHALLENGE
CHARNWOOD FOREST CHALLENGE WALK
THREE COUNTIES CHALLENGE WALK (Peak District).
CAL-DER-WENT WALK by Geoffrey Carr,
THE QUANTOCK WAY
BELVOIR WITCHES CHALLENGE WALK
THE CARNEDDAU CHALLENGE WALK
THE SWEET PEA CHALLENGE WALK

INSTRUCTION & RECORD -
HIKE TO BE FIT.....STROLLING WITH JOHN
THE JOHN MERRILL WALK RECORD BOOK
HIKE THE WORLD

MULTIPLE DAY WALKS -
THE RIVERS'S WAY
PEAK DISTRICT: HIGH LEVEL ROUTE
PEAK DISTRICT MARATHONS
THE LIMEY WAY
THE PEAKLAND WAY
COMPO'S WAY by Alan Hiley

COAST WALKS & NATIONAL TRAILS -
ISLE OF WIGHT COAST PATH
PEMBROKESHIRE COAST PATH
THE CLEVELAND WAY
WALKING ANGELSEY'S COASTLINE.
WALKING THE COASTLINE OF THE CHANNEL ISLANDS

DERBYSHIRE & PEAK DISTRICT HISTORICAL GUIDES -
A to Z GUIDE OF THE PEAK DISTRICT
DERBYSHIRE INNS - an A to Z guide
HALLS AND CASTLES OF THE PEAK DISTRICT & DERBYSHIRE
TOURING THE PEAK DISTRICT & DERBYSHIRE BY CAR
DERBYSHIRE FOLKLORE
PUNISHMENT IN DERBYSHIRE
CUSTOMS OF THE PEAK DISTRICT & DERBYSHIRE
WINSTER - a souvenir guide
ARKWRIGHT OF CROMFORD
LEGENDS OF DERBYSHIRE
DERBYSHIRE FACTS & RECORDS
TALES FROM THE MINES by Geoffrey Carr
PEAK DISTRICT PLACE NAMES by Martin Spray
DERBYSHIRE THROUGH THE AGES - DERBYSHIRE IN PREHISTORIC TIMES
SIR JOSEPH PAXTON

JOHN MERRILL'S MAJOR WALKS -
TURN RIGHT AT LAND'S END
WITH MUSTARD ON MY BACK
TURN RIGHT AT DEATH VALLEY
EMERALD COAST WALK
JOHN MERRILL'S 1999 WALKER'S DIARY
A WALK IN OHIO

SKETCH BOOKS -
SKETCHES OF THE PEAK DISTRICT

COLOUR BOOK:-
THE PEAK DISTRICT.......something to remember her by.

OVERSEAS GUIDES -
HIKING IN NEW MEXICO - Vol I - The Sandia and Manzano Mountains.
Vol 2 - Hiking "Billy the Kid" Country. Vol 4 - N.W. area - " Hiking Indian Country."
"WALKING IN DRACULA COUNTRY" - Romania.

VISITOR GUIDES - MATLOCK. BAKEWELL. ASHBOURNE.

John Merrill's - "My Derbyshire" Historical Series.

A TO Z GUIDE TO THE PEAK DISTRICT by John N. Merrill
WINSTER - A SOUVENIR GUIDE .by John N. Merrill
DERBYSHIRE INNS - AN A TO Z GUIDE . by John N. Merrill
HALLS & CASTLES OF THE PEAK DISTRICT. by John N. Merrill.
DERBYSHIRE FACTS AND RECORDS by John N. Merrill
THE STORY OF THE EYAM PLAGUE by Claence Daniel
THE EYAM DISCOVERY TRAIL by Clarence Daniel
PEAK DISTRICT SKETCHBOOKby John N. Merrill
LOST DERBYSHIRE VILLAGE WALKS - VOL 1 & 2 by John N. Merrill
TOURING THE PEAK DISTRICY & DERBYSHIRE BY CAR by John N. Merrill
LOST INDUSTRIES OF DERBYSHIRE by John N. Merrill
DESERTED MEDIEVAL VILLAGES OF DERBYSHIRE by John N. Merrill

FAMOUS DERBYSHIRE PEOPLE -

ARKWRIGHT OF CROMFORD by John N. Merrill.
SIR JOSEPH PAXTON by John N. Merrill
FLORENCE NIGHTINGALE by John N. Merrill

GHOSTS & LEGENDS -

DERBYSHIRE FOLKLORE.by John N. Merrill.
DERBYSHIRE PUNISHMENT by John N. Merrill.
CUSTOMS OF THE PEAK DISTRICT & DERBYS by John N. Merrill
LEGENDS OF DERBYSHIRE. by John N. Merrill.

PEAK DISTRICT VISITOR'S GUIDES by John N. Merrill

ASHOURNE
BAKEWELL
MATLOCK

DERBYSHIRE HISTORY THROUGH THE AGES -

Vol 1 - DERBYSHIRE IN PREHISTORIC TIMES by John N. Merrill
Vol 3 - DERBYSHIRE IN NORMAN TIMES by John N. Merrill